LYCUS: THE PROPHECY OF ANNIHILATION

I. S. KNIGHT

LYCUS

The PROPHECY *of* ANNIHILATION

This is a work of fiction. Names, characters, places, and incidents either are the product of the author's imagination or are used fictitiously. Any resemblance to actual persons, living or dead, events, or locales is entirely coincidental.

For more information, E- mail address: authorisknight@gmail.com

First Edition: October 2021

Cover Design by *Mirella Santana*

www.mirellasantana.com.br

Ornaments by *Vanessa* / Deposit photos

Map by *Saumya Singh* / Inkarnate

Editing by *Kristin Mullen*

www.mullineditorials.com

Interior Formatting by *CPR Editing*

www.carmenrichterwriting.com/cpr-editing

ISBN 978-1-7775959-1-3

www.isknight.com

ACKNOWLEDGEMENTS

Writing a book is no simple task. Both of us realized this when we started writing this story Mid-June 2018. Words flow through our mind and we write them down. That's how the journey to write this book started. You start with a thought, an idea that evolves and contorts and twists into what becomes the first draft. The first draft that then gets rinsed and wringed into a second draft and so on until you have the final manuscript. Lycus is our debut novel. It is the threshold we cross together in our writing career. Easy as it seems, it is a mountain to conquer that we did day in and day out. It has a piece of our soul. Not only do we love every character, but they will always be a part of us. This task becomes easier with the people you surround yourself with. The two of us have been blessed being surrounded by our friends and family who pushed us to write and bear with us while we endlessly plotted and deleted and re-plotted and planned and unplanned characters, stories and plot points.

Ipen would like to begin with thanking his Grandparents for instilling into him a love of writing and storytelling. *Sardar Karnail Singh* and *Sardarni Surjit Kaur* are the two most significant individuals in making him the writer he is today. His grandfather, who regaled him with stories of his childhood, teaching Ipen the importance of hard work. His grandmother who told him stories and fables from her childhood, instilling in Ipen the love of stories.

The most important figures in our lives are our parents. Ipen's parents *Mr. Lakhbir Singh* and Mrs. Rajmanjit *Kaur* and Saumya's parents *Mr. Narendra Pal Singh* and *Mrs. Madhu Singh*. For never giving up on us, for always pushing us to achieve more. For never letting us settle for anything less than perfection. Without their love, dedication and support, it would have been impossible to finish this novel. Ipen's younger brother, *Jagdeep Singh*, who was always the person he could rely on to provide a challenge. Their struggles to constantly one-up each other pushed Ipen to strive for a higher standard. Saumya's sister, *Surbhi Singh* and Brother-in-law, *Rahul Uttam*, who have guided Saumya and her choices, always caring for her future. Also, Saumya's niece, *Oeshi Singh*, who came to this world while we worked on Lycus, has been an inspiration and joy. *Lucas* is Saumya's most loyal companion and writing buddy.

Our families kept the two of us going to finish this. Family isn't always what we are born into. Sometimes it's also those we choose for ourselves. Our friends, who became our family, siblings we weren't born with but the ones we chose ourselves. Our constant bickering, and parties and coffee shop meetings kept us on our toes and together for nearly 6 years now. Ipen's friends: *Navpal Hothi*, the most culturally in tune; *Noble Sengar*, Jack of all trades; *Pardeep Pabla*, who somehow knew everyone; *Arjun Chahal*, the gym nut of the group; *Alex Raman*, who lost a record 4 phones in a year; *Sandeep Sooch,* who always offered level-headed advice; *Jugraj Singh*, the party fiend; *Pritpal Bansal*, the person who knew all the famous people; *Jaideep Kang*, the person who most in touch with the world around him. These individuals, Ipen's brothers, their support and companionship, could never be understated.

Saumya's friends, who stuck with her through thick and thin. *Jennifer Guleria*, who Saumya met during her first year in university, has stuck with her through the years, listening to me talk about her stories, supporting me and sharing the burden through the years. They have laughed and cried together and those moments they spent together are unforgettable. *Shashithra Basker*, who has her back for the past 6 years that they have known each other; *Suhail Ahamed Akhtar, Jeremy Vasquez* and *Sophia Apura*, who Saumya can turn to for advice. The hours spent together with them are cherished forever. *Soham Patel* and *Christopher Lopez Serrano*, her dear friends who have always helped her, guided her whenever she needed it. All the years Saumya has spent with her friends sharing her hopes, dreams and fears, now Saumya shares with them her happiness. The culmination of 3 years of hard work.

Our families have been instrumental in shaping us and we cannot thank them enough. Along with our friends and families, several individuals we met on our journey to publishing have become important friends and without them, Lycus would not exist.

Emma Burnside, the first person we consulted about the project, who provided her valuable advice and knowledge to us as we scratched together a first draft. Emma was also the very first person to read through the entirety of Lycus for which we are forever grateful.

Tammy Malone, a stranger turned friend who shared with us their valuable time in shaping Lycus to what it is now.

Shannon Hughes, who when Lycus was nothing but a few pages and an idea, created one of the most stunning covers we could have imagined for our novel.

Mirella Santana, an amazing graphic designer who worked tirelessly to create the cover of this novel, giving our book an unforgettable identity.

And last but certainly not least, *Kristin Mullin*, our amazing editor. Who read the first draft, edited and improved and educated us, seeing Lycus through the end. We cannot even begin to thank her enough for her tireless work.

Thank you to all who were a part of this project. Now, turn the page and immerse yourself in Vascya.

Saumya & Ipen

To the ones we love and those who love us.

CONTENT WARNING

Welcome to *Lycus: The Prophecy of Annihilation*.

This novel is a Dark Fantasy and contain themes that are not suitable for younger audiences. As Authors, it would be irresponsible not to label strong triggers. Please be aware that this novel contains graphic depictions of blood, dismemberment, suicide, and sexual assault.

PRONUNCIATION GUIDE

1. Adrian – *Ay-**dree**-en*
2. Adya – *Ah-**dee**-ah*
3. Alistair – *Ah-**lis**-tar*
4. Amae – *Ah-**may***
5. Amarog – *Am-ah-**rog***
6. Belaize – *Blaze*
7. Beleotell – *Bel-ay-**oh**-tell*
8. Canagan – *Kan-a-**gan***
9. Charles – *Charl-**ss***
10. Çatall – ***Chat**-all*
11. Chern – *Shar-**n***
12. Cora – *Ko-**raa***
13. Chetnia – *Shet-**nee**-a*
14. Dira – *Dee-**rah***
15. Draxus – *Dra-**ck**-sus*
16. Eliana – *El-**ee**-ah-na*
17. Erwin – *Er-**wen***
18. Erylesia – *Air-uh-**lee**-zia*
19. Esteve – *As-**ti**-eve*
20. Evette – *Eh-**wet***
21. Eyolf – ***Eh**-oulf*
22. Faust – *Fa-**ou**-st*
23. Fenrir – Fen-**re**-ar
24. Gornikulu – *Gor-**ni**-koo-loo*
25. Honoria – *Hon-**or-ee**-ah*
26. Idaos – *Eye-**day**-os*
27. Illari – *Ill-**aa**-ree*
28. Janus – *Jan-**us***
29. Jennifer – *Jen-**nee**-fer*
30. Kaiser – *Ka-eye-**ser***
31. Laki – *Lah-**key***
32. Lily – *Lil-**ee***
33. Liunella – *Lee-oo-**nel**-ah*
34. Lunaire – *Loon-**air***
35. Lycan – *Like-**An***
36. Marcus – ***Mark**-Us*
37. Maya – *Mah-**Yah***
38. Merritan – *Mare-**it**-an*

39. Morin – *Mo-**ren***
40. Mugiri – *Moo-**gee**-ree*
41. Navar – *Nuh-**vur***
42. Nihara – ***Ni**-ha-ra*
43. Norias – *No-**ra**-ee-us*
44. Novocher – *No-**vo**-share*
45. Orden – *Or-**dun***
46. Rayne – Rain
47. Regvyer – *Reg-**veh**-er*
48. Ronak – *Roh-**nak***
49. Rylsk – *Ry-**lisk***
50. Sundara – *Sun-**daa**-raa*
51. Sora – *Sow-**ara***
52. Tierra – ***Ti**-ey-raa*
53. Mortis – *Mor-**tis***
54. Umbral – *Um-**bruh**-al*
55. Vascya – *Vah-**see**-ah*
56. Vouyen – ***Vo**-en*
57. Walka – ***Vaal**-kah*
58. Xyabolt – *Zee-**ah**-bolt*

Chetnia
Urekiz
The Low Cities
Novoch
Drustuk
Regvyer
Bohzok
Legend
Capital
City
Town
Village
Sanctuary

Koro
River Brahn
Nedev
Mdin
Soloro
Izo
Temple of Sundara
Vascya

PROLOGUE

Idaos

Sunlight peeked through the windows as dusk approached. My footsteps echoed on the pristine marble floor as I hurried along. The walls were daubed with spectacular artwork designed by brilliant artisans from the land of Vascya. The stony hallway grew chilly as I hastened through the cavernous corridors of the towering castle that lead to the chamber of the Council, *the Holy Sanctorum.* Reaching the end of the corridor, I finally saw the heavy wooden double-doors embellished with circular patterns, an intricate design of Lycans engraved in the middle. As I dragged them open, I thought, *The Vascyans and their designs…*

The doors opened to a spiral array of stairs leading upwards. The staircase was carved from marble, flaunting the overall elegance of the place. Its grace and curves were proof enough of the mason's caliber. Continuing up the stairs, I thought – not for the first time – that I was going to change everything. I was going to remake the world; it had to be done. And it had to be done *this* way. I needed to be strong, now more than ever. *The only way*. The thought rang through my mind like a gong.

Reaching the top of the stairs, I continued through the well-lit passage lined with torches. The stunning paintings of the moon and her phases hanging on the walls were a blur as I strode by. Finally, I reached the last set of stone doors. The only thing separating me from the fate of tomorrow, when all would be changed forever. Two wolves of the Vascyan army stood guarding the chamber entrance. They pushed the doors open and shifted to the side, bowing their heads in respect, and sealing them behind me as I stepped inside the Holy Sanctorum, the chamber of *Liunella, the Moon Goddess.*

"You have forced us all to wait too long, Idaos," announced a resounding voice.

My mind was calm as a still pool as I waded to my seat. The sun had set and the tender radiance of the moon illuminated the Sanctorum through a circular oculus in the high ceiling above. The Sanctorum was a large space, its chalk-white walls soaring above all. In the castle's heart, it was protected by towers and thick walls. Before the wolves built the city of Regvyer, it had served as the holy temple to the Moon Goddess once, centuries ago.

Even with Liunella's light, darkness loomed over us. A fire was lit in the hearth that provided little warmth. I sensed the scrutinizing gazes of all the elders upon me. Two women and seven men were all seated around a circular table, sipping on fine liquor from golden goblets.

"Thank you, Elders, for acknowledging my request and arriving on such brief notice. I would not have called for you if this was not a matter of utmost importance," I said, my voice echoing in the chamber.

"Alpha Idaos, our oaths bind us to arrive when the Council convenes. We are the leaders of Vascya. However, I hope that the call was not in vain. I have traveled from the western border to be part of this gathering," huffed Alpha Eyolf.

My eyes darted towards him, taking in his appearance for a moment. He was old. A silver stubble covered his face, though few wrinkles lined his forehead. He was the oldest member of the present Council that ruled over Vascya. I glanced at everyone else seated around the circular mahogany table, somber expressions graced their faces, each adorned in crimson and gold cassocks with intricate embroidery. Besides Eyolf and I, the others were young. Some appeared to be in their late-thirties whereas Olegario and Valio were in their mid-fifties. Beside them were Alpha Illari and Alpha Evette. They were fierce sisters who ruled their territories with an iron fist. The current Council has been in power for a mere hundred years, and was now mostly comprised of alphas from the new era.

Regretfully, they weren't as strong as the Four Winds, alphas of the pure bloodlines, which had become scarce. Vascya now had only a handful of wolves who possess the old blood. The current Council boasted only two, Alpha Ronak, and I. A far cry from when the Council was full of them. Of course, the Council was a lot smaller back then. Four members, but now, ten.

I commanded the rapt attention of the Council. They turned to me, eager and waiting. I let the silence stretch a beat longer. Then I spoke, "I did not mean to cause any discomfort to you, Eyolf, nor to the others."

I smoothed out my crimson robes as Eyolf passed me a goblet of my own. I sipped the wine; the liquor burning the back of my throat. I had called the Council without warning after all; they had to be angry. But it was a necessary action, a passing discomfort.

"This might come as a surprise to the Council, but a fortnight ago I was down in the dungeons examining and studying documents in the old archives. We are all familiar that the archives contain our Lycan history and treasured secrets. While going through some ancient scriptures, I stumbled upon a set of tomes which originally looked of no importance, just a journal, but as I read through them, I..." I retrieved a small worn piece of paper from the frayed pocket of my robes. It was old, crumpled, and yellow. I placed it in the center of the table for the elders to see.

"I stumbled upon a prophecy," I added, my voice brusque. Alpha Amarog raised his eyebrows in utter disdain. He ran his hand through his short black hair in annoyance.

"You called the Council for childish tales, Idaos? This is extremely disrespectful!" Whispered mutterings flowed from the gathered elders, but I held my resolve. I squared my shoulders.

"I believe this prophecy will soon be realized and that, if we do not take radical action now, the whole Lycan race will suffer the repercussions of our ignorance." A surge of confusion and disbelief erupted throughout the chamber.

"What is the meaning of this, Alpha Idaos? You are afraid of a mere prophecy?" Alpha Canagan scoffed in disbelief. "I believe our strength surpasses some words scribbled by an old charlatan!"

"I must agree with you, Canagan. Idaos has finally lost his mind. To call for a gathering in the Sanctorum over a prophecy." Evette chuckled, amused by the slanders hurled at my expense.

"Silence. Idaos has guided Vascya for years towards a better future. Have faith in his blood, alphas." Eyolf said.

"Despite the jeers, I am intrigued, Idaos. In all the years I have known you, you were never one for flights of fancy, so I know this must be important. Do not keep us in the dark," chimed Illari, her voice soft, almost lyrical.

Picking up the delicate paper once again, my insides burned with excitement. I wasn't like other Lycans. The Moon Goddess had blessed me with the ability to perceive the future. The seemingly innocuous scrap filled me with dread, a result of my enhanced, prophetic senses. Despite the mockery of the other Alphas, I knew the moment was here and now. I would change the future of all Lycans. I cleared my throat and spoke.

"Blood turns on blood,
the cull will begin,

Lycans will fall,
Damned, be the sin.
There will come those that rise from the depths of destruction,
To restore what once was,
the bearers of the God of Death.
Two there shall be and their guide will be extermination,
They will hold the key to endless death.
For woe upon this world,
should the two ever mate.
The power and strength will be in their bond,
the Lycans will bow.
The stink of death surrounds us all,
to storm and fire, Vascya must fall."

The same mouths that had mocked my words were now twisted in shock, their eyes wide with horror. Canagan and Valio stuttered, but the words couldn't escape their lips. In all their years on the Council, none had ever imagined such a catastrophe could befall the Lycan race. Only silence graced the room, amplifying the sounds of the crackling logs that still burned in the fire.

"Are you confident that this prophecy will come true?" Alpha Amarog said in a low voice barely above a whisper.

"Elders, I trust you are aware of my gifts. I am blessed with the blood of the Seer. When I read the prophecy, I sensed utter destruction and death. Destruction of our society, territories, and packs. Destruction of Lycans! That is why I called the sacred Council."

An uproar burst from the group. "When will this come to be true, Idaos?" said Esteve. "What will happen now?" asked Olegario at the same moment.

From the corner of my eye, I saw Evette whisper, "Oh, Liunella help us..."

"How do we prepare for such a calamity!?"

The incoherent mix of voices bombarded me. Questions assaulted my ears. I slammed my fist on the table loudly, calling the elders back to order. "Be silent!" I said. "One at a time. I will answer as best I can." They quieted down; their expressions grim.

"What can we do about the mates mentioned in the prophecy, Idaos?" Olegario asked reluctantly.

"I have examined the prophecy closely. It doesn't name any particular wolves, Alpha." I paused. "However, I have a solution."

"Go on, Idaos. We are all willing to hear your suggestion." Alpha Valio urged me.

"I propose we hunt and imprison all wolves with the mate bond. We watch over those who might pose a threat and dispose of them. We must prohibit unsanctioned marriages between wolves. All marriages must be conducted under strict adherence to the Council laws to avoid this prophesied destruction." I had expected a mixed reaction to that; I didn't see it going over easily. It meant a civil war. A massacre.

"Have you lost your mind, Alpha!?" Alpha Illari exclaimed, her voice screeching with disbelief. "We cannot allow such a thing! We absolutely cannot hunt and kill mates. The Lycan race will suffer. The Moon Goddess has always destined a Lycan to mate; we cannot oppose her!"

"I am aware of that. Do you think I am so incapacitated as to suggest such a horrific deed without adequate reason? I have considered all our choices. Believe me, I have explored every avenue. If I had even a single alternative, I would never propose such a barbaric solution."

"I am against any such notion. We are the sacred Council. We are the leaders who are sworn to protect, not to become the jaegers ourselves. I do not support your decision, Idaos," replied Evette. Illari nodded in solidarity with her sister.

Anger filled my body like a wave. I curled my hands into fists. I knew I could not lose control in the sacred chamber. Berserking was forbidden here. The others would not tolerate something like that. My surroundings darkened and my senses sharpened. I heard each of their beating hearts pulsing like drums. The wolf inside me was eager to surface.

Pointing at her, I said, "Look at the damned prophecy and tell me you aren't blind to its words. If we do not act, these wolves will take everything from you."

"I do not care for this prophecy, Idaos. I oppose such a wild 'solution'. Do you have any idea how many wolves we would kill? Liunella would never forgive such a deed. If you go through with this insanity, I will not stand by you. We as elders should come to a judgment together. You cannot single-handedly decide the fate of the lycans!" Alpha Ronak thundered.

"Are you challenging my bloodline, Ronak? I have the foresight. I have seen it." I wheezed in anger.

"You are not the only one who has the blood of the old in you, Idaos. Do not neglect the fact that I have the blood of Draxus, the power of the mind, flowing in my veins. I believe that I will arrive at a better plan of action," Ronak said.

"Time is a luxury we do not possess, Ronak. The bloodletting will start and we cannot stop it. Tonight, in this holy room, we will determine the fate of our land. Each one of you, your home, your family, your people, even your life, is in perpetual danger. If you think this response is extreme, so be it. But this is the only way you can keep yourself safe in the troubled times ahead. My senses, the powers bestowed upon me by The Moon Goddess, do not lie. I was meant to find this prophecy and guide you all. I know the path I suggest is destructive, but it's the only salvation we have! We must protect ourselves from the coming disaster. So, with Liunella, our goddess of tides as a witness, I call upon the Council to vote on this decision, right here and right now!" My voice rang with clarity. It was clear as a bell. I had them. They would bend.

"All in favor?" Alpha Eyolf whispered. I smoothly raised my hand, gazing at the other elders. One by one, with a look of shame and defeat, other members raised their hands in affirmation. However, three hands remained on the table, fists clenched in opposition. Ronak, Illari, and Esteve.

"You cursed fools." Anger seethed in my words as I scowled at the three of them.

"Idaos, on my life, I will not allow you to go through with this." Ronak spoke with chilling clarity. "Allow me some time to come up with a solution better than eradicating innocent people," he said.

The nerve of the bastard. "Ronak!" I yelled. "There is no other way. I have tho—"

"You have thought nothing through," he snapped back. "Why did you invite me to be a part of this Council if you won't even take advantage of my intellect? In your bid for power, you deposed our king in the last revolution a century ago. This time around, I will not let you commit even more atrocities in the Council's name."

"Damn you..." I fumed.

"Alphas, I bid to remove Idaos from the Council," he said.

"But the prophecy!" Eyolf exclaimed.

"Listen to me," I said to the elders. "I cannot lie; my gifts do not lie. Vascya will die."

"Ronak, we must move quickly. We do not have the time to consider your options, as every day wasted makes it harder to counter the prophecy," Olegario said to him, placing a hand on his shoulder. Ronak shrugged it off.

"The majority has ruled," Canagan said flatly. "Your thoughts hold no sway, anymore."

Ronak's eyes went black, his growl reverberating in the enormous chamber.

"You dare taint the sanctity of the sacred chamber by berserking?" I said. "Look at him, he would spill blood in this holy place!" The alphas nodded.

"Ronak, you must leave," said Eyolf.

"We'll decide your punishment for committing this grave sin at a later date," muttered Valio.

Ronak looked stupefied. He slammed his fists on the table and got up from his seat, stomping his foot on the stony floor.

"I'll save you the trouble of deciding anything. I will not be a part of your barbaric schemes. I am leaving the Council." He tore away his crimson robes, throwing them into the fire. His enraged emerald eyes met mine, “This will not end well.”

Ronak turned and left the Sanctorum. Silence filled the large room. The council had agreed to a great civil war. They would do it. They would burn the world to save themselves.

“We shall start the preparations tomorrow,” stated Canagan.

After we adjourned the meeting, I remained alone in the Sanctorum, still seated in my chair, gazing into the hearth fire, staring at the burning robe. My thoughts raced with possibilities. Liunella’s light continued to bathe the vast expanse of the chamber with its silver gossamer glow. I felt a grin finally break out on my face as my laughter echoed throughout the barren room.

THE BLOOD MOON HARBINGER

Charles

Darkness enveloped us in the damp, dense forest. It had been raining throughout the night which made running exhausting, especially since we were running from *him.* With every breath, the scents of the wet forest overwhelmed me. The silence was deafening. The creatures of the night, too, dreaded the monster behind us. In the distance, I heard the startled hoot of an owl and tried to pick up my pace.

The trees were thick around us. They formed a suitable cover, but the tracker chasing us was one of the finest in Vascya. Any cover, shelter or camouflage was useless against him. I was at the end of my strength. My feet throbbed and I wanted to rest, but running was our only chance at survival.

"Faster Lily, please, we have to run faster!" I whispered desperately to the woman running beside me. She was once radiant, with long auburn hair, an angular face, and a button nose. But now dark circles sagged beneath her eyes and fear etched her face. Her hair was streaked black with dirt and haphazardly tied in a knot atop her head. Her skin glowed pale, for we'd been weeks without a ray of sunlight.

"I am... trying, Charles," Lily panted. I knew it drained her to run for hours without a rest. Still, we had escaped him. *Him,* the worst of all.

He had captured us and thrown us in shackles. He'd watched as the

Council guards kicked and beat us repeatedly, wagering with other hunters which of us would die before we reached the Low Cities. They'd injected us both with wolfsbane, the poison which trapped our wolves, preventing them from being unleashed. Although our strength was finally coming back, we were stuck in this form a little longer.

Every time I glanced over my shoulder, I thought I'd see him hot on our heels, grinning viciously as he reveled in the chase. He was a tall man and even taller in his wolf form; a savage and monstrous beast, standing well over twelve feet once shifted. His arms seemed broad as tree trunks, his legs heavily muscled and incredibly powerful. Though he stood and ran on his hind quarters like the rest of us when he let the wolf out, it was easy to imagine him loping on all fours in pursuit of his prey.

The eerie silence of the forest was unnerving. I looked up to the sky. The clouds had cleared, and the stars shone bright in the moonless night. That only made it harder for us. Had there been a full moon, we could have regained our strength earlier. Studying the stars, I guided Lily beside me in the correct direction. We had to keep moving north. Otherwise, we would be lost in more ways than one. Rumor was, there existed a Sanctuary for mated wolves, a place that promised protection. I was determined to reach it.

Finding a mate was Liunella's gift, which the Council had turned into the worst nightmare. Lily would have been safe if it weren't for the bloody elders, the wolves responsible for the creation of this horrendous law some fifty years ago. If only they hadn't started killing off every mated pair in Vascya, we could have been happy. We could have lived.

The memory of the day I met Lily was seared in my mind. I'd been wandering alone, trying to enlist with rebels for the war, but since they moved around so much, I never knew where to look. Of course, that was for their own protection.

I'd seen a skinny girl by a filthy puddle in the dense forest, scrubbing her face clean of blood. Scars covered her arms and legs and her clothes were filthy. My wolf had perked its ears and shown interest in her scent the moment I spotted her. She had smelled so vibrant, like clean sweat and blood with a hint of cinnamon. It was so appealing, so compelling, that I had to approach her. I took a deep breath, my thoughts swirling around in my head. *"Is she the one? Is this my mate?"*

I drew close to her, and as her amber eyes found mine... I knew. Liunella had destined her for me. She was my mate. I returned her gaze in bliss for a moment until I realized the horrific truth.

We were now a target.

I must get her to safety. There's no other way. I had to make her safe or die trying. I won't let anything happen to her. Lily is mine.

My wolf flared inside me, jerking me from my thoughts. This was a glimmer of hope; the wolfsbane was wearing off. But the tremor subsided mere moments after appearing. I realized we were both running faster than before. We were close to flushing the poison from our systems.

No, I thought. *Hope at this time is dangerous.* I casted the notion aside and tightened my grasp on Lily's hand.

"We can make it!" I called to her.

She beamed at me, her eyes shining bright with resolve. Everything was worth it. Even risking death to be with her was a small price to pay. Suddenly, I stumbled over a root and crashed to the woodland floor. A gnarled branch made a terrible, bone-crunching snap as I landed atop it. I cursed the night and this terrible chase before regaining my feet and taking flight. The thick muck was slowing us down. The faster we went, the harder it was to maintain our footing.

"Lily, I feel your pain, but we have to make it farther north. To the river," I panted between strides, "Only then will we have any hope of shaking him off." I glanced at her again. She had that fierce look of determination on her face. She was regaining her strength as well.

My ears perked up abruptly and I stopped in my tracks. I grabbed Lily and shielded her with my body against a tree trunk. I could hear something. My instincts told me it was nothing good. A feeling of dread settled in the pit of my stomach.

He was here. He had found us.

"Lily, look at me. We are almost there. We can do this." I cupped her face in my palms and kissed her, her chapped lips rough against my own, We took off running again with renewed hope. We were so close. So damned close.

Lily placed a hand on my shoulder and cried, "We... we did it, Charles! I can hear running water. It's the river!" I heard the hope in her voice, that dangerous, dangerous hope.

We burst through the thick tree line onto a sandy bank. Water from recent rains had flooded the river, but it was nothing we couldn't swim across. I immediately strode into the rushing water, and as it flowed over my feet, I couldn't help but smile.

"Lily, we did it!" I yelped.

As soon as the words left my mouth, I felt a yank, and in a flash lost Lily's hand as I was pulled under. The icy water flooded my lungs and burned my insides as I choked and sputtered. *Lily!* My thoughts clamored for her. Somehow, I found the strength to heave myself upward, staggering in the swift flow of the channel. I gained my footing and realized I was now waist-deep. I shifted around, shaking my head vigorously to get the water out of my eyes, only to see Lily in the hands of that monster.

"You! Please, just... just let us go! Please..." Her words came out choked with fear. Terror clutched my heart with an iron fist as I watched a diabolical grin stretch across his face. Human now, he was still huge. Just over seven feet tall, he glared at me through a shock of shoulder-length silver hair. A well-kept beard lined his chin ever so perfectly, giving him the appearance of a saint. But he was *no* saint. He was *the Blood Moon Harbinger*, infamous for his strength and agility. The only thing he did well was murder. And now he was holding Lily.

"You... almost made it." He spoke in a deep, mocking voice. I closed my eyes as my soul filled with dread. *NO! We were so close... so close to freedom*. Lily's face flushed with horror.

"Run," she begged weakly, tears streaming down her face.

"No," I replied determinedly, holding back tears of my own. I felt my wolf flare briefly inside me once again, stronger this time, but subsiding just as quickly. He was frenzied, but the wolfsbane still held him in check.

"Leave... leave us alone, please! I beg you! We... escaped. Please, let us go. We won't say a word. We could disappear!" Lily sobbed, struggling in his grasp.

I felt the forest closing in on me, the river water trying to sweep me away. For a moment, I couldn't breathe. My body shuddered in terror. I was afraid of what he was going to do. I was pathetic. I couldn't even protect her...

Suddenly, I felt Lily's presence clearly in my mind, which could only mean one thing. He's free. My wolf is free. Lily must have sensed it, too. I saw the hope clearly in her amber eyes. I felt her thoughts. *"You can escape now. Run, Charles!"* She spoke through our connection, our cursed bond.

"No!" I snarled. I closed my eyes and my wolf began rising. I felt my eyes going dark, my wolf taking over, but I failed to shift once again. When I looked up, I saw his grin widen.

"I can feel your wolf clawing to the surface. *Save me, Charles!*" He roared with laughter, mocking my efforts.

"Charles..." she murmured. "No, no, please don't..."

I felt the shift in energy, that astral distortion, as the monster took on his own wolf form. It is widely known that the wolves with the old blood can distort the world around them when they shift, but I never imagined that the feeling would be so dreadful. It made my vision blur and my stomach clench as if I would wretch. His mere presence oozed power and strength. He uttered a low, throaty growl and my wolf clawed desperately to the forefront of my mind as my muscles bulged. My bones made crackling sound and finally, I shifted.

"Damn it!" I yelped in pain. It was as if I was changing for the first time. My body was free of the poison, but my wolf had trouble emerging. My skin turned dark as my hair protruded. A few more seconds and I'd be able to get her away – get us away. My body grew from a mere six feet to eight. Even in my wolf form, I was a pitiful sight compared to him.

The rumors did not exaggerate when they claimed he was a giant, towering twelve feet tall with rippling muscles, a coarse gray coat, and a chest of silver hair. There were less than six wolves known as *Kaisers*. They were wolves of the old blood, of *the Mugiri of the Strength*. Having always been rare, *Kaisers* had been dying out for decades. Yet here was one now, towering in front of me, holding Lily by the neck between his powerful claws.

We stood facing one another, him on the beach and me in the water. I craned my neck to meet his glowing, red-rimmed eyes. He let out a threatening growl, challenging me, and then tossed my mate to the side like a doll. I lunged forward.

He was incredibly strong, and faster than I expected. Every time I swung my paw at him, he'd gracefully dodge and give me a vigorous shove, toying with me. My attacks grew desperate and wild. Apparently tired of the game, he lashed out faster than my eyes could follow with three incredibly powerful blows straight to my gut, I started coughing blood, rocked, and was hardly able to stand.

Then, I noticed another field of distortion, gentler than before, and saw that Lily was shifting. With the two of us in wolf form, we could escape. I braced myself for another attack, but he ignored me and went after Lily, instead. The horror of the situation hit me as soon as I saw him switch directions. She was in the middle of changing into her wolf, yet the after-effects of wolfsbane still plagued her. She watched as he took long, powerful strides towards her. I lunged to her defense and almost fell. I had several broken ribs.

Fuck, not now! I took another step and another, ignoring the pain. He wrapped his monstrous jaw around her neck. I roared in anger with all my might, but it was too late.

I love you, Charles, run! Her last thoughts speared my mind as I wordlessly screamed in anguish. An instant later, she was torn to pieces in front of me as that bastard ripped her head from her body. He carelessly tossed the head into the river and slurped her blood greedily, lapping at the red flow that gushed from her neck.

I collapsed to my knees as I felt her pain burning throughout my cor. My chest felt hollow, my heart empty and void. Lily, my wolf, my mate, my purpose, was dead. It had all been in vain. Tears streamed down my face as I kneeled before the monster, utterly defenseless, yet no longer caring.

He came closer, his breath hot on my neck. It stank of the blood that dripped from his jaw. Her blood.

"You... Belaize, what have you done..." I whimpered; all my power gone. I sat there, pathetically huddled and crying over the lifeless body of my mate. Then he turned on me, his fangs and claws ripping and shredding my body to ribbons, tearing me asunder, and yet I felt nothing at all as my eyes closed one final time.

"I'll be with Lily."

THE RAID

Belaize

I strolled through the shadows of a gloomy forest with ease. The dazzling stars illuminated my surroundings. This was a dark and moonless night though; a night when wolves are at their weakest. The forest was virtually silent, with only the occasional chirps of crickets, and the snickers of small animals hiding in the thicket. I sensed everything in my immediate area. The big and the small were as distinct to me as they would be in the daylight.

After wiping out the escaped mates by the river, it felt wonderful to stretch my muscles. The pair had actually sprinted quite some distance from the camp, surprisingly. It had been too long since anyone had put up any sort of challenge, and yet those two managed to change into their wolves, even after the Council guards gave them a high dose of wolfsbane. That was, quite frankly, a welcomed treat.

As a Kaiser, one of the rare six granted increased speed and strength to rival the gods, I was the ideal warrior. I was made for the hunt. The sound of combat was music to me, and blood was a glossy finish to my fur. Battle was better than any drug and sweeter than any woman.

Still, shame filled my chest at the thought of my single defeat. On a night such as this, it was hard not to think about. I had been gutted and left to die on a forest floor. Even after twelve years the memory made me feel like a suckling infant. Helpless. Defenseless. *The only fight I have ever lost...*

I grimaced at the massive scar on my arm. It scrawled across my chest, cut me deep too. Even with enhanced healing, the physical reminder of that sudden attack would always exist. I wanted vengeance for it. But I had to play my cards right if that was ever going to be a possibility.

And I admit I had gone searching for it. Just another mission issued by the elders, after all. But I had not expected... *that*. That thing. It had come out of nowhere and I had no chance against it. I went into that forest expecting a ferocious animal, maybe a wildcat, or a bear, but what I encountered was something else, something *way* too powerful. And yet I survived, somehow, but the scar was a painful reminder.

But...maybe it could happen again. No. No, it won't. I will not lose again.

I trudged through the trees toward a clear valley covered in short bushes and tall grass. Soon I reached the camp that the pups had set up. About thirty little tents made of gray tarp extended across the valley. Torches were lit along the flanks, casting the night in a yellow glow. I sensed about fifty-five individual wolves in front of me. Nodding to myself in approval, I left the shadows of the trees behind and started moving towards the camp entrance. The Council guards posted there smelled me before I closed the short distance. I would have punished them if they hadn't.

At least they can do something right, I thought with disdain.

They were still inexperienced and impatient to fight. None of the young guards had legitimate combat training, and they wouldn't last more than thirty seconds with me. Nowadays, the Council was sending these pups to the front lines as quickly as possible thanks to the war.

The Council made use of us all. Women served the realm as breeders for new frontline soldiers, and the runts were plucked from the slums of the Low Cities as soon as they could howl at the moon. They weren't ready for a fight. They weren't good for anything besides target practice. My wolf paced within my chest.

"You smell of the blood of the cunts that fled this afternoon," one of them offered. I didn't bother to recall his name.

"You smell like the shit I took this morning," I snapped back. He knew who I was. They all knew. I wouldn't even break a sweat killing him. I glared at him with fury. My wolf was eager to tear out his throat for that remark. I never tolerate disrespect. The pup closed his mouth immediately, bowing his head and cowering away. I crossed the camp and made my way toward my tent.

"Belaize, you always take the fun out of every wager," called another.

"Go hunt a rabbit, pup. That ought to be fun for you." I paused for a moment. "Now that I think about it, maybe even that would be too much for your wolf."

The small crowd chuckled at the retort. "One day your arrogance will bite you in your own ass, Belaize!" He called out again, hatred evident in his voice.

I stilled. I craved his blood. Turning, I strode towards him. The Council guard was small compared to my colossal frame. Still, in his late teens, he was new to the field and didn't think I would hurt a Council guard. He assumed that the title of the guard granted him immunity. But no one was safe from me. For the better part of a decade, I had been the success behind the Council. These artificially bred wolves were worthless against me.

For a second, I looked down into his eyes. Confident at first, I watched as they slowly became more and more worried. Fearful. Shooting my arms out faster than he could see and wrapping my rough hands around his frail neck, I hoisted him bodily off the ground. My fingers began digging into his neck. I heard every crack of his bones as I simply held him there, aloft. I squeezed tighter and tighter. The wolf struggled in my grasp, flailing his arms and legs, but he couldn't escape me. Blood oozed from his mouth, dousing my fingers red.

"Even if my arrogance bites me back, you won't be alive to see it," I said darkly, staring into his eyes, savoring the terror I found there. I tore his head away from his body with my bare hands. His gurgling scream echoed through camp. His body dropped to my feet, twitching a few times before going limp. Blood poured from the shredded stump. I picked up his disembodied head and threw it outside the camp. I sauntered away to my tent. "Rot. You fuckin' idiot..."

I hauled up the gray tarp covering the entrance and stepped inside the modest but comfortable space. A fire was burning in the center clearing to keep me warm during the cold, damp night. I washed my bloodied hands, scrubbing away the red of today's kill. Well, kills. After changing out of my dirty trousers and into a new clean set of clothes, I walked back to my desk and grabbed a pitcher of water, gulping it all down at once.

I had just eased myself down on my makeshift bed when a wolf entered my tent unannounced. "You shouldn't have come inside," I threatened.

"I know, but I had no choice! Orden is summoning you, sir," responded Marcus. He was an apprentice of Commander Orden, some Council puppet with an exalted title who ran the operation of capturing mates in the Northern part and was, unfortunately, under Alpha Valio's protection.

Marcus shifted his weight nervously. He was tall and lean, but he paled in comparison to me. He'd been around for quite some time now, so I tolerated him, but just barely. "You should know, if it was someone else, I would have killed you by now," I muttered darkly.

"I know, sir, and I am grateful for that. I would prefer to keep my head attached to my body. Commander is calling for you, and he requires you in the briefing area, right now, sir." The anxiety in his voice was rather apparent.

"Sure. I've nothing better to do." I straightened and tossed aside the pile of furs. A brief walk later, I entered a much larger tent. It was taller and significantly roomier than mine, and could easily accommodate eighty wolves inside. In the center was a heavy wooden desk. A middle-aged man sitting behind it. The hair on his head had thinned and his beard turned white. He glanced up, gesturing for me to sit in the chair opposite him.

"Orden," I said.

"Belaize, come here. Sit, I ca—"

Towering over his small frame, I slammed my fists on his desk and glared. "The next time I hear you've 'summoned me,' I'll murder every wolf in this camp — including you. I am not your slave to be called upon." The low growl in the back of my throat only emphasized my displeasure.

He stilled like a statue in his seat. He was a miserable excuse of a Commander. His fear was unmistakable; I could smell it. Satisfied, I nodded, then sat down on the cushioned brown chair.

"Speak."

"I—um—I," Orden stuttered.

"If you have called me only to waste my time, tell me now," I said. He took a deep breath and collected himself.

"Forgive me, Belaize. We just received valuable intelligence, and I thought you should hear of it urgently. I hardly considered how it would displease you. My apologies."

"What is it?"

"One of the ranger teams was scouting the forest areas near the Walkaian border in the northern region. The rangers discovered a mate Sanctuary. They confirmed it is under rebel protection, and that many warrior wolves are moving in and out of the Sanctuary. The Council is convinced that the rebel army is gathering their forces there and will strike the Capital soon. The elders want you to lead a unit and destroy that Sanctuary." Orden spoke quickly, eyeing me with expectation.

"It could be another one of those camps where mated wolves are hiding. I don't have any problem killing and capturing them, but I want my hands bloodied with some actual rebels now. It has been months since our last skirmish. How certain are you that the rebel army is present at the Walkaian border?" I said, yearning for blood, the hunger to kill stronger than ever.

"I'm not that sure, if I'm being honest with you, Belaize. The rebels keep moving all over Vascya, and it's becoming harder to pinpoint their location. Each time we think we are closing in on them, they slip from our grasp. This information could be false, but the elders have instructed us to move out, as we are closest to the border. They have specifically requested that you run the task force as well, considering your..." he cleared his throat, "Accomplishments."

"Killing record, you mean," I added with a wry grin.

"Not what I intended, but that works. So, will you go on this raid?" Orden prodded.

"Fine. Only because there is a promise of kills," I agreed.

"It's settled. You'll debrief your unit tomorrow morning, see them equipped for the mission, and leave for the Sanctuary soon after the first meal."

I nodded once, stood up, and left the command tent. Stepping out into the gloomy night, I looked forward to the bloodbath that tomorrow would bring.

THE PHALANX

Belaize

Waking up to the smell of fresh morning air, I stared at the dark screens hanging high above me as my eyes blinked open. The mellow rays of the morning sun were peeking under the edges of the tent. Last night's fire was long gone and ash lingered in its place. I sensed all the wolves in the valley. Some had probably gone out to hunt for prey. After all, this was the best time to do so.

The task force Orden asked me to lead was aggravating. I worked alone, and yet, I was being "ordered." Their silly rules meant nothing to me. I did what I wanted, killed whoever I wished. But the Council would never let me work alone; I was valuable and highly dangerous for their old ass. They want to keep me under constant surveillance. I resented that.

Finally, I sat up. The bed was stifling and oppressive. It was time to step out, organize, and attack.

I went into the briefing area where I had spoken with Orden last night. Marcus was sitting behind a desk in the tent's corner, scribbling away on yellowed paper. "What are you doing, Marcus?" I called. He looked up toward me, his blue eyes surprised. He crammed the papers in the drawer and stood up.

"Oh, nothing. Just some reports Commander requested for. They are to be shipped out to the Low Cities along with the detainees this afternoon. What can I do for you, sir?" he inquired.

Mannerly, this one, I thought. I cleared my throat.

"I have to gather a team for a raid near the northern border. Bring me nine of the fastest wolves available here. Get the necessary supplies loaded and we'll move out around noon. You will go with me as well. Is that clear?"

"Sir, not to be impolite, but why have you chosen me? I will simply be a hindrance; I am neither fast nor strong," he said.

"I chose you, Marcus, because I think your strategic skills might be useful in the field. I require someone that can supervise these pups."

"Very well. Thank you, for the opportunity. I'll prepare everything. I will meet you at noon with all members at the camp entrance." He stood up from his chair and marched out of the briefing area.

I liked Marcus. He was easy to order around, and my wolf, with his alpha blood, agreed with Marcus's obedient nature. He was a few years younger than me, but he was mature for his age. There was something else to Marcus. He had intelligence far beyond his years, and a wolf that knew when to sit, stay, and shut his mouth.

I decided not to kill him in the foreseeable future unless he provoked me.

Exactly at noon, I sauntered towards the camp entrance. I sensed exactly nine wolves assembled there, along with Marcus. They were standing together in a group, bags filled with supplies. Upon my arrival, every one of them bowed. Perhaps yesterday's kill taught them some respect. Every wolf present looked to me expectantly, waiting for instructions.

"As you already know, the mission is to wipe out the rebel base. Information suggests it's near the Walkaian border. we'll take a straight route through the forest, to the town of Novocher, where rangers are expecting us. After briefing them, I'll decide the plan of action.

"Frankly, I don't believe you're the best wolves suited to carry out this operation; you don't have adequate experience. However, you are fast, and therefore less of a hindrance. If anyone steps out of line..." I looked directly at Marcus. His jaw twitched, but he met my gaze. "I'm warning you now. I will tear your limbs off and leave you to rot." A low growl escaped my lips. "You would be wise not to test me." I searched the faces of all ten wolves before me, who only nodded silently in agreement.

"We should reach Novocher before dark. Tonight marks a new lunar phase, so don't expect moonlight to aid us. I wish to arrive as soon as possible. Rebel corpses await us."

I shifted, morphing into the monstrosity that was my wolf. The popping of my bones and pulling of my muscles felt incredible. I shifted faster than all of them, and the pride of it burned in my chest. I shook out my coat, knowing I made an impressive sight. As each wolf finished their transformation, I smelled fear in the air. Their attention turned to my silver mane, the mark of the Kaiser, one of the old blood.

Their wolves stood half my size, and I could smash every bone in their bodies if I wished it. My eyes flickered to Marcus. He was more built than the others. He had a jet-black coat that contrasted with his sea-blue eyes. He stood at maybe nine feet tall. And perhaps in a certain light, he displayed peculiar traces of an alpha.

Impossible, I scoffed at the idea.

The attributes of the old blood flared in wolves at an early age, before they go through the first shift. I am sure I showed the traits at a mere age of five. That is how most wolves find out that they are bestowed with the old blood or cursed with the tainted blood of Jackals. The origin of Jackals is still unclear, as some wolves are born weaker than others, with limited shifting abilities, and are thus more affected by the lunar cycle. I showed signs of being a Kaiser before I had even turned.

Marcus was undeniably stronger than he let on, but he could never match a Kaiser. And yet as he moved through the group, adjusting armor and packing supplies, I noticed how exact he was: he never moved more than he needed to. He never slipped or faltered. I would be careful to watch him. He was dangerous, that much was clear.

I waited a moment, then stepped to the helm of the group and howled. I crouched down low like a spring coiled tight. Then I let my wolf take over. I sprinted into the woods with the others on my trail.

Trees rushed by me as I ran. I loved sprinting through the forest and flaunting my agility. The world was a blur and the breeze whipped at my face as I jumped over a fallen tree trunk, ducked below another, diving deeper into the forest. The cool air filled my lungs as I analyzed my surroundings. The camp's scent, the woodsmoke and shit, slowly faded as we headed for the river Brahn.

The shortest distance to Novocher involved swimming across the mighty river, although it wasn't as broad toward the forest of Chern, so it wouldn't be the hardest of crossings. The prisoners I slew last night made it to the same river.

The evergreen forest was yet damp from yesterday morning's rain. The forest floor was a thick, sludgy muck. The others were stumbling and staggering. Even the fastest of the lot was having trouble keeping up with me. I flung a steady stream of curses in their direction.

Then sun was dipping below the western peaks when I heard the dull sound of running water. We were only six miles away from the Brahn. I stretched my awareness toward the Council guards that accompanied me. A few, including Marcus, were beyond my senses, lagging far behind. Marcus wasn't of the warrior bloodline, nor was he equipped for speed. It was his mind that I put on the team, not his strength, but I made no effort to slow my pace.

Soon I halted in front of the flowing waters of the river. It wasn't as flooded as it had been yesterday, the runoff water long gone, but it was unquestionably deep. The water flowed west with a current that could kill just as swiftly. I briefly glimpsed the blurry image of my wolf in the water, the scar on my arm was an angry red tear in the distorted reflection.

Panting came from the tree line as one wolf appeared behind me, followed by everyone else. They emerged from the woods looking haggard and worn, covered in sweat and scrapes.

I turned toward the river and jumped in, signaling the rest to follow my lead. Kicking hard with my legs, I swam faster and soon crawled up the other side of the steep and muddy riverbank. Dropping to all fours, I shook myself vigorously, shedding my sleek fur of water. Then, mostly dried, I stood and shifted to my human form and dressed myself as the rest gained the riverbank and started changing back as well.

"Five of you will remain here with Marcus. Light a fire and rest. Everyone else, go hunt. Be quick about it. We rest for an hour. No breaks after this," I ordered. The wolves scrambled to their tasks at my words.

I stalked off in the opposite direction along the riverbank.

Frankly, I couldn't stand their company. I was the ultimate rogue and assassin. Wolves have an instinct to remain together, but I preferred to be alone. I'd never made the pack bond, and I never would. I'd only ever trained to fight. *I am the one who slaughters*, I thought.

All I needed was a challenge. The entire population of Vascya, or what's left of it, paled in comparison to my might. But it... that *thing... What was it?* My thoughts chased themselves as that night came rushing back to me.

Running. I was running towards the woods of the forgotten gods. I'd heard the stories. No one comes back from these woods, they say. But I was determined to prove that the beast within woods was just another challenge to fall short of me. Yet, the woods were ominous, like they had a presence of their own. Something stalked me through the moonless night, just as I hunted it. In a blink of an eye, a white flash came out of nowhere and threw me to the ground with ease. I lay disoriented and confused. I smelled the iron of blood. Where was it coming from? My chest burned. The woods spun around me, and the flash came again.

A searing pain took hold of me as my arm burned with phantom agony. My head was pounding and my eyes blurred. This happened sometimes, when I was alone, my thoughts are pulled back to that place. The memory alone frightened me.

Suddenly, I heard a howl coming from the direction of others, pulling me out of remembrance. The smell of fear-sweat lingered in the air. Surely, the wolves would smell it, as well, and that could not be allowed. I took a quick dive into the river beside me, washing myself of the stench. *Why did that night torment me so much?* I clenched my teeth. These idiots were supposed to hunt. And I had to lead them.

I closed my eyes, sensing others. "Nine, ten, and... thirteen." I realized the pups had brought back more than game.

Walking back to our brief camp, I saw four of the wolves sitting around the fire cooking a boar for lunch. The scent of charred pork filled the air, attracting the attention of small scavengers nearby, hidden away from sight. Rats, stoats, and the like.

Turning aside from them, I concentrated on the 'men.' "Well, well, well, what do we have here?" I glanced at the three captured wolves. Two females and an adolescent boy stood huddled together and bound to a tree.

"We discovered this lot wandering about two miles from where we were hunting. They were trying to hide, but considering our speed, these idiots didn't stand a chance," the young guard said.

I studied the three of them intently.

"Who are you?" I asked nonchalantly. They were covered in rags which could hardly be referred to as clothes. They were filthy and clearly starved – for Liunella knows how long. The two women gazed at the damp ground covered in rotting leaves beneath their feet. The kid stood wailing and weeping, irritating me to the end of my patience.

"Boy!" I snarled. I felt the pull of my fangs as they became sharp, canine points. "Why do you cry?" I asked with malice in my voice. One of the she-wolves flailed in her binds, trying to break free.

"You can't protect him, especially from me." I chuckled at her attempt. Marcus caught my gaze. He was studying me... No, he was telling me something. "*Let them go*," his blue eyes said with silent words, his gaze full of meaning. I just smiled.

"Loosen the boy and bring him to me," I ordered. The guards obeyed and shoved the boy in front of me.

The woman struggled in her restraints. "Don't touch him, you filthy Council bastards. Don't you dare!" She protested, screaming vile curses.

When that failed to elicit a response from any of us, she sank within herself and groveled, begging, "Please, my son! My only son! He's innocent! We are all innocent!" She sobbed, knowing the danger all of them were in. Frankly, it was a pitiful sight.

"Quiet, now. Be still...," I drawled, circling the kid. He was trembling and weeping, barely able to stand from fear. His hair was greasy, his cheeks gaunt. I heaved him up to my face with one hand. He struggled briefly in my grip, and whimpered with pain. "Have you turned yet, boy?" I asked him.

The boy shook his head in denial. "And pray tell, how old are you?" He glanced toward the female who I presumed to be his mother, with tears streaming down his face.

"I'm... thirteen," the boy gasped. Hidden claws grew from my free hand. I traced one gingerly across his frail neck and looked over to the she-wolf. "You are raising a weakling." I spat.

Everything was silent, except for the woman's wails that echoed throughout the forest. The other she-wolf remained silent, all but paralyzed at the events unfolding before her. Catching a glimpse of Marcus, whose eyes still pleaded for mercy, I dropped the kid. He rose, scurrying to his mother's side.

A bitter laugh escaped my lips. "Let's play a game, shall we? It'll be entertaining, I assure you. If you, boy, can make it to that tree," I pointed in the distance toward a pine tree standing tall within the forest, about a hundred feet away. "If you can touch it, I will let you and your companions go free."

"You may want to start running now, before I change my mind," I taunted.

The kid glanced at the two women tied up. In a split second, he took off sprinting. He was fast, I'll give him that, even with his feeble body. Perhaps he was close to changing. The Council guards roared with laughter as he ran. He even made it to the tree, but I stood rooted in place, a smile upon my lips.

The skinny boy turned to look at his mother. Instantly, blood drained from his face as he witnessed his mother's severed head in my hand, dangling by her hair. His face echoed the pain and agony she must have felt in her last moments. The blood was still leaking from her sundered neck, dripping in the dirt. The horror of what I'd done crashed upon him as he cried out in anguish. I tossed him her head. It rolled along the ground, coming to rest at his feet.

"Untie this one and let the two go," I said sadistically. "Let's not say that Belaize is not a man of his word."

Then, the boy rushed towards me, even faster than before. *He was going to swing at me.* The thought was hilarious.

He jabbed at my chest, but I caught his hand in mine and wrenched it. I heard the crack of his wrist as the bones split and tore. He shrieked in pain and fell to his knees. The other woman rushed to the fallen kid, who now lay unconscious on the ground from the pain.

"Get out of my sight," I said, disgusted. Without word, the woman picked up the boy and sprinted away into the forest. I watched as she disappeared into the trees. She was heading north and I made a mental note of it.

"Marcus!" I shouted. Marcus immediately stood in front of me, awaiting instruction. He was nervous. Even though he hadn't protested me, I knew what he wanted. *Forgiveness? Mercy? Ha!* I scoffed at such cowardice. *If you're going to kill,* I thought, *it should be for the joy of it.*

"Yes?" Marcus inquired.

"Tell one of these wolves to pursue them. I want to know how far the Sanctuary is. Stay close but far enough not to be detected. The rest of us will move when we've eaten."

"Yes, sir," He answered and left to set up the arrangement.

I wandered to the river and started washing myself again. Blood covered my hands. It didn't bother me, as an alpha, that's expected. The weak perish. That is how the world works. My reflection rippled in contorted waves of water. "Who are you?" it said.

"Death." I replied solemnly.

REBEL

Marcus

I left Belaize standing where he was. Scanning the riverside, I spotted Xavier, his peculiar copper colored hair was easily spotted from afar. He was perched on a boulder and feasting greedily. Xavier had a runner's build: tall and lean; one of the fastest wolves in Commander Orden's camp, at that.

I forced a calm exterior, but my body was covered in a sheen of sweat. My throat felt raspy and it hurt to breathe. I was the last to cross the Brahn. I admit, I am stronger than most wolves, but my speed has never been an asset. Apparently, I was in charge of strategizing, but it felt more like I was that bastard's servant. I didn't belong on a fucking strike force.

"Xavier," I called to him. He looked up but kept chewing meat off the bone.

"What?" he replied.

"You saw what happened." The flashes of the severed head and their screams echoed through my mind. I shuddered, but I kept my voice hard as stone, "Belaize wants you to track down the pair that ran away."

Xavier's lips curled into a snarl as his eye twitched. "I'm in the middle of my meal. I don't want to go after them. Go find someone else. Or better yet, go yourself." He spit a bone fragment at my feet.

"Oh wait, you can't track them because you're the slowest of the bunch. Fucking useless piece of shit." The other guards sitting around us snickered. My muscles quivered as I clenched my fists.

Cracking my knuckles one by one, I bared my teeth; my sharp fangs elongating, "I will not tolerate insolence."

All Xavier did was laugh louder than before, patting his thigh alongside. "I am not scared of you, Marcus. You are just Belaize's slave, you know? Yes, sir. No, sir. Just a little bitch that fulfills his master's every command. Maybe you are his bitch. Our camp doesn't have any she-wolf warriors anymore. Belaize has his needs too." He cocked his head to the side in disgust. "We all hate Belaize, but you are just as vile, if not more. Wagging your tail like a pet around him."

At that moment, I lost it. I transformed into my wolf, my body changing, growing. My senses sharpened as I grew taller. Within moments, I stood opposite Xavier in my wolf form. My feet rooted to the ground and ready to strike. Compared to Belaize, my wolf was nothing, but I could compete with others in strength.

I jumped on Xavier, throwing him down. His food splattered to the ground, forgotten, as he growled and shifted into a dark copper coated wolf. I had a clear advantage in size, but him, oh, he had *speed.*

Once more, I growled and attacked, but he slipped right under me. His jibes lacked strength, but he made up for it with his slender frame and agility. We circled one another then, clinging to a brief pause in combat. My wolf was cold and calculating, taking in his movements.

I pounced and watched and repeated. Noticing the ripples on his muscles as he moved, and how he favored his left leg but only slightly. Everyone flocked around us now, watching the quarrel. They jeered and hollered. I sensed Belaize standing in the shadow of the trees by the river. They assumed I'd lose, that I was weak because I did the work, because I was slow. Because I didn't show my anger.

Wrong choice.

I concentrated on Xavier, waiting for his attack. When he bared his fangs to strike me I jumped high and opened my jaw, revealing sharp fangs of my own aimed right for his neck. He instantly skipped to his left to dodge away.

Wrong fucking choice.

I dug my right claw into him. Blood oozed from his shoulder and he stumbled. That was my cue. I jumped on him, hurling my body over his, applying my weight and pinning down his wolf. I snarled and grabbed his neck, ready to sink in, waiting for his surrender. He stopped moving and leaned his head to the side, ultimately accepting his defeat. I released him and changed back to my human form.

"Next time do what I order you to do, because Belaize isn't the only one with anger or the ability to kill. He might be the leader right now, but I carry out his instructions. You'll do better to keep that in mind," I huffed out with annoyance.

"Go wash up and after that, trail that boy and she-wolf. If Belaize hears you wasted his time, he won't be lenient."

Turning, I wandered to the riverbank away from all the wolves. I needed to be alone. Sitting down over a jagged, sturdy rock, I listened to the serene silence of the forest. It cooled me, just a little anyway. I resented fighting; I was good at it, but I loathed it, too. Especially this war.

All I wanted was peace.

I recalled looking at Belaize earlier, hoping, wishing he would not murder the poor she-wolf who wanted to protect her child. But he was ruthless as a demon. The rumors spread throughout Vascya were true. He loved to kill.

I had been around Belaize for over a year. Observing him. Noting his strengths, weaknesses, and his intentions. Trying... trying to overthrow him, to kill this monster who impersonated death. Time was running out; I swear every day Belaize just got stronger and stronger. His black heart was filled with rage, and the Council knew exactly how to use that. Belaize was the deadliest weapon the Council possessed. We had to beat him, to... kill him. That was the price of victory.

And... I had found a way. The only way.

My thoughts drifted to Ronak, his patient leadership, his steady guidance. He was a deserving Alpha, and he needed this information if he was going to save us. Save all of us. This just might be the slight shift in current that would change the tide of this war.

The plan had been to run away from Orden's camp once I had more intelligence, but I couldn't just leave them behind. Charles. Lily. Unfortunately, their escape had been discovered, and with the patrols on high alert there was no way that I could've made it out safely. *No way you could've saved them either, right? Their death was your fault,* I thought bitterly, acid in my throat. No. Now I was stuck with Belaize, carrying out his orders and killing for him. Every fiber of my body was against it. To hurt others, to fight the innocent. War was horrendous. I pawed at my face briefly.

I would make it out soon, but till that time came, I'd keep hidden away.

I had to be careful, extremely careful.

MATES

Belaize

A ghost of a smile emerged on my face. It was obvious who would win the round, even before it had truly begun. Marcus's stance was perfect. He had gauged his opponent from the start, unlike the guard. A fight without weighing your odds was simply idiotic.

I was different. No matter the odds, I would win. People trembled upon hearing my name. My wolf relished the fear that struck their hearts when they realized they were going to face me.

I eyed Marcus as he walked away after defeating the Council guard. *Well, he is carrying out his orders nicely*, I thought.

I settled against following Marcus to the river. He needed time. While I reveled in the thrill of a fresh kill, Marcus was a different brat. He didn't want me to kill that she-wolf, but I didn't have such a delicate heart. I was molded to be a vicious killer; death given a physical form.

About an hour passed when I went back to the others.

"Get off your lazy ass. The time to relax is over. Get your supplies packed within five minutes, we are leaving. Novocher is about a four-hour run from here. I'd like to be there before sundown," I barked.

Within minutes we were on the move. I was running fast through the dim forest. Most of the others kept up with me after being rested. They weren't too far behind, although they couldn't match me step-for-step. Perhaps they know better than to get too close; they knew their place.

Marcus still lagged compared to the others, but at least he was running parallel with the rest of the wolves now. It was remarkable how he had adapted in a short amount of time.

A couple of hours had passed, and the sun was hidden behind the mountains of the Walkaian Range, the Frozen Fingers. The sky had turned varying shades of cinereous as the night approached; a few stars already twinkling.

The trees had thinned out. I could sense the town's energy. We were nearing the small town of Novocher. Even amid the war, towns like this thrived well. The wolves living there had co-operated well with the Council. Most had collectively surrendered the mated wolves that lived in their towns to avoid carnage. But many wolves had turned against Council's decision. *The rebels.*

I halted in a clearing carpeted with grass and changed, waiting for the others to assemble. Soon, all nine wolves had gathered. I remained in the center, encircled by them. "We are a couple of miles from the town. We will walk from here on. Someone will meet us at the town entrance. We are going on the raid tonight, so when we get there, rest, otherwise, you will not survive the fight," I cautioned. It was necessary to prepare them for later.

I took to the trail heading toward town. I stayed in front of the pack, and the others traveled wearily behind. I could sense their nervous unease around me, how they stayed closer together, eyes averted. We carried on that way until I spotted a broad flat stone symbolizing the town's entrance. 'Novocher' it read.

As the trail gradually widened, it became smooth. I felt the pulse of life around me, and one standing apart from the rest. An old man was waiting at the edge of the trail. He walked towards me and bowed. "I am Lazarus, and I welcome all of you into the humble town of Novocher," he squeaked in a high-pitched voice.

He was an old man. Age had withered his face, wrinkles spider-webbed from his deep-set eyes and his cheeks sagged loosely. He had a nearly bald head with only a few whiskers on this crown. He looked like a man who has seen a lot of blood in his life. Yet, he was receiving us like old friends.

"I'm certain you know who we are," I said, asserting my dominance. He nodded.

"Yes, of course. You are the mighty wolf, Belaize. I received word from Commander Orden yesterday informing me you and the others would arrive shortly." He gestured to the other wolves beside me with one frail hand.

"I am sure the long run must have tired you today. Come with me and I'll show you to your quarters. Dinner awaits there." He motioned for all of us to follow.

I started walking and fell into step with Lazarus. "What do you know about the rebel base?" I inquired.

He drew a deep breath and sighed. "The wolves living here, they just want peace. The town is under the protection of Alpha Valio. He made the transition through these arduous times much easier. And I assure you, we do not associate ourselves with the rebels, otherwise the Council would see to our eradication. We abide by its rules-" he paused as a wracking cough shook his small form. He pulled a cloth from his tunic and wiped at his mouth.

"But the rebels are troublesome. They raid us every month or two, looting and disrupting the trade. The Council has equipped us with elite guards for protection, but it's not enough. These rebel warriors are different. They are meticulous. Their leader knows efficient tactics to bend every battle in their favor." He gave a knowing look at each of the young men behind me. I shifted my weight and moved my shoulders to block his view, towering over him.

"So I have heard from my travels throughout Vascya. Ronak has made quite an impression with the Council," I acknowledged. My wolf was eager to tear the rebel leader apart.

"There was only a handful of rebels before. Now, it's like nothing I've seen before. I had mentioned this to Alpha Valio. That's when they sent those rangers here." Lazarus finished.

"Where are they?"

"Ah yes. One of them is waiting for you at the tavern. He will deliver the information and lead you to the base," the old man responded.

We walked down a barren street. Novocher was not a small town. It stretched far and wide, dotted with clusters of brick buildings, and cobbled streets. I saw the shops were closed, not a soul in sight. Everyone was inside the safety of their homes.

False security.

We walked along the side of a narrow, rundown building. It looked rusty and old, like the entire town. The red brick street was crumbled and worn. A stone sign beside the building read, 'Morin's Tavern' in the slight gleam of light coming out from the windows. The wooden door was closed, but hung loosely from a broken hinge.

The old man climbed the steps in front of the door then knocked. A scrawny boy pushed the door wide open. "Oh, uncle! Come in. You're a little later than I assumed you would be. It's alright. Come in. Come in, everybody," he said warmly.

The kid was small. Weak. He looked about fourteen. He had a head of unruly black hair, and his freckled boyish face beamed as he greeted us.

"Welcome to Morin's Tavern. Please take your seats and I'll bring you some food and moon wine. My sister will be down shortly with food." He grinned pleasantly, turning to Lazarus.

"Uncle, should I call the other guest downstairs?"

Lazarus turned toward me. I silently nodded and sat down on a gray upholstered chair. The feather padding was a bit much, but it was comfortable. Lazarus turned to the boy again. "Yes, of course, Rowen. Hurry with the wine."

Rowen quickly shuffled away. "He is a decent kid. He helps his sister around the tavern. After the Council... took their parents away, they are the only ones left for each other. I have known them since their birth, yet I share no blood with them," he said gently. His eyes softened. Clearly, he was fond of the boy.

I studied the old tavern. Tawny colored paint covered the walls, which was peeling away. Across from me were wooden shelves filled with bottles of assorted wines and liquor. The smooth wooden tables and chairs were old as well. A fire blazing in a narrow fireplace in the room's corner kept the tavern comfortably warm. It seemed like a nice place for regulars and merchants to wash away the day's work with some wine. Even though it was old, the siblings kept it nice enough.

The other wolves were lounging around, resting after the long, hard run. The boy, Rowen, arrived with glasses full of moon wine. I picked one, lifting it to my mouth and sipping slowly. The crimson-colored wine burned down my throat as I swallowed. "Excellent wine." A good moon wine always leaves a burn.

The stairs to the far side creaked, and a man stepped into the room. He was about six feet tall but had little muscle. His brown hair was drawn in a braid down his back. "You must be the ranger. Sit." I gestured to the chair in front of me.

He strode across the room and sat in front of me comfortably. "I have heard you found a rebel base." I shifted in my seat, resting my head on my hand, sipping wine with the other.

"Yes, that is correct. My name is Darin. Three days ago, my partner and I were scouting the border. The elders had sent us to find one of the rumored mate Sanctuaries. We stumbled upon one, alright. We confirmed that it was a rebel operation's base not long after. The number of rebels hiding there is astonishing. A constant flow of wolves comin' and goin'. Unexpectedly, we saw about two hundred, maybe even closer to three hundred fifty wolves arrive." He halted for a second, reaching for a glass of wine from the server boy and sipping it.

"I was absolutely shocked to witness so many wolves at once. Rebels normally travel in small numbers. It seemed like the rebels were gathering there. Immediately, I traveled to Walka to contact the Council. They informed me that your group was the closest. And here we are." Darin finished.

"Did you see their leader, Ronak?" I scratched my rough stubble, wondering what he looked like. The rebel alpha was the greatest pain to the Council, Ronak, the wise.

"I'm not sure who was in command there, but one of 'em was ordering the wolves around. Might've been that one. He was a couple inches taller than me, long dark hair till about this length." Darin pointed a little below his shoulder. "He had a small build. Looked a little lanky, to be honest."

"How many wolves do you estimate in the whole Sanctuary?" I drilled on.

"I would edge on, hmm... about four hundred, including the rebels that arrived. Might've changed since I left. My partner is still at the location. When we raid, he'll tell us the correct number." He hesitated, looking at me with inquiring eyes. "Are... these the only wolves you have accompanying you?" he said.

I arched my eyebrow, my gaze meeting his. "Your... point?" I growled.

He shifted nervously in his chair. "I... uh-uh... It's too few for raiding the Sanctuary."

I shoved the table away and seized the man by his neck. Our glasses fell to the floor, shattering. I knocked him against the wall. Everyone stilled. I sensed their fear, especially, Darin's. His pulse beat heavily against my palm. My wolf grinned in my head, reveling in the power.

"Do you think I am incompetent for such a miserable task?" I paused as I continued to choke the ranger with my hands. "You should never forget who I am, wimp."

I sent him flying across the hall like a rag and sat back down, gesturing to the scared-looking boy to bring me more wine. I looked over at Darin. He was coughing and wheezing on the floor. After a minute or two, he caught his breath and stood up. He gawked at the others present, as if awaiting them to say something. But all he found were their lowered gazes.

I could see sudden realization spread across his features. Everyone feared me. And they did so with good reason. He staggered a little. Finally, he pulled the chair in front of me. "I didn't tell you to sit." I glared at him.

He let go of the chair, head bowed again. He was rooted to the spot. I swirled the wine in my glass, not bothering to hide my smile.

"Marcus," I called. He immediately shuffled out of his chair and stood in front of me.

"Yes?"

"I want us to plan the attack. I will need you to strategize. Take Darin and get the map of the area. We'll decide how we'll proceed after eating." I continued, "We will storm in the dead of night."

I glanced at Darin inquisitively. "How much time will it take for us to reach the Sanctuary?"

"About an hour and a half hour from here," he replied with a wince.

"Fine. After planning, we are to immediately move out." I turned to the scrawny boy standing in the corner who was listening to our conversation.

"Get us the food now. Rowen, is it?" I asked while lightly brushing my beard.

He nodded. "Yes. Yes. I'll tell Morin to bring the food. So-sorry for the wait." He hurriedly ran out of the room.

I sipped the wine again, relishing the burn. *It was a damn excellent wine*. I wondered how it ended up in a small tavern like this.

"You have... authority in you," the old man observed.

"You have to be strong to use the power."

"What power is it you speak of?" He inquired with curiosity.

"The power of death." I smiled wickedly.

Soon, the boy returned. He had some bowls and plates of meat on his serving tray. It smelled delicious. A young woman entered the room in tow with him, carrying more plates.

The girl was slim with straight brown hair. She was wearing an old tattered red dress, covered in dark smudges of oil. She placed the food down on the table for everyone and she smiled.

"I'm Morin. I hope you all enjoy the food." She spoke cheerfully. She almost turned away, but abruptly stilled.

I could sense something was off. My gaze followed hers as she looked at one of the wolves that was with me. He was one of the Council guards, new to Orden's camp. His name was Norias, I recalled. He had been idly chatting in the corner before he caught her attention.

I could see him staring at her. With lightning speed he bolted from the chair and wrapped his arms around the girl, holding her close. "Mine," he whispered, but we all could hear him clearly as a wolf's howl.

Mates.

Just what I needed, I thought disgustedly.

In the old times, perhaps, it would have been a joyous affair. To find your mate, the one you would be with for life, the one chosen for you by the Moon goddess herself. They say the mates, the couple, are... perfect for each other. They complement each other. To mate is to mingle your souls, and to share every emotion, every thought – in perfect harmony.

A weakness.

The royal emblem of Vascya, too, was based on mates. The history said when the original Council was formed to govern the land of Vascya they came up with the seal, mused by mates. It signified the pure connection, the gift of the moon goddess. Now, it was a curse. The flags were burned and the paintings destroyed.

The couple edged away to the corner of the room. Norias was standing in front of her protectively. He knew the fate of the mates better than many. The fate determined by the Council. The fate decided by his own masters. He was, after all, a part of the Council's army.

No one moved. Silence flooded the room. I could sense the unease. I glanced at the terrified kid standing shocked beside me. He knew what happened to his parents; they were taken away; the old man had said. Now, his sister faced the same horror.

For a moment my chest tightened, and I almost felt bad but sobered up quick when I saw Norias snarling at us.

"Stand down, Norias. One more snarl from you, and my mood will go right downhill. And, you know by now what I am capable of," I said, my voice echoing in the silent room.

He didn't move a muscle. I kept glaring at him, challenging him. He drew a heavy breath and lowered his head in submission, still shielding the girl. I served some meat onto my plate and took a bite. Everyone was looking at me bewildered. Especially Marcus.

Marcus was soft. Merciful. Naive. I knew he would plead with me again, but there was no question as to what I would do. I took a bite of the tender meat and chewed slowly. "I don't feel like killing. Especially, when the food and wine taste this nice." I took another sip of the wine and gazed at Norias.

"You have two choices." I spoke slowly, taking another bite. "First of which is, you wait for me to finish my food, before I slit both of your throats." I paused as Norias growled in frustration. I rolled my eyes before taking another bite. "Second would be to voluntarily surrender yourself to the Council.

"Now, neither of the choices are great. But you should be grateful that I am even granting you one. Usually, I snap necks." I laughed as I clicked my fingers. "It's because of the girl. The food is quite delicious, and I couldn't just kill you after such a lovely meal."

"Now, I assume, being killed is the worse choice, but you, Norias, being a Council guard — you know what goes on in Regvyer and the Low Cities where they hold captured mates. Your mate might just become a surrogate."

I leaned back in my chair, folding my arms. "Running away is useless. So, what will you do, Norias?"

He was shaking. I had seen this before. The options were cruel, of course. The Council was ruthless. The girl was clinging to him. Tears were streaming down her face as she held him. He turned to face her. I knew he was crying as well. Tears. Weak. He was weak. Nothing should make you weak.

"Belaize, sir, I think... I might provide another choice," Marcus said abruptly.

I watched Marcus with interest. "And what may that be?"

"They... can be our bait."

THE CARCASS

Belaize

"They... can be our bait." Marcus's words echoed in the silent room. The firewood was crackling, it was deafening.

"Go on." I wondered what he was thinking. I had placed him on the task force for his mind after all. He cleared his throat. Every wolf in the room stared at him. Norias snarled at Marcus. He clung to his mate.

"Never. You will never use us. This is outrageous." Norias screamed, his fangs grew and his voice shook with terror.

Sweet love, I scoffed at the thought of it. The Moon goddess had made us weak by giving us mates. *Weak.* I grimaced.

"Well, clearly, he doesn't want to be a lure. That leaves only two choices again, die or let your woman become a tramp. Which do you prefer?" I taunted.

He let out a low-throated growl in defiance. He knew he couldn't stand up to me; I was too strong; I was a Kaiser, the strongest of them all, and no matter what, he could never measure up to me. Never. I smirked at both.

The girl looked me dead in the eyes and stammered. "If we-if we-we do what you say, will you let us go?" She had hope in her eyes. She thought it would all end in a fairy tale. They'd live happily ever after.

What a load of crap.

I laughed bitterly. My expression turned stone-cold in an instant. "This is not a negotiation, girl. You are captured or dead. Why would I let you go? Especially when your 'mate' here is a Council guard. I'm sure, they'd want their property back. You'll just be an addition to the stock of bitches they control."

I saw her spirit break before my eyes. Tears rolled down her cheeks as she buried her face against Norias' neck, weeping. It always happens this way, first the groveling and then the slow, bone deep realization that death was here. Death was waiting.

I felt a tug on my arm. I saw Rowen standing beside me. "Pl-please... Don't take... my sister away. Make-make him leave. Everything was okay when- he wasn't here." The kid pleaded.

With a jerk, I pulled my arm away, glaring at him. "Listen, and listen well, kid. The world is a dangerous place. You're either strong or you're dead. Your sister and her mate are weak. They are dead. Go mourn them." In that moment, I saw his eyes reflect complete and utter misery.

My scowl turned into an expression of regret. *He's just a child, like you once were,* said a faint voice in my head. Blurred images of torture, punishment, hunger, and death entered my mind. A memory of a boy clinging to a woman's hand, wailing and crying as a tall dark man tore him away from her. Scenes of more torment and loneliness washed over me. I closed my eyes, cleansing the momentary weakness out of my mind before anybody realized what was going on. I ran my fingers through my long hair and shifted my attention to Marcus. "Tell me your plan."

"Well, as you said, I drew up a rough map of the area. We can let them go to the Sanctuary. While they distract the rebels we'll surround the area and attack them. They won't even know what hit them." He stopped and peered at the mates. I followed his gaze. They looked like they'd seen a monster.

"Not... bad. I have to hand it to you Marcus, you are quick on your feet."

The girl unexpectedly yelled. She was livid. She raised her head and shrieked in rage. "We will not be your toys. We will not go in there and support you. You are a demon. What makes you think we won't confess to the rebels of your attack the moment we step into that wretched Sanctuary?" She sobbed and wept harder, tears covering her face.

But I didn't care. I chuckled at her outburst. Everyone was studying me warily. I felt their eyes upon me. I gulped down the rest of my wine, smiling maliciously. "You won't say a word," I said, "Or I'll pick your brother apart joint by bloody joint."

"You... wouldn't... no, you wouldn't! You're lying, you're bluffing. He is just a kid!" For a second the images threatened to return, but I pushed them back. I looked at her dead in the eyes, and I felt my wolf surfacing.

I growled, "I don't make empty threats, girl. You'll do well to remember that."

She flinched away. Everyone knew I never back down on my word. If I made a threat, it would come to be.

"You'll lead the way, Darin. We leave in half an hour. Once we get close, we'll split up and surround the Sanctuary. These two-" I waved my hand in their direction. "They will march into the middle of the Sanctuary and distract the rebels while we launch our attack. Everything should be done with precision." I turned to the old man.

"Lazarus, you will keep this boy here. If these two go astray, I'll know exactly where to find you and the boy."

I rose and left the bewildered wolves in that tavern. I walked out the wooden front door and into the chilly night. The night was young. The temperature would go down soon. It was perfect for running.

When we ran as wolves, our bodies often overheated from muscle strain. But a cold night made it easier. We weren't far from Walka. It was only an hour's run to Walka and another a few miles beyond that to the Frozen Fingers.

Beyond the natural mountain range of the Frozen Fingers, existed the land of darkness. Even though I had travelled everywhere in the Land of Vascya, the land beyond the border was a mystery. It was said in old legends that the Moon Goddess had forbidden everyone to go beyond the borders. No one knows why. I have heard tales that some wolves that go beyond never return, as Goddess claims the wolves. Other stories suggest that they come back from the land beyond rabid and insane.

I wandered in the dingy alley at a slow pace. I liked to be alone, and I knew others were constantly anxious around me. The girl, Morin, and Norias. They needed time, time to say goodbye and accept their cruel fate.

Mates. I don't need a mate. It would only make me weak, and I cannot be weak. Only power rules the land, and power is everything.

Everything.

Minutes ticked by until eventually, it was time to go back. I returned to the rusty old tavern, slamming the door open with one hand. "You'd better be ready to go. I want to get this done as soon as we can."

I glanced around at everyone. They had packed the supplies. The girl was standing beside her mate. Both were dejected.

"Out. Now," I ordered. Everyone shuffled out of the tavern in a line. I studied Rowen. His eyes were red and swollen, his cheeks were tear-stained. He was standing beside Lazarus. "Keep an eye on him," I instructed in an undertone. He nodded. Turning away, I walked out of the tavern.

It was time to start a bloodbath.

We walked through the series of alleys and streets unit we reached the northern end of Novocher.

I indicated everyone to assemble. "Darin," I called, looking through the group for him. He stepped forward, bowing his head.

"You will run beside me on the way to the Sanctuary. Once we get close enough, we will split up. The rest of you will continue onwards and surround Morin and Norias. Do not let them flee. I believe the mountain range start soon and therefore it'll be easy. Either save your own head or theirs, the choice is yours." I gazed at them. They looked away, unable to meet my eyes.

I shifted into my wolf, standing tall at twelve feet. I could tell the girl was petrified by my devilish appearance. Within a minute, everyone turned, and we started running, continuing our journey.

Running through the dark forest was easier than it had been the day before. The rain hadn't hit this region, which left the soil dry. I didn't run too fast so that Darin kept up with me. Sometimes his copper brown wolf would disappear from my sight, but he was never very far.

Soon the terrain of the land changed. It became steeply sloped, with splashes of fir trees every couple of miles. The night was dark and moonless. I saw the glow of the tiny town far from the high mountain where we were. The lights shone in the night like stars in the dark. Tiny buildings littered all over the town. We had reached Walka.

The excitement and the bloodlust were calling my wolf, I felt excitement flooding through me, pumping euphoric adrenaline through my veins. I wanted to go as fast as I could to reach our destination and taste the blood of those filthy, weak mates. I smelled them; their scent was thick in the surrounding air. The others had picked it up as well. Their ears were perked, instantly alert.

I wanted everyone to be together as a group to lower the chances of our prisoners escaping, and if discovered, we could attack the rebels instantly, allowing more time to get inside the Sanctuary.

As we were running toward our destination, the air around us grew colder. Darin motioned for us to stop. We were under the cover of the thick trees overhead, concealed from plain view, but I saw the signs of a clearing ahead. The animal trails were well defined, cutting through the forest floor. The paths grew wider in the distance.

Everyone gathered around. They were panting from the long run, their breath misting in the air in front of them. I shifted my form and watched for everyone else to shift too. "Where is your partner hiding?" I asked Darin.

Turning away he pointed in a north-easterly direction. "Can you see those dense firs? We were hiding there. I told him not to move from that location as it gave us the best view of the area. He should be there."

I glanced where he pointed. From our place on the peak, I could see a large clearing down in the valley that indeed looked like a rebel base. Just before the clearing, I noted the cluster of trees that Darin indicated served as the ranger's hideout. Neither were far, but we could go undetected from this distance.

I smoothed out my long hair. It was wet with mist that had spread in the forest.

"Okay, so this is what we will do. Darin, Marcus, and I will go to the hideout. The rest of you will quickly surround the base, but you will keep your distance. You are to attack only when we give the signal. We will light a flare from those trees." I pointed in the direction Darin had mentioned. "By that time, every one of you should be in position."

Everyone nodded in agreement. "Now, you two--" I tilted my head toward our bait. "You will walk straight into the camp. We will have eyes on you, remember that. You will walk in there, and you will distract as many rebels as you can." A demonic smile graced my lips.

"It's time now. Move everyone." I told them curtly, turning to walk towards the hideout with Darin and Marcus.

Darin shuffled quickly to lead the way. We moved silently through the dense wood. Darin was a competent tracker, his eyes always scanning the ground, the canopy. The cover was thick. We kept a steady pace toward the ranger.

I paused, my senses perking up.

"Stop," I said lowly. Both were a couple feet away from me by now. They halted in their tracks and looked at me with inquiring eyes.

"Something is wrong. I don't sense anyone besides us." I continued to walk towards the makeshift hideout.

"But- But I told him to stay here. He has to be here," Darin said tensely. He looked gaunt, his face turning white, no doubt concluding to the worst possible fate for his partner.

I moved to examine the area. As soon as I reached the tree a rotten stench hit my nose. I followed it, which led to a crumpled body.

The ranger's corpse.

His head had rolled face down in the mud, ripped away from the body, along with his limbs. The stench was worse up close, sickening. Flies surrounded the corpse, and worms ate away at it. Blood had seeped below, the ground darkened with death.

Marcus showed up after me. The moment he saw the corpse, he lowered his head and stepped back. His weak core couldn't stomach it. He'd never been good with gore. I heard him wretch a few feet behind me. How could he expect to fight if he could not bear the blood that followed it? How would he ever be able to cope with it?

The ranger's savage death meant one thing. Rebels had found out about the spy and knew we were coming. I turned back to the others. Both were looking down at the ground, unfocused. We didn't have time to lose. If we didn't get this done the fucking Council would have my ass.

"Both of you, snap out of it. We must charge right now. The corpse looks about a day old, so I don't think many are left at that base, but we must capture or kill. Give the signal now," I ordered Marcus.

He looked as white as snow. "Now!" I yelled impatiently.

His hands trembled as he took out the flare. He was taking his sweet time. We had to attack. I bared my fangs in anger. "Stop wasting my fucking time." I snarled, grabbing the flare from him and raising it high so that they would see its flash. A second later a green flash lit up the sky directly above us, followed by a loud boom.

"Get your shit together, Marcus," I growled and changed into my monstrous wolf, my silver hair glimmering in the darkness of the night.

Let the culling begin.

INTERLOGUE

Laki

The night was dark and becoming colder. The frigid winds were stinging my face. The chill seeped into my bones. I clutched my thin leathers closer, as I blew on my hands in a futile attempt to keep them warm. Living near the foothills of the Frozen Fingers wasn't easy. But tonight, the dread of death loomed in the crisp air. It was the lull before the storm, the calm before everything falls into chaos.

I was patrolling along the border of our base. The Sanctuary spread over a vast expanse of the valley. We were tucked into the lowest part of the hills and hidden from the towering violet mountains, the jagged peaks of white reaching up like a frozen hand towards the sky. A narrow waterfall pooled near the westernmost edge of the base, which served as the water source for all those who lived here.

This rebellion was our only hope to go back to the time of what once was. The Council had been ruthless with the Lycans. They announced the orders for capture of all the mated wolves of Vascya. Initially, everyone had co-operated, but as the days passed, the Council started killing mated wolves. They wreaked havoc in our lands. It was an absolute massacre. The raids decimated village after village. People abandoned their homes, their businesses, and their families because some old fools with their powers thought it was necessary for survival. Despite bloody protests against their rule, the voices of innocents fell on deaf ears.

Going against the will of our own Goddess was out of the question. Yet these old fools sat on their chairs and controlled the fate of our country. The rebels opposed them. Our country is amid a civil war. No one is safe. Peace is far out of our reach, a distant dream.

I sighed, my breath sending wisps of mist floating into the air. Thinking about the rebels, the peace, and this war made my head hurt. Not to mention the looming threat coming our way. Everything was going wrong all at once. The warning from one of the rebel spies arrived two days ago. "Evacuate, take what's necessary. Leave fast. Death follows on swift feet." We thought we had a few days at least, but that was just wishful thinking.

I remembered the announcement from yesterday. It was nearly dawn; the sky was a brilliant shade of crimson, when the call for a meeting came. Most wolves had retired to the comforts of their beds early in the night. Those left were on duty guarding the Sanctuary. I had woken up, sweat covering my body, when I heard the howl. It wasn't the first time I had woken up in the night to run from raiders.

Minutes later, everyone had gathered in the training arena, which served as a meeting point on occasions. Rayne was standing tall in the center with a grim look on his face. His clothes were wrinkled and threadbare; his sandy brown hair was filthy. Blood glinted on his chest in the glow of the torches. I shuddered; my heart was gripped with fear. I knew the others around me felt the same. Rayne's green eyes were cold and hazy. Everyone was staring at him, waiting.

Waiting for him to confirm what we already knew.

He took a deep breath as if preparing for the chaos. "Evacuation of this Sanctuary starts in an hour." He said. With a jolt, fear spread around, causing everyone to dishearten. "We have found a Council ranger near our base. It is safe to assume that an attack isn't far behind. Everyone round up your things and meet here. You know the drill. We will make groups of six, each accompanied by a warrior. All the warriors immediately report to me, I will assign your next destination. You are not to travel in more than a pack of seven." Rayne sighed.

"I know the news isn't good, but we have to work together to win this war. It is my fault that we must leave this place. Being so close to the border was my idea. I thought the rangers wouldn't find us here, that we could go undetected. It worked for a while, but... it is time to say goodbye. Be swift. We have till the coming evening to save ourselves from the clutches of the Council... if we are lucky." He finished and walked out of the arena, leaving us all in fear of the future.

I sighed, so this was it. We had to leave this place too. I liked this Sanctuary. We had settled in two other camps before this, but for once it felt like home. The soft fir trees, the valley surrounded by mountains, the fresh air of the forest. Everything pleased my wolf, especially the wilderness. And now it was time to leave.

I turned back slowly, walking back to my tent. It was a big tent, supported by one long pillar in between. I lifted the cover to go inside, to my family. My child, Jake, was asleep in his mother's lap. He was small for a nine-year-old boy. In a few years, he would turn and become a full wolf. The thought of Jake and I going on runs made me smile for a moment, but sadness hit me as I remembered that we must run again for the safety of our lives. I looked at his mother, my mate. She took one glance in my direction and sighed. My father was lying on the other side of the tent, resting. He was old and frail; his gray hair was matted against his head. Wrinkles etched his face and loose skin sagged from his hands. He would die any day now. I couldn't bear to leave my father behind in such a state. It killed me to move from place to place to survive, with him in tow, but even after our misfortune, all he gave me was his toothy grin.

I couldn't take him with me this time. Maybe if he were stronger... But he could barely lift himself up on the bed.

I sat down beside Catherine, my mate, my purpose. I said nothing, just wrapped my arms around her, taking a deep breath as her intoxicating scent washed all over me. "What happened, Laki?" She whispered softly, her slender hand stroking my curls.

"You and Jake... you have to evacuate now. Rayne... he thinks raiders will attack us tomorrow. Evacuation will start soon. You need to leave, my love." I choked back a sob. I was... so helpless. I couldn't protect my family. All we could do was run. That's all we had done for the past two years. Fuck the Council, fuck their methods. I'll protect my family with my life.

"What about you, Laki?" She croaked.

"I'll... stay with father. I must. He is dying. I cannot... I won't leave him now in his last moments. Leave with Jake. I'll find you at the next Sanctuary. Maybe I can fight here and help the others too. I... cannot run away, not yet." I said, while holding her, as if it was the last time I ever would.

"We are not leaving you behind. I am not leaving you behind, Laki." I looked down at her face, determination clear in her voice.

"Please Cate, Jake... at least I can rest easy, with both of you away from this... threat. Please..." I tried to persuade her.

"Laki, no matter what, I will not leave you. I am ready to protect you and Jake with my life if I have to, but I cannot bear to be without you." A single tear trickled down her cheek.

I felt her sadness right in my core. It killed me to be apart from her, but these circumstances forced us against each other.

"What about Jake?" I tried once again. She lifted her hand and caressed Jake's soft brown hair. His innocent round face and soft features. He was barely nine. So young yet caught amid this war.

"You know I will protect him with everything I have." She said with sincerity, nothing but love in her voice. Love for him, for us, for our small family.

I held her harder in my arms, accepting her decision. My Cate was a stubborn woman. I kissed her forehead softly, sinking into the little calm we had left.

My father had passed away a few hours after that. I had lifted his dead body in my arms; he was so light, a far cry from the powerful smith he had once been. I carried him to the small waterfall and the river it formed nearby, where I let the water wash over his face. I continued wading deeper into the icy river where the current was slow, but the water was deep.

The Moon Goddess was the queen of the tides. When all wolves passed, that is where they went, for she claimed their souls for her own. My arms struggled to let go. Tears streamed down my face and a hollow pain throbbed in my chest before I finally let Liunella carry him to the afterlife.

I'll see you again father. My last thoughts floated after him as his body was carried away by the river. My father... deserved a better end. A happy end to his life. Instead, he had been ill and on the run with me. As I waded back to shore, I reached for the family I had left and held them close.

I went and talked to Rayne, telling him we wanted to be on the next team to get out of here. Rayne said our turn should be in two hours, that is when the warrior wolf who will escort us will leave, till then we must sit tight and hope for the best. I was worried; it was getting late. Merely fifty people remained in the Sanctuary, while over three hundred had fled to the foothills.

If only Cate had agreed to go, I would have been long gone. But here I was stuck patrolling. Soon I'd be out of here and we'd all be safe. I sighed and huddled closer to the fire which burned nearby. I looked at the dark forest, the shadows of the tall trees playing their tricks.

Suddenly, I saw a flash of green light up the sky. Its eccentric color and brightness amazed me. Seconds later, a loud boom followed. The sound tore through the Sanctuary like thunder. My body trembled with fear so strong all I wanted was to lie down on the floor and hold myself together.

The attack had finally commenced.

Catherine! Jake! Fuck. My mind stopped working; my body moved on its own. I changed into my dark brown wolf, my senses becoming alert. It would start any minute; I had to get Jake and Catherine out. I howled loudly, warning the wolves. My voice was immediately followed by a series of howls from other patrol guards. They had witnessed the flash too.

Cate be ready, it's starting. Protect Jake. I'm coming! I pushed these thoughts to her through our bond with urgency as I ran swiftly to the shelter, where they were waiting for me. I rushed past three rows of tents and took a sharp turn past the well. In three leaping strides I bounded over fallen logs, skirting the outer edge of the Sanctuary. My heart beating loudly in my ears. Finally, our tent was in view. I skidded across its entrance. There huddled in the corner, hiding beside the small bed. My family, I needed to protect them.

Run towards those mountains! I pointed at them by tilting my head. *Be careful with Jake. I'll cover you both. Run! Now! We have to get out.* I said in my thoughts. I knew she would hear them.

She nodded and picked Jake up in her arms and started running.

We had run a few hundred steps, when the first screams broke out. Soon, more screams followed. Everybody was in the center of the Sanctuary, running around, fighting the guards, some people were running, few children were huddled together, crying. The attackers, they had begun killing and capturing. It wouldn't be long until they came for us. We had to get out of here. NOW!

Another five minutes. That's all we'd need to get out of the base. I glanced around, scanning my surroundings for any immediate threat. The warriors left in the base had already engaged with the enemy. I saw one of the warrior wolves fighting another. The scent wasn't familiar, he was the enemy. I would have helped him, but my priority was Catherine and Jake.

We were edging quickly towards the western border of the Sanctuary when I saw an enemy wolf sprinting. He saw us, changed directions started approaching us. His teeth were bare, mouth covered in nothing but blood.

I dashed in front of Cate, stopping her. *Hide between those tents!* I screamed in my head. *Be careful, Laki!* She responded and hid herself.

Within seconds, my wolf was on top of the enemy. The fairly slender wolf hadn't expected it. He thought I would run the other way because my mate was close by.

Never. I will protect them at all costs.

He pushed me off and smashed his claws against my chest, tearing the skin. Blood dripped down my torso as pain shot through my body. I struggled and threw him on the ground. pounced on him, my fangs bared, lips pulled back. I snarled, aiming for his throat. My teeth pierced through the soft flesh, and his blood pooled in my mouth. With force, I ripped out a chunk of his shoulder muscle. His gray wolf trembled and soon became still. He was dead.

I spit the blood from my mouth and checked for Cate, they're safe for now, I sensed them, but she wasn't in sight yet. I took in my surroundings; the raiders had set shelters on fire. Screams filled my ears. They were begging for mercy, for help. But I headed towards Cate.

I heard a scream near me. It shocked me to my core.

Laki! Her voice clouded my head.

“Cate, fuck! I’m coming! I’m coming!” I ran towards her. What I witnessed made my soul whimper.

The monster. *The blood moon Harbinger was here.*

He was here. And he had cornered my family. There stood the devil. His monstrous wolf, chest covered with fine silver hair, glinting in the fire’s glow. His long canines were sleek with blood. It dripped from his mouth and down his chin. Cate had wrapped her arms around Jake, hiding him against her.

Run away, Laki. Now! Her thoughts whispered in my mind.

Never. Not without you. I replied. He looked at them, scrunched his mouth in disdain and turned away, walking away from my family.

I slowly got closer to him. He strolled among the chaos as if choosing his victims. Who he would enjoy killing most. It made me sick to my stomach.

Laki! No. Please! Come back! We have to go! Cate pleaded. I glanced at her one more time. Fear etched her brown eyes. Fear, and worry for me.

I must try. I cannot run. Cate be safe. Keep Jake safe. I replied. She hesitantly nodded, clutching our child closer. I turned my attention back to the monster.

I had to do this quickly. One swift attack and maybe... this war will be over.

Before I could advance, Rayne and his guard appeared; warrior wolves rallied beside him. We could win. A small hope filled my chest. Rayne was nowhere near as large as the Kaiser; however, he was strong and had numbers on his side. The harbinger cocked his head, his expression interested. The blood lust was almost palpable. I looked to where Cate was. She was staring at him in shock. *Run!* I yelled, but she stood rooted to her spot, embracing Jake.

Rayne and his guards were nervous, pacing, but not advancing on the monster. The Harbinger’s reputation was horrifying. It happened in an instant. Rayne attacked, holding nothing back, followed by the five warriors who flanked him. The Harbinger laughed as he picked off the warriors one by one like they were frolicking pups. Edward was the first to fall, followed by Taylor, and then Gren. They didn’t stand a chance. He wasn’t even trying.

He danced around their swings, kicks, and lunges. Thrusting his claws forward, impaling another wolf called Alexander. He lifted his hand and picked up the wolf as if he weighed nothing and sent him hurtling through the air fifteen feet into a burning shelter. Alexander’s screams filled the night, serenading the chaos. Rayne froze in place, standing opposite to the monster. Only he and Felton remained of the six that faced the Council’s greatest assassin, the Blood Moon Harbinger. He was no monster; he was no wolf... he was death incarnate.

He changed to his human form. Blood and sweat covered his titan-like body. His blond hair was tied at the back of his head. But most terrifying was the sight of blood dripping from his mouth. He licked his lips, savoring the taste of victory. Moving slowly, keeping Rayne to his left and Felton to his right. He looked at Rayne and finally spoke. "You look strong, I'll save you for last. Stay right there." He turned and faced Felton, dropping his guard to Rayne.

This is your chance, I thought, hoping Rayne would attack him. Felton faced him valiantly. But he didn't stand a chance. As Felton's corpse hit the floor, the blood moon Harbinger turned to face Rayne. "So, tell me, do you still have the courage to stand before me?" He laughed demonically. Rayne was frozen. His eyes darted, looking in every direction, taking in his surroundings.

Then he turned and ran. Rayne, the right hand of the leader of the rebellion, abandoned his people and ran. The monster laughed; his haunting voice followed Rayne out of the camp. He turned his back, kicking the dead on the ground with his feet, and once more stalked through the Sanctuary for more prey. Not running wild like his companions. He was cold and meticulous.

I followed him with silent steps. Swiftly, I got closer to his side, but out of his view. I only needed one clear shot at his neck, a wolf's weakest point. A tent on the monster's right succumbed to the blazing flames, drawing the Harbinger's attention. This is it; this is my chance. And I ran. My vision tunneled to focus on him. My eyes tracking the movements of this insane murderer. The Blood Moon Harbinger.

I snarled seeing my opportunity, baring my fangs, I ran as fast as I could. This is it; this is for all your sins.

"Die!" I screamed as my teeth were inches from his neck. Suddenly, the air was knocked out of me, and I was thrown sideways. I howled in pain, my shoulder and collarbone were broken. Another slender rusty wolf came out of nowhere and attacked me.

"Xavier, you fool, I was waiting for him to make his move and you took the fun from me!" He growled with anger, crossing his arms.

Those words hurt more than all my injuries. He knew I was watching; he knew, and he would have slaughtered me. "Kill him before I kill you." He said, not giving me a second glance.

Cate... I love you. My last thoughts to her, as I felt my death approaching.

The one named Xavier had changed into his human form, glaring at me. His lips were upturned in a smug smile. He was enjoying this. I tilted my head in agony. Cate was standing where I last saw her. I looked at her face, and my little Jake's face one last time.

Tell him that his father, he didn't die in vain. He died trying to protect everyone from this war. I whispered to her, hoping she would hear.

In the next moment, all I heard was a terrible scream as my death ripped my heart out.

Darkness and pain engulfed me.

Father, I'll see you sooner than you would have liked. I hope I made you proud.

SLAUGHTER

Marcus

The decaying body of the man rested behind me. Brutally murdered. The insects were picking him away. His head and limbs separated from the body; his insides spilled onto the ground in a bloody heap. It turned my stomach. I tasted the vomit in my mouth. I stepped back, unable to look at the man that once was. Unable to look at the dead. The images of all the innocent, the loved ones, Rowen, Norias, Morin... Everyone... whirled around in my mind. They wouldn't stop.

My mind was a whirlwind. This fucking war. This fucking war between rebels and the Council. The fucked-up choices of the elders. The damned killing of all the innocents. My heart ached for peace. To stop this destruction. I don't want any more death. *Just fucking stop!*

The green light soared brightly through the sky. I couldn't bear to face it. I closed my eyes. I... can't. The signal just meant more death. More killing of the innocent. More destruction. My body shuddered with overwhelming emotions. I couldn't...

I couldn't harm anybody. I couldn't strike civilians. They didn't deserve this. I turned my head slowly to peer at Darin. He looked just as miserable as I felt. With one last glance at his partner, he too changed into his gray-colored wolf and followed Belaize.

I stayed rooted at the spot, alone and in the darkness that devoured me. Innocent wolves would be captured and killed. Tears welled up in my eyes. I scrubbed them off with my wrist.

No. I can't. No. This is... war.

I should run away. Run away right now. I could hand this information to the rebels which would dispose of Belaize, and the Council wouldn't stand a chance. It might be the key to end this war. I had to run. I transformed into my black wolf and twisted in the opposite direction of the Sanctuary.

I only made a few hundred feet when a faint shriek of a woman came from behind me – from the Sanctuary. It was so faint... but it was a scream of a woman in agony. It stopped me dead in my tracks.

I can't leave them. If I can help them, I will. No matter the cost.

In mere seconds, I was sprinting with full strides towards the direction of that scream. I felt powerful for once, adrenaline poured through my veins like a drug. I leapt through the tree line, bursting into the scene of a massacre. The smell of blood and ash was everywhere. It was putrid. It was a demon's grotesque nightmare. The shelters were aflame and bodies littered the ground. Those who weren't dead but injured were screaming in agony. I saw people scattered in every direction, trying to escape. But it was a futile attempt. The team... I had assembled was working efficiently. They had surrounded the entire base and quickly taken control.

My eyes blurred with tears. *I caused this. I planned this... for him. But they were supposed to get out by now!* My mind screamed. This couldn't be happening. No one was supposed to be here. I had already sent a warning.

Just this morning, I was working and Belaize came into that briefing room, demanding me to assemble his team. I had sent the tip to clear this base days ago. However, from the moment I learned Belaize would lead the assault, I had issued out a notice for immediate evacuation. No one was supposed to be here! I failed everybody. I caused these deaths!

Horrified shrieks plagued me as I stilled, witnessing the destruction. My legs refused to carry me forward. All I wanted was to flee.

A shrill cry cut through the air once again. It came from a woman right in front of me. With some struggle, I lifted my gaze to look at her. My soul shuddered with fury. A wolf was beating the woman. I squinted my eyes, willing the tears away to get a better look. I realized it was Morin. He was hurting her!

Somehow, I broke out of the paralysis that tormented me. I closed my eyes, running in that wolf's direction. I shoved him down hard. My speed and momentum enhanced the impact of his fall. He didn't realize what hit him.

I covered his body, stopping him from getting up. I twisted my head towards Morin. She was a wreck. Her clothes were torn, her black hair was painted with blood. I saw a wide slash on her arm. She stared at me with bewilderment.

"Find Norias. Run. RUN!" I screamed at her. She nodded and scampered away. The wolf under me was thrashing, trying to get me off. I raised my body up long enough to punch him hard in the face and knocked him out.

My body was shaking horribly. I eventually rose, taking a deep breath, concentrating. I couldn't be weak now. I had to help. Running across what used to be the courtyard, I rounded a corner and barreled right into another person. He stumbled forward and lost his footing.

The night was dark, but the shelter fires lit his face in a warm glow. It was Xavier. Behind him was a she-wolf protecting a cowering child. The woman looked exhausted. She was injured and bleeding but shielded her child. Between Xavier and the woman was a mutilated corpse of what must've been her mate.

Xavier hauled himself back up, dusting off his hands. He snarled at me.

"You?!" he said and spat at my feet. He was wounded. The dead wolf must've put up quite the fight. But a civilian was no match against a Council guard. Xavier turned his attention back to the woman and child, getting ready to attack her.

Quickly, I jumped between him and the woman. "Leave her alone!" I growled as I towered over him and assumed a defensive stance. He turned on me, slashing at my face. *Always the quick one*. I winced as the pain shot up my cheek and my blood spattered the ground. I grabbed his right hand, twisting it around his back, holding him in my iron clad grip.

Xavier took a quick glance at the woman while struggling in my grip and back at me. "What the hell, Marcus? What are you doing? Why are you protecting them?"

Momentarily, he stilled, not moving a muscle, making my grip on his hands loose. The next instant, he exploded outward and broke free, stumbling away. He got a couple feet away from me, just out of my reach. "You're a fucking spy?" He spat at me, baring his bloody fangs.

I didn't flinch. He faced me, standing tall and ready to strike. In his amber eyes I saw malice, hatred, and contempt. He swung at me with his left hand. I crouched under it and swiped at his hip. He stumbled and cried out in pain. His hip already had a deep wound. His blood smelled foul. I jabbed at him, but he hooked my arm with his hand and hit me with a savage kick on the right side of my chest. I felt a few ribs break. Hunching over and coughed blood, I tried to catch my breath.

"You're pathetic, aren't you? Groveling at my feet," he said, putting his foot on my head and pushing me down in the dirt. "N-no!" I said smiling as more blood dripped from my mouth. "You're just fucking predictable."

I grabbed hold of his leg and yanked him down hard, making him lose his balance. He did a feeble hop-step to get his leg back under him.

My arms moved rapidly and cupped his head. I looked into his amber eyes, which widened as he realized he had lost this fight and his life. He couldn't help himself. The foul odor of piss filled the air.

In that moment, I failed myself when I closed my eyes and twisted his head left. I heard a sickening crunch as his spine uprooted itself from his neck. He was dead before he hit the cold, hard ground.

I felt sick. It was so simple. So fucking easy to murder him. I assessed the nasty, purple bruise on my chest. I wiped my eyes clear of the tears and blood that were sliding down my cheek.

The she-wolf fell to her knees in front of me. She was devastated. Tears streamed down her face. She was clutching her child hard against her chest. "Jake." I heard her whisper. When she released him the boy stumbled straight to the corpse. He was old enough to understand what had happened. His muddy face was steaked with tears. "Father..." he said, his voice cracking. "Get... u-up," he choked. I motioned for the woman to see to her child. But when I saw her face, she was equally distraught.

The woman had felt every blow to her mate. She went down on her knees, kissing her mate one last time. She was sobbing but reluctantly left her husband's still form behind.

"Come on, we have to go." I barely choked the words out. I had a throbbing headache. *I killed him. I killed them all. I am not better than Belaize.* The thought kept repeating in my head, but I couldn't focus on it, not now. I needed to get these two out of here. Gathering my composure and putting my arm around the two of them, I ushered them forward. "We can't stay here, I can fight the others, but if Belaize shows up, we are finished."

We started walking out of the base, turning in and out of a series of allies, and away from the destruction. We kept walking as fast as we could despite our injuries. I realized that a remarkable amount of time had passed. The sun was rising as the first rays kissed the horizon. The fight was over. There were no more screams. Smoke from dead fires rose into the sky and grey ash covered all that remained. The stench of death hung everywhere. I couldn't believe that this place had been a tranquil and bustling Sanctuary less than twelve hours ago.

When we were quite a distance from the wreckage, I turned to them. "What were you even doing here? You had evacuation orders!" I strained my voice to keep from shouting. The she-wolf held her head down and continued to move. "My mate, Laki, he couldn't leave his father. He was near death and it would have been impossible for him to be evacuated. Laki stayed by his side until the end. When he eventually said his goodbyes, we were ready to leave, but then the attack started. And we ran into that monster. My mate would've..." she choked back sobs.

"Laki? Shit. Catherine! I didn't realize you and Laki were in this

Sanctuary," I said, surprised. I hadn't recognized her before. The woman that Laki had described was a shadow of the woman before me. Her face was caked with ash and worse. In the massacre we had left behind, I hadn't realized who I was protecting. I knew Laki. We had trained and worked together before in another Sanctuary in the east.

"My father would have slaughtered him had the one you killed not interfered," the boy said with hatred in his voice.

Xavier, you bastard.

I had developed a strange resolve while working with Belaize. I was stronger than before. I despised him, but I still respected him. It was because of that resolve I could help these two. Somehow, I had saved them.

After we left the Sanctuary behind, we made it to a mountaintop, far away from that place. I hardly saw the burning ruins, but I still glanced back to see them one the last time.

"You should keep your eyes forward; you never know what you might run into." I stilled. A chill ran down my spine. I turned, gawking at him in disbelief.

There he stood, leaning against a tree, his legs crossed as if he was expecting us. Waiting for me. The magnificent man with blond hair tied back in a ponytail and dark, black beard. His muscled arms folded across his chest. His hands and mouth were covered with dried blood. He looked massive with the sun at his back, like an emissary of the angels. However, he was no angel. Belaize, The Blood Moon Harbinger, stood before us in all his glory, smelling of blood, death, and excitement.

DESPAIR

Belaize

I had been waiting for him here for a while. After I ran to attack the rebels, I killed wolves left and right. My wolf hungered for their blood. I had ripped apart many throats in the dark hours of the night, selecting only victims worthy of being ended by me. What a pathetic fight it was. In the middle of the fight, I had sensed Marcus come to the burning Sanctuary. I knew he would have another breakdown. He was weak and vulnerable.

"Imagine my surprise, Marcus, when I stopped sensing you. For a moment, I thought you were actually dead." I stared at him, my gaze unwavering. I was furious at his betrayal. I wanted his blood spilled this instant. It had been a while since I had felt the anger so strong. It was hard to even control my wolf. He was yearning to gain control and kill. But I had restrained him. I needed to have a conversation with Marcus first.

"Clearly, you were wrong," he replied stoutly. I sensed his agitation. I knew he wanted to keep his companions safe. It was a she-wolf and her boy. I saw the resemblance they shared. Blond hair, angular face, and freckles. I vaguely remembered her. She was in the Sanctuary and I had walked away from her and the child, as I wanted to keep them as prisoners for the Council. The elders required me to show some result of this mission, especially when, once again, the rebels had slipped right out of my claws.

The woman was limping before they had come to a stop in front of me. No wonder that I had found Marcus here. The woman and her child were slowing him down.

"Yes. You're not dead. But you will be after I'm done with you," I said, mocking him.

"I considered you many things, Marcus. Loyal, obedient, respectful. You carried out my orders perfectly all these months, and you made a fine assistant for Orden. Imagine my surprise, when I found out that you, out of all people, were a filthy traitor." He snapped his gaze directly towards me. My gaze he met his cold blue eyes.

"I'm not a traitor. You hear me? I am not a traitor, Belaize!" He spoke with determination. It was clear he had finally gotten his shit together, but for the wrong side.

"Really? You're a fucking spy. No wonder all those rebels slipped right out of the Council's – no, my hands. Even now, here you are, running away like a fucking coward. Face it, Marcus, you might have the tactics up your sleeve, but when the Council relied on you all you could do was cower away like a dog with his tail between his legs." I spat on the ground.

Marcus was in a protective stance between me and the she-wolf with her child.

"I'm not a coward. And you know what? I'm glad that I was a spy. Do you know what my true purpose was being under Orden? You." Marcus stared at me. My wolf was rioting, I felt Marcus challenging me. And I never back down from a challenge. Ever.

"You have been the rebel's target since the beginning, Belaize. The mighty assassin the Council bred and trained. The Council's ultimate weapon. The only thing stopping rebels from attacking and eradicating the Council is you. Because you are outstanding at what you do, Belaize. Killing." He took a visible breath as if he couldn't believe what he was saying, and there was venom in each word.

This was the first time Marcus had ever talked back to me. He had grown a spine, or had that been an act to slip under the Council's nose?

"You kill, without a care in the world. No matter the consequences. You don't care who you kill, a father, a mother, a child, an innocent, no one! And yet you live without remorse. That's what I learned about you. They assigned me to kill you, but it was not possible to do that on my own, I realized. I am weak compared to a Kaiser. I've accepted that.

"So, I stayed to spy. I leaked information on every major attack you led. Salvaging whatever I could. Saving the innocent. Putting my life on the line to protect the good and create a path of peace in Vascya. In my eyes, I'm not a coward, I'll never be. But you know what I will be, I'll be the wolf that guides Vascya to peace, because –" he was nearly shouting but then his voice became cool and quiet. "Because I know you

Belaize. I know everything about you."

The hair on my neck rose and a slight shudder went through me. *He knows everything. Could he?* My mind raced.

"You don't know shit, Marcus. You should be concerned about one fact only: that I am going to kill you," I said, keeping my expression neutral.

"That's where you are wrong. I know about that scar on your shoulder. The scar that makes you freeze every time you look at it," he said.

My blood grew cold. *How? No one knew how I had gotten it.* Flashes of the white creature abruptly emerged in front of my eyes as if I was hallucinating the moment all over again. The uncertainty, the anxiety I felt. It all washed over me.

"It's just a scar," I said, trying not to show the inner turmoil of my mind, my fists clenching, nails digging sharply in my palms as I tried to stay calm.

"Is it? I don't think so. It's your weakness, Belaize. You know it, and I know it. I have travelled with you long enough to know. The one who gave it to you will be our weapon against you. We will destroy the Council. The rebels... Oh, the rebels will relish it." He taunted.

My wolf craved his blood. His challenge. He knew about that night. *Fuck, I can't let him run. I must kill him.*

"It's still just a scar."

"I did my share of work, Belaize. That is not 'just' a scar. That is the single piece of evidence that you failed a mission given by the Council. Someone overpowered you. You were beaten. The rebels will be joyous to know that."

"You'll die trying to run away from me before you can do anything, Marcus. I'm your death. You should accept that now."

"Even if I die, I'm not going down without a fight," he said.

"I am going to lay down the details clearly for you. You are going to lose, Marcus. You'll be on your knees begging for mercy while I'll laugh in your face. And your assumptions were right, I won't ever have any remorse. I'll relish killing a coward like you." I moved to stand in front of him, but out of arm's reach. My tall figure towered over him. He was rigid with tension like a coiled spring. He would attack, I knew it.

"Go. Take Jake and run. I'll stall him. Run away now," he said in a low voice. He shifted his stance, and moved closer, accepting my challenge.

The she-wolf was trembling with fear, clasping her child. She stood rooted in place, unable to move.

"Listen! Your mate didn't give away his life so you could too. Don't let his death be in vain. Run." Marcus stared at her with his steely blue gaze, his jaw clenched. She nodded and scooped her child in her arms and shuffled away from us, stumbling into the deeper forest. I laughed at them. "You are trading your life away for that weakling."

Marcus turned, focusing solely on me. I saw the change in his body movements. They were more... calculated. He was ready for whatever I threw at him. He was ready to fight me, even though he knew he could never win. He was fighting to protect that wolf and her child. A new respect bloomed inside me for Marcus. Whatever side he had picked in this war, he was not a coward. He had the courage to face the consequences. I... respected that.

"She won't run far, Marcus. I will give her to the Council once the flies make a home for your corpse," I said with a smug grin. Then I changed.

He changed into his own black wolf. His icy eyes stared me dead. My wolf loved this tension between us. The air was electric, making the hair on my body stand. I let the tension wash over me. It was something new, something exciting. I had to kill Marcus. He knew about the scar.

That night flashed again in my mind. I felt the hostility in the air, but in that fateful moment, I was the prey, and the predator was ready for his attack. It came in a flash so fast that even my Kaiser bloodline, blessed by the Goddess, couldn't do anything.

I bared my long, sharp canines, my lips curled back. I growled deep, and my feet shifted from right to left. His wolf moved and, in a blur, he pounced on me. I moved my head to the right, aiming for his neck. But to my surprise, he moved to the left, leaping away from me. I swiped my claw to injure his side, but he had estimated that move too. As he landed on the ground, he rolled over and then quickly regained his footing.

I growled at him again. My wolf wanted to toy with him. I waited for his next attack. He waited a few seconds before moving to attack me. This trick differed slightly from the last. Marcus always had his tricks.

He charged, but I waited for the moment his bared fangs were near me; I stood tall, my body stretched, and slammed my heavy body right on top of him, trapping him. He moved, trying to force his way out. I enjoyed this. He wriggled out of my hold, but not before I bit him hard on his shoulder. His blood poured in my mouth as I dug my teeth hard. He let out a painful whine. I moved away, licking my teeth clean of the iron taste of his blood.

I gave him a moment. He could barely stand now; it was painful to watch. But he slouched into another fighting stance.

This time I moved. My speed was fast, and like wind I was behind him, shoving so hard that his body slammed against the trunk of a thick fir tree. He let out a groan and scrambled to stand up, but wasn't quick enough. I attacked him again, my claws pricking the right side of his abdomen.

I was playing with him now. With every swipe and jab his spirit broke. He dodged me once or twice, but with obvious exhaustion. The pain of his wounds was slowing him down.

He stood trembling with pain or fear, I didn't know which. I looked one last time into his icy eyes; they were still determined.

Pain. It was pain. I didn't see an ounce of fear in him.

He was still trying to stop me, or to stall me at least so that the wolf and her child could run far away from me. *Why was he protecting someone he barely knew? He will give his life away for them. Why?* I wondered.

Not that it mattered now. He was done. The last attack was mine. I headed towards him; my fangs visible, ready to tear out his throat. Ready to kill. Suddenly, my body was slammed to the side. In a whirlwind, seven wolves surrounded me.

Rebels. Fuck.

For a moment I was so focused on Marcus, I'd forgotten to keep my surroundings in check. My Kaiser wolf was mad with bloodlust and nearly beyond my control. The seven warriors stood at around nine feet tall, seasoned and vetted. They looked poised to strike. Now, things were a little amusing.

I waited... muscles tensed, knees bent, and ready to leap. A smile played at my lips. "Run." One of them said. "Marcus, El is waiting for you. Run!" I watched them keenly. Marcus was dumbfounded. He was ready to break. They blocked my vision. I focused on them.

"Tell me, do the odds suggest your victory?" I asked, glaring at the wolf in front of me. He said nothing. It happened in an instant. The wolves pounced on me at once. I lunged forward and grabbed one by the throat while the others crashed into the ground where I stood.

I squeezed my monstrous claws, my nails digging and curling all the way around him, I lifted him from the ground as his feet kicked feebly at my chest. I brought him to eye level and let him stare into my eyes. His courage left him then, the urine pooled on the ground at my feet. I threw him as hard as I could onto a tree, his body crunched sickeningly on impact.

"Disgusting," I spat out. I turned toward the other warriors. Hesitance marred their still faces. I smiled wickedly and tore into them. Then I slashed the largest of them and clawed at his chest. He howled in pain as his blood drenched the ground. I noted how quickly the blood was absorbed.

A wolf with a black coat swung at me. That was the last time he'd ever use that arm. His arm went flying, trailing blood. It arched over me and landed with a splat. I couldn't help but laugh at the sound. I kicked another wolf with an amber coat so hard that I felt his ribs shatter as he flew backwards from the impact. Two of them jumped at me with their fangs bared. I gracefully sidestepped to the right and ripped out one's throat. He fell to the ground, dead before he hit the floor.

Two of the surviving wolves caught my arms in their jaws, teeth piercing me. The third approached me. He was visibly exhausted. "This is it." He spoke between slow pants. "Beg Liunella for mercy, for you shall never receive it from us."

"Oh please! Let me go, I swear I'll never kill again!" I mocked and laughed at his face.

"You righteous fool, you had the perfect opportunity, but you would much rather get the last word." I swung both my arms forward, sending the two wolves holding me into the third. I walked towards them as they struggled to comprehend my strength. I pressed a single clawed finger into the brown wolf's chest, and I pierced him between his ribs. I went to the next and did the same. The last remaining was the fool.

"You, tell me where the rebels are," I commanded. He shrugged, and I snapped his neck, twisting it almost a hundred eighty degrees.

My silver chest was stained red with their blood. No one can defeat me in battle. I'm the Blood Moon Harbinger for a reason. I took a deep breath, scouring my surroundings. The forest was clear and silent.

Realization hit me. *Marcus; he's gone.*

My wolf was furious. Someone who knew my weakness was alive. A mix of anger, fear, and anxiety washed over me.

Fucking Marcus.

Rays of sunlight now covered the mountains. I looked up at the golden brilliance of it.

This isn't over yet, Marcus. You will die by my hands. I will come for you.

FOR THE FUTURE

Marcus

After being thrown into the tree, I hardly had the energy to stand. I was tired and in pain. My shoulder, my side, and my chest were all bleeding heavily. The blood dribbled down my fur into the soft cool ground.

I was dizzy and faltering on my feet. My body trembled hard as I somehow kept myself upright. The pain was taking over, and I knew I only had the capacity to endure one last attack. *I'm going to die,* I thought.

Belaize was coming for me with the resolve to slay me in his red-rimmed eyes. This was it. I saw my end approaching.

I was calm, at peace. I had overheard people talking about the experience that one goes through before they die. Your life flashes in front of your eyes. All the memories of your life pass through your mind in seconds. One final taste.

For me, it was different. The calm spread all over my body. I knew the pain and the heartache I felt because of this fight, this war, were finally at an end. *This was it*, I thought.

Belaize, he ran towards me. I closed my eyes. I sensed him approaching me. His dark, deathly aura filled my senses. Only one picture came into my mind that second, a small, thin girl with brown hair cascading down her shoulders, framing her round, plump, rosy cheeks. Her soft emerald eyes twinkling with mischief as she ran down a hill calling my name. *Marcus.*

Marcus. Marcus! Someone patted my face.

My eyes flickered open. I wasn't alone. The last thing I remembered was Belaize readying for another strike at me, but the scene changed somehow. I was surrounded by wolves, now. Their great forms were covered in the rebel insignia. Rebel warriors, here.

I studied the person beside me, the one who had urged me to move. He had a full head of black curls and an angular face with a scar across his cheek. As he came into focus, I recognized that scar. It took me few moments to comprehend that I was the one who gave him that scar. *Adrian.*

He wasn't tall, but back when we had trained back at the rebel base, his strength made up for his size. In a fight with him, you wouldn't know what hit you. I smiled at the thought. He was saying something to me, fervently pushing me, and leading me away.

"Marcus, come on, we need to run now!" I heard his raspy voice, barely above a whisper.

I finally moved as he willed me to. Away from the exchange with Belaize.

Adrian pushed me forward again. "Marcus, we have to go. Now. Our warriors are buying us time, but we have to move! You want their bravery to mean nothing? Come on!" He urged me on ahead.

I nodded my head. I didn't shift back, because if I did, I would have passed out from exhaustion. The adrenaline in my veins was the only thing that kept me going. We staggard deeper into the woods. Adrian supported most of my weight, careful to avoid the broken ribs. He was guiding me away as quickly as possible.

I reasoned that the rebels had to get me out. Of course, they couldn't leave a spy alive amidst the enemy, especially after Belaize had discovered my identity. I wouldn't have survived after that. I shouldn't have.

I knew Belaize had been toying with me. For him, fighting wasn't about trying your hardest to win, or concentrating and calculating every choice. It wasn't about pitting your will against your enemy. No, to him it was a game. It was for amusement.

My life was amusing to him.

I was weak. I was weak compared to him. He was the most feared assassin of Vascya for a reason. The Council had trained him, molded him into a weapon. Other Council guards were trained differently than Belaize. They didn't have his skill or his bloodlust. I could fight many Council guards, but Belaize... I was no match for him. White hot pain shot through my ribs with every step.

Adrian was saying something. But I was groggy. All I could do was move my legs as he ordered me to. My mind was foggy, but one thing was clear, I was barely clinging to life. I had accepted my fate. My end. I had admitted defeat. I was weak.

But I didn't want to be weak. I never wanted to come this close to death. There was a war to win. People to protect. The lives of innocents at stake. I'd get stronger and better. The next time I faced Belaize in battle, I would be his equal. Or damn well as close as I could become. I'm done hiding and running away. *Look at me now,* I thought bitterly. *Running away with my tail between my legs. Just like he said.*

"Never again will I surrender to death..." There was blood in my mouth. *Had I been muttering out loud?*

"Marcus what are you talking about? Marcus watch your footing!" Adrian cried as he pushed me hard to the right, shaking me out of my thoughts again. We would have tumbled into a thick fir tree.

I realized we had walked quite far from the Sanctuary. I could still smell the smoke in the air as ash hung in the wind. We were at the top of the mountain, far away from Belaize's reach now. The great vastness of the Walkaian range spread out before us. The green, lush forest was alive in the light of the new day.

The massacre of the night had ended with many casualties, but I wasn't on that list. The thought was bizarrely hilarious to me. As I leaned against one of the many large boulders that littered the mountain top, I chuckled madly. Somewhere in the back of my mind I knew that blood loss was making me delirious. The pain was overwhelming, and shock had set in.

"What are you doing, Marcus? We have to hide!" I heard Adrian say. I ignored his banter and hopped onto the boulder, the rough surface was jagged but plain. I hoisted myself up in the Sanctuary's direction and let out a howl. A mighty howl. It echoed all throughout the Frozen Fingers.

The sound paid reverence to the dead. The ache in my voice acknowledged the sacrifices made for the safety of innocent. Instead of diminishing, my song seemed to dance between the hills. It grew and changed and stretched. And before the final note could die, I filled my lungs once more, arched my head towards the sky, and let out another. It was a call for hope. It was a call of peace for the future of Vascya. Most of all, it was a challenge. *A challenge for Belaize.*

As the sound died away, I stayed a few moments more. I took deep gulps of air into my lungs, but I was dizzy. I stumbled off the boulder and fell to the ground. My vision darkened as unconsciousness took over. The last thing I remembered was Adrian calling my name over and over. My still form shifted as he heaved me from the rugged ground.

I gradually opened my eyes as light flooded into my pupils. I shielded my eyes with my arm. As I moved, my body protested with waves of pain. The pain was so awful that I doubled over, sending more spasms of pain rocketing through every inch of my body. Everything ached. I racked my brain struggling to figure out what happened, and soon it all came crashing back.

The ruined Sanctuary, Catherine, Jake, Adrian, and the wolves who saved me. The sudden thoughts prompted me to get up. As I tried to stand, my legs couldn't handle the weight of my body and I collapsed to the floor as the pain engulfed me.

As I laid there, someone approached me. Adrian's scent washed over me as he lifted me off the ground. "Marcus!" he said with relief. He helped me get back into bed. "You gave us a scare. It has been three days."

"Where am I?" I wondered. My voice was a hoarse murmur.

"I carried you back to the main base. Stay still now. El wanted to see you as soon as you woke up, I'll bring her," he said, turning me to my side. He turned and ran out of the room. I slowly took in my surroundings. I was in a wooden cabin. Low evening sunlight illuminated my room through dusty windows. The small space was sparsely decorated. Another empty bed covered with white sheets was beside my own. I noticed a table a few feet away which had some medicinal herbs and a pitcher of water resting on top. I tried to move, but another wave of pain overpowered my senses.

A few minutes later, Adrian rushed into the room with a girl at his side.

"You damned fool," she said, tears welling in her emerald eyes. "You're so stupid," she repeated over and over again. Her hands cupped my face as I managed a feeble smile.

"Water," I said, my voice barely rising over a whisper. Adrian huddled over to the small table beside me and poured me a glass, slowly raising it to my mouth. I drank greedily, the water rolling down my cheeks as I gulped. "You're spilling more than you're drinking," she said.

After I had finished, I tried to sit up. "No!" she said, pressing down on my chest to keep me still. It sent pain throughout my body, I yelped, and her hand quickly recoiled. "I'm sorry," she said, her eyes glistening with fresh tears. I couldn't believe someone as strong as her was so sensitive. The thought made me smile lightly.

"Did anyone make it here?" I inquired.

"Of everyone that lived in the Sanctuary, hardly three hundred people made it out. We sent most of them to the southern camp with supplies," Adrian said. I nodded; the southern camp was perhaps the most heavily fortified.

"Before me, did a mother and her child make it here?" I asked with hope.

"Catherine and Jake, you mean?" Adrian guessed. I nodded.

"They're here. They're shaken up, and the boy wanders aimlessly; Catherine, she's strong but she's breaking without her mate," he said flatly.

A heavy and dreadful silence settled in the room. "You think it'll end?" I said, "The war. Will it ever end? Will Vascya see peace again?" They didn't respond.

"Get some rest," she said. She stood and moved towards the door. Adrian got up as well.

"Eliana..." I called. She paused at the door, angling her head towards me slightly. "I'll never lose again."

Her emerald eyes met mine, reflecting determination and strengthening my resolve.

"Good!" She responded with a tender smile as she closed the door behind her.

THE TEMPLE OF SUNDARA

Belaize

The rebel corpses were scattered at my feet. The stench of blood filled my senses. Unfortunately, the rebel warriors weren't much of a challenge. But in the end, they had extracted Marcus at the cost of their own lives. I don't know if that was brave or just foolish.

I drew a sharp breath before wiping my bloody hands clean.

Now, I'd have to answer to the old asses on the Council. They would be furious that I had let the rebels slip away once again. They might just have my hide for letting a traitor informant escape. My wolf would certainly like to the see them try. *Marcus, huh. Who would have dreamed it would be him?*

I've had enough of the Council for a lifetime, yet their missions never lack blood and battle. I chased the adrenaline and fear. I played the part of a puppet, sure, but only to feel the roaring surge of power as I stole life with my just my two hands. Each and every victim held fear in their eyes. Everyone except *Marcus*.

Marcus... He was something else. I looked forward to facing him in battle again. But till then, I'd have to be careful. He would convey to the rebels the significance of the scar.

I lifted my hand, running my fingers through my hair in annoyance. My fingertips trailed across the scar on my shoulder and down my chest.

It felt jagged, deep. The skin had healed, but it was an unmistakable vestige of that night, plaguing my memory. *What was that thing?*

I remember it was an exciting day. It was full of the scents of a fresh kill. I had barely finished my meal before the old men in their long crimson robes came to me. They told me about this... thing... that lived in the sacred forests of the Moon goddess. It was near the city of Rylsk, in the southern part of Vascya. A barren place, the worshipers of the goddess long since captured, killed, or starved.

I had laughed at their faces when they told me about the task. They needed my strength to put down a feral animal, apparently. How ridiculous. I was so wrong. So, fucking wrong.

My wolf was agitated, but I willed myself to walk deeper into the heart of the sacred forest. Even the quiet rustle of wind against the withered leaves had set my nerves on edge. Why was I so restless? This had never happened before. It was an enveloping presence that surrounded me, threatening to choke me.

I saw a vague trail leading me somewhere deeper inside the thick forest of Sundara. I walked slowly towards it, taking in the faint scent of pine and fresh earth, letting it wash over me, while scanning my surroundings. I walked and walked for hours, encountering nothing but small creatures, a few deer, here and there. Nothing remotely of sort that the mighty Council was scared of. But something about this place made me cautious as a whisper.

Eventually the trail opened into a plain grassland. The area had hardly any forest cover. It was an enormous field; the grass stood about two feet tall. The ground felt damp with evening dew, and dusk was approaching fast. I scoured my surroundings, still nothing. The sense of dread was stronger than before. I glanced over my shoulder to make sure I wasn't followed.

I stood still for a few quiet moments, reassuring myself, and then I continued to tread ahead. Soon I spotted a rocky structure. Moving closer, I saw it was a building of sorts. Although in shambles, it appeared to be made from engraved white stone. The ruins of a castle, I thought. I stepped through the crumbling outer gate. It was covered in a flaky, iridescent moss. Rubble had accumulated in large scattered piles. I tried to imagine this castle in all its past glory. The halls must have been huge, the pillars sculpted to perfection. I saw the manifestation of its beauty as it must have been.

The moon was high now. Its dim light illuminated a ruined altar at the far end of the hall. The altar shined, mirroring the goddess' glow. Gigantic pillars engraved with the images of the moon in its lunar cycle were still intact beside it. Pebbles, dirt, and dust blanketed the place.

I shuffled closer to one pillar and traced my fingers along the phases of the moon. I moved to examine the altar next. I climbed the white stone steps, only to gaze upon an engraving of a woman etched into the stone floor. Remnants of what once were the womanly curves and long hair falling down her shoulders. My eyes lifted to see her face. But it... it was destroyed as if someone deliberately smashed it. I realized I was at the temple of Sundara, the sacred altar of the Moon Goddess.

It was well known all over Vascya and every wolf, young or old, knew about it. It was said that this was where the Moon goddess had created the first wolf, named Fenrir. But that was nothing but an old wives' tale. Long before the war, people came here from all over Vascya to worship the goddess, but the rebellion left this place barren and lost to the elements.

According to the scriptures, a wolf with the blood of Mugiri led the rebellion. Moon Goddess' wrath was unquenchable. She removed the wolves with evil intent from the land. It was whispered that because of this rebellion Kaisers were exceptionally rare, compared to alphas of other bloodlines. I was proud to be Kaiser. My skills were enhanced astoundingly through my training. The Council had put a lot of effort to make me who I was. I sighed and stepped down from the altar.

I meandered around the altar, gazing at the moon high above. Our goddess was looking down on us. I wandered inside the ruins, the Council's mission was a distant commitment. I doubted I would find the creature anyway, so I explored more.

In a corridor to the left of the altar the walls were torn apart, but what was left of the place was stunning. I must've been the first to find this place in centuries. Dust covered the walls; I traced the inscriptions on them with my fingertips. The white carved stone depicted many tales I had learned during my childhood. One of my favorite had to be the legend of the four winds of Fenrir.

Beleotell the Ghost, Çatall the Sight, Draxus the Mind, and Mugiri the Strength. These four wolves were said to be created by Fenrir himself. Though Fenrir's existence can be disputed, the Four Winds were a historical fact. They spread throughout the land of Vascya and thus began the Lycan Empire.

You could hardly call the Lycans an empire now. We were squabbling like pathetic infants instead. The Council's plans to capture mates had led to an insurgency through the nation.... I scoffed at that thought and continued to follow the carvings. A large block was in the center of what seemed to be remains of an atrium. A large obelisk of white carved stone stood in the middle. I encircled it, peering closely. It showed what I thought was the disappearance of Fenrir, but it was difficult to tell.

The block still stood tall with few cracks, but something had clawed its surface. The deep gauges were massive. I speculated as I changed into my wolf. I measured what was etched on the surface with my claw. It dwarfed my hand in comparison. Whatever or whoever did this, it was absolutely monstrous.

What happened next was a blur... or a dream... I don't know. I saw a flash of white and was sent hurtling into the back wall of the atrium. The wall must've been about fifty feet behind me. Nothing in this world could have done that to a wolf my size. Nothing! Yet, I found myself dazed. My head had hit the stone wall hard. Blood was trickling down from the wound, and my head was pounding.

I growled and looked forward, but there was nothing. I saw nothing. Black spots appeared in my vision, but I rose up on my feet. Running to the center of the chamber, I roared louder, turning left and right in a frenzy. I was anxious... and scared. I hadn't been scared in a long time. The last time... my thoughts stilled when I saw it again, a white streak. This time I felt it rip into my flesh as a searing pain enveloped my body. It took every ounce of my strength not to pass out.

I felt the darkness inch closer, threatening to overcome my sanity and send me to the afterlife. I willed myself to stand. As I did, I saw it; I saw death and howled loudly.

A rush of adrenaline hit my body with a surge of strength. I sprinted from the atrium, from the temple, from the ruins and back into the dense forest. I ran hard and true, right through it, and only when I knew I was close to the edge of the forest did I let myself slow down. But I was a prey, and the predator was hunting me with all his might. With another white flash, I collapsed on my knees and snarled; my fangs bared. I saw the flash again, but this time slow enough that I made out its eyes. Red. Red like someone had drowned the moon in blood. Then it was gone.

The pain came back as the adrenaline wore off, and again I was sent to the brink of the gathering tide of darkness. Somehow, I stumbled out of the forest, my body drowsed in blood, and one hand clutching my stomach wound closed. My eyes blurred; my feet faltered. I fell into the arms of unconsciousness.

I had woken up several days later. the Council healer said I had danced with death and come back from the brink – not once, but twice. They demanded to know what had happened in the forest of Sundara, and I had no answer for them. A white flash was all I could tell them. Some began to fear the woods like a plagued tick.

But, I needed to know. It took me three weeks to completely recover. Time had moved slowly then, and my waking thoughts were consumed with that place. All mention of the Sundara temple had been scrubbed from the Council library, so the scrolls at my bedside were of little use. At night, it was much worse. The dreams stole my sleep, and a bit of my sanity.

When I finally found myself staring at the entrance of the woods, I had neither the strength nor the will to cross the thicket. I came back several times and each time my feet stopped before the trail leading into the woods. Was I afraid? All I knew was that the closer I got to the woods, the more this damned scar on my body burned.

I traced the scar up and down on my body. My face contorted into a frown as the memory of that day faded from my mind. I found myself sitting on a wooden stump next to the bloodied carcasses of fallen wolves. I stood up finally and prepared for what was to come next. The Council... I would have to face them. I took a deep breath and gathered the bodies. Lifting them on my shoulders, I made my way to the narrow, serene river close by and dropped them one by one into it. I turned my back towards them, leaving them in the care of the queen of the tides.

THE SPLINTERING FACTIONS

Idaos

They say that Fenrir himself laid the first stone of this castle, just as he created the first Council's robes from his own heart's blood. Old tales fit for children and the enfeebled. The true artistry of it was in the masonry. Each tile was of elegant design, every garden immaculate, and every bit of silver a bright, polished finish. That is the way I ran the Capital.

I was raised within these luxuries, as was every member of my long bloodline of Çatall's chosen. This castle was meant for us, and the others of the original Four Winds. Scholars believed Vascya was born here within these walls. Here, the Council would live, learn the art of leadership, and guide the land through the centuries.

But times had changed. The Keep stayed empty throughout the year. The Council, along with their families, preferred to stay with their packs in their territories. Vascya was now divided into ten states, and a Council member commanded each one. Now, the alphas only gathered at the castle of Regvyer for dull discussions on trade, taxes, and rebels.

Even so, the lycans here were loyal to the cause. The thick, stone walls promised a measure of peace, and I kept the wolves here well supplied and cared for. I kept the security and the army meticulous. Constant drills and patrols ensured that the Rebels had yet to attack the Capital. My strength and brutality were unmatched behind this stronghold.

As I trudged through its stony hallways, the reverberations of my footsteps against the polished floor were deafening. My crimson robe flowed behind me. Occasionally, I spotted a few guards, who bowed before me as I passed by.

The halls were bustling today with servants. The arrival of the first Alpha had been early this morning, pulling me from my bed before the crows called the sun. The rest trickled in at a more reasonable hour – after morning meal. I had bid each and every one of them to await my presence in the sacred chamber of Liunella.

I strolled to the end of the hallway and turned right. The stone doors were magnificent as ever with intricate, engraved swirls like that of a whirlwind. Two Council guards were standing outside, guarding the door. They bowed when they spotted me and pushed the doors wide. A far departure from my hurried entrance some fifty years ago.

"You are getting in a habit to make us wait, Idaos." Alpha Canagan's voice echoed. He was perched on his chair sipping wine from a golden goblet. Even though fifty years had passed since the day I unveiled the prophecy, Canagan had barely aged, except for the dark shadows beneath his eyes, no doubt a result of the numerous rebel uprisings. The other alphas had assembled around the large mahogany table.

"I'm sorry, Canagan. These old bones of mine have started to give out." I smiled as I seated myself at the center of the table, between Eyolf and Valio. *This used to be a much smaller table*, I thought regretfully. Granted, I had driven the new Council's formulation, from the original four to now a party of ten, but still. That hadn't come without its share of headaches. This room did feel crowded at times.

I glanced around at everyone in the vast room. The walls were the same chalky white. Bright rays of midmorning sun illuminated the room. My eyes glazed over the single, empty chair at the end of the table resting beside Alpha Illari.

I shifted in my seat, getting comfortable, and turned to face the others. My voice drawled through the great room, "So, as to the matter at hand—"

"Ahem... I would like to start the meeting today," said Alpha Illari. Her stern face flickered with a shadow of uncertainty without the leering presence of her sister. Her golden hair was up in a graceful knot. Her lips were painted a shade of ruby, matching her robes.

"My territory is facing difficulties with the Council guards. They haven't been following strict orders to not harm the mates. Instead, they make it a sport to kill the helpless wolves. I have brought this up many times to all of you, yet we never have come to a better solution," Illari said.

"It is the same in my territory. As a result, many wolf packs have taken up with the rebellion. We have tried to make the process as smooth as possible for the innocent wolves, but we have failed," said Esteve from the other side of the table.

"No reports have been received and without more evidence, I am afraid I can't do anything. I can only keep track of wolves once they've been admitted into the Low Cities," said Alpha Remus, who was sitting three spots to my right. His brown hair was curled atop his head, his eyes a steely gray. The young alpha who had replaced the seat vacated by Ronak.

I observed him for a moment, taking in his tense posture. "You need rely on a written report instead of the words of an alpha? Oh Liunella. What has become of this Council! We are meant to lead!" Illari said with disdain.

"It is not my place to ignore your words. But we have to uphold the laws. The wolves of Vascya know they have to come to the Low Cities for inspection if we want to find those mates. When they choose not to do so, willfully and by their own accord, measures must be taken. I have tried my best to monitor them and release those who I can, but the rest remain in confinement. As for the guards, I do not know. My responsibilities end after I send them to Regvyer," Remus said coldly.

"I am afraid I am at fault here, Illari. With help of Canagan, I sent guards to each state. The actions of those guards fall on my shoulders. But in these troubling times, I am afraid that calling troops back to the Capital for martial punishment would be useless. An unnecessary waste of supplies, even. I can, however, remind my commanders to keep them on a tight leash," I said.

"Your passive actions are worthy for an applaud, Idaos. This meeting holds no importance to me if you dismiss my concerns so easily. You have left me with no choice. I will co-operate with the Council, and deliver mated wolves safely to the Low Cities, but no Council guard will step a foot in my territory." Illari's voice echoed in the room. I looked in her gray eyes and only found cold fury.

"You will do no such thing, Illari. That would deny the Council's law. You will be made an enemy of the state if you are not careful," Eyolf chimed beside me.

"I don't care anymore! My words fall on deaf ears. I did not support your decision back then, and yet I cooperated. Loss of life is something I cannot bear, especially for sport. Either the guards face the consequences of their actions, or they do not enter my territory. I give the Council five days to do so." Illari stood then, tall and proud. Her fingers clenched into a knuckled fist and she stormed out of the Sanctorum.

Canagan sighed in his chair, taking a long swig from his goblet. "Well... Illari and Evette's opposition has always been clear," Olgario said, while stroking his long black beard.

"We cannot go back on our actions now. We must find those mates," I said. "Let's continue."

Remus was reading a stack of mission reports. He spoke without looking up, "The commander of the Low Cities requests that the other alphas hold off on calling more soldiers for aid. He says he needs more time to train wolves, otherwise the rebels will always have the upper hand in battle." He shuffled pages briefly, squinting. "Additionally, more security is needed within the Low Cities. Rebels focus their efforts there in hopes of releasing captives."

"We can wait for the warriors to mature. But I am afraid time is not a luxury we have. Remus, train them harder. Ronak's warriors are on another level. His knowledge of the Council means we need every available advantage," Amarog said.

"What about the wolves I sent two weeks ago for training? They were the best of my pack," Alpha Valio queried.

Remus looked in my direction, but his gaze stayed on Valio. "Training has begun, but it will be at least two months before they are ready for battle."

"Two months?" Valio spit the words out, his nostrils flaring.

"I know, alpha. But the rebels... they are just getting stronger and stronger. Ronak is sedulous and strong. Whenever he trains a warrior, that warrior can take down at least ten Council guards. I have instated the most capable commander training new guards, but even they're not enough. Numbers. Our victory lies in numbers. We must overwhelm their forces, otherwise, all of this was for nothing," Remus said distastefully.

Alpha Remus trained and supplied the guards for all over the Vascya. He volunteered for the task after replacing Ronak and assuming his territory. We chose Remus not only for his inheritance of Low Cities but also for the blood that flowed in his veins, the blood of Mugiri. He was a Kaiser, the only one on the Council.

"If only, Janus were alive today. We would have more weapons at our disposal, others like Belaize," Alpha Eyolf muttered beside me, but I knew everyone heard precisely what he said.

I felt a wave of agitation ripple through the Council. We knew how Janus, the best Master of Arms of Vascya, died. A slight shiver ran through me as the memory of his dead body, which was ripped into pieces, flickered in my mind. Blood was splattered everywhere. If I tried, I wouldn't have been able to make out the man's face. It was clawed that badly; the eyes had been pulled and crushed. The heart was shredded. It was gruesome. *Yet...*

We knew who had killed him, because only after Janus's murder, did he earn his name. The Blood Moon Harbinger.

Janus had been the one to oversee his training. We didn't truly know what Janus did to Belaize, but we had demanded Janus for a weapon and he delivered. Belaize was unmatched, but our control over him was slipping day by day. My throat seized for a moment, and I found it difficult to swallow but my face was a mask of composure.

Alpha Esteve broke the uneasy silence that had settled in the chamber.

"Janus may have been great at what he did, but the only thing he has left with us is trouble. You know that, Eyolf."

"Yes. But you must admit that we got what we needed. And right now, we need more wolves trained like Belaize." Eyolf huffed in his chair.

"We need stronger wolves who can fight the rebels effectively. Belaize is strong, always has been, but he is absolute chaos. We cannot control chaos," Canagan stated. I sensed aggression in his voice.

I stroked my stubble which had grown gray over the years. Canagan was right indeed. Belaize was chaos. The rebels feared him. When he first set out every mission was a success. He singlehandedly captured twice the number of mated wolves than any other squad. But even that paled in comparison to the number of wolves he had left dead in his wake.

For the last year and a half, his missions hadn't been effective. He ignored orders. He even killed Council guards faster than we could recruit them. It was a waking nightmare.

I cleared my throat, "What is the report from Belaize's last mission?"

"It was a mess, Idaos. I know that rumors have swirled, but let us address why we are all here: It's imperative that every member of the Council is made aware of this disaster," Remus said, his voice sent a chill through the room.

I didn't like this at all. I sensed that something was... off. The blood of old had given me the power of foresight and I could feel the stirring of energy within me. My body was slowly filling with dread. Something was going to happen.

Something...

A crisp knock came from the door. A heartbeat of silence. "Enter," Amarog murmured. A Council guard entered our chambers and bowed before us. Everyone's attention diverted to him.

He lifted his head and said, "Elders, Belaize is outside to see you, may I brin—" He was pushed from the entrance when the tall man entered the room. The Council guard lost his balance and fell. He snapped his head in the man's direction and growled. "I told you to wait outside while I announce your presence!"

"I don't wait around for anyone," he replied coolly. I took the sight in. Belaize was tall. Taller than most wolves. His blond hair was neatly tied into a ponytail. His clothes were new, tawny-colored trousers and black shirt, and his muscles rippled from beneath the thin fabric. His face was lined with old, fading scars and short black stubble.

The Council guard stood up, huffing. His pride was clearly bruised. Without a word he walked to the corner of the room with a stony, hard face.

"Belaize, you're here. I was expecting you." Remus chuckled, but the smile didn't reach his eyes. "I was in the process of updating the elders about your last mission. Though, I am sure you'd like to tell the tale yourself."

Belaize shifted uncomfortably.

He took a deep breath and started talking. "Orden told me that all of you wanted to dispatch a task force to Walka. I assembled one, and we travelled to the Sanctuary. One of the rangers scouting the area met us on the way and led us there. When we reached the Sanctuary, we found the ranger's partner dead at his post. I immediately realized the rebels knew about our mission and I ordered the others to begin the attack. We captured about seventy wolves alive. Many died fighting, from our side as well." He stopped.

Remus shifted in his seat, putting his elbow on the table and resting his head on his hand. His gaze fixed on Belaize.

"How convenient of you to deliberately leave out crucial details." His voice was low and hard. He shifted in his seat to address those seated at the table.

"Alphas, Belaize – on his own will – let the Chieftain of the rebel base go, because— let me quote from the report—" he shuffled through papers and plucked one out, reading, "Because 'he was a scared little cunt.' Belaize, this is why you were summoned. We are with a mere handful of prisoners because of your incompetence! You could have found information on Ronak and ended this war on your own, but you just had to have your laugh! You let him go because you found it fucking funny!" Remus's voice was raised now. His face was beet red in anger.

The alphas each wore a somber expression. Sunlight danced around the room, yet a dark aura had settled in. Belaize was chaos.

Belaize's expression turned furious, but he was restraining himself. "I let him go because he wasn't the leader or anyone important," he grumbled.

"How do you know he wasn't?! He was commanding the base. He was probably their chieftain, the one who directly reports to Ronak. He would have known Ronak's location. But you still let him escape. Why? Answer me now, Belaize," Remus said, with the power of an alpha clear in his voice. One Kaiser to another.

I studied Belaize. His posture emitted the strange energy of defiance. His wolf rioted that someone was commanding him. "I let him escape because of the exact reason I fucking stated in the report. He was a scared cunt running for his life. The rebel leaders are fierce, or so I have heard. They are brave and courageous, not weak like that wolf. He was a rebel, sure, but not a leader, and not worthy of being killed by me. That's exactly why I let him go."

Remus cut in, "So any scared wolf you'll see, you'll let them go? Is that it? No wonder we aren't getting many prisoners from you these days. The monstrous Belaize here, is turning soft!" Remus lip curled with disdain.

Belaize snarled at Remus. In a blur, he moved to the edge of the chamber and punched a large crack through the stone wall. He was breathing heavily, attempting to control himself. His brute strength was unimaginable.

"Don't push him, Remus," I breathed in a whisper. The room was silent except for Belaize's heavy breathing.

"Push him? I haven't even begun, Idaos. This is only the half of what transpired in Walka. Belaize, had a spy, right under his damned nose, and didn't even know. For the last year the spy has leaked Council secrets to the rebels! And Belaize, oh so conveniently, let the fucking spy escape, as well."

Remus was furious now. Belaize's outburst hadn't phased him an inch. No. Remus matched Belaize in strength, A pair of Kaisers in the same room was powerful as an earthquake. The raw strength they both possessed was something to behold.

Neither were backing down. Remus sent the reports flying from the desk. "Belaize, you clearly have lost your touch. You couldn't even smell a spy around you. And when you found out, you didn't outright kill him. No, no, no, no... you had toy with his life, because killing the rebels wasn't fun enough. This isn't a damn playground! This is a war. I would have let the leader slide because, for once, I believe you are right. The rebels are fierce, but this? Belaize? Really?" Remus had left us all speechless.

After a moment Alpha Amarog said softly, "Do you have anything to say in your defense?"

Belaize stood still, tension clear in his body. "Answer your alpha, Belaize. You're incompetent in completing tasks, but the least you can do is answer your superior," Remus bellowed.

"No," he croaked.

"Look at this failure in front of you, Eyolf. You were just saying that if Janus were still alive we'd have more weapons like him. But, guess what? He is a damned failure."

As soon as he finished that sentence, Belaize lunged at Remus. With great speed, he clawed at his throat. The alphas shuffled quickly around the table. The Council guard, who stood silently in the corner till now, was quick to shove Belaize aside, but it took Canagan, Amarog, and Esteve to pry Belaize away from Remus. They held Belaize down. Remus's clothes were bloody. His neck gashed open. I shivered a little, looking at the crimson blood. I knew something would happen in this meeting, but this wasn't what I expected.

Remus coughed blood. Rubbing it on his sleeve, he sat up. "Look at the rabid wolf in front of you, elders. This is the Blood Moon Harbinger. A fucking nightmare," he said, clutching at this throat.

"I will kill you. You think you are so high and mighty just because you are on the Council? I'll squeeze you like a fucking insect. It's not my fucking fault we had a spy. He worked with efficiency. He was Orden's assistant. I didn't know shit about him. Blame Orden for this mess, not me." Belaize snapped.

His fangs sharpened and his eyes shifted to a blood red hue as his wolf surfaced. He was struggling to tear himself free of the other alphas. Five of them were holding him down now, and they still barely kept him away from Remus.

"I have the old blood too, Belaize. You are not the only Kaiser in this sacred Sanctorum." Remus glared at Belaize, his fangs elongating as well. It was a battle for dominance over the other.

"This is a Council assembly! Stop it, both of you. Remus, go to Infirmary. This meeting is over. Elders escort Belaize out, right now. We do not spill blood in the Sacred Chamber. Liunella will not forgive us." My voice boomed.

Canagan immediately shuffled out of the room with Remus. I followed the others out with Belaize. They still gripped him tightly, so he wouldn't break loose in his bloodlust. After a few minutes, I spoke to other elders. "Elders, please leave Belaize and myself, alone. I would like a word with him."

Shock and reluctance displayed on all of their faces. "B-but Idaos, you saw what he did!" Olegario said, immediately.

I nodded at him and looked at Belaize. He was taking deep breaths but was calm enough to converse. "Remus, frankly, was an idiot to push him. I just want a conversation with him. Leave us, please. Afterward I want to address other issues, as well. Please await in the chamber once the others have assembled."

Slowly, he nodded, and everyone shuffled out of the corridor. I waited patiently beside Belaize. He was gazing at the cloudless cerulean sky through a great window. I looked at him for a moment. He was half a foot taller than me. His blood sang of strength.

"I'm sorry for the way Remus acted. It wasn't worthy of an alpha. We have been under great strain, Remus especially. The rebels relentlessly attack the Low Cities. He just wanted a win, to show off his hard work," I mumbled.

"I don't care what he wants. Yes, that Chieftain, or whoever that was, was my fault. But Marcus, he wasn't. I was going to end him, but the rebels extracted him." Belaize spoke, his face expressionless.

"Well, now the spy is gone, I believe the next mission will be more successful than the last one. Go rest, Belaize. You deserve a day off," I said, patting his muscled back.

The moment my hand touched him, dread filled me. Shivers ran through my spine, and cold death surrounded me. I stumbled away, trying to keep my expression neutral. "I- I should go now. Elders are waiting for me." I turned, my crimson robes swirling in motion as I sped away. Dread, fear, and anxiety gripped my heart harder each second.

I focused on getting away. Getting away from Belaize. One foot after the other I walked out of the corridor, all my energy drained. A dark silhouette loomed at the end of the hallway and before I could register what it was it melted away. The stench of my fear filled the dead halls of the castle.

I was panting by the time I finally entered the chamber once again. I closed the door quickly and faced the empty room. Eyolf came to my side immediately, his face twisted with worry. “Idaos! Idaos! Are you okay? Did Belaize do something!?”

I gripped his hand tightly and shook my head. The words felt trapped in my chest, constricted by horror. “No. No! I- I saw a vision... he... Belaize... he is our... death. He is... our end. We have to kill him, otherwise... we all are... doomed.”

HARBINGER VS. MORTIS

Belaize

The Capital smelled of sewerage and sweat as I roamed the crowded streets. Dusk was approaching fast. The sky was a shade of orange; flames danced along the silver clouds. Generally, the weather was clear in the southern states of Vascya, and Regvyer was no exception. In the beginning of the Lycan race, Liunella created the first wolf, Fenrir. He was the leader of the Lycan race, and he was the one who set the first stone of the Capitol. He had chosen and blessed the Four Winds to guide Vascya to prosperity. As such, the Winds lived and ruled Vascya from this city.

I was pacing aimlessly in an enormous alley. The stone buildings, the complexes, the bricked side streets, reminded me of the magnificent castle at the city's heart. I sensed wolves all around me, getting on with their everyday lives. The streets were scurrying with life. I saw people selling trinkets, fabrics, paintings, everything one could imagine lining the walkways beside the old buildings. Children ran along the alleys, their laughter subsiding in the hustle of the city, their mothers ushering them toward home. Despite a rapid decline in the Lycan population, Regvyer remained densely populated.

Sure, the Council's decisions and the war had altered the lives of these wolves forever, but they had been quick to get back on their feet. Cities like this renounced mated wolves to keep out of the war. The

Council did release mated wolves from Low Cities from time to time, but they never returned the same.

Last week's meeting had been disastrous. I had tried to restrain my wolf, but when Alpha Remus ripped away my abilities and integrity... I shook my head and continued my stroll. The shadows were looming in the alleys now as merchants closed their little shops and departed to homes or bars or another's comfort.

A gentle breeze caressed my face. It was warm and salty. I ran my fingers through my hair, my fingers wet from the humidity of the south. I decided I liked the north better.

Regvyer, unlike the other small towns and cities, was one of the most heavily fortified against the rebels, second to the Low Cities.

The Low Cities weren't far from here, hardly a four- or five hour run. The Low Cities were two cities situated so close to each other that they were one. They used to be a trading hub like Regvyer, but now functioned as breeding grounds for the Council. To maintain the number of wolves constant in their forces, they kept the female prisoners and bred them. It was vicious, but I had filled the prison cells inside the Low Cities myself.

A boy, who was barely four feet tall, tugged at my trousers as I passed through an intersection. I looked down. Dressed in rags, his hair covered in dirt and filth, he tugged at my pants again with his tiny fists. "Please..." the skinny boy stammered. His face was gaunt and hollow. He was more bone than skin.

"What?" I said, pulling my leg loose from his grip. "Hungry... I am hungry."

"Where are your parents boy?" I gritted my teeth. I didn't want to be disturbed.

"Taken. They... were taken away. Please." He tugged at my pants again. I shook my leg away with force this time. The skinny boy stumbled and fell down.

"Run along, boy," I scoffed. I fished out a few diras from my pocket and threw it on the filthy street in front of him. "Don't bother me anymore." As I turned away, I saw the vagrant boy picking up the money hurriedly. He gave me a grin, a tooth missing from his mouth, and then was gone.

I continued to my quarters further down the alley. *Why did I do that?* I was lost in my thoughts. The Council was weighing heavily on my mind. Not to mention the child I was witnessing in my visions. *Who was he? And those visions, why were they becoming more vivid?* In a wrong fight, these distractions could get me killed.

I halted when I reached the center of the city. The capitol's high walls loomed in the distance. In the center of the square was a granite statue of the Four Winds. Fenrir stood protectively in the middle, his gaze fixed toward some distant land, some hidden truth.

A fountain pooled at his feet. The evening sun made eerie shadows against the water droplets as they fell on the lifeless wolves. The fountain seemed to glow with an almost celestial light. The hum of the flowing water was mesmerizing. The expressions of each of the Winds were so realistic. Too realistic.

My eyes focused on my forefather, *the Mugiri*. His massive bronze wolf was fearsome, even the fangs were sculpted beautifully. The fountain was said to have been made by *Keda,* one of the most prolific builders to have ever lived. He was descended from the bloodline of *Draxus* of the Four Winds. The famous *Navars*.

The people sought Navars for the bloodline's unparalleled intelligence. They are exceptionally skilled and quick-witted. Ronak, the leader of the rebels, was one of the old blood, a Navar. Killing him, another wolf of the old bloodlines would be riveting. I smirked at the thought and peered into my blurry reflection in the ripples of water.

I don't know how long I spent staring, but a movement broke the trance. It was virtually imperceptible, and most would have missed it entirely. But not me.

"Faust, I can smell you." There were others too. Ten to be specific.

"So... this is what the Council wants. To kill me," I said, turning to face the empty street. I saw a flicker of movement from the corner of my eye. An enormous shadow slowly stretched before me.

There he was. His rust brown wolf standing at the end of the street. He was large by most standards, well over ten feet tall. In the steel armor he had on, he was a menacing sight.

"This is what I want," he called out, challenging me.

My wolf howled in delight as I gradually let him come to the surface. I shifted, my bones and muscles snapping and reshaping as my body grew. My limbs stretched, darkened as hair sprouted from once bare skin. My brown tunic was torn to rags, my briefs stretched and strained before ripping and falling off. I glared at Faust, dead on. He tensed up. He was ready to fight.

I analyzed his stance. He was likely to make the first move. He stood prepared to kill me. His much like my own.

That armor would be a problem. Faust's and his battalion, *the Mortis*, were infamous among the assassin's that served the Council. They were vicious, efficient, and the preferred killers to whom the Council handed their dirty work.

I was one powerful wolf. But these, they were ten brutal executioners who preyed on the single target assigned to them. If I could put a number on it, I would say their kills number in the thousands. But, of course, wolf for wolf, I was better in every way.

My eyes flickered to my surroundings as I glimpsed two silhouettes on the rooftop. They were armored as well. This was going to be a challenge. I sensed movement behind me and I tilted my head to the left.

Four of them guarded the streets that split from the central courtyard. Three more left... somewhere. If they were smart, they would hold back until the last second. As the thought finished, I saw a glimmer of black armor and spotted the remaining three wolves trying to circle around a building to my right. *I guess they aren't too bright.*

The armor worn by the Mortis was tough. I had tried it on myself during training once. Iron claws were a particularly useful feature. They were gauntlets that were worn over the paws, and I had heard stories of these gauntlets; the Mortis had been using them to subdue rebels. At the cost of speed and power, the armor gave a relatively impenetrable defense. But I knew its weaknesses.

"Pitiful, that your own claws aren't enough to win," I jeered at Faust. His expression grew colder.

"What would Janus think?" I mocked again, licking my fangs with my tongue. He slowly walked towards me.

"He would be damn proud of me once I kill the one responsible for murdering him in cold blood."

I smiled wickedly. "Faust, you aren't even a shadow of what Janus was. Quit trying to impress your dead father." The other wolves started closing in. Every hair on my body was alert as I felt them surrounding me.

The tension was palpable, the smell of fight always sent me into overdrive. Faust's eyes were a pale silver, as always. His gaze didn't waiver, but I knew he feared me. He had always feared me. Behind his bravado, he was just like the others. They all feared me. In a blink of an eye, I lunged forward.

Faust leaped back, evading my claws by barely an inch. *He shouldn't be able to move this fast*, I marveled. Not with that armor. The other wolves charged toward at me, trying to catch me off guard. *How?*

A wolf sprang at me from behind, I jumped and leapt over him in an arc. I landed gracefully and when he turned, I planted a firm kick to his chest, shattering the armor. It dawned on me. This isn't the steel armor I thought it was. It was lighter. I couldn't help but grin. Ah, these fools had sacrificed defense for speed. Big mistake.

The wolf I kicked flew over ten feet and landed with a thud. His body skid limply on the cobbles. That kick should have shattered all his ribs. Then another wolf was on me, slashing at my back with the iron gauntlets. I moved out of the way and caught him off balance, but before I could deliver a decisive hit, another wolf was lunging forward. I dodged his blow and gripped the other hard. I slammed him into the wolf I had just evaded. They were impressive wolves, large and heavy, but they were nowhere near strong enough to face a Kaiser. I sensed movement from behind me. Faust charged me, trying to ambush me while I was fighting his other wolves. Typical Faust and his gulls.

Two more wolves rushed at me from either side. In another three seconds they'd be upon me, I jumped into the air, Faust had expected as much, but the other two followed me with their eyes focused solely on me, and barreled into one another. I must've been ten feet in the air when Faust and I clashed. His momentum sent me flying backward. We crashed into the granite fountain behind me. I stumbled a little but kept upright. I stomped on Faust's head, holding him beneath the water.

Looking up, I saw that the two wolves from the roof had scaled down and were running toward me. I let out a grunt and hopped out of the fountain. Water shot upwards in a stream behind me. Faust coughed as he caught his breath. He was wheezing. Rubbing the water out of his eyes, he quickly heaved his soaking form out of the fountain, ready to follow me again.

There were too many of them. It was frustrating. The heat of my anger surged and I let out a heady snarl. The wolves from the rooftop didn't falter, even after watching the skirmish from above. *Good, I like a brave set of challengers.*

The wolves coordinated their attacks, striking when one had already done so, to prevent any openings for me counter with. Pathetic. One wolf swung at my chest, I let him connect his iron claws against my chest. They raked at my flesh and blood poured from my body. I grimaced at the pain, but grabbed his arm and ripped it right off. His blood splattered my face. He let out an agonizing scream.

His partner realized what was happening, but it was already too late. I caught him as well. I uttered a growl, low and deep, as I twisted his head, hearing the satisfying crack. His muscles tore as bone ripped through flesh and blood spurted from fresh fractures. The wolf howled in pain, toiling in my ironclad grip but to no avail. Grabbing him by his helmet, I lifted him off the ground and smashed his head on the stones. His shit armor crumbled along with his head. I turned to the other injured wolf. I saw his gnarled and misshapen arm lying beside him as he whimpered.

Unexpectedly, a boy came to my mind. The one who I had so brutally maimed in the forest of Chern. Whose mother I had killed in front of his own eyes. I felt my legs give out underneath me as I dropped to my knees.

"Why?" I screamed into the night; my hands clutched my head. It throbbed painfully as if someone was hammering a nail over and over again.

I struggled to keep my mind present. Dimly, I was aware of Faust walking to me casually, a savage grin on his face. "Belaize, how the mighty has fallen," he said mockingly. I took a deep breath and stood up slowly to face him.

"You haven't won. Three of your men are dead. Two are injured. What part of this looks to you as I've fallen?" It was difficult to keep my voice from slurring.

"Oh! We never meant to kill you." He said, grinning smugly. "Only capture."

"Capture?" I quizzed. "The likes of you could never hope to arrest me," I stated defiantly.

"Oh, but we have, even as I speak the wolfsbane runs through your veins, sapping away your strength. You're finished, Belaize."

Wolfsbane! When? I thought, and my mind sped back to when I took the hit from the wolf. My eyes flickered to my chest wound, now soaked with blood. My silver fur was wet, now a deep crimson.

"They coated the gauntlet with it," he said with a pompous, proud smirk.

"It doesn't seem to work," I lied, my expression still stone hard. I felt it, though. The wolfsbane was eating away at my wolf.

I needed to get out of here before the wolfsbane completely scoured me of my strength. I stood over a corpse and lurched down, tearing a gauntlet off the dead wolf's claw. I hurled it at Faust. It made impact and shattered his armor. The claws were buried deep inside him. It wouldn't kill him, but it would give me the chance I needed desperately. As the chemical tore through his body, I seized his neck.

"I'll kill him if anyone moves an inch," I said to the remaining Mortis fucks, feeling a wave of weakness wash over me. Faust was struggling in my grip. I felt his agitation. I had beaten him even though he had me cornered. I grinned even as my vision blurred.

"Damn you!" He shrieked, choking and wheezing. The wolfsbane had him too.

"You, inject the others with the wolfsbane," I said to one of them. They all looked at him, and he looked at Faust. Piercing Faust's skin with my finger, enough to draw blood, I said, "I'll kill the bastard!"

Faust's body tensed, and then eased. "Do as he says. Now!" he said to the wolf. He pricked the remaining seven wolves with his gauntlet. They began to groan and wheeze as the herb overtook them. Faust's lips had turned a purplish hue, and his mouth made twisted, gasping motions as he struggled for air. I casted him aside like a doll. Then I ran from the courtyard as fast as my legs would carry me. I dashed through the winding streets, fleeing Regvyer. The forest, I needed to go to the forest.

I sprinted through the fields, not caring about the direction. All I had to do was put one foot in front of the other. Again and again. The Council... the elders, who had used me over and over again for their benefit, ordered those petty wolves to capture me. I pushed the thought out of my mind and kept running.

The night air was cool and stung the wound on my chest. My speed had dulled substantially. I wasn't entirely under the heavier effects of the wolfsbane yet, but soon... I would be helpless. The wound would heal, it wouldn't even scar, but the thought that my negligence had brought me so close to death sickened me.

I smelled a river nearby and veered towards it. I dove in and propelled myself forward with my strong legs. After swimming a good distance underwater, I came up for a breath. They would follow me, I was sure. They would be close by now. The river should cover my tracks. My body felt weightless in the flow of the current.

I threw myself onto the riverbank on the opposite side then ran some more. When I didn't have any strength to continue, I sat down under a tree. The moon was up high and it was a starry night. Sweat covered my body, and I was panting. Finally, I changed, no longer a wolf. It wasn't the first time I had been attacked with wolfsbane, but the idiots had used too much. Faust knew it would take a lot to incapacitate me.

I got up and looked around my surroundings. The soil was damp and was covered with small grass. Trees littered here and there. I was still in my underclothes; they were loosely hanging around me after having been stretched. Blood covered my chest as I saw a deep gash. My body felt heavy as lead now. The forest swam drunkenly around me. Only blackness remained.

I woke up with a start as the sun had just dipped below the horizon. I groaned as I sat up. It was a struggle to keep my eyes open. Damn! I had slept through the day. I had let too much time slip by. *Trackers will find me soon*, I thought.

Lifting my hand, I stroked my face clean of dirt. My skin felt hot under my fingertips. The wolfsbane had yet to flush out of my system. I sighed heavily and rested my head against my hand. I thought of the events of the previous night; it made me lightheaded. My head spun, and I almost fell to the ground again. I was running a fever.

"This was absolutely great," I thought out-loud. "Not only did I disgracefully run from a fight, I'm sick. Next, I'll be swooning over a mate."

I scoured the forest floor, hoping to find Acana, the medicinal herb. It grew around the roots of certain trees. It helps with pain and fever. I could use it as a paste to close the wound on my chest. It took me a few hours before I finally found the small bell-shaped sorrel herb.

All the effort took a toll on my body. My vision was blurry. Paste. I needed to make a paste before I rest. Tearing the leaves off and ripping the root apart, I separated the two.

I found a hollow log and broke it into the general shape of a bowl, placing the leaves inside. Using a smooth stone, I ground the leaves. I sniffed the air. At least, I had the sense to keep close to a stream. I walked until I reached the mossy bank. The flowing water of the small stream distorted my reflection. It was grotesque; I had to admit. My hair was disheveled, covered with grime. Dried blood covered my chest. My red-rimmed eyes were hollowed from exhaustion.

I grunted and poured some water into the bowl and made a paste. I had made enough to last me a few days. Applying it to my wounds generously, I bit down on my lip, trying not to scream. I tossed a few extra Acana leaves into my mouth to help with the delirium, and I drank some water from the stream.

I sniffed the air again, and this time smelled blood. A fresh kill, somewhere. Getting up without thinking, I started following the scent. The exhaustion was catching up. Just a little longer, I willed myself. I stumbled along the way as I followed the scent of meat. My stomach growled, my body was giving out, my vision was growing blurry.

Walking into a clearing carpeted with grass, I saw a wolf. It was a she-wolf, her face buried in a fresh kill. It smelled like a moose. I swerved in her direction. I tried to change, but the exhaustion combined with wolfsbane had me beat. I let out a string of muttered curses.

The forest around us made gentle melody. A bird song. Leaves rustling in the distance. But this was secondary to my maddening hunger. Strength, I was losing strength. My mouth was watering. The she-wolf turned her head toward me. She stood slowly and walked towards me. In a shimmer of shadow and light, she changed. Long auburn hair cascading down at her sides. She was stark naked. Her body was muscled like that of a warrior. But her eyes… she looked at me with soft emerald eyes.

My eyes went wide, as I heard my heart beat outside of a battle for the first time in my life.

A TWIST OF FATE

Eliana

The Sanctuary was bustling with people today. It was late in the morning; the sky was a clear blue, cloudless. The Sanctuary had a vibrant energy. Children were playing in the open grass in the middle of Sanctuary. Their laughter was infectious as they ran around mischievously. Every member of the Sanctuary was busy with chores. Some wolves patrolled around the borders, some trained new warriors. Some were builders who helped during the establishment and expansion of the camp, and a few were skilled enough to cook food for everyone.

People in the base lived peacefully, as much as possible that is, and thrived within their daily duties. It was more or less an established community. I couldn't believe that so many of these people had been through hell and back in this war. For years, the Council had been hunting rebels, but every time these people had fought, bled, and survived. Together, they forged the living soul of this Sanctuary. Despite such loss, they were determined to live.

Children who should grow up playing on the streets were exposed to the horrifying brutality of war. Just the thought of having their parents killed before their own eyes... it brought me to tears. It was too much for such innocent beings. Even infants were targeted. Protect and serve? No. They just killed and captured.

I sighed; my shoulders hunched. Looking up, I saw Marcus from across the courtyard. I was sitting under the cool shade of a fig tree. My back rested against its rough trunk. Marcus had physically recovered; I knew that, but his heart... I know he had suffered a tremendous blow in his last fight.

After his return from the base in Walka he was shaken up. Although, he had changed. I saw... an... unknown determination in him. I hoped he wouldn't become too reckless. The war was far from over and we needed to win it, somehow.

Marcus was with a boy. They walked casually in my direction, engaged in conversation. I couldn't help but feel sad for the kid. He looked hardly thirteen years old. He was yet another casualty of this wretched war. He would have been a brilliant soldier if only he had two hands. He arrived at this Sanctuary with others a couple of weeks ago. That monster... He did that to him. I remember the day he arrived here.

He was accompanied by two other wolves, a warrior guiding them safely here, and a girl. They were one of the last teams to evacuate from the ruined Sanctuary; the boy, especially, was a mess. He was covered in blood and was tired—left barely with any strength to stand. His broken arm was bent outwards at the elbow and a deep shade of black. Infected. The healers weren't able to heal his arm, and now all that was left was a rounded stump. When I looked into his eyes, they reflected hurt, pain, and determination.

I closed my eyes, and felt the cool breeze striking my face, making soft sounds as it rustled the leaves above me. Marcus was a good man. I couldn't help but smile fondly as I thought of him. I often caught myself wondering what it would be like to be his mate.

He was kind and courteous, caring and understanding. How would it feel to be his? He made me feel at... peace. But the Goddess hadn't destined us together. Maybe after the war, we could be something... more. It wasn't uncommon to bond with someone who was not your mate. But that was in fate's hands.

I must have gotten lost in my thoughts because I was startled when Marcus put his hand on my shoulder. I looked up at him wide-eyed and tried to push him away from me, desperately hiding my flushed cheeks.

He must have noticed, because the next thing he said made my heart beat faster. "Damn El, you daydreaming about the day I'm going to sweep you off your feet?" He winked and smirked at me knowingly.

I gained my composure and shot back, "You wish, a scrawny little thing like you could carry me away, let alone thinking I'd let you." We both laughed and for a second that's all it was. Marcus and me and our joy. *Our peace.*

The boy came up to Marcus from behind and tugged at his shirt. Marcus turned, and he kneeled beside him, ruffling the child's hair. He'd make a great father. Is this what finding one's mate felt like? I felt at ease around him. He made me smile. People always described it so differently, but this had to be it, right?

I shook my head free of warm thoughts and focused on what was at hand. We were in the middle of the war. A war! I don't have the luxury of thinking like this.

"Marcus! When will I be ready to train?" The boy said agitatedly. He was eager to get stronger.

Maybe with two arms the boy may have made a great warrior, but with just one he would only get killed. "What's your name, little one?" I asked, kneeling beside Marcus. He looked at me and Marcus. Marcus nodded at him, encouraging him, and he finally spoke after a lengthy pause.

"Erwin. And I'm not little. I will change soon, you'll see!" he said stoutly. I looked at him and found it hard to not stare at the raw stump where his arm would have been. He caught me looking. The boy's face turned to one of anguish and fear, then to one of hate, as if he were reliving the memory of that day.

"The big one, with the red eyes. He did this, you know. He killed my mother, too. That's why. I want to get stronger. I want to train so I can change!" he said. He was shaking. Marcus put a hand on his shoulder, trying to comfort him as best as he could.

"It is okay, Erwin." Marcus said calmly. "You don't have to be afraid anymore."

I saw the look on Marcus's face. My heart felt so heavy. I wanted to reach out to the child and comfort him.

"I'm not afraid," he said, "I want to kill him!" The conviction in his voice was palpable. But this path that he had chosen would swallow him whole. I turned to hide the disgust on my face. There was no end to his cruelty. He slaughtered the old and maimed children. The notorious Blood Moon Harbinger.

"We'll start your training next week, Erwin. It will be difficult, especially with... one hand," Marcus visibly swallowed. It was hard on him to point out Erwin's disability too, but he kept his composure. "But we will make you tougher. Okay?"

Erwin nodded slowly, "Okay. I know what I am now, Marcus. But I don't care. Somehow, I'll help everyone." He said and walked away from us.

We were left speechless for a while. I looked at Marcus. He was lost in his own thoughts. Marcus, too, was determined to get stronger. He had been at the brink of death a couple of weeks ago, but right now he was sitting beside me. Marcus... if only there were more people like him, perhaps this war would never have happened.

"Will it always be like this?" I whispered to Marcus.

"I don't know, El. I wish..." He trailed off, unable to continue, but I heard him loud and clear. He wished for peace.

"Where is Adrian?" Marcus inquired.

"He has gone with the warriors to another Sanctuary in the east. Father has sent some new instructions to the chieftains. You know how he is. He sends only those he trusts as messengers. Keeps his cards close, otherwise," I replied. I was painfully aware at how close our bodies were. So close to touching, beneath the cool shade and away from the scorching sun.

"He should be back in a couple of days. It is not the same around here without his hot temper." I grinned.

Marcus looked at me and flashed me a smile. "Don't let him hear that. His ego is already big enough, especially after he got me out alive the last time."

My smile faltered at the mention of Walka. "Do you think we can defeat the harbinger?"

"Maybe. Ronak has sent out wolves looking for the creature that scarred the mighty Belaize. Yet... I don't know, El." He sighed as he clenched his fists.

"Maybe luck will shine on us soon. Who knows?" I said as I ran my fingers through my long hair. *I needed to trim it soon*, I thought.

"El... I'm leaving in a couple of days," Marcus said. I turned to look at him. He was staring at the ground ahead, avoiding my gaze. I felt my face harden.

"You just escaped death, Marcus. Don't go on another mission so soon." My words were hollow. I knew Marcus. I'd known him since I was a baby. We grew up together in the middle of this war, and yet his heart was pure. I hadn't anticipated that he would leave so soon, but I should've.

"Don't Eliana. You know..." He trailed off.

I did know. I knew too well. I grabbed his hand and gave it a tight squeeze. "I do."

I saw him turning towards me. His eyes were as blue as the summer sea and they were trained on me. I felt blood rush to my cheeks. *Oh Liunella!*

Out of the corner of my eye, I glimpsed enormous shape appear from the shadows a few trees to our right. I released Marcus's hand and turned away.

The enormous shape was a man that I knew all too well. He was the only Kaiser in the rebel army. He was also my mentor. "Glad to see you return, Romulus," I said with a warm smile.

Romulus walked as if he was floating a few inches above the ground. He was close to seven feet tall, if not larger. He was large-chested with broad shoulders and had an aura of power that practically oozed from him. But Romulus was quite humble for a man of his size and reputation. He was a mystery, not a man of many words. I barely knew anything about him, yet I trusted him with my life. Supposedly, he once had a twin, but he was tight-lipped about his past.

As he drew closer, his features became more visible. For a Kaiser, he lacked body hair. He liked to keep a clean-shaven face, and the only hair he had was a tousled mop on his head. It was a handsome mix of gray and black that accentuated his silver-gray eyes. I would be lying if I said he was not handsome for his age. A man of few words with a proud heritage, he dressed the part too, with a long flowing emerald colored robe with golden buttons. He wore a gray shirt underneath with the top two buttons open, exposing the top of his sculpted chest.

"Eliana," he said sternly as he walked up to me. I already knew why he was here. It was time to hunt.

"Let's go," I said, wasting no time. Getting up, I dusted the dirt off my trousers, standing up straight. "I'll see you later," I told Marcus. and with a smile I turned away. I followed Romulus out of the Sanctuary, into the deep woods. For as long as I can remember, we had gone hunting once a week, whenever he was in the Sanctuary.

It took us about an hour to get to a dense part of the woods. I don't know why, but a strange feeling hung over the woods today. A feeling of fear. It made my wolf anxious. Something was terribly wrong. It was almost suffocating me. Romulus felt it too. I saw it in his stance. The way he moved forward, caution in his every step.

"Move forward child, I will follow you from a distance," he said and disappeared into the woods. He knew I didn't like being called a child, but Romulus only called me that when he was trying to shelter me. That's how it had been with us. Over a decade, now.

I took in the eerie silence of the forest, letting my senses flood with the nature. I sniffed the air. I looked around me, but Romulus had melted away into the dense bushes with such ease that I couldn't detect him. I knew he was watching my every move.

He was a menacing hunter with honed skills and a lethal ability to sneak up on people. This was his way of training me when I was younger. He led me to different parts of the forest. He would watch me hunt or fight with the Council guards, if any came close to the Sanctuary. Romulus believed in one thing: dedication. *Because in an actual fight, when your life is on the line, you must give everything you've got in order to win,* he would lecture. I was a trained warrior now, my skills honed to perfection, but I was more than a mere warrior. I was an alpha.

I kept walking aimlessly and came upon a clearing. I smelled an animal, nearby. My wolf howled with delight in my mind, and I let it surface. It was time to hunt.

It felt good to stretch my muscles again. My wolf was about nine feet tall. Smaller than most wolves, especially the males. My fur was dark brown, darker than my hair. I was told that even my eyes were different in my wolf form. They changed to forest green with a hint of silver. But the most striking feature of my wolf was the mark of Navar on my forehead. All wolves with the blood of Draxus had a ring with three markings crossing it vertically.

My father had told me it signified the ability of Navars to focus all sensory information on one thing: the mind. I was quick to reason and calm when others acted with their emotions. Even though I was small, I was more agile and tactically superior to most wolves. I knew my swift speed was my strength and I harnessed that ability against the enemy with ease.

I lifted my snout and sniffed at the air. It smelled sweet. The soft bluestar flowers smelled vibrant, airy. But there was something else. Along with the scent of fresh spring in the air, a hint musk of a moose lingered. It had to be large and possibly aggressive too.

I moved forward silently; my paws moistened in the fresh grass. I heard the moose before I saw it. It burst through the tree line and into the clearing.

The moose was a massive hulk of a beast. Its head towered over me as it sensed the danger I posed. It lowered its head, shook its brown antlers, and snorted. I braced myself, tensed my legs, getting ready to leap over it.

The gigantic beast charged towards me. In another few seconds, it would be in range. As it approached, I jumped high over its head and onto its back. I leaned in and kept my weight centered. While hanging on, I slashed its neck with my claws. The moose groaned but kept up its blind charge. I dug my claws into the muscles on its back as it buckled and ran headfirst into a tree.

The wood splintered, but the tree held. The majestic beast slumped, its breathing was labored and blood pooled from the wounds I had made. I closed my eyes and said a silent prayer. I found its heart and pushed my hand deep into its fur covered chest, ending his pain.

I buried my face in its belly and ate. I gorged myself; I didn't realize how hungry I was. The meat was tough and savory. The blood and the thrill of the hunt made was exhilarating. It took me a while to eat my fill. I changed back and realized that my face was covered with blood. I heard some rustling in the bushes behind me. I brushed it off as Romulus coming back, but all of a sudden, I heard a crash.

The crash echoed loudly among the trees. I shot up to see a colossal man covered in blood and bruises stumbling through the brush toward me. His steps were staggered, he could barely stand. I felt him trying to shift. He was powerful. The astral distortion was tremendous, but he couldn't do it. Somehow, he couldn't shift. I saw the wound on his belly. It was smeared in a grey paste and caked with dried blood. I froze.

I saw him clearly now. He stood over seven feet tall; he had white-blond hair and, strangely, a black beard. Even under the blood and bruises, I made out his muscled body, a chiseled chest and thick, strong limbs. He was not a man, but he was power. Pure power. It surrounded him, even in this state. But his most striking feature were his eyes. They were a deep crimson red. No, they were black with a red ring around the pupil.

My heart raced, I heard it ringing in my ears. I felt an incredible urge to be with him, to be with this man. To hold him, to protect him, to love him, to care for him, to mate with him. So many emotions overwhelmed me, all at once, but only one thing filled my mind. Mate. *Mate!*

I saw his features soften, and his eyes grew wide in surprise. I felt our hearts beat in sync; the blood rushing through me. The hair on my body stood at attention. My body ached to touch him.

My eyes took in his sight greedily. *Mate!* My wolf howled in my head with such happiness. Crimson eyes... those gorgeous crimson eyes... wait a second. I looked at him again. He took a step closer towards me and it hit me.

My heart sank as I realized who he was. Belaize...

The thought didn't even get finished in my mind, when without warning, three fully armored wolves exploded through the tree line. *Shit! I should have paid more attention to my surroundings. Romulus will lecture me for this.*

The wolves wore Council armor and had the royal crest etched onto their chest plates. They were definitely the tracker squad. Were they with Belaize, too? Maybe trying to get to the Sanctuary? It didn't add up, especially since Belaize was injured.

Belaize turned from me to face them. I felt the distortion again as he tried to change. Again, the distortion subsided. Something... was wrong.

One of the wolves growled and snapped at me. I stood my ground and bared my teeth, telling them to stay away. "What do we do with the girl?" he asked the others. "Leave her be. We only want this traitor. Dead or alive."

Traitor? I thought, confused. My mind raced. These were Council guard's but... that's Belaize. He is the Blood Moon Harbinger. How the hell can he be a traitor? Belaize was being hunted.

As the realization hit me, my wolf rose to the surface, taking complete control of me. We jumped in front of Belaize, shielding him with our body. *Why was I protecting him? Wasn't he the enemy?*

"Run away, girl," one of them taunted, "Before, you become another dead body for the crows to feed on." I growled and bared my teeth in fury at the three guards.

"Try me," I said.

I felt a heavy hand on my shoulder. My skin tingled at his touch.

"Move girl, you'll just get in the way," he said, his voice deep, full of pain and exhaustion. He could barely stand, yet he was ordering me down.

"Stay the hell down!" I said, pushing him away from the armored wolves. He almost fell, barely able to recover his balance. The other wolves chose this moment to jump at me.

They surprised me for a moment. Their armor was lighter than it looked, they were nimbler than I had expected, but I gracefully dodged each of their attacks. They were quick, yes, but I was quicker. I swung at one, and my claws grazed the armor with nothing more than a scratch. This is going to be tough, I realized. I heard Belaize laugh. He proceeded to have a bloody coughing fit, doubling over in pain.

The other two circled behind me and I found myself trapped. I turned quickly, not leaving an opening for them to get me unaware. Belaize slowly straightened and, for someone his size, moved swiftly despite his injuries. He grabbed one wolf from behind and snapped his neck without hesitation.

My jaw dropped, and my eyes widened. He was on the brink of unconsciousness, his eyes drooped and his head lulled, but he snapped a nine-foot wolf's neck with his bare hands. His strength was frightening. The other two ignored me and jumped for Belaize. He tried to dodge, but one of the wolves slashed at his belly, opening a fresh wound. He stumbled and dropped to one knee. My heart sank when I saw that much blood. My mind went blank, my wolf took control, and I changed. All I saw was red rage. I tackled the wolf that wounded Belaize.

The tracker froze in shock; that was his first mistake. I dug my teeth into the back of his neck, where his spine connected to his head. I bit down and blood rushed into my mouth. Pulling hard, I tore his flesh away, bones, muscles. Flesh and all. He was screaming in pain, writhing underneath me, trying to shake me off. This time, his armor did nothing to stop my rage. I gorged out his eyes, relishing his painful scream. As his body stilled, I shifted my attention to the last wolf.

The last guard was standing opposite of me. He stood there wide-eyed. He finally looked at me. Taking in my appearance. Blood trickled down my jaw, staining my fur, and I saw the shift in his stance. The realization struck him hard. He wasn't facing just any she-wolf. No. He was facing an alpha.

My legs tensed, I was ready to pounce. But then I felt a familiar presence in the clearing. "Romulus, stay away. He's mine," I said without breaking eye contact with the Council guard.

Romulus entered my line of sight. "That's enough for today, child. Go back to Sanctuary. I'll handle both of them." He moved, standing in between me and the guard.

"No! I'm not going anywhere," I thundered with anger. I had never talked to Romulus like that. Ever. *What was happening to me?*

He gazed at me thoughtfully, his eyes squinting with consideration. He finally nodded grimly. "Make it quick."

I leapt at the guard instantly. He was waiting for me. He moved to dodge my attack, but I was faster than him. Swift. Without his armor, he might have dodged, but I had already calculated the maximum reaction time that armor allowed. The metal armor was nothing more than a piece of junk. It was pretty damn shit, especially in a fight with me.

My blow pounded his shoulder, and I knocked him down. He tried to get up quickly, but I shoved him down again. He swung an armored claw to strike my face, but he missed by inches. As soon as he tried to hit me again, his claw was ripped off of his arm. I darted my eyes in that direction to see Belaize standing above me. But he was... helping me?

"Hit the sides and it'll come off," he said, pain was evident in his voice. I did as he said, and hit the side of the wolf hard. The armor crumpled and the guard's defense was gone. I ripped through his chest with my claws, puncturing his lungs. Moments later, it was over.

I moved away from the dead body. I was breathing heavily, my heart raced faster than it had ever before. It took a few moments before I calmed down. I changed back, and I saw I was covered in more blood than before.

I glanced at Romulus. He was standing opposite to Belaize, glaring at him. Two Kaisers, battling it out. Dominance. Authority. It meant everything to an alpha. "Come on. We must go," Romulus said, backing away slowly toward the base.

"Romulus... we can't leave him here," I said. In a split second, Romulus tore his eyes away from Belaize and met mine. I felt shivers run down my spine at the coldness of his stare.

"You are right. We cannot leave him here. It's time for me to end this war, once and for all, right here and now. I should kill you, Belaize."

"No! You can't kill him!" I stepped in between the two of them.

"Are you really defending the Council's puppet? Do you realize what you are saying? He is the reason we are losing this damned war! Give me one reason not to kill him!" Romulus growled, clenching his fists by his side.

I turned my head to look at Belaize. He stood rooted to the spot. He was watching us. No, he is watching me.

"Romulus, trust me. I want to win this war as much as you do. I want him to pay for what he did to the countless victims of this war. But killing him today will solve nothing! The Council will keep making new assassins. They will be merciless, just like him! If we want an upper hand on this war, we need to imprison him, and pry all the information we can out of him. Otherwise, Romulus, we will lose no matter what," I finished. I waited for him to say something, to counter me, to argue. But Romulus didn't utter a single word.

"Fine," he muttered finally. I knew he didn't want to agree with me, but he had made his choice to support me despite that.

"I don't need your pity, girl. Kill me now. Get rid of me. It will be the best decision of your life, otherwise you'll regret it," Belaize thundered.

I glared at Belaize. I felt my teeth elongate in anger. "It's not fucking pity. Now, shut up and start walking." I said, disdain clear in my voice.

I don't know if it was my imagination, or what, but I saw him flinch a little. He regained his posture but I saw pain in his crimson eyes.

"Now," I said stiffly. Belaize lowered his head a fraction and closed his eyes. He took a step or two in my direction, as if approaching me. His eyes flickered, and he stumbled. I saw him losing consciousness as he fell at my feet. His dirty hair splayed around him like a halo in the dirt.

I dropped to my knees beside him. I pressed my hands on his open wound. He was losing blood very fast. "Shit. He is unconscious! We need to get him back at the camp. He needs help!" I said hurriedly to Romulus.

"He needed medicine yesterday. With the state he is in... Eliana, I don't think he will live to see tomorrow," Romulus muttered. My head throbbed as my wolf howled in pain. I tried to ignore it. But it was too much. No. NO! My head spun more as everything came crashing down on me. NO!

PANCHAYAT

Eliana

My heart raced, echoing in my head, as I jogged swiftly. I was running late for the meeting. Although I had woken up early this morning, I didn't have the will to face the day. I had stayed in my tent staring blankly at the changing shadows.

The clearing came into view as I rounded a corner near the middle of the Sanctuary. Almost all the rebel wolves had gathered today. Meetings were held periodically to update everyone about the war. Our wins and losses were declared here. Every fortnight we would gather and praise the fallen, plan, strategize. I sensed everyone in the area waiting for it to start.

For a moment, a rush of nervousness coursed through my body. I felt a flush rise to my cheeks. I finally stopped at the edge of the crowd and squared up my shoulders, ready to take on the battle I had to fight ahead. *Just to keep Belaize alive*, I thought.

I stepped to the center of the clearing; the crowd was bustling with chatter. I felt the collective anxiousness in the shifting body language of the attendants. As I got closer, the wolves quieted into a soft murmur and parted ways for me. I saw my father sitting on a red leather chair across a wooden table in the shade of a large open tent. Scraps of paper were spread out before him, and he was completely engrossed.

Beside him sat two other wolves, Romulus, my mentor, and a woman.

She looked older than usual today. Her hair was a flat grey, though streaks of white caught the morning light. Her face showed wrinkles now, I noted. She looked at me with her scrutinizing gaze. "We've been waiting for you, El." She spoke softly.

"I know, Amae. Hopefully, I haven't kept you waiting for long." I flashed an apologetic smile.

My father looked up at me with striking emerald eyes, which mirrored my own. A small grin played on his lips as he watched me approach. "No Eliana, you haven't. We should start soon, though. Everyone is getting restless."

"Yes, father." I nodded and took my seat at the table. My father, Ronak, he was the leader of the rebels, and the guiding force of this rebellion. He looked old, but he was a great warrior for his age. He had the strength and the experience to guide the lycans through these tough times.

It had been a couple of weeks since I had last seen him. He never stayed in one Sanctuary. He always moved from one base to another, instructing different missions to turn the tide of the war. For such a rebellion, we were going strong, and that was because of my father.

He was one of the best tacticians in the country. After all, he had the blood of Draxus in him. He was a Navar like me. The alpha bloodline that typically handled all the plans and missions for the old Council. They are master tacticians and seasoned logicians. Any plan of attack an average wolf made, a wolf with blood of Draxus could easily counter in five different ways.

It's with the blessing of Liunella that my father has kept so many innocent rebels alive. *The Council has strength, but father has his mind.*

But as honorable, kind, and patient as I knew him to be, I couldn't help but worry how he would take this news. Perhaps it would've been best to talk in private first, away from the citizens he protected. *Wouldn't it be best if they not know?* I wondered. *Wouldn't it be safer for... him?*

But this was a community, that's what I believed. And I would not hide in the shadows like some sniveling Council dog. I had to be better than the elders, so I had to be honest. And besides, this was the first and only opportunity I had to tell father about Belaize. It had to be now, I couldn't wait in this in-between world any longer.

"If we are done waiting around for my sister, should we get this meeting started or not?" my brother said with a scowl on his face. His face had changed in the weeks since I had last seen him. the line between his brows was deeper, and his jaw was set.

We looked alike. We had the same angular face and pointed nose. I had deep emerald eyes, like father, but Rayne's were a shade lighter. In contrast to my auburn hair, which I'm told I inherited from my mother, he had father's sandy blond hair. Rayne was strong and large, but he had an aura about him that always radiated negativity.

"I wasn't that late, Rayne. Take the damn stick out of your ass, for once," I muttered and crossed my legs, taking a deep breath, calming myself.

It'd always been like this between us. He was older by merely two years, and he used that leverage to act like an egotistical ass. He sat down beside me without a word. I knew he wouldn't argue right now because father was here. We fought a lot, but when dad was around, we kept it to a minimum.

I loved my brother and deep down I knew he cared for me too, but that never eased his jealously. I was a Navar, but Rayne was just a normal wolf. It was quite rare for two generations consecutively to have the blood of the old. No one had expected me to be an alpha. But when I turned, everyone was shocked. Rayne hated that it wasn't him. I tried not to show it off; he worked hard to be father's right hand, but in tough times, father always planned missions with me instead.

I glanced around. The gathering had grown quiet. Amae stood up from her seat and cleared her throat. "I'm grateful, that each one of you assembled here today. Ronak has returned to deal with urgent matters. He will give us an update about the war first."

My father nodded and picked up a thick sheet of paper. "I hope all of you are well," he addressed the crowd, "I was busy establishing a new Sanctuary, after we lost the last one. Most of the warrior teams made it out safely and were directed to the new base. It's near the east of north-west border.

"Despite that loss, we have maintained the onslaught over the Low Cities. The Council Guards are acting up, but they cannot match to our skilled warriors. If things go on like this, it won't be long till we take the control of the Cities and cut off the supreme power of the Council." He paused for a minute as the rebels cheered and hooted. It wasn't victory for us yet, but it was a step closer to it.

Rayne cut in, his voice raised, "If the entire rebel force attacked the Low Cities and the Capital together, this war would be over a lot sooner. Why are all of you cheering over this, anyway? We didn't take complete control.

"All we are doing is sitting around hoping that Council will fall short. Father, I have heard that every ten days the Council sends over a hundred wolves to the Low Cities to bolster their security efforts. Every time we decrease their numbers, a fresh wave enters. I'm done with this cycle repeating all over again. We need to attack, and we need to do it now!" When he finished there were a few howls of agreement for him.

I had to say, it was bold of Rayne to voice this idea to public. *Bold but stupid.*

I ran my fingers through my hair. I gazed at our father. His expression had turned into stone. He was trying not to get angry at Rayne, but deep down he was furious.

It was a natural response. My father's wolf felt challenged by Rayne and his outburst. This was one of the effects of having the blood of the old. If it felt like a confrontation, any small action could set off an alpha to show their dominance.

"Rayne, mind your manners. Your actions won't always be tolerated," I said at a low volume, but I know most of the wolves heard me.

"I'm not scared, El. I feel that this should be the next course of action for us, and I'm putting forth my opinion at a damn meeting. You don't always get to talk down to me. This is my right!" he exclaimed.

"You should realize that I'm not taking your rights away. All I am saying is that you should respect father in front of others. What impression do you think this gives wolves when the leader's own son is questioning his decisions? Haven't you realized by now that father has already considered your plan?" I said.

"Well, I'll tell you why we haven't done exactly what you so graciously laid out in front of us," I said venomously.

"It's because if we split our forces and attack in that manner, we will be setting up innocents for sacrifice. The Council is increasing its troops every day. We already have a hard time chipping away at their guards. This is not a war of power. We care for each and every life because they matter. Signing their death sentence is not the way to victory."

"Not only that, the chances that this would work are low! What if we fail? The blood of so many innocents would be on our hands, and we wouldn't be any different from the wretched Council who use their soldiers for their own comforts and luxuries." I finished and looked away at the ground. Silence settled in the clearing. Rayne was wrong. Older or not, I wasn't afraid to stand up to him.

"Enough with both of you squabbling here! This is an official meeting. If you cannot behave for two seconds, I swear to the Moon Goddess, I'll kick both of you out of here myself. You don't want to test me," Amae said, furious at us. She was right, but it was Rayne who was an idiot. He'd always been such a hothead.

"Ronak, continue." She huffed at my father, making sure everyone was paying attention to him.

"Rayne, there is some wisdom in your plan, but Eliana is right too. I know this is upsetting to hear, but this entire war is a gamble. Sometimes, we will have victories, other times we'll have losses. We have to make sure that every life taken is not in vain."

I was lost in my thoughts for the rest of the meeting. I tuned everyone out. As the end of the meeting approached, I knew it was the time to bring up... *Belaize.*

"We are done with the updates. If anyone doesn't have an agenda to discuss, this meeting is at an end," Father said. He paused, looking at everyone gathered, giving them a chance to speak up. From the corner of my eye, I felt Romulus' gaze trained on me. It was time.

I stood from my seat and moved to stand ten feet ahead, in the middle, surrounded by everyone. As I met their gaze I felt my mouth move, but I couldn't find the words. Perhaps I hadn't accepted it myself. My thoughts were racing.

"Speak, Eliana." Father's voice boomed. He always called me Eliana when he meant business. I looked at him, his emerald gaze unnerving me.

"I want to discuss the fate of a prisoner I captured two days ago while on a hunting trip with Romulus."

"You know the standard procedure for that. We take the prisoner to the encapsulated area so we can question them. What is this truly about?" Dad said, always straight to the point.

"Before I tell you who the wolf is, I want you to know that the wolf was on the run and being hunted by the Council. I believe the Council wants him dead," I said, pushing a lock of hair back behind my ear.

"Honestly, El? Council's enemy is our friend. Why did you capture the guy?" Rayne laughed while making the snide comment.

I closed my eyes and geared up for it, ignoring Rayne. "Because I captured Belaize."

It felt like the calm before a storm hits. For a few seconds no one believed what they had just heard. Then a great roar erupted from the Sanctuary.

All I could make out were screams and bloodthirsty chants. *Kill him now. Kill the monster. Kill the monster and win this war. Torture him for all the lives he took. Make him feel the pain of every wolf he killed.* Tears threatened to spill from my eyes, but I stayed strong. *No. No. No one will kill Belaize.* My wolf was ready, just on the edge. She was rioting. Hearing all this about her mate made her furious.

I opened my eyes and looked at Romulus. His gaze was still fixated on me, as if he knew. I glanced at Rayne for a second. He was shocked. He couldn't say a word. It was as if he had seen a ghost.

Someone yelled from my right side. The boy. It was Erwin. He ran up to me, standing beside me, tugging at my hand. "I want to watch when you kill him." His stump was peeking out from his shirt, which loosely hung over his body. I couldn't look at him. I just couldn't. He wanted revenge. He wanted to see Belaize in pain.

I heard Amae trying to get everyone to settle, but to no avail. The crowd was riotous and ready to spill the blood of the enemy.

"Silence!" my father roared from his seat. Everyone shut their mouths, taking their seats again. They respected my dad. He was their leader, the alpha.

Once the camp had settled, my father continued. "Explain. How did you find him, Eliana?" I knew he was angry at me because I hadn't informed him about Belaize as soon as he arrived. But this was necessary, because before we can extract any information out of Belaize, I needed to make sure they did not kill him in his sleep.

"Romulus was present when I saw him. He appeared from the thicket and was being chased by Council guards. They had called him a traitor, which makes me believe that somehow, Belaize is a threat to the Council. That's why I captured him and brought him back here."

"Where is he, now?" Rayne piped up. His voice was barely a whisper. He almost sounded scared.

"In the Infirmary. Romulus believes they poisoned him with wolfsbane." I glanced at Romulus. He nodded.

"Yes, he is. The amount that has been injected in him... it's a miracle he is still alive. Although, I have my doubts he will be of any use to us, anymore. A normal wolf would die if he were in this condition. He's on the brink of death." Romulus' face stayed expressionless.

"Exactly. That's why I brought him in. I believe he might help us." Turning, I faced the other wolves and I witnessed the disgust on their faces. Erwin stared at me in disbelief, tears welling in his eyes. He turned and ran out from the area. I saw Marcus standing beside a tree in the back. He saw Erwin, as well. My heart broke for the poor child, but if we wanted to win this war, we had to accept what fate brought us.

"I know, each one of you have survived the horrors of this war. Everyone has lost something. Your family, your home, your children. We have spent the last few years running away from the Council. The Blood Moon Harbinger has been the worst weapon of all. Famous for his ability to kill without conscience. Right now, we have him in our hands. As much as, I want him dead too, like everyone else-" I paused and took a deep breath, "We cannot kill him. He is an asset. If he's being chased by the Council, he must know – or have done something – to put a target on his own head. But we have to know, because that might be the turning tide of this war. After all, as Rayne said, the enemy of our enemy is our ally.

"You don't have to trust him or consider him your friend. I don't know why he appeared here, either. But I request that everyone put their anger and hurt aside. Think of our future." I worked frantically to keep the clawing desperation from my voice, pausing to look at my father.

He sat stiffly in his chair, but he caught my gaze and I saw his eyes soften a little. He agreed with me. *Please, please*, I prayed, *you must agree, you have to.*

After a minute there were murmurs of approval from some wolves, but many remained deep in thought. I didn't blame them. Giving the person who destroyed so many lives a chance at life was a lot to ask for. But I wanted to end this war. Even if it meant co-operating with an enemy. My wolf had... hungrier notions just beneath the surface. I forced them down. I was Navar. I value my mind over everything. *Right?*

"There is no point in keeping him alive. He is already on his deathbed.

We will not get another chance," Rayne said.

"Yes. I agree with Rayne. The harbinger just attacked Walka Sanctuary. He has killed so many. We should not take any chances." A wolf from the crowd spoke loudly.

Another set of chants to kill Belaize, torture him, to parade his head on a spike, rolled through the camp. The images hounded my mind.

"I think we should kill him. What if all this is a ruse? What if the Council sent him to kill us all? To attack this Sanctuary as well?" Rayne spoke with defiance.

"You, of all people, should know he wouldn't have to come sneaking into our Sanctuary to kill us. He would publicly execute you and have fun with it," I retorted. His demeanor changed as his face turned red with anger, but he couldn't counter me, I was right and he knew it.

"If he were faking it the Council would've already attacked us," I continued. Another set of whispers of agreement came from the crowd.

I watched my father sitting at the high seat. I waited for his decision. He sighed, clenching his fists. "Okay Eliana. I agree and stand by your decision. For now, we keep him captured. You are responsible for any incidents that occur by his hands. Guard your prisoner well. We'll see if we can get information out of him. For now, this meeting is over. If anyone has anything else to discuss, come to my quarters," he said as he stood up to leave.

"I still think we should kill him. Guard him well, El." Rayne said with a hint of threat as our father left, along with Amae and Romulus.

I wandered away from the meeting area without a word. I didn't realize until I was standing at the base of it, but my feet took me to a large red brick building. A wooden sign above the door was etched with the word Infirmary.

I sighed, pulling the door open. The building was well supplied with resources. We believed the injured always needed special care, so even when the rest of the camp was makeshift and could move within hours, this building... it would stay put and protect the weak, no matter what.

My footsteps echoed within the silent hallway. I moved through the building as if in a daze. Down another hallway. Left turn. Careful on the third step of the staircase, it tends to squeal. I kept moving until I reached a solid wooden door down the hall. I stayed outside. I didn't have to go in, anyway.

One-way glass was attached to the outer wall, and I peeked inside. The ceiling window illuminated the room in a stark, white glow even though we were currently underground. In the middle of the barren space laid Belaize, heavily strapped to a bed. He was still unconscious. The healer said that he'd woke up thrice in last two days but passed out again within minutes. The wolfsbane was still weakening him. From where I was standing, I could see the crosshatching of his wounds. The healer had stitched them, but the scars remained. His blond hair spilled onto the pillow.

He was monstrous, but at this moment, he looked peaceful. I was itching to touch him and just sit beside him. But I couldn't. *No. I couldn't*. Not until I knew he wasn't the enemy. My wolf was angry with me for doubting our mate, but I couldn't help it. I had heard everything about the Blood Moon Harbinger, his ruthlessness, his strength, his power. He would have killed Marcus that day. He can kill anyone with his bare hands. The memory of him killing the Council guard two days ago rushed through my head. He killed so... effortlessly.

My mind and my heart were in turmoil. I leaned against the cool glass, my fingertips pressed against it. My sole focus was him. I didn't know how much time had passed, when I felt a hand on my shoulder.

I stiffened for a moment, but realized Marcus was standing beside me. He was wearing black trousers and jacket. His black hair was a mess, as if he had been constantly running his fingers through it. But that wasn't the worst thing.

He looked gaunt. Through the glass, he saw a ghost of his past –one he thought he had outrun. Finally, Marcus's gaze caught my own. "I was looking for you, El," he whispered, his voice gentle.

"I came here because, Marcus… I-I have to guard him." I was shaking, but I tried to maintain my composure. My heart was in shambles. I kept looking at Belaize, as if I couldn't take my eyes off him. We stood there a while in silence, the sounds of our breath echoing through the corridor.

"Why?" Marcus insisted.

Why? Why? Why!? That word kept running through my head. I felt his questioning gaze on me. His stormy blue eyes usually made my heart flutter. For nearly a decade I would try to steal glances, be worthy of his praise and attention. For a decade I had craved Marcus. But today, I felt nothing. Today all I saw was the pain in his eyes.

The pain. I was making him relive his worst fight. I knew it. I didn't want to hurt anyone.

A single tear slipped from my eye, rolling down on my cheek. I looked at Belaize again. "Because, he's, my mate," I said, my voice hollow and cold as ice.

MAYHEM

Eliana

Three days had passed since the last Sanctuary meeting. But it felt like a lifetime. The rebels had witnessed my claim to let Belaize live. My father had supported my decision, yet when he had called me to his quarters, he was furious. Both Amae and Romulus had witnessed his wrath.

"Why did you not tell me immediately, Eliana?" My father had asked. I had no words for him. Why hadn't I? I wanted to protect him. It was my nature now, but I still had my doubts. I needed for him to wake up. I was hoping that he would have some explanation. But I couldn't deny hard facts either. He was the Blood Moon Harbinger.

"Because I know you would have killed him without thinking it through. Even now your wrath clouded your good judgement as well. I wasn't wrong. You know that. He can be an asset." I was trembling. Lie after lie. Shame was enveloping my core.

"We have decided. Child, go look after Belaize. He needs to be alive for this," Amae had said. That was the last time I had seen father. I did not have the energy to lie to him. Or anyone else. They were my family.

Since then, I was holed up in front of the Infirmary. I was playing at guard, monitoring who went in and out. I didn't take breaks; the anxiety was overwhelming. I was sitting under the shade of a tree and my eyes darting about nervously. I hadn't seen Marcus since I'd told him the truth.

But when I told him, he was speechless. We both were. How could this have happened? We'd never know what the fates had planned. He knew Belaize was destined to be with me. His reaction was not what I had expected. Marcus had asked me one question. That's it. One question.

"Will you accept him, Eliana? Will you accept the bond?" he had asked.

I didn't have an answer for him. He had left me there alone then and hadn't returned.

For three days, I had been lost in my thoughts. No one dared to talk to me. Sanctuary wolves, my neighbors, my friends, all of them glared at me whenever they passed. A few children had come around demanding to see Belaize, demanding to see the monster. I had driven them away. Yet, I knew the stares and the snide comments would not stop. Not until Belaize woke up.

It was late in the evening. The sky was a beautiful shade of orange mixed with crimson hues, and for a moment it reminded me of Belaize's red-rimmed eyes. The wind blew softly, rustling the leaves above me. The dim light of the evening sun made the scenery exceptionally beautiful, but I didn't have the heart to appreciate it as I would have a few days ago.

I stood up for the first time today. My thighs and back ached from sitting too long, but I had nothing else to do. I slowly stepped inside the gate of the bricked building, the Infirmary.

I didn't go downstairs where they kept Belaize chained to his bed. An image of Belaize lying there wrapped in bandages came to my mind. I shoved the thought aside, and instead climbed up the stony stairs, where healers lived. I knocked on the second door on the right in the well-lit corridor. A woman answered. She was short and beautiful. A little older than me, with brown hair and a heart-shaped face. When she saw me, she opened her door wider. "Come in," she murmured.

I stepped inside, glancing at the beautiful room. We didn't have much luxury, but she had made this little room her home. It was painted yellow and decorated with plants along the small window. She had a bed, and a small table with a wooden chair beside it. Dutifully, I marched to the chair and sat down. It was a ritual now. Every evening I would come in and repeat the same question.

"Honoria... How is Belaize?" I asked, again.

She walked to her bed and sat facing me. Her long straight hair was framing her face.

"Eliana, I am doing everything I can. I have given him every form of herb I know that works against the effects of wolfsbane. It should be purged from his body by tomorrow, that's my best guess. His life still is in danger though. His wounds are not healing fast enough. If he lives through the night, I might save him," Honoria said slowly.

"Thank you. The other healers…" I trailed off. The other healers had refused to help Belaize after they learned his identity.

"I know. I told you before, Eliana. Being a healer is part of my heritage. I will not turn away from someone who is dying. I come from a family of healers and we pride ourselves on it." She gave me a weak smile.

I nodded stiffly. Rising from my seat, I took a last glance at the beautiful, cozy room. "I'll leave now. I don't want to impose."

Walking to the wooden door, I had just opened it when she grabbed my hand. I halted and looked back at her. Her hazel eyes reflected… pity. "It will be better. Liunella watches over us."

For a moment, I felt she knew. She knew why I was here every day. I nodded in response, unable to say a word. When I had made it a back to my perch beneath the tree, a familiar scent washed over me. I whirled around and saw him standing five feet away.

"You look like hell, El." He chuckled. I ran to him, into his open arms and wrapped my own around his neck, hugging him.

"Where have you been, Adrian? You gave us a scare. You were supposed to come back four days ago!" Releasing him, I took a step back. I scanned him for any visible injuries. Adrian has always been taller than me. His light brown hair, which matched my own, was short. A beard graced his high cheekbones, but most striking were his mischievous violet eyes. He grinned from ear to ear while I checked him out.

"Wipe that smile off your face, ass." Turning back around, I sat back in my spot. Adrian joined me, sitting on the dirt.

"I know you are happy to see me, El. Don't lie."

"Only because you aren't rotting somewhere in Council territory." I shoved my elbow in his chest sharply. I smiled for the first time in days when he groaned in response.

"What happened though?" I inquired. Father had sent Adrian to the Sanctuaries in eastern states to deliver messages. Adrian was one of his most trusted warriors beside Marcus, Rayne and I. The four of us had grown up together in the Sanctuary. We were the rowdy troublemakers.

"Our squad had a run in with a unit of Council guards when we were returning. We wiped them out, but a few wolves were severely injured. So, we had to stay hidden till they healed. The Council was crafty and used iron claws with wolfsbane." He shook his head in disdain.

"I am glad everyone returned home safely," I murmured. Dusk fell over us. The canopy birds had quieted, returning to their nests. Calm silence fell between us as we looked at the ever-changing hues of the sky.

"El, I heard what happened here. Why… Why are you doing this?" Adrian asked me softly. *Why? Why? Why?* Fresh tears threatened to fall from my eyes, but I took a deep breath to calm the turmoil I had inside my heart.

"He… can be an ally," I said through gritted teeth.

"Stop with that excuse. I know how strongly you feel about everything. The war. The Council. And the Blood Moon Harbinger. He is a killer who has single-handedly destroyed the lives of thousands of innocents. Hell, what he did to Marcus was horrifying. I got to him in time, but I was afraid for my life when I saw him, El."

"You don't hope for friendship with a wolf like that. No. You shove your claws in his chest and rip his heart out. So, what is the real reason, El?" Adrian's words cut me deep. He was right. He was so fucking right. Yet, I felt my wolf rioting inside me. She was furious.

I wrapped my arms around myself, barely holding myself together. I glanced at Adrian. His eyebrows raised in confusion. He held my gaze and anxiousness washed over him. He put an arm around me. I laid my head on his shoulder as tears finally fell from my eyes.

Minutes passed by as he comforted me. "He is your mate," he concluded. Pulling away, I rubbed the tears off with my hand. I couldn't face him.

"I don't know what to do," I admitted.

"You keep him alive, El. That's what you do. Till he becomes our ally." Adrian's voice had a hint of determination. He squeezed my shoulder. He stood up from the ground and extended his hand forward.

"Let's go. I am starving, and you need to eat something. You look like a skeleton right now."

"Yeah, yeah. Prick," I said, grabbing his hand, and standing up as well. He had eased the storm within me. That was Adrian. *My best friend.*

I promised myself that I would be back in fifteen minutes and reluctantly left the Infirmary. Adrian and I walked to the Kitchens near the center courtyard. Many wolves helped daily with cooking and serving food to the Sanctuary. Even before we entered the pavilion, the aroma of spices and delicious meat wafted through the air.

A mixture of warriors, builders, and children were already standing in line in front of tables filled with food. A few wolves behind the table kept the line flowing as they heaved massive portions onto waiting plates. Adrian and I stood in line, plates in hand. Soon enough, our plates were filled with rice topped with gravy and meat, and a side of vegetable salad. We found two seats along a table near the back and started eating. The sound of conversation and laughter drowned us.

I looked around, but Marcus was nowhere to be found. I saw Romulus at one end sitting with his group of trained warriors. My father usually ate late at night in his office. I sighed and took another bite of meat. I chewed as my taste buds sang. Tonight, the food was great. Sometimes when supplies were low, we didn't get food like this. Those days were hard.

From the corner of my eye, I saw three wolves approach us. In the middle was Rayne. He had a scowl on his face. I sat up straighter. Noticing my movement, Adrian looked up and saw Rayne coming toward us with his friends. "So, is he dead yet?" Rayne said, as the three of them sat down across from us.

"No. He is still in terrible shape," I said coldly. Rayne had tried to convince me to kill Belaize after the meeting, but I hadn't changed my decision. He had been spiteful since.

"You should just gut him, El. Don't draw out his misery. He will die eventually." His friends beside him laughed. I gripped my spoon harder. Suddenly, I'd lost my appetite.

"You don't get a say in this Rayne. Father has agreed with me. End of story." I retorted.

"Navar or not, both of you are fools, El. He will die."

"Honestly Rayne, this is pathetic. You have no control of this situation, yet here you are taunting your sister. Stop acting like a child." Adrian defended me. More love and respect bloomed in my heart for Adrian. Even after knowing everything, he still supported me.

"Stop with the act, Adrian. We both know El's affections are saved for Marcus alone," one of Rayne's friends said with a sneer. I growled at him in anger. They were testing my patience.

"Another word from your mouth and you'll be sorry that you have a tongue." My voice was dangerously low.

"Don't Ambrose. It is not worth a fight. She's too smitten with men to focus on the war." Rayne said and got up. "Whether it's up to me or not El, he will be gone soon." Rayne just laughed and left Adrian and me on our table.

I pushed my plate of food away. "I don't want to eat anymore." Adrian took my plate and piled my leftovers over his own. We left the Kitchens a few minutes later, taking the long route back to the Infirmary.

Night was upon us. Stars were glinting in the sky. A crescent-shaped moon had risen. Liunella was watching over us all. I silently prayed that Belaize would get better. Even if it was selfish, I wanted him to wake up and answer me.

We arrived at the Infirmary and I was about to sit down when I noticed something amiss. An eerie feeling crept into my mind. The door of the Infirmary, which was usually closed by this time, was wide open. I looked around, scanning my surroundings, but the feeling didn't go away. I walked to the gate. "El, what is it?" Adrian questioned.

"Something isn't right. I should check on Belaize," I said as I headed inside.

My footsteps echoed along the empty corridor. Hurriedly I dashed inside, running downstairs to where Belaize was. As I reached his room, I smelled another wolf inside. Belaize was in danger.

With lightning speed, I pulled the wolf away from Belaize, who was choking his unconscious body with his bare hands. I threw him out into the corridor. My wolf snarled, eager to come to surface and rip the wolf's throat out. I focused on him. He was wheezing. I had thrown him against the wall hard. He glared at me. His fangs elongating as well.

"Why do you protect that murderer? Why? He took my mate away. Do you know that? He took her away to the Low Cities. I feel her pain every day in my mind as they rape her and won't let her die. I will kill him," he thundered.

I stood between Belaize and the wolf. He was right, Belaize... the harbinger. Yet, I owed him one chance. One chance because of my faith in Liunella's gift. *Just one.*

"You will not harm him until father decides his future," I said irrefutably. He growled and changed into his wolf, ready to fight me, to kill me. He growled and as he pounced at me, I saw Adrian shoving the wolf hard, sending him flying at the end of the corridor. Adrian grabbed the wolf hard by his neck, dragging him outside. I heard the wolf howl with anger, but Adrian kept dragging him away.

Hearing the commotion, healers came running. One of the healers rushed to the wolf's side restraining him. My head throbbed with pain. An attempt to kill Belaize. Rayne's words came crashing in my mind. He... all of them, they all loathed Belaize. I was the only one willing to protect Belaize. I clenched my fists; I was shaking.

I felt burning rage. Everything was going wrong. This wasn't supposed to happen. I felt my wolf take over. My fingers elongated to claws and I smashed the glass that separated Belaize's room to the corridor. The glass shattered completely.

Honoria entered the room. She grabbed my arms and shook me. "It is okay, Eliana. He is fine. Belaize is fine." She hushed smoothy, like an adult calming a child. I pushed her away and punched the wall in front of me. The seething rage took over. I wanted to kill that wolf who attacked Belaize.

Adrian came next. He glanced behind me at the bed, where a broken Belaize laid unconscious. He reached for my shoulder and pulled me out of the room. I growled at him, threatening him to release me. But he dragged me outside. Outside the room. Outside the Infirmary.

I was pathetic. The entire ordeal has made me despicable. Adrian just put his arm around me as I fought him, pushed him away, yet he held me tight. "I am here, Eliana. I will help you. I know. I know." He repeated those words over and over until I finally calmed down, finally succumbing in my friend's embrace.

THE MIST

Marcus

I woke with a start. The scream broke out from somewhere in the Sanctuary. It was horrifying. It made my gut twist with fear and pity. The scream was full of pain; it made me nauseous. The agonizing cries echoed throughout the entire camp, the sounds of a wild animal in the throes of death. *Are we under an attack?*

"Shit." I scrambled out of my small bed and tore away the tent's cover. I tried to move in the direction of the scream. Whoever was howling was in desperate pain. I saw others coming out of their tents as well. They looked around frantically, moving quickly, asking the same question. *What's going on?*

Another piercing cry clawed at the night. I took off in the direction of the Infirmary. It took me a moment to realize it was coming from the inside. I scrambled past the crowd of wolves that had gathered and ran straight downstairs. It was something to do with Belaize, there was no doubt.

The wretched sound continued. I put my hands up, covering my ears. Eliana came into my vision. She was standing down the hall, her hands and face pressed against the door, looking inside. "El! What happened?!" I yelled.

I came to a stop beside her and saw her tear-streaked face. She was a mess. I hadn't seen her since after the meeting. I didn't have the heart to face her. Adrian was standing close by as well. He had gone pale. He was in shock. I focused my gaze inside the room. What I saw... I knew it would haunt me in my dreams.

Belaize was lying on the bed. They had strapped him tight to the frame so he wouldn't break free. He was moving as much as he could in restraints and just writhing in pain. His chest was covered with scars. Fresh, puckered stitches had burst open on his abdomen. He was covered in gore.

What scared me the most was his face. A dark shadow loomed over him as if the devil himself were trying to rip his soul from his body. His mouth was open. Saliva trickled down his unkempt beard. His eyes... his eyes were open. But something was wrong with them. They weren't red anymore, they were silver and glowing with a bright silver aura. Blood streamed from his eyes like tears. The Blood Moon Harbinger had finally lost it.

Bile rose in my throat when he cried in pain again, but I controlled and calmed myself. "What is wrong with him, El?" I asked. She sniffled a little.

"I don't know. They won't let me go in," she said in a hoarse whisper.

I looked inside again in confusion and saw two healers beside him. They tried to hold him down but were failing miserably. One of the healers reached madly for a filled syringe and stabbed the needle into Belaize's arm.

His back arched into a bow and he seized. He fell to the bed and then slowly stilled. He weakly protested for a full minute. I felt it stretch before me like a long road, each heartbeat a step. I don't think I took a breath that entire time. My lungs burned.

Then his eyes closed and the dreadful thing was finally over. I stood there with Eliana and Adrian. The healers moved through the room with practiced efficiency, fixing the straps and righting the table. A couple of minutes passed in silence. I heard footsteps walking hurriedly down the stairs. I craned my head to see Ronak with Amae in tow.

"What happened?" Ronak questioned. Despite the late hour Ronak was well groomed and looked the part of a leader. I glanced at Eliana, but she was in no state to speak. She was still looking inside.

"I don't exactly know. I ran in here and saw him screaming in pain. I don't know why. Maybe the healers know." I shrugged and put a hand on Eliana's shoulder. She flinched, and I retracted my hand, my fist clenching.

"I was here, guarding him." She sucked in a deep breath and continued, "I must have closed my eyes for a little longer than I intended, I guess. The next thing I know, he started screaming. I yelled out for healers and they told me to stay outside." She trailed off, never taking her eyes off of him.

At first, we all stood like that, stony and peering through the window.

But as the hours passed, we took to sitting instead. I was fidgeting with my shirt sitting beside Eliana. Adrian sat beside me. All of us sat in silence, as the minutes ticked by. The first rays of the morning sun had brightened the dark corridor when the healers stepped out of the room. It was visibly hard on them, too. To witness such horror. Ronak looked at them expectantly.

"Right now, he's stable. We ran some tests on his blood," Honoria said. "I had assumed that the wolfsbane had cleared out of his body earlier, but that is not the case. The wolfsbane hasn't drained from his system, and that's causing some sort of side effect. That's my guess, at least."

"We will try to give him some more Acana and herbs, but I'm not sure how long he has. We gave him some sedative so that he can rest," she informed. She moved to put a hand on Eliana's shoulder, as if reassuring her, and finally walked away with her companion. Maybe she knew what it meant to Eliana.

Ronak was the first to move. "I should inform the others on the matter. Everyone is worried. El, keep an eye on him," he said and left in a hurry. Amae stepped forward and grabbed Eliana's hand, squeezing it. My heart broke for her. I didn't give a shit about Belaize, but El didn't deserve this... this torture. Amae turned to leave.

El abruptly spoke, her voice echoing in the corridor. "Silver. His eyes. They were silver and... they were glowing. He..." She trailed off. Amae stilled, her body went rigid in an instant. With her frail fingers, she lifted Eliana's chin and looked her dead in the eyes.

"Did you say glowing?" She quavered.

"Yes." El nodded. I saw Amae's expressions change. The initial shock turned to fear, clear as day on her face.

Without a word she released Eliana and quickly sped away. I immediately followed her, leaving Eliana and Adrian behind. My instincts told me something was not right. "What's wrong? Amae! Hold on! Tell me what's wrong!?" I yelled after her. I took hold of her arm before she exited the building. "What do you know? Is he going to die? What is it?" I pleaded.

"I don't know if he's going to die or not, child. But, if this goes on he will soon. He's lost, my child. And time's running out," she said. She was heaving; I realized she was scared. *But why?*

"Lost? I don't understand? Do you know a way to help him?"

"I know a way but... I have to prepare myself. It used to be so easy. But now, it will be one of the toughest battles for me. You will know soon, Marcus," she said, muttering to herself as she walked away. She left me standing on the steps of the Infirmary more confused than before. I trusted Amae with my life, but I felt like the steadfast foundation of our Sanctuary was crumbling away.

I didn't go back to Eliana's side after that morning. Or the next, when

Belaize's screams tore through the camp again. They shook me to my core, yet I couldn't bare to look at him. I condoled the state he was in, yet I hated him. Was it possible to pity the Blood Moon Harbinger? I didn't know.

I woke up with my body drenched in my sweat. The cool breeze coming in through the thin slats underneath the cover of my tent made me shiver. I slowly sat up on my small bed. I slept on a thin, rundown mattress. Luxuries weren't something affordable when you were in the midst of a civil war. The scream was excruciatingly painful, and it made me sick. It was awful. Belaize was screaming again.

It wasn't the first time, and it certainly wouldn't be the last. I was worried for Eliana. The news that Belaize was her mate had left me shocked. I knew she wasn't destined for me – we both knew. But, sometimes, I thought that maybe after the war, we would accept each other. I had always loved her and cherished her while we grew up together.

Both my parents had died when I was very young. I don't remember them much, but I knew it was because the Council had started poaching mates. My parents had handed me to Adya, Ronak's mate. When Adya was pregnant with Eliana, the small group managed to escape to the woods before the Council's influence had overtaken their small town.

Ronak had taken me under his wing. I had seen El being born. She was an adorable girl with bright, wondrous emerald eyes and soft auburn hair like Adya. We grew up together, Rayne, Eliana and I, and somewhere along the way Adrian had become a part of our little family too. As the years went by, Rayne became bitter and spiteful, but our bond only deepened.

Through all this, I knew I wasn't meant for El. I'd accepted years ago that Liunella had someone special for her, and I had hoped she would meet him one day too. But fate was cruel to her. Belaize. Destiny had kept the most ruthless killer among the lycans for her.

Eliana was a powerful warrior and an alpha. She was kind; she was one of the most intelligent wolves in Vascya. I had fought and trained beside her; she was strong, agile, and a true warrior. She was everything Belaize wasn't. I never wanted Eliana to be in such a situation, I wanted to protect her more than anyone else.

I sighed and ran my hand through my drenched hair. Another scream broke out, and I flinched. It was just as grotesque as the previous one. Before the sound could die away, another began. Whatever was happening to him was worsening. I was tired. I hadn't slept well in half a week. The entire Sanctuary hadn't. We were restless and on edge. It was terrifying to see such a great monster succumbing to such agony.

Romulus had informed us that Belaize might not make it through the next couple of days, that it was a damn miracle he was still alive. That amount of wolfsbane would kill any wolf within an hour, but Belaize was still hanging on to life. Honoria had claimed that the wolfsbane was out of his body completely now, but she didn't know what was wrong with him.

When I heard that Eliana had captured him, there was a dominant part of my wolf that wanted to kill Belaize, to tear him to pieces. I had tried, and I had failed miserably. I was feeble and weak compared to his strength, that much was clear. But to see him in such a state... I didn't know what I was supposed to feel.

"Marcus," a voice called out from outside of my tent. I broke away from the trance and focused to my surroundings. My back felt stiff from being in one position for so long. "Marcus!" another call came from outside the tent.

I scrambled out of my bed and stepped outside. The Sanctuary was dark except for the scattered light of fire-torches. The stars twinkled softly in the sky. It was a moonless night. I saw Ronak pacing in front of me, waiting. "Ronak? What is it?" I asked, moving closer to him.

Worry was etched into his face. He was a mature and intelligent wolf and rarely I saw him in such a state. Even through the war, his composure never cracked. "I don't know about it myself, but Amae has summoned you to the Infirmary," he replied. I followed in step with him.

"Why didn't you send someone else, Ronak? You shouldn't have come yourself," I muttered.

"Amae told me to do so. She told me to keep this quiet. I don't know, Marcus. She has been secretive the last two days."

We quickly reached the brick building in the center of the sprawling Sanctuary. As we sped through corridors and down the creaking stairs, I felt nothing but doom. It tightened my stomach and made my palms sweat.

As we entered the stark, white healing chamber, I saw Amae, Eliana, and Adrian standing beside Belaize. He was even more gaunt than before, if that was even possible. His face was yellow and sunken.

"We are here now, Amae. Tell me, what is this about?" Ronak said. His voice was sharp and irritated. I had heard rumors that Ronak had lost his mind keeping Belaize alive. Some wolves thought it was madness to keep the killer so close. An attack on Belaize had occurred already, earlier in the night when the screams had started. They wanted him dead.

She sighed, and a look of resignation shadowed across her face. She slowly walked over to a chair and sunk down.

I saw Eliana from the corner of my eye. She had been such an energetic, cheerful person only a few days ago. Now she was serious and quiet, staring glassy-eyed at the bed. It made my heart burn. Adrian stood close by too. He had stood by her since he'd returned from the last mission. It had been hard for me to be present for Eliana. Facing Belaize was one of the hardest things I had ever done and he had nearly killed me. I was glad that Adrian had stayed with Eliana throughout. Even if I had fallen short, I knew she was protected. They were my family.

"It's time to tell all of you the truth." Amae fidgeted with her gray cotton robes. "I'll start from the beginning. El, Marcus and Adrian... what do you know about our world?" she questioned us. I glanced at both of them and shrugged. El was confused too.

"What does that have to do with this?" Eliana said.

"We don't have time for history lessons, Amae," Adrian muttered.

"Child, I only ask because I must know where to start." She huffed a little.

"Well, Lycans live in the land of Vascya. Liunella punishes whoever strays from Vascya. I know that our world is in the Tierran Realm. We exist here. I have heard that there exists another realm, but those are just rumors." I trailed off, cursing myself for running away with Adrian in the middle of lessons when we were young.

"You're right, Marcus. Our world is a grand place, and the realms are an important part. Lycans, and every being in this world, is a part of the Tierran Realm. But there are two other realms besides that. The Astral Realm and the Sacred realm. The Astral Realm is an overlapping space between us and the gods who reside in the Sacred realm. Liunella too inhabits the Sacred Realm, but sometimes she visits us here. No creature other than a god can enter the Sacred realm, but... they can enter the Astral Realm."

"Entering the Astral Realm is a learned skill, but it comes to some easier than others. Wolves with very little astral energy within them tend to struggle the most. This task is about focus and discipline." She paused for a moment.

"I still don't understand, Amae," El insisted.

"I'm telling you this because Belaize has somehow transcended into the Astral Realm. That realm drains your energy much faster than this world, and Belaize has been gone too long from his physical form. His spirit is being consumed by the force of the Astral Realm, the hunger of it," she replied.

"Wait! How do you know he is stuck there?" Adrian asked, bewildered.

"El told me his eyes were glowing when he was screaming. I didn't believe her at first, and I had to see it for myself. The next night when it happened, I was there to see it from my own eyes."

"Have you seen something like this before? Amae? Can we help him?" El's voice was small, hardly a whisper.

"I have seen wolves go into the Astral Realm. They have glowing eyes, too. Wolves have gone to that realm before, child, and come back. But consequences are severe when they stay too long. Belaize... he has been in that realm too long."

"How do you know all this?" I questioned. I was leaning against the far wall, looking at her.

"Because, I have the blood of *Beleotell* in my veins. I am an *Umbral*, child. My powers help me access the Astral Realm. Not only that, I have the gift of soul-sight. Because a lycan soul is made up of Astral essence, I am able to see beyond the realms, and judge a soul's vitality. He is very lost and terribly sick."

My jaw dropped and my eyes widened in surprise. This was something that I never would've expected, especially from Amae. A wolf who can peer at someone's soul... I shivered a little. The hair on my arms stood up.

The ghost. They called them the ghost. The wolves of the blood of Beleotell were rare. Very rare. At one time, Umbrals had been hunted and killed out of fear. To be standing in the presence of one made me uneasy. I felt naked somehow, too exposed, vulnerable.

"Umbral... Damn Amae, I didn't know you were an alpha when you kicked my arse in the courtyard two summers back. No wonder it hurt," Adrian muttered. Amae shot him a glare, and he recoiled. His hands up in the air in surrender.

"So... how can we help Belaize?" Ronak asked, scratching his jaw. He wasn't as surprised as I was. I believe he knew about the blood of Amae. But it was a new revelation for the three of us.

"I would have done this myself, but I cannot. I'm not ready to face the past I left behind decades ago." She let out a sob. Amae's hand moved to rub a tear off from her weathered cheek. Ronak moved to comfort her. Something must have left her traumatized, otherwise she wouldn't have kept this a secret from us.

"What do we do?" I asked her softly. She glanced at me. Her tear-stained eyes caught the light. Belaize was lying unconscious, breathing softly. Eliana stood still, as if she weren't even breathing.

"He... Belaize, he's lost in the realm. If we don't bring him back he will have a worse fate than death. He will be lost forever. Claimed by the creatures of the Astral Realm. Someone has to pull him out." I felt her gaze on me.

In an instant I realized that Amae had summoned me so that I could go instead of her. "No. I won't do it. Ronak can do it, heck Adrian can. Amae, you don't need me!" I thundered.

"Marcus. It has to be you. I can transfer your mind to the Astral Realm. I would go myself, but... I can't." Her voice cracked with emotion, but she continued.

"Ronak, El, or Adrian, none of them can go. Ronak might not survive, and El was instrumental in his capture and imprisonment here. Her presence might destroy whatever's left of him just by that fact alone. Adrian has no direct ties to Belaize. I called you here for this reason. I know he tried to kill you. I know he savored every minute of it, I have heard the stories. But you are bonded by your hate. You know it's there, you feel the pull. I can see it. Straying so close to death can mark a soul, bind it. You two are bound in such a way. It has to be you."

"B-but..." I muttered and trailed off. *Just let him die*, my wolf growled. *Why should we even bother?* But Eliana's tear-stained face etched with worry came into my mind. I swallowed hard and squared my shoulders.

"I'll do it." I gave Eliana half a smile. She was gazing at me, stunned. She knew I was doing this just for her. Even Adrian looked perplexed. "Marcus..." He tried to say something, but I lifted my hand.

"I know. I am the only one who can bring him back. As much as I hate him, I will do it," I said. And after a beat, "What do I have to do?"

Amae sighed and the tension left her. "Fall asleep." She replied.

"Wait, what?" I asked with confusion, but Amae ignored my question. *Damn this woman.*

"Adrian, roll a bed inside." Within a minute, Amae had ushered me onto the bed. She sat in between me and Belaize. She grabbed my hand, and with her other hand grabbed one of Belaize's, connecting us three.

"Marcus, the astral realm is unlike anything you've imagined. Wolves in that world appear different, too. You'll know what I mean when you see them. Remember, this realm is interconnected with ours. You might see different creatures or people. Ignore them. They are shades or dangerous astral entities. If you see one, run. I'll guide you in there, but I cannot guarantee you'll find Belaize right away." She softly squeezed my hand.

"I know this is difficult for you, but you're our only hope if we want to save Belaize."

Eliana stepped closer to me and touched my arm. "Don't get lost in there, Marcus. I'll be waiting right here," she whispered, kissing my cheek. Adrian just sat in the corner and stared. He was unusually quiet.

I nodded and closed my eyes. "Ready?" Amae hesitated a moment then gave me a reassuring smile.

"As I'll ever be," I said. I squeezed my eyes shut. My mind emptied. No Eliana, or Belaize, or Amae, or Ronak, or Adrian. No one. Just the darkness surrounded me. I waited.

I waited for something to happen. *How would I even know it worked?*

Everything was still, I felt my hair stand on end. My heart pounded wildly, but I willed it to slow. I concentrated on my breathing. Nothing happened. *Was Amae being truthful? All I had to do was sleep?*

I opened my eyes a moment later and gasped. Mist. All I saw was a mist.

GHOSTING

Marcus

It took me a few moments to realize that it wasn't mist alone covering the area. A silver, shimmering aura blanked the landscape. I turned in a full circle, and just as the mist was displaced, more crowded in. It covered everything in a white, foggy haze. The ground was solid with patches of grass here and there glossy with dew. The world appeared silver, as if an argent lens had settled over the vast expanse. Even the small rocks had a silver polish to them. I squatted down to pick one up. I ran my fingertips across its smooth, velvety surface. *How?*

I didn't know how or when the transfer happened, but Amae had used her powers to send me into the Astral Realm. Focusing on my muscles and my body, I spent the next few minutes gaining control over my new form. I tested a few fighting stances, whirling and tumbling through the mist. A lifetime of training had forced me to develop an intimate connection with movement. I stretched slowly, calming myself.

Another dimension between our world and our goddess's, I thought. The Astral Realm was absolutely enchanting. As I looked around, Amae's warning echoed in my mind. *Shades*. I had to be careful of something called shades.

I wandered through the Astral Realm. I had to find Belaize. I couldn't deny the possibility that even I might get lost. I knew nothing of how to navigate this place. Maybe the Umbrals like Amae only knew how to travel through the realms.

I was lost in thought when I saw a bright light ahead. It wasn't far from where I was standing. It wasn't moving. Trudging ahead slowly towards it, I was wary. I looked around, but the shrouding mist made it impossible to see far. The horizon was an unattainable blur, but the light kept getting brighter and brighter as I drew closer. I shielded my eyes from the intensity. It was so striking, yet magnificent.

As I neared it, I realized it resembled the shape of a stone. It wasn't bigger than the size of my palm, but in my gut, I knew this was different from the other cobbles I had seen lying on the ground before. I leaned down and grazed it with my forefinger.

"Shit!" I retracted my hand back instantly and stumbled, falling down on my backside. I cursed under my breath. A shock had run through my body when I had touched the luminous rock. It was something otherworldly. Some kind of energy source, perhaps. I shook my head and got back on my feet. Better to stay away from it.

Although, the realm was interesting, and as much as I wanted to explore, I needed to focus on finding Belaize. I moved on again, trying to find somewhere distinct. If I could find something with form, like a landmark, then I could measure my journey. *Where would Belaize be?*

How could he be stuck here? A shiver went through my spine. What if he stayed here and left our realm on purpose? What happened to those who left? Amae had said they met a terrible fate. The memory of Belaize's agonizing screams and his grotesque, shimmering eyes passed through my mind. If that was just a start, I didn't want to know what would happen if he decided to stay here forever.

But would he purposefully leave Eliana? Why? Everything I knew of the mate bond told me that it was unbreakable, that it would draw two people together indefinitely. Surely, he couldn't resist her pull. I needed to bring him back so that he would stop hurting El. She didn't deserve the pain that he had brought into her life.

I raised my eyes, my surroundings were still covered in the wondrous mist. I glanced back at the bedazzling wonder, and then left it behind. As I moved, I saw more radiance that called out to me, beckoning me to come forward, but I now knew to stay away. I noticed that the silver grass wasn't affected by my weight, either. No impressions or footprints appeared on it. The mysteries of the Astral Realm amazed me.

I kept wandering and soon lost my sense of direction. The hours ticked by, though it could've been merely minutes. Time was immeasurable here. There was no change in the brightness of the day.

Suddenly, the air felt colder than it had a few moments ago. I was briefly confused. I smelled it before I saw it. Fear gripped my gut. The putrid scent of decay assaulted my senses. I gagged, bile rising in my throat. The creature was dead. Yet it was... walking. It looked like a man, standing on two legs, yet his shoulders hung low. His hair was a mess. His skin was sickly and dark gray, with wounds that had long stopped bleeding. His eyes, they were black. Completely black. He was coming towards me, groaning.

I held my breath. Amae's warning echoing in my head. *Shade. Shade! It was here. It was here in front of me.* I had to run. I willed my legs to move. I ran ahead, not caring where I was running. I just ran. Away from that thing.

I hadn't gone far when another shade appeared on my left. This time it was a woman, or it looked like one anyway. "Fuck," I cursed and changed my direction yet again. I had to stay away. I lengthened my strides and focused on my breathing. Adrenaline soured through my spirit as I sprinted.

After some time, I stopped running, catching my breath. I was panting, sweat dripped down my neck. My throat was parched. I was tired. I hadn't been able to find Belaize, and I was just wasting my time running away from the shades. I kicked at the ground in frustration. "What the hell am I supposed to do, Amae?" I yelled into the empty, silvery expanse.

That's when I noticed something different. I saw roots. They were... tree roots. I hadn't noticed anything like that before. The roots burrowed into the ground, but I couldn't see the source of them. The roots were shining with a soft luster.

I started following the root system. It should lead me to a tree, I reasoned. Maybe I could climb it and look around. There was nothing else for me to do, really. As I followed, the gnarled roots thickened until they were as wide as I was tall.

Soon, I saw a silhouette of a bright, silver tree illuminating everything in sight. The glow reminded me of the moon on a bright, clear night I was far from the main trunk, but I saw the tree clearly from where I stood. It was enormous, at least several thousand feet tall, and put the mountains of Walka to shame. The leaves sparkled as if a cluster of stars in a far-off galaxy had accumulated to form this... brilliance. I was in absolute awe.

But something was odd about it. I couldn't put my finger on it. There were six major branches protruding from the massive base. The entire tree was flourishing well, but one branch on the right side was drying out as if it was dying. But how can just one branch die, and others still glow like that?

Everything in Astral Realm was so... pure. I didn't notice at first, but I realized that this place was filled with a sense of hope. It was as if every blade of grass and gnarl of wood was its most uninterrupted form. This place was completely unspoiled. There was no blood to stain the soil.

Yet I knew it was deadly. The shades themselves were a reminder that something otherworldly gripped this realm. I knew whatever phantoms stalked this weightless expanse would desire to have me stay forever.

I sighed, it was a tedious walk to a seemingly ever-distant tree, but my curiosity had won over. I willed myself to move ahead. Gradually the mist cleared as I neared the tree. I looked to my left and saw a vast lake. The water reflected the shimmery light like a mirror. It stretched as far as I could see, merging with the white horizon. I was only a couple of hundred feet away from its trunk now. The tree was at the bank of the lake, its roots stretching in every direction. It was a sight to behold, truly.

Suddenly, I sensed him. My astral form became rigid. I urged closer to the base, until, finally, he came into focus. He was sitting at the base of the tree, his mop of blond hair in stark contrast with the textured bark.

I broke into a light-footed jog. I felt like I was floating over the rough, uneven terrain. As I got closer, I noted that he was deep in thought. He wasn't... stuck... like Amae had said he was. His chest was rising evenly as if serene. *But why wasn't he getting back to our realm? Our world?*

Stopping in front of him, I took in his appearance. Belaize looked disheveled. His blond hair was greasy, his clothes torn up. The wounds that were raggedly torn open back in the Infirmary were now smooth, silver scars. He was sitting with his elbow propped up on his knee, eyes closed... thinking.

He didn't even notice me. "Belaize..." I mumbled. No response. *What happened*!?

Leaning down, I put my hand on his shoulder and shook him vigorously. "Belaize!" I shouted. My voice echoed in this lonely place.

Finally, his eyes flickered open. They were embedded within deep-set dark circles. Though less unnerving than the silver glow, his crimson eyes reminded me of death. He looked gaunt. Sickly. "You," he said.

"Out of everyone in this world, you are the last person I was expecting to see." I curled my hand in a fist, anger unfurling within me.

"Do you think I want to be here? Huh?" I said through gritted teeth.

"Well, why are you here?" Belaize prodded. I sensed a hint of curiosity in his tone.

"Because you are dying. I have to save you. That's why I am here."

"Oh please, Marcus. Drop the bullshit act already. You hate me. I know that well. You don't care if I live or die. You want to kill me with your own hands. I know. I saw the determination in you when we fought. Yet here you are spouting utter crap about saving me. Leave me alone."

"You're right. I hate you. You're a monster. But right now, you are imprisoned and on your deathbed. I came here to bring you back to our realm so that you can heal. We need information to win this war, and whether I like it or not, you might be the key to turning the tide in our favor. So, get up and let's go. We have to get out of here," I muttered. I hated Belaize. My nails were digging into my palm as I tried to restrain myself from beating sense into his thick skull.

“I am not going anywhere. I chose to stay here in the Astral Realm. This isn’t the first time I have been here. I’m staying right here, Marcus. You may leave,” he said stubbornly.

Swiftly, I grabbed his throat with my hand and threw him against the massive trunk of the tree. He was weak, I realized. It was hard to hold him there even in his weakened state, and I struggled to maintain my grip.

“You’re going to listen to me, Belaize. You’re fucking dying. Do you understand?! Dying! Have you ever thought about what you’re doing to her? Huh? You wanted to know why I am here trying to rescue you? Well, now you know!” I yelled in his face and released him, stepping a couple of feet away from him. I was panting, shaking with wrath.

“You love her,” he finally said, after a few minutes of silence. My back was towards him. I couldn’t bear to look at him.

“Yes,” I whispered.

Belaize, he looked even more distraught than before. It stung to my core. They were mated, and I was powerless to it. I stepped towards him. “Come on, Belaize. We have to go. I will not let you die right now. She is relying on me to bring you back.” I wrapped my fingers around his arm, trying to pull him up.

“I won’t die, Marcus. I am death. I cannot die,” he said. I looked into his crimson rimmed eyes. They seemed to reflect jealousy.

Suddenly, a person leapt from the canopy above and landed smoothly in front of us. He dusted himself off and looked in our direction, a smirk clear on his face. “Who the hell said that you are death?” said the stranger.

Something felt familiar about him. I had seen him somewhere. The strong build, the copper brown hair, that angular jaw. That’s when it hit me. I had seen his lifeless body. The body we had left to rot in the burning Sanctuary. He was the spitting image of the child. The she-wolf and her child I had saved.

“Laki...” I whispered in utter shock. The stranger just smiled.

EVOCATION

Eliana

All my life I had been on the run. I never had a stable home. From one camp to another, I travelled with my family, surviving and perpetually avoiding the clutches of the army. The Council had fucked up Vascya years before I was even born into this world. I grew up in the shadow of my father. Ronak was one of the most intelligent wolves alive. My father had once been part of The Council but left to start the rebellion against those old fools. He led the rebel warriors into war; he kept the fight going between those in power and those who lacked it. He dedicated his life to this cause. One of the strongest Navar in Vascya. Yet, he was a soft person who had always showered Rayne and I with love, despite his tragic past.

When I was little, I would sit in his lap almost every day during his meetings with the different Chieftains and rebels. Like clockwork, I would crawl up to him, demanding to be lifted and he would hold me close while he attended to various matters. I didn't know he was such an important and high-ranking wolf in our country. He was just my father.

He had suffered a significant loss too. After my mother, Adya, passed away. It must have been hard for him. Amae told me once she died while giving birth to me.

I always knew not to ask about my mother. I knew it would cause him pain. I had seen so many people lose hope, lose their laughter and will to live, after the death of their mate. But my father was different. He gave himself over to the war completely.

I remembered when I was in my early teens and I was talking to other wolves my age about mates, how wolves described the entire experience. How once they gaze upon their soulmate, passion and love flow through them. I wondered what it was like for my father.

That night I prepared myself to finally ask father about her. After eating dinner in the Kitchens, I had left Marcus and Adrian, and I trailed behind my father as he went about instructing wolves for night duty. It was a dark night in the camp, but it didn't scare me like it once used to. People were chattering among themselves as they strolled lazily through the camp.

I walked in the shadows of the tents, believing in my stealth, as I followed my father. I wanted to talk to him alone, but I didn't want to get in his way, either. Crouching low behind one tent, I was lying on the ground when I heard his voice.

"I know you are there. If you are trying to hide, you are failing miserably. Why are you following me, Eliana?" My father said in a stern voice.

I bit my lip, squeezing my eyes shut. Oh crap, *I thought. Crawling out of the space between the ropes of the tent that kept it upright, I stood up straight and walked to my father, facing him. A small smile played on his lips. He was tired after a long day, but I knew he was happy to see me. His sandy blond hair was short and his face was unkept with slight stubble.*

"I wanted to talk to you but... I thought you were busy," I said sheepishly, looking down at my feet.

"So, you were following me to find me alone in the middle of a meeting? Am I right?" he inquired.

I just nodded in response. I felt guilty taking up his time just to satisfy my stupid curiosity.

"What do you want to talk about El? Don't worry, I am not busy at the moment." He laughed while ruffling my hair a little.

"Are you sure, father? I can come back later." I trailed off again.

"It's fine, El. Don't worry that little head of yours yet. I'll find a use for you later. For now, ask away. You look so worried. Is something the matter? Has Rayne done something again?" he inquired.

"No. No. Rayne did nothing other than usual. He went off with his friends after dinner." I shook my head. I didn't want to get Rayne into trouble. He used to be a good brother, but ever since the Draxus blood showed its trait in me, he was jealous and wasn't too shy to show it. My father signaled to follow him and started walking towards one entrance of the base. I trailed behind him.

We sat atop a thick log far from the base, so others would not disturb us. His gaze was upon me as he patted the seat beside him on the log,

"Come. Sit. Now tell me what's going in your mind? I bet your thoughts are running wild." He chuckled.

I took a few steps and sat down beside him. I was embarrassed and felt terrible about asking him. "I...I..." I started but couldn't bring myself to ask him the question.

"Eliana, tell me. I'm here," he said and wrapped his arm around me. His body felt warm, and I scooted a little closer. Taking a deep breath, I spat the words out.

"I wanted to know about our mother."

I felt his body go rigid. I turned my head to look at him and witnessed a pained expression on his face. Tears filled my eyes, threatening to spill. I had caused him sadness. "I'm sorry. I'm so sorry, I won't ask. I didn't mean to. I just... I was just..." I trailed off. I started to get up but my father, he only tightened his grip around me and held me closer.

"No. El. Stay. It's okay. I just... need a minute," he said.

So, I stayed. I sat there waiting for my father to say something. Anything. Some time passed, and we sat there perfectly still. "I miss her. Your mother," he finally said. I gazed at him, listening to every word he spoke. It was the first time he spoke of her.

"She... was something. Adya. Her name was Adya." He breathed, as if reminiscing with each word. It was as if he hadn't uttered her name in years.

"Yes. I know her name. Rayne told me once when we were little."

"She was my mate, El. Right after the Council declared the capturing of mated wolves, I launched the rebellion. I wasn't able to stand by in cowardice while those foolish alphas controlled our fate. A few months after that, I met her. She was a beauty, your mother. You have her hair, too." He softly ruffled my hair again and smiled at me.

"When I first saw her I didn't realize you can feel so many emotions all at once. She was helping some wolves escape from a burning village near the East border. I didn't have a stable home back then. Though I suppose you couldn't exactly call this stable, either." He was looking up at the stars.

"I'd just strolled into the village when the Council guards attacked. She was helping an old woman get out of her house, which the guards had set on fire. I remember, my wolf was so restless. And unexpectedly, I saw her coming out of the burning home accompanying the woman. Her hair matched the flames behind her, her face was covered with ash, and her scent smelled sooty. But I couldn't look away, El. I couldn't look away from that woman because my wolf told me she belonged to me." He lifted his hand and put it over his heart.

"You feel it in here, El. Whenever you'll look at your soulmate, you'll feel their presence here."

"Adya... she was extraordinary. Your mother was a peaceful person. She would kick my ass." He laughed again. "But, she loved me for all

my flaws. I miss her every day, El. I feel the hollowness in my heart that reminds me she is gone. But, I have moved on. Not many wolves can. They don't survive the loss of their mate, but I did because I had responsibilities. You and Rayne are my family. Marcus and Adrian too. I lead this war because I have the ability to do so, but I don't do it because of that. I'm a leader because your mother once told me she wanted peace in our country, in our home, in Vascya, so we could raise our children in a happy, loving home. She wanted to protect you and Rayne from the horrors of this war, El. But..." He trailed off. I hugged him hard from the side. I knew what he was feeling, even if he didn't say the words.

"But... I failed. You're growing up. Rayne is growing up too. And yet, I couldn't end this war. I lost her, too, but I have dedicated myself to make her dreams come true, and I'll do so until my last breath. She lives in my memories. She will forever." He took a deep breath again and went silent.

"How will I know that someone is my mate?" I asked him.

"From the moment you see your mate, you will die to protect them, no matter what."

My father's voice rang loud in my mind. I opened my eyes and stepped back into the reality that was my life now. Steady breathing fell upon my ears as the man who lay before me clung to life. His face was covered by an even thicker beard. It had been over three days since Marcus went into the Astral Realm. Yet I had no clue, no sign, of what was going on.

My head throbbed with pain as I relived the last few weeks. Why wasn't Belaize coming back? What happened? The uncertainty of the situation was making me dizzy. At least his screams had stopped after Amae sent Marcus. A small mercy.

I lifted my hand to my forehead, massaging my temple with my fingers. My mind refused to think of anything else, it opened and reopened the wound with each passing minute. I couldn't stop myself from worrying about Belaize. Slowly, I trailed my fingers over his bandaged hand. Why was I so helpless? All I could do was just sit here!

"Let him take his time, El." I jumped instantly, hearing my father's voice. I looked behind me and saw him standing against the door.

"I don't know what you mean." I shrugged and sat up straighter than before.

"One of the smartest wolves with blood of Draxus, doesn't know what I mean? Eliana, you need a better excuse." He chuckled and stood beside me, ruffling my hair like he used to do when I was a kid.

"I don't know if he has enough time left," I whispered; insecurity was clear in my voice. He walked up to the glass window. He was staring at his own reflection. We stayed silent for a while, both lost in our own thoughts.

"Even if... he doesn't have the time left anymore. All you can do is pray to Liunella for his safety and happiness. Belaize is lost somewhere. He is... a prisoner to his own mind. Unless he is able to break the chains holding him back, he won't come back to you, El. So, pray that he is brave enough for you." He said with a solemn look on his face.

"Brave enough for me?" I asked. *How does my father know? Did Marcus tell him? Did Adrian spill my secret?* My mind raced with questions. They wouldn't do that! How does he know!? Dizziness overwhelmed my senses. I gripped Belaize's fingers with my own, reassuring myself that he was still here.

"Even a fool can tell what he means to you, El. Only time will tell what will happen to him and to you. But, that's for later."

He answered my unspoken question and reassured me. He walked out of the room, leaving me alone once again with Belaize. I looked at him. His wounds were healing a little, but according to Honoria, it was slow progress.

I was losing hope. I had asked Amae what would happen if both Marcus and Belaize remained in the Astral Realm for eternity. Her reply just made me shiver with fear. She said that if they remained there too long, their souls would completely transcend into that realm. She said that the beings of that realm, the shades, would capture their souls and feed until nothing was left. As for the physical body, it wouldn't decay. It turns stone cold and hardens, and the vessel remains trapped in this realm forever. Images of Belaize and Marcus laying still as stone in this room plagued my mind.

Sometimes, tears would stream down my face. I didn't want to cry, I barely knew him. All I knew of him was ruthlessness. I knew that he hurt people, tortured them. He was a tool, he was a murderer, a killer. Yet, here he laid in front of me, and all I wanted was to protect him from any harm. Because I couldn't help it.

My conflicted thoughts circled in my mind day and night, again and again. What had I become? This mate bond... Belaize, I realized, was ruining me. I didn't even want to imagine what my father went through after the death of my mother. But now I could.

It was the middle of night. It felt like an eternity, honestly. My eyes were tired. I needed sleep, but I just couldn't leave him alone. I had changed his bloody bandages. I tiredly laid my head beside his arm, holding his hand. This simple touch comforted me. Just being there with Belaize gave me some measure of peace. My father didn't come back. He had told me to pray and have faith. Faith. But right now, mine was dwindling. *But what was I keeping faith in? Him?* I sighed.

"Come to me, Belaize. Please. I'm... afraid, but I'm still waiting. Just for you," I softly whispered, choking on my words. In all my time being at his side, those were the first words I had spoken to him. I closed my eyes and laid my head down. In my heart, I knew I would wait forever for him. For my soulmate. For... Belaize.

ALIVE

Belaize

Marcus's words whirled in my head. For the first time in my life, my mind wasn't settling down. I focused on the serene calm of the Astral Realm. I was sitting against the World Tree, *Ygdrasil*, my back leaning against the base of the giant tree. The Astral Realm was a wondrous place. Whenever I came here, I always felt a sort of calm and peace. But this time, peace was the last thing on my mind.

I remember as though it were yesterday, the first time I had transcended here. The sudden burst of anger and the energy within took control of me. The horror, the thrill, and the love of my first kill, had pushed me over an edge – of sorts. Janus. He had pushed me too far. I still heard his laughter ringing in my ears while the blood splattered from his mouth as I tore him apart. I... didn't exactly know how, but my blind rage transformed into peace.

My vision had brightened as the angelic glow of the Astral Realm came into my view. I didn't know it was another realm back then, I assumed I was dead, actually. For the first time in my life, I had felt a calm aura surrounding me, flushing my senses.

I had been here a few times since then. I still don't exactly know how I come here; I just do. When I stumbled upon this great tree my second trip, I was able to riddle out what this place was. I had remembered a story of a legend of the World Tree, Ygdrasil, when I was a child. It was an old wives' tale yet, here it stood, in all its glory.

This time, however, the Astral Realm did not provide its calm and serenity to soothe my mind. Everything had changed. This place used to calm me and fill me with absolute content. Now, it was suffocating me.

It was chaos.

I felt my wolf urging me, demanding me to go back to the Tierran Realm, but I refused. Time flowed differently in Astral Realm. Perhaps that had been a day ago, perhaps it had been several. I willed myself to stay here, fighting against the pull. I couldn't... I just couldn't go back.

I shut my eyes tightly, blocking the angelic lake from my vision. I just wanted to shut everything out, but my wolf was making it difficult, very difficult. The darkness surrounded me. That's all I needed. Darkness. Death. Power. *I am death.*

The mantra lulled me for just a moment, but Marcus's words slammed into my mind again. My wolf was pacing within, yearning for her. And then the light took over, the ever glow of the lake. Marcus was here, talking. He was here. Yet all I thought of was her.

The image of the lush green of a forest came into view. The scent of fresh kill clear in the air. She entered my line of sight. Her. That girl. The girl with the auburn hair and soft emerald eyes with golden specks that made me want to lose myself in her. It made me want to surrender at her feet and beg for her. Her.

No. NO! I'm not weak. I'm not weak. I'm not weak! The pounding in my head took over. The wound, healed here in this place, burned with a phantom ache. My wolf. Oh, he was conflicted too. He wanted to be by her side and to protect her, as she had protected us. He wanted a chance to prove to her his strength. Why, though? Why did he need to do that? *I'm not weak!*

I felt darkness taking over me. I was tired. I shut my eyes closed. I just wanted to escape. I didn't want to feel... I was weak. I couldn't afford to be weak. *"Only the strong, the powerful survive in this cruel world, you're strong, aren't you, Belaize?"* The whispers invaded my mind.

I am not weak. I am not weak, I thought. But Marcus... he loved her. He... loved her. He loved her. He deserved her. But... Liunella chose her for me. My mind was swept into memories of her. Her scent. Her soft face and her striking emerald eyes. *No. No. No. I can't!*

"Come on, Belaize. We have to go. I will not let you die, right now," Marcus said. I did not respond. *I should have killed him. I should have killed Marcus when I had the chance*, I thought. My wolf snarled, but not out of anger. It was battering me to listen to him. *Think of what you're doing to her,* Marcus had said. But every time I returned to the thought that he might be right, that I might be dying, Janus's mantra repeated in my head. *"You cannot die. You are death itself, incarnate,"* said the specter of my dead master.

There it was again, the mantra. "I'm not going to die, Marcus. I'm death. I cannot die." I spoke out loud this time.

I heard something fall through the air and land with a soft thump on the root I was lying against. I snapped open my eyes, gazing at the stranger. "Who the hell told you that you are death?" he said as he sat down and crossed his legs on the root.

I had seen him somewhere before. His face, it was familiar. Marcus had the same look of recollection in his eyes. I understood, then. The hint of a smile playing upon his lips was vastly different from the look of fear and horror that I had last seen. The wolf from the Sanctuary in Walka who tried to attack me. But he was long dead. *How?* I looked at the stranger.

"Laki..." said Marcus, wide eyed. So, Marcus knew this person too.

"Ah, so you do recognize me," he said with grin. "Or at least the body I'm wearing right now." He wasn't even on guard; he was completely vulnerable. But what did he want?

"What do you mean the body that you're wearing?" Marcus said. I watched the exchange between the two men.

"Well, I had to wear something to appear before you," the stranger said as he stroked his stubble.

"Who are you?" I said. I knew the Astral Realm differed from our world. It had many unexplored secrets of its own, but this man... something was off about him.

"I am no one... a stranger in the night... a wandering collector of memories, of sorts," he said. "I am the beginning, and I am the end."

"Don't speak in riddles. Tell me who you are, right now!" I said louder. I was agitated. The hair on my body was standing on end.

"Feisty," he said. "Truth is, it doesn't matter who I am. What matters is who you are. Both of you," he said as he pointed his finger toward us.

"Us? What do you mean, both of us?" Marcus interrupted.

"Shhhh. Just listen, I'm talking now," he said, smiling at Marcus. "You two are important, in the grand scheme, neither of you will die before your time." He paused.

"So... we're both dying?" Marcus questioned again. A shadow crossed the man's face and his eyes flashed red. It was as if a demon possessed him.

"I said be quiet, boy!" he said sharply. Marcus immediately stilled. There was something dangerous about this man, I couldn't put my finger on it. Laki, Marcus had called him, but he was just wearing this wolf's body, apparently. How was that possible, though?

"Marcus... look in your heart for the courage, boy. You are in a state of change. Metamorphosis. There is a fire smoldering within you. You will burn bright," Laki said. His voice sent shivers down my spine. Marcus was perplexed.

"What in the world do you mean?"

"You have my gratitude for the future that may come. The fates love you dearly," Laki said cryptically. Before Marcus could say anything, Laki touched his head and Marcus vanished. He disappeared in front of my eyes.

Where did he go? I wondered. I didn't understand. *Who was he? What was he?*

"I sent him back to Tierra. He wasn't needed anymore," he said simply. Laki focused on me.

"Belaize." He stared into my eyes. They were red pits of nothingness. "Belaize... Belaize... Belaize..." He spoke delicately, but it sent chills down my spine. "I don't know who fed you this death nonsense, but you are not death," he said, laughing.

"In fact, you are now next on his list." I stared at him silently, listening to him. Between one blink and the next, he was standing beside me. I hadn't heard him. I hadn't seen him move. I jerked back reflexively, but not before he placed his hand on my forehead. I squeezed my eyes shut, waiting to disappear, waiting to blink away.

"Oh... someone fucked you up good, and I know how he did it," he said shaking his head. "And no, I'm not talking about the wolfsbane, if you're wondering. I'm talking about your mind," his hand glowed as heat flowed through me, filling my core. Suddenly everything was clear.

The heat coalesced in my chest. I felt pain, suffering, sadness, constricting my heart. I fell to the silver ground on my knees. Tears were streaming down my face but my eyes were wide open, my heart was racing. Then darkness.

Sometime later, I slowly sat up, taking a deep breath. I was still in the Astral Realm. The lake was in front of me, a little farther away from Ygdrasil. I felt his dark presence. It was incredibly powerful. More powerful than anything I had ever felt, or even imagined. I lifted my head but as I my vision cleared, the presence vanished.

"You're awake again?" I heard Laki's voice. He was sitting at the top of a gnarled root, his legs folded while he sat. "I didn't expect you to be up for another hour, at least. You are brutishly strong," he said with a hint of admiration.

"What did you do to me?" I asked. My voice was coarse, my throat ached.

"To put it simply, I un-fucked your mind. A compulsion kept your mind imprisoned. You'll be able to recover now," he stated nonchalantly.

"I... don't want to go back," I murmured.

"You have to, son. The world... Eliana needs you." My eyes snapped to him. He was looking straight ahead into the vast world of angelic glow.

"Eliana," I softly whispered her name. My head filled with thoughts of her again, but this time, they were filled with longing. I needed her.

I needed Eliana. Liunella, even her name was beautiful.

"The world is out of shape, too many people are dying before their time. Find out why. We will meet again when it is time." Before the sense of his words was clear, he vanished. My head felt lighter. It wasn't clouded anymore. The pain... it was gone.

I closed my eyes. I was lost again. I thought about those soft emerald eyes. I smelled her sweetness. I let her presence wash over all of my senses. I wasn't pulling away from her anymore. My wolf guided me toward the light. Toward... hope, to her.

She was holding my hand, hers were soft, slender, and felt so small against mine. I focused harder, and I saw myself. Bandaged and beaten. My breathing was shallow. My blood had stained sheets through the bloody bandages. I realized she had been dressing my wounds. She was taking care of me. She... was waiting for me. At that moment, I knew. I knew I had to go back to her. To Eliana.

I closed my eyes, and I felt my soul return to Tierra. My soul felt heavy, as it always did when I returned, but this time, I felt pain flooding over me as I regained consciousness. I groaned softly. Eliana stirred as she heard me groan. She quickly pulled her hand from mine, looking at me with those wondrous eyes.

Within a moment, she dashed out of the room. I moved my head a little. My muscles felt stiff. It ached terribly to even move, but I did it, anyway. Taking in my surroundings, I realized I was in an Infirmary, of sorts. The room was bright, and a small pile of herbs rested on the bedside table. Shortly afterwards, Eliana returned accompanied by a short woman. Eliana stood by the door as the woman approached.

The woman asked me questions. Did it hurt when I lifted my fingers? Could I feel the sharp pinch at my calf? She buzzed a light into each eye and checked each ear. But the entire time my gaze was trained on Eliana. She stood in the hallway staring at me, her face expressionless, as the healer reviewed my vitals. Soon the short woman left, and once again silence graced us. But Eliana never came back inside.

I looked at her. I couldn't pull my gaze away. She was right there. But something was different. I felt different. The rage, the bloodlust, that I had once felt every moment had abandoned me. The need to kill was no longer there. It left a vacant space in my chest. I was thinking clearly. I never knew that a veil was on my mind, but that stranger had torn it free.

I felt Eliana. Her presence. I was at... peace. The one I only knew in the Astral realm. I was free. I wasn't death. I was no longer bound to the ghost of my dead master, which had tormented my thoughts for so long. His words didn't haunt me anymore. I wasn't death. For the first time in my life, I felt alive.

I am alive.

IMPRISONED

Belaize

A loud sound of tapping against an iron door woke me from a deep slumber. The deafening screech of metal sliding into my cell grated against my ears. My eyes flickered open, but only darkness greeted my vision. I was laying down, facing the cracked cemented ceiling as usual.

“Eat up. Although, I’d rather you starve to death. Half the wolves in this base support that notion. If only Ronak gave us permission,” Alver said venomously. I saw him standing just outside the door through spiked bars.

I chuckled in response. “I know you want to get your hands on me, but in actual combat, a maggot like you wouldn’t stand a chance.”

This was my daily banter with Alver. He was the warrior wolf appointed to guard my prison cell, unfortunately. He was older than me by a couple of years, I could tell by his stature. An unruly dark brown beard covered his face, and his head was shaved. He had a strong build; it was no wonder he was the one guarding me. Not many could stop me. He hated me, like every lycan out there.

Alver snarled in response and left me in the cell to stand at his position down the hallway. I sighed. That was my only interaction with another person. I reached out and grabbed the plate of food Alver had left. I nibbled on a bite of stale bread. I didn’t like it, but I ate anyway.

Starvation isn't something my body could handle right now. Finishing up, I slid the plate back out, the screeching echoing in the dark hallway.

I moved back to my spot. I traced my fingers on the scratches that I had made on the wall beside me. "Twenty-four days," I whispered. Twenty-four days since I last gazed upon Eliana's face. I shook my head, trying to occupy myself, trying to keep her out of my thoughts.

Twenty-four days, but I still couldn't change. I cursed under my breath and tried to force my wolf to the surface for the hundredth time since my imprisonment, but I just... couldn't. I sensed my wolf inside, but I couldn't change.

Sure, I'd heard of wolfsbane killing the wolf spirit within a lycan. I knew it was possible. But always in those stories the physical form would diminish as well. Lycans are spiritually connected to their wolf-spirit, and one cannot survive without the other. And yet, here I was. Frail. Weak. Slowly recovering from my time in the Astral Realm.

Something was blocking my transformation, but what? The damned wolfsbane had cleared from my blood apparently, so why couldn't I change now? I rested my head against the scratches on the wall, caught up in the confusion. Alver must have felt the astral distortion because he walked back in.

"Still can't change, can you?" he said taunting me. I didn't reply. My back faced the door.

Rather than walk away with the empty plate as usual, he stood there. I felt his glare boring into my skin through the rusted iron bars. "It's a damn shame." He sighed, dejection clear in his voice. "Someone like you, with so much talent, so much innate potential, to be wasted on killing and rampant murder."

I squeezed my eyes shut, trying to keep out Alver's words from my mind, but his words cut deep. Ever since Laki had cleared my head in the Astral Realm, I had felt immense guilt. He said my mind had been tampered with. I had deduced that this was all Janus's doing. *But does that absolve me?* I wondered.

I turned to face him from my shadowed corner of the cell. My eyes met his gaze. "Why do you fight?" I questioned him. For a second Alver just stood there, as if trying to comprehend my question.

He finally spoke up. "My father..." he said.

"I fight for him. I fight for the countless innocents: mothers, daughters, sons, brothers, fathers, friends, neighbors. For everyone!" he said stoically. I scoffed at his list. Fighting for anyone other than yourself made you weak. It made you predictable. I wanted to speak my mind, but I just nodded and held my tongue.

"What about your mate?" I inquired. "Do you fight for her?" He tensed for a moment before letting himself relax.

"She's gone." Then he left me in the eternal darkness of the cell.

Another victim. So many people had lost so much, some of them because of me, but all of them because of the Council. I couldn't remember how the Council justified the killings, but I knew Alpha Idaos was behind it. I knew there were plenty of meetings about it. I knew I had even been in some of them, but when I tried to push my memory back that far I just reached empty, blank space. I felt hollow. Since the new Council had come to power by killing off the descendants of the old, there had been unrest in the nation. That unrest turned to outrage once the Council began to cull the population.

I looked around my cell and spotted the small metal fork that had been worn nearly to its base. I began scratching another line into the wall, completing the twenty-fifth tally. The sound of metal on stone echoed through the cell and down the hall.

Once the tally was complete, I stood before my reflection in front of the scum-covered mirror in the corner. It was cracked, and I imagined that prisoners before me had tried to break it, but only a crack remained to tell the tale.

In the reflection, I saw a ghost of my former self. My face looked sunken, with dark harrowing circles underneath my eyes. I lifted my shirt and looked at myself from top to bottom. My entire body was covered in scars, my ribs were showing. The mark of the bloodbane gauntlets tore great streaks across my abdomen. The scar of the creature from the ruins of Sundara twitched when I traced a finger on it. A cut was bandaged near my lower abdomen that had yet to heal completely.

I cursed silently. I took the loose shirt off and began my routine. I worked out hard and fast. Working my core and chest, I had nowhere near the stamina I once possessed, but I had to get back there, soon. I could not be weak. I hated the state I was in; my wolf was too embarrassed to even show himself while I was in this pitiful state. The thought made me push harder.

I grunted in effort as I pushed my body past the seven hundred and eighty-fourth push-up. My body was glistening in sweat, my chest was tight, but still far from the once sculpted muscle. I heard the iron door at the end of the hall creak open as I completed the next push-up.

"Alver, go do your rounds outside, I want to talk to him alone." I heard an unfamiliar voice. Alver stalked off into what I assumed was the middle of the day. I stood up and used my shirt to wipe my body of sweat. I watched as a stranger came into my view through the spiked bars of the iron door. He had sandy brown hair that lazily draped across his forehead and deep green eyes, which reminded me of Eliana. Strangely, he smelled familiar.

"My sister should have killed you." He spoke with contempt clear in his voice.

"I don't know what she and my old man are thinking. But you don't deserve to live, not after the crimes you've committed." He spat the words at me.

I silently watched him pace back and forth in front of my cell, and I formed a picture in my head. I had an encounter with him before. I looked at his face again, trying to remember, when suddenly an image of a wolf running away entered my mind. He was the coward from the Sanctuary at Walka, the one the ranger had told me was the leader. A small smile formed on my lips. He stopped pacing to look at me. He stepped closer to the bars and gripped them tight.

"What are you smiling at, you pathetic waste of life?!" he yelled. He made no effort to hide his hatred. "I am going to murder you, watch me!"

"You are more than welcome to open this door and try. I won't even need my wolf to snap your neck," I said, my voice was deep and rough. He stared at me, dumbfounded. For half a second, it was as if he might actually try to open the cell. "You won't, though," I said proudly.

"You're a fucking coward. That's your reality. You ran from the fight before. You were afraid of me. You ran from the Sanctuary before, and left wolves burning, to die, and to be captured by me. I have no doubt in my mind you'll run from here too. I wonder... if your old man knows. Or worse, your sister. You already live in her shadow, don't you?" I smiled at him. He stood frozen in front of me, white as snow. It was a look I knew well. Fear.

"Your biggest mistake was assuming that I am a weakling, even if you have imprisoned me in here." I said. "Someone like you wouldn't be able to lay a finger on me."

"Try! I dare you!"

In an instant, I was at the iron door. I smiled malevolently and slammed my hands against the bars hard. The bars shook and vibrated with intensity, the sound echoing in the empty hallway. He flinched, falling backwards on the stony floor. Quickly scrambling to his feet, he stood up but he pressed his body against the far wall. As far away from me as he could get. I laughed out loud. His lips contorted as if unable to speak. Before he could, I spat on his pristine shirt.

"Get lost and come back when you have more balls than your sister." I dismissed him and moved to sit on my makeshift bed on the icy floor.

He hesitated, and then fumed out of the building. I watched as his shadow faded from the hallway. In a few heartbeats, Alver returned to his post.

"Is it true?" Alver demanded. He crossed the distance to my cell with quick strides.

"Is what true?" I questioned in return.

"About Rayne?" he said. He looked as if he had seen a ghost.

"I see no benefit in lying, Alver. Rayne is a coward," I told him. "When I attacked Walka, he confronted me. He saw his men die brutal deaths," I said, walking closer to the bars again, so I was face-to-face with Alver. I stared into his eyes.

"I killed his comrades one by one, wolf by wolf, and what did Rayne do? The son of the smartest wolf in Vascya, the great Ronak the Wise." My lips cured into a snarl. "He ran like a damned coward." Alver rocked back on his heels as if stricken.

"It's a shame I wasn't there," Alver said after a moment of silence. "I would've killed him, and you." I couldn't help but laugh at the ludicrous statement.

"You couldn't kill me in the state I'm in now." It was his turn to laugh.

"You're vain and selfish. You think you're the strongest in the world, yet all you've seen of the world are the weak and defenseless. You pray upon women and children and cowards and speak of your strength, your might. But the reality is that you're just a weak man."

His words cut right through the iron bars of the cell. I couldn't say anything. The words refused to escape my tongue.

"For some reason Ronak wants you alive and I will respect his decision; however, give me one reason and I will kill you without a second's hesitation," he said with a confidence that made even me feel small.

I realized in that moment that whatever Alver was, he was powerful. But more than that, he was brave. I looked him in the eye, still inviting him to attack me. But he was smarter than that, a lot smarter than Rayne was, anyway. He turned his back and walked away without saying another word. I heard the door slam shut. But it opened again right away.

"Back again so soon?" I questioned.

She was old, perhaps in her late fifties, and not at all who I had expected. She had a weathered face and grey hair. She was incredibly short, perhaps only reaching my elbow. Each step was slow and patient as it echoed down the hall, and I thought there was something different about her. Leaders have a certain way about them.

"Who are you?" I asked. I took in her scent. It oozed an ancient strength. It was the unmistakably scent of an alpha. But that's impossible, she didn't look like one.

"Your name is Belaize, yes?" Her voice was soft and sweet. I would say it flowed like honey, which was surprising, and maybe even a little refreshing.

"Who are you?" I asked again, less hostile than before. Her presence, as powerful as that of an elder of the Council, was calming. I heard the soft jingle of the keys as she opened the cell. I just stared at her. She walked in, closing the door behind her and sat on the floor cross-legged, and motioned for me to sit down near her.

I did. As emaciated as I was, I still towered over her. "My name is Amae," she said introducing herself, "I am a spiritual healer, of sorts." She smiled sweetly.

"You are one of those freak preachers that claim to access a higher state of being," I said with more venom in my words than I had intended.

She had a cheeky grin on her dimpled face. She playfully replied, "I don't claim to access anything. But since you mentioned it, you've been there, haven't you?" Her aged, gray eyes twinkled as she spoke. "The Astral Realm?" She clarified.

"Yes." I nodded slowly, "I've been there."

"Have you unraveled how to get there at will?"

"At will? Have you gone senile, old woman? No one can go there at will. It's a primal place that can only be accessed when our primal instincts kick into overdrive. It might never happen to some, but to others it could happen several times. Except for Umbrals. Before they were hunted into extinction, they could travel to the Astral plane with but a word," I said. How such a ludicrous thought came into her mind was beyond me.

She chuckled lightly and shook her head. "And what if I told you, that in fact, it is a skill that can be learned and honed just like fighting and running?" I looked at her dumbfounded. *What she was saying was preposterous.*

"Impossible," I said to her.

"Possible, because all Umbrals aren't dead yet, child." Her eyes twinkled. "What this freak preacher can do, son, is not only teach you to access the Astral Realm, but I can also help you access your memories. I can even find out why you can't change," she mumbled. I stared at her silently. My mind whirled with confusion. "All it'll take is for me to touch your head, and I can see what's holding you back." She got onto her knees and reached for my head. I slapped her hands away.

"No!" I yelled in defiance. "Stay out of my head!"

She recoiled a little, then softened. "I've seen some of what you've been through when I sent Marcus to find you." I grew angrier as she spoke. *How can she see inside my mind?*

"You've seen the monster I am, so why come back?" I seethed. She stared at me with pity in her eyes. There was a pulsing sensation in my head as she swiftly touched my temple with her wrinkled white hands.

The children and women I had slaughtered, their screams, their agony. "You're in my damned head!" I screamed. "Get out! Get out!" She clamped her hands on my head harder. The screams were deafening, and then there was silence. All of that anger and agony dissipated. Nothing but white existed. Nothing but peace and calm. The kind of peace I have known before.

I slowly regained my composure. Amae was still in front of me, but we weren't in the cell anymore. The silver glow and the hazy mist greeted my vision as I realized where I was. The Astral Realm.

"Impossible." The word echoed in my head until it disappeared. "Do you believe me now, child?" I didn't know what to say or think.

"The blood of Beleotell hasn't left Vascya yet, son. I am an Umbral. I can help you. Let me help you," she murmured.

We stood in silence for what seemed like an eternity before she finally spoke again. "When I brought you here, I saw someone in your head. Someone that haunts you." She started walking in a random direction, motioning me to follow her. I fell in step with her. She was hesitant. I gazed at her. The look in her gray eyes. Loss and heartache lived there.

"Who are you talking about?" I asked, half knowing the answer. She paused as if she was choking on the word.

"Janus!" She spat.

My eyes went wide, "How do you know about him?" I asked in disbelief. For the first time, she looked away from me.

"He..." she paused, I saw a tear glisten in her eye. "He killed... he killed the man I loved and tore apart his body," she said. "He defiled him in ways I could not even begin to describe, in ways a wolf should never witness, let alone experience." Her voice lost its softness, and a chill crept up my spine. While she spoke, she didn't sob or cry. She knew pain, but she had gone past it. Though Janus plagued her mind, too.

"If it makes any difference to you, I killed him," I stated. She sighed and looked up to the empty white expanse of the Astral Realm.

She must've been praying because several minutes had passed before she looked back at me. "Killing Janus doesn't bring him back," she said, finally.

"But confronting him just might bring back your wolf," she said.

"Do not ridicule me any more than you already have, Amae. He's dead. I killed him with my bare hands. I can't confront him anymore." I said.

"There is a way, but are you ready?" I looked at her dumbfounded.

"Even if that's possible, why do you want to help me? I'm your enemy. Every wolf in Vascya hates me. What is your purpose of bringing me here?" I asked.

"Because Eliana sees some good in you, Belaize. And talking with you here, I see it too. Let me help you, and maybe you can start repenting for what you've done." I stood in front of her, feeling like a guilty child in her presence. *Why did I feel this way? What did Laki do to my head?* There were so many questions, and to answer each of them, I would have to trust Amae.

"Okay," I said. This was the only way I would have answers to my questions and bring my wolf back. I felt empty without him close to the surface.

She motioned for me to kneel. I did as she bid me and dropped to my knees. She lifted her hands, pressing her fingers to my head. I saw her eyes flicker to a shade of golden as they glowed and... it was over as soon as she had begun.

"That's it?" I asked. It took me a second to realize, but she wasn't there anymore. I was alone. I stood and turned frantically. "Amae!" I yelled and heard my voice echo in the emptiness of the void.

"Child, this is the inside of your mind, your subconscious. This place is where your thoughts exist, far away from your feelings." I was more confused now than ever before. "Be ready child, some things you will see, are buried deep inside the annals of your mind. Suppressed even to you, because of Janus."

"Why do you call me child?" I said, annoyed.

"Is that not what you are?" She replied. Her voice came from everywhere all at once. I looked at my body. I was small. I had become a child, somehow.

"What is this?" My once calloused hands had turned into the small, slender hands of a child.

"This is your mind's perception of yourself. You see yourself as a child trapped in an expanse of space." *Is that why I cannot change?* I thought to myself.

"Yes, that's exactly why. And before you panic further, understand that I am inside your head, though you cannot see me."

The space before me began to shimmer. Flecks of light wobbled and shifted. It looked like something was pressing against the empty air in front of me, like a hand behind a curtain. The air was bending. No, something was materializing in front of me. "What is that?" I asked her, warily.

"Your fear." Amae said. *My fear?* My thoughts rang loud in my head. Just when I thought the entire fabric of my mind would tear, the shimmering stopped, and, in its place, stood a tall broad-shouldered wolf. He had brown skin, black curled hair. His face was angular with a deep scar on his chin. He had a set of intense silver eyes.

It can't be. This wolf, the scent, those cruel eyes... Janus.

SHATTERED MEMORIES

Belaize

Janus was here; he was standing in front of me, that evil smile playing at his lips. He was towering over my small body. There was a twinkle in his eyes which I had grown to dread. The sound of blood rushed through my ears as I staggered back, away from Janus. I couldn't breathe. It was a hallucination, surely, but so real. So fucking real.

"You're not delusional, Belaize." The soft, gentle voice spoke, which I recognized as Amae's. She was watching it all. Everything.

"You will always choose fallacy over reality, because you are weak, Belaize," he said, mockingly. Janus. He was here. Wearing his official Council uniform as Master-of-Arms. The maroon velvet jacket embroidered with silver and gold thread. The crest of wolves of Vascya on his breast pocket was as crisp as I remembered. He was standing tall and smiling at me with familiar arrogance. But... I still didn't understand. *How was he here? How could I see him?*

I knew I had killed him with my own bare hands. He died at my feet when I tore his heart from his chest. For an instant, a flash of blood, the ancient castle of the twin wolves, the flag of Vascya hoisted over its walls, came into my mind. A courtyard with white granite floor, and blood splattered everywhere. It was still wet, and I heard an echo of his last laugh as the blood dripped down his scarred cheek. I ripped out that wretched heart of his with unrecognizable anger and tore it to pieces. I winced at the thought. My hands were now smaller than I ever remembered, and they were shaking. *But why?!*

"Fear." Amae's voice echoed again. Janus stepped toward me, but I stood firm. I forcibly planted my feet. I couldn't move away from Janus. I didn't want to. I wasn't afraid of him.

"Oh boy, but you are afraid of me," he said. His mouth stretched into a wide, sickly grin. I shook my head in disagreement.

"No, I'm not. I don't fear you, Janus. I murdered you."

He began to slowly circle me. "Look at yourself. You're weak, Belaize. You have always been weak. Even now, you're as trapped as a damned child in your own mind! Such weakness," he said and pushed me. I stumbled a bit but stood tall.

"No. Janus. You're dead. I don't know what Amae did with my mind, but you're merely my imagination," I said, hiding behind the words I spoke.

"I raised you like my seed, Belaize. I taught you, trained you to be strong. But you? You have never met my expectations." His voice came from behind me as if he was whispering in my ear. A shiver ran through me, and I bit down on my tongue.

"Strong. Be strong, Belaize." Amae's soothing voice echoed through my mind.

"Death. I created death. You were my prized possession, boy. Look at yourself! Nothing but a child. You don't deserve to be called a Kaiser. You don't deserve to have the sacred blood of Mugiri flowing in your veins." He hustled me against a sudden, solid wall in the empty expanse. Air was pushed from my lungs like a punch to the gut. I tried to defend myself by pushing my hand toward him, but he overpowered me, cutting my palm with his sharp teeth. Biting my cheek as pain shot through me, I shoved away from him. Blood dripped down my hand. I looked at Janus to avoid his next attack, but he just stood where he was. He licked his lips clean of my blood.

"You taste like shit." Janus spoke. Those words... they felt familiar.

I stayed silent and alert in case he assaulted me again. *But how? I am strong! How could he wound me so easily?*

He laughed at me. "Don't you see yourself, Belaize? I created death. Me! But, you? You ended up being a fucking disappointment. Such a shame. Failure. You were not strong enough to kill, so a little bitch had to come and rescue you. Even a jackal is better in combat than you." He spat on the floor as he kept degrading me.

A light flashed in front of my eyes, and suddenly I was in a forest clearing near a creek. Grass and a fresh kill filled my senses. I recognized this place. It was where I first saw Eliana. It was the place where she fought the Council guards. I saw her wolf jump in front of me, attacking the guard and ripping him apart.

"Pup." Janus's voice pulled me from the memory.

"No," I said in defiance. "I was under the influence of wolfsbane. I don't know why Eliana protected me!"

"But you do! Because you were a weakling."

"Belaize, he will try to trick—" Amae whispered from some distant corner of my mind.

"I," Janus said intentionally cutting her off. He was trying to overpower me I knew. My thoughts were frantic. "Always thought you were better than Faust." He sighed in regret. "I should have raised him like you, Belaize. You always excelled in my tasks and missions, but trickery is something I never taught you. Faust always begged for my attention, but I focused on you. But you have been such a baffling disappointment."

"I always fought fairly. I have never used trickery. You're wrong, Janus. Get out of my mind."

He chuckled. "Don't you remember your fight with Faust? Don't be pretentious, Belaize. It was just deceit that saved you from Faust that day. Death himself, trying to save his own life. Such a disgrace."

Janus paused, "You were supposed to be..." He had a crazed look about him. His eyes twinkled unnaturally. "Supposed to be perfect," he finished. He sounded almost sad at that thought. "Instead, you're just broken."

We stood in silence. Our surroundings shimmered. It was if the world was tearing apart. My vision blurred from the intense light that bathed us. The shimmering turned into violent ripples of varied colors as my surroundings stretched and morphed into a large, cavernous hallway.

My vision finally cleared, and I stood in the hallway now. It was dark and old. I sniffed the stale air. The hallway was littered with doors on either side, as far as my eyes could see.

"What is this?" I said in awe and curiosity. I couldn't even describe the sheer immenseness of it. The ceilings ran so high that they blended with the eternal darkness.

"This is what you need to see, Belaize. Somewhere in this hall, behind one of these doors, is the reason your wolf doesn't surface." Amae's voice echoed in my head. I looked over at Janus, he just gave me a toothy grin. He was enjoying himself.

"What will we find behind this door?" He said and walked to the first door. He slowly pushed open the rustic wooden door and lazily stepped inside. I stood still, anticipating his return, but all I heard were his fading footsteps. I stared at the half-closed door for a moment then followed him inside.

It was darker than I expected. I found myself in a familiar place. A spring breeze flowed through the trees, and light mixed with shadow through the thick canopy. It was as if I had just entered a forest. There in the clearing... a wolf was hunched over a fresh kill by a creek.

"Eliana..." I whispered. This was the day I met Eliana.

"The she-wolf. What is her name again?" Janus asked. I turned toward him and shoved him forward with every ounce of strength I had, but he didn't budge. I snarled at him.

"Don't you ever bring her name to your lips."

"Oh! Is the whore so important to you?" He smiled maliciously. "That's the bitch that put you to heel, eh?"

"These are your memories, Belaize. Don't let him get under your skin," Amae said. Just as Amae's thought finished in my head, I saw myself crash into the clearing. A stumbling mess. The rags that hung loosely off my body were soaked in blood. My face was a sickly shade of white. It wasn't until I saw myself from this unprecedented perspective that I truly realized the grave danger I was in that day.

"This memory is of no concern," Janus grumbled as he turned and walked back, vanishing through the door from which we came. I moved to follow him back through the door, but stopped once more to look back. Eliana was protecting me from the Council wolves now. I watched for a moment before stepping through the door. The darkness slowly faded as my eyes adjusted. The cavern reappeared. Janus had already walked several doors down. I quickly caught up to him as he settled on another door to open.

We stepped through together this time. Suddenly, there was a boy weeping at my feet as I held the severed head of a she-wolf in my hand. Janus laughed. "Ah! This is you Belaize! My magnificent creation," he bellowed loudly, taking in the gruesome scene before him. *I should not have killed the she-wolf*, I thought. I felt a twinge around my heart. Remorse. But I watched intently, as if unable to tear my eyes away. I had killed that wolf, and I had maimed that boy beyond repair.

"Do you see Belaize?" Janus continued. "You are my masterpiece. You are mine!" he said maniacally. "Nothing more than a cold-hearted murderer." Janus licked his lips. I couldn't help but think that what Janus said was the cold, hard truth. I was a killer. There was no redemption, not from this.

"You are not that person, Belaize," Amae countered.

I turned my back to the grisly murder and walked out. Janus followed close behind. "What's wrong? Can't take the truth? Or has your bitch made you soft?"

His voice echoed through the hallway as I strode away from him. These... were my memories. Memories of every murder I committed. Every wolf I had assassinated for the Council. Every piece of my life was in this hallway.

As I moved deeper into my mind, I noticed something. The slow signs of age were subtle. The doors were dirtier, more worn down. Some were cracked and splintered. Dust lined the handles and cobwebs stretched across the paneling.

I stepped to the closest door and traced my hand on it. My fingers left streaks through the dust. Looking back in the direction from which I came, I saw that even the hallway itself was older, the stones were lined with grime. I continued exploring this bizarre hallway.

Janus had followed me too, and we had walked quite a distance from the previous memory. There were thousands of memories in here, in my mind. After a few more paces, I paused and tried a handle. It was stiff. I tried to push it open, but it wouldn't budge.

I pushed on the door harder, using all the strength I had, and it moved marginally with a loud creek. This damned child's body was so fucking weak. Janus laughed as he watched me. "Move aside, you pathetic dog," he stated and kicked at my legs. I landed against the wall on the other side and winced in pain. My body throbbed.

He kicked the door next. A loud bang echoed and the door shattered into pieces. The temperature dropped the second the door splintered. I felt goosebumps rise on my skin. An ominous feeling ran through my body, making me shiver. *What's behind this door?*

I saw Janus grinning as he silently walked into the doorway, disappearing into the blackness of the void. I stood up with some effort, wincing as I limped behind Janus into the memory.

The scene in front of me was of a dungeon. The walls were made of bricks as old as the temple of the Liunella. I looked around, taking in surroundings. The dungeon was dimly lit by oil lamps. I saw that my body was strapped to the opposite wall. My arms were cuffed above my head and my feet barely reached the floor. My head hung low against my chest. I was fading in and out of consciousness.

Janus was there, sitting on a chair still wearing that same scarlet jacket. He was silently working away at a table, reading an old tome. Craning his neck in my direction, he looked at my limp body. Then he pushed the chair back, the sound made me wince. He stood tall and grabbed a glass of water from the table. He slowly approached, and when he was just foot from me, when I could smell his sweat, he threw the water at my face. I could barely lift my head in his direction.

"Boy. You're a disappointment," Janus muttered in my memory. He moved away to the other end of the dungeon. Tracing his hands over a rusty-looking trunk, he popped open a lid and removed a velvet box. He closed the trunk and placed the velvet box on the table beside his old, worn book.

Finally, opening the small box, he smiled devilishly. He slowly picked up a cloth from inside. I stared at his hand intently. Wait, no. Not a cloth, but a stone maybe, wrapped in cloth. The stone was glowing. But... how? Why? These bizarre questions rushed through my mind as I stared at the unfolding memory. Janus came closer to me and touched that glowing stone to my head and spoke in a strange language I had never heard.

I turned to the Janus that guided me through the hall. "What is that stone?" I questioned him. He didn't answer, instead he kept staring at my memory-self, weak and imprisoned.

"Amazing." He smiled maliciously.

"Tell me what it is. Tell me, now!" I said in an aggravated voice.

"He does not know the answer, Belaize. He is only an image in your head," Amae whispered.

I growled impatiently. "Tell me!" I lunged at him. He caught me in the air and slammed me to the ground.

"Belaize, this is not the real Janus, this is just your subconscious mind trying to make sense of this," Amae said with a greater sense of urgency. Janus let me go and stared again at the scene in front of him.

"It's beautiful, isn't it?"

It slowly dawned on me. Laki, in the Astral Realm, had told me about this. *The compulsion*, he had called it. This must be how Janus controlled me.

"Do you want to see how you got here, boy?" His smile was almost ear to ear now. That's when I realized something else. I had no recollection of this memory. In fact, I had no memory of my childhood, or years that followed, either. All those memories, my entire past, was locked in my mind somewhere. In this memory, I was young. I was shorter. I lacked the toned muscle I had grown over the years, and… the scar. The scar on my shoulder and chest was missing.

"What do you mean?" I questioned.

"Belaize, be careful!" Amae said. "You mustn't change based on what you see." She was helpless as I paid her no attention and searched instead for answers from my former master.

Janus turned on his heel and took off, sprinting through the door. I ran after him. We ran faster and faster through the hall. Thousands of doors blurred passed us. They were nearly falling apart as we withdrew further into the recesses of my mind. Memories I did not know of.

I looked ahead and saw that Janus had stopped. The hall had ended. One more door rested beyond this. Unlike the rest in this part of the hall, this door was perfectly maintained. It shone with a brilliant, golden glow.

"What is this?" I said as I slowed to a stop and traced the pristine handle with my fingers. It was made of solid gold. It was vibrating softly as if having a life of its own.

"This is a memory that is all yours, boy. Yet it was supposed to remain hidden," Janus said cryptically. I wanted to see what was behind it. I tried the door. It didn't open. I kicked and punched, but it didn't move even an inch.

"It will not open, boy! Today is not the day that door unlocks," said Janus, "besides, we came here for this." He gestured to a pile of rubble gathered beside the golden door.

"There's nothing?" I said confused. Janus began sifting through the rubble. I looked back at the door once again in intense anticipation, as if it could open on its own. A heartbeat passed. And then another. Nothing. I sighed and moved toward Janus. I helped him move the rubble aside. After several minutes of scrapping and shifting the loose mounds of stone, a hole appeared in the wall.

When the hole was big enough to pass through, Janus said, "The door to this memory has long since vanished, replaced by the rubble that is your mind. This..." he paused for theatrics, "this is the day your life changed forever." He smiled and stepped into the sheer darkness. I hesitated for a moment, glancing at the rubble, the dust, the endless hallway behind me and the doorways to memories it possessed. Taking a deep breath, I stepped inside the void, letting the darkness wash over me.

MEMORY LANE

Belaize

This memory was different from the others I had witnessed. The darkness didn't give way to light like before. "What is this?" I called out, but no answer came. "Damn you." I cursed him under my breath. I took a few more cautious steps forward into the darkness and suddenly, memories came back to me in a flood of visions and voices.

Someone was arguing... I heard their muffled voices, which were becoming clearer by the second. I guessed it was a man and a woman arguing. *Who were these people?*

"We can't keep him!" yelled a deep voice.

"What do you expect us to do?" yelled a softer feminine voice with equal vigor.

"He has no one else in this world except us! I won't let you take him away. He's our... sweet child." Her voice broke on the last word.

As sound became words, so too did their image coalesce in my mind. I looked at both of them. The man was massive; he had a head of black hair and a small black beard covering his face. He was dressed in rags, torn and filthy. The woman was short in contrast. She had blond hair tied in a loose, knotted bun. They both were tired. They had been running.

The couple was standing in an old cave in the mountains. I looked, saw trees and creepers covering the walls. These two were alone, hiding away.

"You have to understand. He has to go to the Sanctuary. Only they can protect him." The man urged with an aggressive tone. His name brushed against my mind. He was called Arthur.

What were these two arguing about? Who were they? A moment later, I noticed a small boy clinging to the woman, hiding behind her, his small fingers wrapped around her leg. He was small, no more than five years of age. I stared at the boy a little more. He seemed timid and afraid. But... he was familiar. He was the same child from my visions!

Impossible! And why are these people in my memories? Wait, is that boy... is that me?

My head began to pound. It made some sense now. Why I kept seeing him, why he hounded my sleep, my dreams. They were my own memories. I saw him through the space between the woman's legs. A blond mop of hair on his head, an angular and innocent face. I caught a glimpse of his glistening eyes, they were red, like my own.

"Don't be foolish, the Council will murder us! They'll murder you if they find him. We barely made it through the last attack."

My eyes went wide as I looked at the woman more closely. The same blond hair, the face resembling my own, the voice which was so calming, soothing. My heartbeat accelerated... M... Mother!

I saw my young-self clutch her legs harder. "I have to take him with me to the Sanctuary. He will be safe there," the man said. He must be my father. These people... they were my parents.

My mother leaned down and picked the boy— no, me— up in her arms. She was crying. My father stepped close to her and hugged her from behind. "You know I'm right. He will be safe. Safe from the Council."

"I know," my mother croaked with grief and pulled me closer to her. After a moment of embrace, my father pulled me to his arms. "Come on. We have to go on a trip."

I looked up at my father. "Where are we going, father?" I asked curiously.

"Some place where you will be safe," he replied and stepped a little further from my mother.

"What about mother? Come! Mother! We will go with father," I said with a smile.

"No. She isn't coming. You won't see her for a while," Father said. In urgency, my young-self glanced back at my mother. She was sobbing as she fell to her knees, feebly hugging herself.

"Keep him safe!" She screamed in pain as my father left her.

I stood paralyzed as the vision followed my father and I. "Where are we going, father? Why won't mother come with us?" I questioned again. But he kept walking silently. Without a word, he swept me onto his broad back. Changing into a gray wolf, he was impressive. But nowhere near what I am capable of now. My father and I continued the journey silently. Father ran for hours, and the sky above him darkened.

Many clearings, creeks, and forests passed us by as we moved. It was around dawn when I saw buildings up ahead. They were huge. I realized they were castles. Castles that I have seen before. I have been inside these castles, I realized. A shiver ran down my spine as I realized my father, who had me sitting on his shoulders, was running right towards the Low Cities.

"Father, what is this place?" I asked him. He let out a low growl and said, "I'm not..." He trailed off, the words dying in his throat. "Just be quiet."

I wondered why was he taking us there. What was happening?

It took him a few minutes to complete the last stretch to the Low Cities. When we arrived, he strode through the gates, down winding alleys, passed stalls and vendors, until he reached the Twin Castle's courtyard. A pristine lawn, lined with hedges.

When father arrived there, he knocked on the familiar, massive wooden door and shortly thereafter a guard appeared. My father grunted something to him, and the guard shut the door and disappeared. What was going on? I was overwhelmed with nausea as the memory unfolded.

Another few minutes had passed when the door opened, but this time Janus appeared. My eyes went wide. Janus? But... how did my father know him? What was happening? My thoughts swirled and I felt ill. Something terrible was on its way, and I couldn't stop this memory.

"Ahhhh come, come!" he said calmly. "So, this is that boy, you spoke of?" he inquired.

"Yes, Lord Janus," my father said.

Father put me down on the ground and urged me forward. "Go to him, boy." I looked warily at Janus. He was young in the memory and dressed in those wretched crimson robes. I stepped backwards into my father, waddling on small feet.

"I want to go back to mother," I told my father.

"You're never going to come back to our life," he said with such a grimace that it made me sick, and then he shoved me forward. I fell at Janus's feet.

I was crying in my memory. Janus helped me to my feet and knelt down beside me. "Look at me," he said. We held each other's gaze. Tears were still rolling down my face. "The blood moon eyes. So rare. You know they are a sign of one of the four bloodlines. Such strength, your child."

My father coughed to get Janus's attention. "Lord Janus. I have delivered on my promise... please, help me," Arthur said. His face was deeply set with worry lines, and his posture was stooped. His hands were clasped together as if to keep them still. He was practically begging.

Janus reached into his breast pocket. He took out a pouch that jingled with metallic sound and threw it at my father, who scrambled to catch it. "Lord Janus, what of my mate?" my father asked patiently. Janus stared at him.

"Fear not, I will ensure the Council turns a blind eye to your small home."

My father grinned with relief and bowed. He ran outside as fast as his feet could carry him, leaving the younger me far behind. Nothing more than a memory. My eyes glistened with fresh tears and I tilted my head up to Janus.

He grabbed me by my neck and dragged me inside the inner chamber. This was before I knew to scream, to cry. This was before I had fully grasped my new place in the world. Alone. As he threw me to the floor I did not cry. I just stared back at the door through which my father left.

I wondered, if I had known then what would become of my life, what I would have done. I would've clawed at that wooden door until my hands were bloody. I would've begged for my father to come back. I would've spat in the face of my captor, my mentor. I would've taken a blade to my wrist. Anything was better than what I had become. What I had been made into.

Staring at my small form crumpled on the stones bubbled a slow anger within me. I was seething. All I saw was red. I was panting, and I wanted to kill. My own fucking father! He... he sold me to that monster. The memory vanished and suddenly I was standing back in the shimmering white space.

"Belaize! Fear not, child, it was just a memory. It cannot harm you," said Amae, trying to keep my anger at bay. Her voice sounded strained.

Janus reappeared before me. "You see Belaize, even your father wanted nothing to do with such a cursed child. No one wants you, Belaize. Your whore is better off without you, too."

My anger surged like a ferocious tide, it washed over me, blinding me. I felt the restraints within my mind shatter. "Belaize, Eliana is waiting for you," Amae blurted in desperation. Janus just laughed maniacally.

Amae could sense my thoughts, my anger, and she immediately snapped me out of the Astral Realm. There was a sense of inertia, of movement. Visions and half made memories, lights, sounds, colors, blinded me as I was slammed back into my body. I felt heavy and limp. We were back on the icy floor of the cell.

We had an audience now. Alver and Ronak were standing in the outer corner of my cell. I looked at Amae, she was panting. I reached out and put a hand on her shoulder, trying to stabilize her.

"Amae," I called to her.

"I'll be fine child. I have not done this in years and I am thus rusty."

I helped Amae to her feet, and she looked at me with pity in her eyes. Something else lingered in her eyes too, but I couldn't quite put a finger on it.

"You saw them," I whispered. She nodded in response. I just looked away. She had seen a part of me that even I had been unaware of.

The world was closing in on me.

My parents. No. Just him. My father. How could he? And what happened to mother?

I felt dizzy and in the next moment darkness engulfed me, giving me a break from the chaos of my past. Giving me peace.

INQUISITION

Eliana

Something loomed in the air this afternoon. A feeling of dread enveloped us. My wolf felt agitated and on guard, just near the surface. I was walking toward the old building that we used as a prison. It was smaller than the Infirmary. We rarely held prisoners in this Sanctuary. Warriors usually killed any enemy before they make their way to the heart of the Sanctuary. Soon, I saw the small gates of the rundown building. It was finally time to face Belaize.

It had been over a month since I had last seen him. He was imprisoned on father's orders as soon as he was conscious and well enough to stand. I hadn't had the courage to visit him.

But it was necessary now. I sighed. Last night, Romulus called for a meeting at the assembly area to plan the next attack. I gave my input on tactics that could be used to our advantage and set Romulus to train the warriors accordingly. He drilled them on formations and fighting stances. But the space between each warrior was wider now that our numbers had gravely thinned.

The rebels had executed many attacks at the center of power for the Council; the Low Cities, that is. Yet, every single attempt had been unsuccessful. The Council was producing and training Council guards at a rate that we could not keep up with. The insidious breeding program and rigorous training methods stacked the odds against us. That had been the case for years now.

Usually, Marcus and Adrian joined in these meetings as well, along with Rayne and his friends. But yesterday I was alone. Marcus and Adrian and gone out with the supply party to get rations for next month. Rayne, well he was Rayne. Training probably. It had been a while since we sparred, and he hadn't attended a meeting since father called him out.

As I headed toward his cell, I strengthened my resolve. It was necessary. I knew that. I had known that for a while. But I didn't have the courage in my heart. So many questions bothered me. *What was he like? Would he accept me as his mate? Was he still working for the Council? What if the only reason he came here was to lure us all into a trap, but something had gone wrong?* I wondered what the ruthless killer would do next.

These questions revolved over and over again in my mind, but none were answered. Because I wasn't ready to face him. Day after day, I prayed I could just catch a glimpse. Or that he was somebody different, or that we had met under different circumstances. Maybe, without this war, we might have been able to live a better life. But, alas, that wasn't my luck, Liunella.

Focus, El! I took a long breath that I hadn't realized I was holding and entered the building. The old musky scent hit my nose. A gloomy stairway descended sharply and I climbed down, my footsteps echoed around me. I smoothed my brown locks with my hand and reminded myself to remain calm.

Alver was sitting in his chair. He looked up, scanned me inquisitively, and then nodded. No one questioned my presence because of my rank. Daughter of Ronak, and an Alpha. I commanded my father's units in the battle. On many occasions, I had even helped our warriors slip out from under the Council's claws. I held the respect of many wolves in this Sanctuary.

After all, two minds with blood of Draxus working together was the reason why so many rebels were able to strike back against the Council. It was the reason those old asses could hardly manage a victory. Father had pressed me to be chieftain in a different Sanctuary, but Rayne had protested. He thought Father favored me on principle alone, rather than fully considering Rayne's efforts and victories.

"I need the keys to his cell," I told Alver as soon as I reached his desk. He arched his eyebrow in a silent question. He was met with silence. A few moments had passed when he finally shifted from his seat. He stood tall, much taller than me, with a stoic expression on his face. Alver moved to the end of the hallway and returned with a set of heavy iron keys.

"Word of advice. Be careful," he said as he placed the keys in my palm. I nodded, clutching them tightly as I walked further into the enclosure.

I selected the longest and heaviest key and pushed it into the metal door that separated me from Belaize. My heart was beating fast. I heard my pulse in my ears. The rusty key made a creaky noise as the door opened. “Oh, Liunella,” I whispered under my breath.

As soon as I opened the door, I smelled the heavy stench of sweat. It hung in the air. I saw Belaize behind the second barred door. I paused momentarily, taking in his appearance. He was in a better shape than a few weeks ago, back when he was in the Infirmary. However, nowhere near what he was in when I first stumbled upon him. He had become so thin.

I opened the barred door as well and stood at the threshold. Belaize was sitting against the stony wall of the cell with his eyes closed. His chest moved heavily as he breathed. He had been working out, and it showed. Sweat glistened on his body. Before I could say anything, he spoke, “Will you just stand there and stare?” he said in an abrasive tone.

His voice pulled me from my thoughts as I closed the door behind me with a loud thud. We were alone, finally.

“I was testing your senses. It has been a while since you needed to use them,” I shot back. I watched him intently as his eyes slowly flickered open. Something was different in his eyes. They... had lost their intensity. The coldness was gone, I felt its absence. It seemed that his eyes mirrored his emotions. Right now, they were soft, and perhaps a bit lost. But that day, the day I first met him, they were fierce. They had a hunger in them. A Bloodlust.

He stood up and stepped closer toward me. I had forgotten how incredibly tall he was. He towered over me. I had to tilt my head upward to look at him. His blond hair was longer, dirtier, tied in a messy bun. He had grown a beard as well.

“What do you want?” he asked. His closeness was making me nervous, but I kept my cool. I put my hands on his chest to kept some space between us. His chest felt hard beneath the touch of my fingers. Sparks ran down my back.

“I need to ask you a few questions,” I said.

“Ask. Be done with it,” he said. His face was blank, but his eyes locked onto mine. They were clouded, deep in thought. I ignored the indecent thoughts my wolf was suggesting. She wanted to claim her mate. Right there and now. But I willed myself to stay calm.

“Why were the Council guards chasing you that day?” I began my interrogation. It was ridiculous how we were standing so close together. But my wolf was enjoying my discomfort. I never knew she could react in such a manner.

“I don’t know,” he said after a pause.

“Elaborate.”

“Hmmm... I had a meeting with the elders, and I probably pissed them off. They've wanted to eliminate me ever since. They ordered assassins to kill me but failed."

"That doesn't feel right," I mumbled. Why would the Council want to kill their best asset? That would just leave them handicapped.

"What do you know about the elders?" I inquired.

"That question is a waste of my time," he said with a short laugh. "You already know about the elders. Possibly more than me. Otherwise, this rebellion of yours wouldn't be as successful. Get a list of better questions."

"Do not degrade what I say. You know that every question has significance, Belaize. Insight from the prisoner about their master is some of the most valuable information we can gather. So, stop deflecting and answer me," I shot back.

He leaned a little closer to me, his gaze unwavering. "Feisty. What if I don't answer?"

"You'll rot another couple of weeks in this cell till you see my face again and answer the same questions. So, what will it be?" I said, arching my eyebrow at him. There was no way he was getting out of this cell, that was just a fact. He would answer. I knew that as surely as I knew that Liunella blessed the wolves.

Silence surrounded us, but I swear I saw a twinkle of mischief in his eyes. My hand was still touching him and I registered that closeness again. Sparks and vibrations flowing through our touch.

"As you already know," he said dramatically, "The Council is composed of elders. Only Idaos and Eyolf are alpha from the old Council. Each member is assigned different tasks to manage the rebels, which again you already know. As for my insight, I'd say Idaos is the one governing Vascya at this point. He is well respected. Plus, he has the blood of *Çatall*, if I recall correctly. Other Alphas are strong, but only Remus is a Kaiser. Does that answer your question, Princess?"

The nerve of him. What a prick! "Not quite. If the Council doesn't want you, does that mean you're now the rebels' ally? Or are you still loyal to those old dogs?" I prodded. It was important. I needed to know.

All of a sudden, he moved away from me. The warmth of his body under my fingertips was gone. The closeness was lost. He turned his back on me and walked to the other end of the cell. This was my first genuine interaction with Belaize. I felt... I don't know what I felt. He looked alright, but what happened?

I waited for him. I waited for his answer. He knew I wouldn't leave without one. I stood there looking at his back. Seconds turned into minutes with no words exchanged. I was patient. *He needed time*, I thought. *But would he join us? Join me?*

"You deserve someone better than me, Eliana. Not a monster. Not a killer," he said in a low tone. My heartbeat lurched. It was the first time he had said my name. His words were thoughtful, contemplative. He must've had hours alone to think about it, just as I had. That would mean he felt the same pull. I held close that small gift of acknowledgement. He... accepted that we were mates.

"Liunella thinks otherwise. I trust her. I have faith in her," I took a deep breath, knotting my fingers together as I finally said, "But, can I trust you, Belaize?"

He turned around to face me, finally. I saw his scarred body, injuries old and new, covering his chest. My eyes settled on his harsh gaze. "Never trust your enemy."

"Are you my enemy then?" My voice quavered. I wanted an answer. I told myself that I hadn't come in here with any hopes, but I wanted the cloud of confusion and uncertainty gone from my head.

"I have yet to decide whether I am your friend or foe. I have all eternity to waste in this cell while I choose," he said.

"Time is not a luxury that we have. You could be a wave of hope for everyone. You could help us end the war. You could help me end this war!" I exclaimed. Why couldn't he understand that?

"It's my choice. However weak or entrapped I might be in this godforsaken cell. Tortured. In pain. Or even dead in a ditch. It'll always be my choice, on my own terms. Remember that. I don't want to play fetch with you as my master. And don't assume that's what the Council did, either. I have killed men, women, and children alike. Why? Because I felt like it. I have a certain skillset to offer. The Council recognized that and offered me a good value for it. You have nothing to offer me, and I will not risk going into a battle for nothing worthwhile." His voice was icy cold as he glared at me.

My heart was in shambles. I had entered this cell for answers, but all I had received was disappointment. But why? Was I hoping that he would have changed? I probably was, but I hadn't accepted it.

"B-but... we're mates," I whispered. I felt... guilty. Guilty of a crime which I didn't commit. Bound to the fate our goddess had chosen for us, yet using it to sway his decision selfishly. I closed my eyes. I wished he would say something. Anything. What happens next? Was it possible that I was wrong about him? Was I just so caught up in my own wishful thinking? How he could have changed? Tears threatened to well up from my eyes. Frustration turned to anger, and I wanted to lash out at him.

But before I could, I sensed him coming close to me. Belaize leaned down and touched his lips to mine. For the slightest second, everything vanished. It was just me and him. The briefest, gentlest touch made my wolf flare inside me, eternally excited by our mate. And as soon as it had begun, he stopped.

"Forgive me," he said parting away from my lips. I looked at him. His eyes. His red-rimmed eyes were full of emotion, need, and hurt. He was hurting. He was pushing me away.

"For everything. You deserve someone as kind as you are." His voice was heavy but kind. I... wasn't wrong about him. He was different!

I was stunned by his actions. I lifted my fingers to trace my lips. I felt the lingering heat of his breath against my own. I was bursting with happiness, my knees almost felt weak. Is this what mates feel? I opened my eyes. I looked into his bewitching red-rimmed eyes filled with tenderness. He... could be a different person someday.

A loud rustling outside shattered the illusion of privacy and we both jumped back. The metal door of the cell dragged open and the peace we had was lost.

"You?!" Belaize said with a flash of anger clear in his voice. Belaize immediately went on guard, I felt the shift in him. My wolf's primal instincts urged me to protect my mate. I whirled around and saw Marcus. He was injured. His face was bruised, his clothes were torn and streaked with blood. He was drenched in sweat. Dread came over me.

"Marcus!" I called out, shocked. He looked at me.

"What happened? Why are you here?"

"I looked everywhere for you! It's Adrian!" He screamed, practically frantic. Alver rested a firm hand on his shoulder, trying to stop him from coming further inside. "We were returning with supplies. They attacked us from behind. It was like they'd knew we would be there at that exact time! Adrian, he sacrificed himself to get me out. El- I, Adrian- He-" Marcus stammered.

No! The implications of that statement were... Adrian. *Adrian. No!*

"We have to get him!" Marcus said to me. "Adrian. Shit. El, I have to go. I have to save him."

I looked at Belaize and saw a grim look on his face. "Prove to us we can trust you!" I said to him, pleading. "Help us get him back." His expression didn't change. "Help me!" I said desperately.

"Your friend is dead! Don't throw away your lives for a dead man," Belaize replied coldly.

"You arrogant bastard!" Marcus grabbed him by the throat, shooting daggers with his gaze. "We saved you! Brought you back from the brink of death, the least you could do is help us!" He yelled. I saw his eyes glisten with tears.

Adrian had saved Marcus. He had supported me when I needed him the most. He was our best friend. Adrian was family. I glanced up at Belaize, hoping he was making a cruel joke, but his expression didn't falter. I felt disgusted at myself for ever thinking he could be redeemed.

I held back the tears in my eyes. How could I be so naïve!? It felt as if the kiss was from some different life.

"Listen and listen good! All of you. Your friend is dead!" Belaize bellowed. This wasn't the soft-spoken man from a few moments ago. No, this was the Blood Moon Harbinger.

"If by some grace of the Moon Goddess he is still alive, he is in a state worse than death! I know exactly where he is, but getting him to side with us is next to impossible!" His voice was deep and commanding. It wasn't fear that stopped him from helping, it was this truth, his truth. I felt it sink in with the gravity of his tone. "You can ever so carelessly throw your lives away, however I will not! Your cause demands you stay alive. If you go for him, you will not come back!"

"Where is he?" Marcus said. His resolve did not weaken. "Tell me where he is! Or be damned, you foul creature." Marcus was close to losing it. I had never seen him so emotional. So furious.

"The Low Cities," Belaize said grimly.

THE SEVEN

Marcus

It was almost as if the news did not register in my mind. The Low Cities... the cursed name lingered in my mind as an ever-looming terror.

Why did it have to be him? My mind was a whir of emotion, anger, sadness, and frustration. "Belaize..." I pleaded, knowing with his help this was possible. I wanted to laugh at this absurd fate. I never thought I would wind up in a situation to ask for his help. I was grasping at thin air. Not only did he want no part of this, but he also advised against it.

"No!" he replied coldly. "You'll be a dead and damned fool if you go."

There was gravity in his words; however, they fell short of registering in my mind. Adrian... he was my best friend! My eyes blurred as thoughts of his smile rushed through my mind. We had grown up together in the camp during the war. After Eliana, he was the only family I had.

"Marcus..." Eliana spoke up meekly. I looked at her. I knew she could see my helplessness. "We will find a way," she said. She turned to look at Belaize with a disgusted expression. Belaize simply sat down on his rugged bed. She immediately gripped my hand hard and began walking out of the prison.

"You will die if you go there," he said.

"Better the death of a warrior than the life of a coward," Eliana said with such a chill to her voice that it scared me to my bones. I walked in a daze. My vision was blurred, and my throat felt tight. I felt like I was being squeezed, like I was losing myself. This was it. This was all I could take. My mind was buzzing with thoughts of Adrian when I realized Eliana had led me to her fathers' quarters.

"Father!" she said, announcing her presence as she entered. "Adrian has been captured and sent to the Low Cities." Ronak looked up from his desk and absorbed the information silently. He met her eyes and said the words I was already expecting. "You will not go there. None of you will go there."

"We will mourn his loss, but I will send no one to their death knowing he is in that place." It was as if the weight of the world was crushing me.

"Ronak..." I mumbled. I looked into his emerald eyes, which were full of compassion and empathy, but also a determination. He was an alpha. His decision was final.

"He came for me when I was going to die the death of a fool." My voice was hoarse and full of emotion.

Ronak sighed visibly. He walked up to me and placed a hand on my shoulder. He squeezed gently. "Listen. Son, I miscalculated Belaize's strength when I sent Adrian to get you. I sent him with seven of our best, and only you two came back. He told me that Belaize alone slaughtered all of them like cattle. Remus, who is a Kaiser, and hundreds, if not thousands, of Council guards patrol the Low Cities. I consider both you and Adrian my children, I will not send another one to die in that place. Give me time. An attack on Low Cities is to start in ten days. Please, give me time," Ronak said.

The weight of his words crushed me. He was right. I looked towards Eliana for support; she was tense. She would never speak back to her father when she knew he was right.

"Father, only Marcus and I will go. We would be in and out with no one ever knowing we were there. In ten days, he will be dead. I will not accept that. He will be back with all of us, alive," she said with defiance.

"Don't be foolish, Eliana!" Ronak exclaimed.

As he finished, there were footsteps at the entrance of the tent, and Amae and Romulus entered the chambers as well.

"Marcus," Amae said and touched my bruised face with her fingers. "What happened?" she asked worriedly.

"The Council guards, they captured Adrian and sent him to the Low Cities." Amae's face filled with compassion.

"He is lost, child," she moved her gentle hand to my shoulder.

"But... he came for me! When I needed him!" I yelped. I could feel my face contorting, tightening and twisting into a grimace.

"I'll do it myself!" I said. I rubbed the tears away from my eyes. I was about to storm out of Ronak's chambers when Romulus spoke.

"Stop! You're walking to your grave. You're so callously throwing the life away that Adrian gifted you!" he said harshly.

I looked at everyone in the room. The tension was palpable. We stood in a circle, each warring for control. They were right. But I would never leave him there. "I owe him everything! I will get him, with or without your help.".

"I'm with you, Marcus, he is family," Eliana replied and stood beside me, facing her father.

"Eliana!" Ronak roared.

"No, Father!" she retorted, "You would have come for me if I was trapped in the Low Cities." Ronak went silent. His face fell. He knew he couldn't argue with that.

Ronak cursed under his breath. He was angry, having been challenged in front of Amae and Romulus. He turned to me. "Then you should come back alive," he said coldly and waved us away.

We stepped outside of his chambers, and I turned to Eliana. "El, thank you! But I need to do this alone. You can't risk –" I hadn't even finished the thought when she swung at my face, her palm hit me square on the bruised cheek.

"Shut up! Or I swear to Liunella, I'll strangle you myself," she said. I stood awestruck, rubbing my cheek.

"I... I'm sorry," I muttered slowly. I noticed again how beautiful she was. But she was destined for another. I grew angry at the thought of him. Belaize didn't deserve her. Eliana softened and drew me into her arms, holding me close. "We will bring him back!" she said as she released me and rubbed tears away from my eyes.

Romulus stood before us. He was deadly silent for a man of his size. "The Low Cities," he said. "I can get you inside, however, we'll need a larger team." I was stunned.

"What?" Eliana replied.

"How can you get us in?" I asked him.

"There are some secrets best left unanswered and questions best left unasked, child," he asserted. "Eliana." Romulus took command immediately. "Ask Alver to meet us at the edge of the encampment in thirty minutes." Without another word, Eliana left.

"Marcus." Romulus paused. "People will die, and you will need to kill. Can I count on you?" It was no secret that I avoided killing on missions, but for Adrian, I would go to hell and return victorious.

"Yes!" I nodded immediately.

"Remus calls the Low Cities home, and he might be there," he said.

That would make things a lot harder. I was at a loss. "There is a possibility, however, that he may be in Regvyer with the Council." Romulus finished, but what he said was of little consolation.

"Belaize?" He hesitated. I shook my head. He nodded in reply. "Meet me at the south edge of the encampment, bring rations, and call Luthor!" I nodded.

Luthor was Romulus' disciple. He was strong, but he had no control over his temper. He loved Romulus as a father and would do anything for him. I left to find him.

Almost half hour later, everyone gathered at the south edge of the Sanctuary. There were seven people in the company. Eliana, Romulus, Luthor, Alver, Eric and Armina, the twins, and me. "Listen!" Romulus' voice cut through the anxiety like a hot knife through butter. "Is everyone aware what our mission is?"

"Raid the Low Cities and bring back as many survivors as we can!" Luthor replied. "What I don't understand is why there's only seven of us!"

"Because this will be a stealth mission unlike others. Our primary target is Adrian," Romulus answered.

Realization dawned on Luthor's face. "We are going there to get one man," he said. "Romulus..." He was silenced quickly by the older wolf.

"Silence. Now is not the time." Luthor huffed and turned around.

Luthor had striking gray eyes and a head of bright, fiery hair. He shifted his weight so that his shoulders faced Eliana instead. Alver spoke next. He was the most experienced fighter among the group besides Romulus. "Romulus... does Ronak know?" he asked.

"Yes," Eliana said with a scowl and Alver just shook his head.

"Listen." I finally spoke up. The entire group was split. Everyone knew this was a suicide mission. They radiated nervous energy. "Adrian would have come for any of you! He wouldn't debate whether it was worth it!"

"We have been trying to dismantle the Low Cities for months now, attacking supply lines and disrupting their operations as much as we could. Today, we are going to destroy the Cities, the seven of us can do it.

"Eliana can plan the entire attack once she understands the layout within the city walls. Romulus can get us in without being seen. Eric and Armina are the deadliest killers in our ranks, and there are only few that can match Romulus and Luthor in strength. Alver, your experience is priceless to us in battle. If everyone believes in themselves, we'll succeed. Liunella will do us right!" I said.

Luthor interrupted. "That leaves you! You're useless to us. You're acting out in guilt," he said. "Stay here, and we might bring him back." I couldn't believe what he was saying.

"Luthor, Marcus has courage. Can you say you've gone toe to toe with the Blood Moon Harbinger and lived to tell the tale?" Romulus questioned.

"Hmpph, I've seen that waste of a man. I could pin him with one arm," Luthor said with a cocky attitude.

"Now you might, but the day Eliana and I captured him, he was under the effects of wolfsbane. He was heavily injured. Must have lost a lot of his blood as well. Even in that state, he snapped the neck of a nine-foot wolf as if it were a child."

That shocked everyone. Even I didn't know he was that strong. It was nearly incomprehensible. "Now, we should leave." With those last words, Romulus shifted, followed by the rest of us.

Romulus and Luthor were large, by any standard, but having stood face to face with the monstrosity that was Belaize, they were small.

The other wolves yipped and growled, restlessly. I changed too; it had been some time since I had last changed. My wolf was eager to surface. I touched my arm where Belaize had left a scar. I tested it and stretched. I growled my readiness to Romulus, who took off. The others followed with excited howls.

We ran for hours without a break. When we finally stopped, we were far from the Sanctuary, somewhere in the middle of a forest. Everyone was exhausted from such a long run. Even Romulus was sweating. We changed forms and sat huddled around. We all knew there would be no fire to keep us warm tonight. The forest was cast in dim shadows.

Eric and Armina were on the first watch. The twins sat on guard nearby. They looked exhausted as well, but sat dutifully, back-to-back, scanning the tree line. We had left the safety and comforts of the Sanctuary and were now in dangerous lands. I walked up to their small perch on a log and sat beside Armina. "Thank you!" I said, "For helping us... for helping me."

Armina looked at me curiously. She was a petite woman with soft golden-brown hair. She had amazing eyes, a calming amber, and they graciously complimented her face.

"You don't have to thank us," Eric replied. Armina just stared back at me with her head tilted to the side as if asking a silent question.

"Have you forgotten Marcus? My sister cannot speak." She smiled warmly at me.

By the goddess! I had been away from the Sanctuary for over two years, and when I had finally come back, we hadn't had much of a chance to reconnect.

"I'm so sorry!" My cheeks flushed. Armina's smile reached all the way to her eyes, and she placed a gentle hand on top of mine. That's when I saw it. The scar on her throat. It began just behind her left ear and followed the line of her jaw under her chin, vanishing abruptly before her right shoulder.

I spoke to the twins for a few more minutes before letting them continue their watch. Eliana put a gentle hand on my shoulder. "We will find him," she whispered. "Get some rest, we need you to be top form tomorrow!" she said, smiling. I nodded and took her advice. I chose a tree and sat against it. Slowly, I laid down in the dirt and watched the twinkling stars. Before I knew it, I had drifted off into the realm of dreams.

I woke up few hours later. Dawn was approaching fast. Everyone was stretching, preparing for the last stretch of the journey. Romulus gathered everyone. "We are almost to the Low Cities, be prepared for a fight!" he said and changed into his wolf again. The group shifted with him and took off. The landscape blurred past me as we continued to make our way to the Low Cities.

We had run much further than we had intended, when Romulus caught the scent of a patrol. Luckily, we were downwind and could divert our path. Had we have been upwind, we could have stumbled onto a massive host. The smell of excrement and smoke were rife in the air. Romulus stopped ahead of us. Everyone fell in line.

Romulus changed and said, "Eric, Armina, follow the host downwind and find out what's going on. Why are there so many?" His voice was gruff. The twins took off without hesitation. Romulus motioned for us to keep running. We sped on ahead, hiding away in the trees.

We scouted for another two hours. Every few minutes we would change position because of wind, or patrols, though we never so much as lost sight of the Low Cities. The grey stonework rose tall and proud into the skyline.

The Cities were originally villages situated many miles apart from each other. But as they grew and expanded, they eventually merged into one great, sprawling city. It was a massive complex of stone structures embedded with a clear glass. An enormous watch tower loomed just outside the city walls. It looked like a beacon, declaring, "This is the Council's will."

"We will move under the cover of darkness. But first we must wait for Eric and Armina to return," Romulus stated.

My gaze didn't leave the Cities ahead. *I'll find you, Adrian!* I swore, with determination flowing through my veins.

PURPOSE

Ronak

I sighed as I sat down on the wooden desk in my chambers. My head was throbbing. I rubbed my temples with my fingers. Eliana was going to send me to an early grave. She was too willful for her own good, but that was, perhaps, the Draxus blood in her. When we choose, we commit.

"She is a stubborn child," Amae said. She had folded her small, aging form into the chair beside me. Her hand rested on her temple.

"Yes. I know. She is courageous too, Amae, just like her mother," I muttered with half a smile as silence surrounded us.

My heart was gripped in fear, though. Fear for the life of my child. I knew the fight between my children and the enemy in this war was inevitable, but watching her walk willingly to her death with such a little possibility to make it out alive... I sighed. Sadness clouded my mind, and for a moment, it was hard to breathe. When I closed my eyes, all I saw Eliana smiling, but the image would shift into Adya. I couldn't lose another member of my family.

I felt a hand on my shoulder, pulling me from my thoughts. "Be strong, Ronak. You always knew a day like this would come. You can't always protect your children. Eliana has grown into a beautiful woman who is not only strategic but an exceptional warrior too."

"She will always be my little girl. I don't know what to do now. How do I protect her?" I said, as my voice broke.

Out of the blue, I felt a light smack in my head. I looked at Amae, curious.

"Blood of Draxus, and you're here spouting utter nonsense. It's not your duty to protect her alone anymore. You share that responsibility now," Amae finished as she turned around and walked out of my chambers.

It left me stunned for a moment. She was right. *That old woman was absolutely right!*

I shuffled out of my tent and walked straight to the prison. The last time I saw Belaize was when Amae looked into his mind. I didn't want his help, but for El I would make that sacrifice. Stepping down into the gloomy hallway from the old staircase, I took the keys from the cabinet and sped to Belaize's cell. The door opened with a high-pitched squeak. As I stepped inside, I heard his booming voice.

"I will not help you."

"I need information. What do you know about the Low Cities? When I was on the Council that was not my territory. They have changed drastically since the war, and you know how they work. That is valuable to us," I said. But he just stared at me blankly. His face was cast in deep shadows.

*I'll have to use a different tactic. He require*s *patience, and he need*s *to realize the severity of the situation,* I thought. But as I considered my options, weighing our choices, I heard him speak. "Why should I help you? I am merely your prisoner here. I don't have to help you at all." Belaize huffed as he sat on his bed stoically.

"We both know you are past the point where you can act like that. You don't have anywhere to go. You don't have a purpose anymore. The Council wants you dead. They sent assassins to kill the Blood Moon Harbinger they created. Yes, they failed, but their intention was clear. That is... to eliminate you. I don't know why they made such a decision, especially when you were a great puppet at their disposal."

"I don't know what you did. But what I offer is a purpose. A purpose to fight from the side where you can achieve vengeance on the Council for what they did to you. Don't you want that?" I said with seriousness. Time was running out. The company of seven had already left an hour earlier. *Time was my enemy.*

"What the Council does is none of my concern, Ronak, the wise. If I choose to help you, it'll be on my own terms. I haven't chosen a side yet, and I believe I won't, either. I am done playing with elders and rebels alike." I looked at Belaize. His decision wouldn't waiver.

"The Cities are the center of the Council's power. Two operations take place in the Cities: the breeding program and the training program," I tried again. Belaize's face twisted in a snarl, and it seemed like he was only willing to finish my thought out of spite. He would have the upper hand.

"Let me make it clear, it is brutal. Once you are captured and sent inside, you are good as dead. They maim the wolves alive and use everything that a living person can offer. From the organs to the seed, they are brutal. The place is heavily guarded. There are over one thousand wolves for each watch. I told Marcus it was no use going to rescue one person. They are walking to their deaths," Belaize finished.

My stomach dropped. I slumped against the wall. He was right. He was damned right! Infiltrating the Low Cities with seven people was an act of absolute foolishness, yet I had allowed Eliana to go there. *What if...?* I couldn't even form the thought in my mind.

"I should've been more strict," I said. My words were hollow and soft. "So you see, the mighty rebel leader has a soft will where his family is concerned." I knew he could hear my bitter regret. My next words were more for me than for him. I felt as if I was somewhere else. Somewhere warm and light. "She is just like her mother. Absolutely fearless and full of conviction." A tear slipped from my eyes. I lifted my hand to rub it away and caught Belaize's gaze. He was confused.

"She went with Marcus. Eliana went to rescue Adrian with him." My voice trembled. A change appeared in his stature. A chill surrounded us, pulling me from Adya's memory. If I made one wrong move Belaize would go feral. I was in a cage with a monster.

"You didn't think she would be the one walking to death. That was foolish. She is a Navar, yes, but here is the truth of it--" I mused and scratched my stubble. *Oh Liunella!*

"El would never leave anyone behind. She grew up with both of them, Adrian and Marcus. They have a bond greater than friendship. It's that of a family. You might not understand her perspective, but she would die for any of them. I couldn't have stopped her." I finished. The truth brought me little comfort; hard honesty is like that.

I stepped closer to the entrance and tossed the keys into the far corner of the cell. They landed with a thud. Belaize's gaze was trained on me. I had surprised him. "If you are not on our side, then you are no use to me. You are a waste of space. I don't want an attack by the Council on this Sanctuary because of your presence. Protecting a wolf who isn't even on our side is witless. You now have a choice to walk away or involve yourself in the rebel's cause," I said, and turned around to walk away.

Amae's words echoed in my head, "Have faith." *Oh Liunella, protect my children from harm,* I silently prayed.

Out in the courtyard someone grabbed my arm and yanked me to a stop. Belaize was standing tall beside me. He wasn't as muscular as before. In a few weeks, he would achieve his form again. I knew it.

"Remember, Ronak, I don't owe you anything. I am not doing this for the rebels," he said. I saw fire in his eyes. He wanted blood. My mouth went dry. The monster was free.

I nodded and stepped aside to clear his way. "Liunella gave you a purpose long before you could decide for yourself. Following her, protecting her, is your destiny."

Without a second wasted, Belaize ran into the tree line of the forest surrounding us. A spark of hope bloomed in my heart. *At least she won't be alone.*

BEHIND ENEMY LINES

Romulus

The distant hoot of an owl in the thick forest had everyone on their toes. The tension was palpable. We had been moving around the edge of the Low Cities for over twenty hours now, evading the patrols guarding the castle walls and the outer rim.

It had been decades since I stepped foot in here, but that was still too soon for my liking. I couldn't believe the forces assembled here. There must be thousands of wolves, easily. Maybe so many as tens of thousands. I never could've foreseen these circumstances. That my ass would be on the line because of those impulsive brats.

I glanced at them. Marcus and Eliana sat huddled together nearby. I overheard them whispering to each other. It brought the memories of the trio back into my head, when they would run and play, innocence etched on their faces.

I cleared my throat to gather everyone's attention. "Time to move. It's been two hours now," I commanded. Within seconds, all of them were ready to march.

At every two-hour mark, we had been shifting from our location. It was too dangerous to stay in one spot for long since the patrols were so frequent. Eric and Armina had been gone for an entire day now. I knew everyone was getting agitated, but we had to wait for information. It wasn't the time for us to march inside the Cities just yet.

We walked in a single file in the shadows of the trees along the outskirts of the Cities. The Low Cities weren't located too far from the sea. Just a quick run headed west to reach the immense rocky cliffs that protect the Cities. The Cities are heavily guarded, bound by walls specially made to withstand wars through the ages to come. These had always been Vascya's pride through the centuries, built by famous twin Kaisers in their day.

"We camp here. Stay put," I commanded. And they did stay, but that didn't mean they stopped moving. Marcus was fidgeting like a flea, and Eliana wasn't any better. I thought they could use more discipline, this close to the enemy you don't pace around, snapping twigs, and Liunella knows what else.

Luthor though, he was good stock. He might not be of a bloodline, but he was near as strong as me. And fast, too. Had a quick, angry head on his shoulders, and he knew how to use it in a fight. Could spar with the best of them. Fact is, I'd won a fair bit of coin thanks to his matches. He was one of our best fighters, fucking lethal.

For a normal werewolf, that's a marvelous achievement. He worked hard through the years. Training sessions day and night had made him capable of the most important thing in this war, that's killing. I knew he was itching to get his hands on the Council guards, but he climbed a tree and sat still instead.

We waited around another couple of hours when I noticed them. A rustling in the leaves near our flank. "It is about time," I muttered. Eric and Armina popped up from behind the thicket.

"Any trouble?" I questioned. Eric and Armina both sat down in the dirt beside me, and the rest gathered too. They had returned without a scratch. I leaned against the tree beside me, my hands folded.

"Just a little, but we disposed of the guard quickly. He randomly stumbled upon us. We were hidden, but I believe he'd lost his way. Armina snapped his neck before he knew what was happening. We hid his body far enough so that he won't be discovered soon," Eric said with a sly grin on his face.

"What about the other Council guards?" I asked.

"The host of the army was about two thousand wolves. We followed them discreetly and saw them leave Remus's territory around the Low Cities. I believe they just sent out a new shipment of guards to Regvyer, based on their current direction. Afterwards, we traced our old trail here. We monitored the wall of the Cities, too. They shift the wolves every two hours."

I nodded in agreement. Least that hadn't changed. "The outside batch patrols every thirty-five minutes." This gives us our window to enter. I glanced up at the sky. The sun was high for now, radiating brightly in the sky, with no clouds in sight, but night would fall in about three hours or so. It was time to move.

"Everyone gather around."

I picked up a stick. "Look at this," I said and made two circles enclosed within a larger oval. "I know the Cities, like the back of my hand. Whatever I say, you'll follow that without question. Now, these –" I pointed in the dirt, "-are the Twin Cities and we are here." I marked a point with the stick's end on the left edge.

"This point here is near the western cliffs that bank the Cities." I gestured. "Now, as soon as night falls, we'll move as a group. Be fast, we can't afford to be spotted." I swept my stick in a wide arc towards the cliffs before marking our point of entry. "We'll move in and time it right so the outreach patrol and the guards on the wall aren't around. That's the best possible way," I said.

"I really hope we aren't climbing that wall," Alver piped up from my right side.

"Fortunately, no. We are in luck. Close to a point at the wall, just about here..." I gestured again to the last mark, "There is a small trap door, which will lead us into the heart of the Cities."

"How do you know about it, Romulus?" Eliana inquired. I knew the question was coming soon enough.

"Because... I used to live here." Immediately, everyone's expression changed. Confusion and chaos.

"Wait? How? When?!" I waited for them to quiet down.

"I don't have to answer you. Only thing you need to know is that I grew up here. Just before the start of the civil war, I left," I said. That was the end of it.

"Quiet and pay attention. We will move out in single file. I'll lead, of course, and Luthor you'll be at the end of the line guarding our rear. Rest of you will keep a lookout for guards on our left, right, and on the top of the wall. As soon as we are near the entrance, I'll open the door and we'll be inside. The keynote is not to make any noise. Don't shift unless you are engaged in battle. If any of you get left behind or spotted during the process, well, I won't risk everyone getting captured. So, keep in mind none of us will come to save you. Am I clear?" I looked at everyone. One after another, they nodded in agreement.

I stood up and walked to the edge of the tree line and looked up at the sky.

"Couple hours more. Rest up, it's going to be a long night."

Night had fallen, and the stars glimmered in the sky. A light breeze blew in my face and scents of the forest washed over me. It had been a while since I had been here, and I was feeling a hint of nostalgia. The Cities, the castle, the people, I suddenly missed them all. I shook off the feeling and stood up. "It's time that we hit them hard," I whispered to the night.

Everyone moved instantly and fell in line. Good.

I lead them forward through the dense trees toward the wall. We made a wide, westerly arc and soon the wall was in our sight. The darkness made it look like a black beast swallowing all light. We moved silently through the area. Not even hearing a single crunch of leaves from our footsteps.

Just beyond the tree line, the ground leveled out. Dense, packed dirt with little vegetation lined the wall for maybe a few hundred feet. I spotted few fire-torches aglow high on the wall. "We will wait here," I whispered.

The air smelled of wolves though the stench was an afterthought. I always said, scents tell stories. Seemed like we timed it right and the outreach border patrol had left a few minutes ago. Our window was here.

The last set of wall guards on the left moved toward a down-ramp. During the change of shift and we would have about one minute to cross.

"Now!" I said and started running. I ran fast. The trap door was a couple hundred feet away. I took great mouthfuls of air and sprinted faster. I could hear the others behind me making the same mad dash. One solid line.

Twenty seconds left! I increased my speed. The dirt beneath my feet made it a little hard to gain speed, but it would be enough. I focused ahead and saw the trapdoor. No Council guard could have spotted it, but I knew it like the back of my hand. After all, I had created it.

I was the first to reach the base of the wall. I was breathing fast. Quickly, I pulled up the small iron door on the ground and slid inside. Eliana followed right after me along with the others. Luthor came barreling in last, and I quickly shut the door.

Everyone was heaving. "We did it!" Marcus said. There was a bit too much crazy in his voice for my liking.

"Quiet. We need to move inside. Follow the same order and don't make any noise. Come," I ordered and went ahead.

It was a small tunnel. It barely fit us. My head grazed the irriguous earth above. The tunnel was dark, but I knew the layout perfectly. "Watch your step and don't fall behind or you'll get lost."

We walked for hours in the pitch dark. These tunnels weaved below the Cities, connecting the two. There were entrances almost everywhere, but most had been sealed shut. They were created for quick use to get from one city to another during the war. Few knew about them.

Gradually the dusty tunnel widened. By the time I could finally stand straight my back ached. Later still, the rough ground switched to a smoother, mossy stonework. Finally, we reached the first staircase. "Liunella blessed," I muttered.

I climbed the staircase first. It was long and spiral. The old stone steps were centuries old and worn smooth. We reached a small wooden door. I pulled it open and entered a larger hallway hidden beside a pillar made of white stones.

I waited for everyone to pile out and looked around for any sign of guards. It was quiet here, luckily. "Gather around everyone," I said lowly.

"Marcus, Eliana, and Luthor. All three of you will head out through this hallway. Keep left. By the end, you'll find another staircase. Go down, it'll lead you to the dungeons. There, you'll find prisoners and maybe Adrian."

"Eric, Armina and Alver, you'll hug the right side of the hallway. Go upstairs and start disposing of the Council guards quietly and quickly," I said and then paused for a moment. "Both teams, you are required to create as little commotion as possible, otherwise we won't get out of here alive. Do not underestimate the enemy. Eliana, release the prisoners only after you have cleared the area of the guards." I looked at all of them for confirmation. They nodded silently.

"What about you, Romulus?" Eliana questioned.

"I have some unfinished business. Now, off you go. Stay safe. May Liunella give you strength," I said and watched both groups head off in their designated directions.

I stood for a while, listening for their footsteps. With each passing moment, their presence diminished, and finally I was alone. I sighed deeply and stood up straight. I walked from my hiding place back into the tunnel. Making my way downstairs, I took up a different path than before. I kept walking, taking an occasional turn. Finally, I reached a door. It was wooden and dusty. Light spilled from the small crack beneath. I pressed my hand onto the aged latch and pushed it open.

Light flooded my eyes, and I immediately cast them toward the wooden beams at my feet. It only took a moment for them to adjust to the soft glow.

"Just as I remember," I said with a slow smile as I moved past the hearth. I was in a spacious room, lit with oil lamps. The walls were covered with books. Right in front of me was an age-old desk with a map of Vascya engraved on it.

"You're early." The voice cut through the silence. I dusted myself off and pulled out a chair to sit.

"I know," I responded nonchalantly.

"You weren't supposed to come here for another three months, Romulus," said the man. He moved and sat in front of me, opposite to the desk.

"I know. But I had to deal with the demands of a few brats. So, I had to come," I replied, and folded my arms.

"Really? You jeopardized the entire plan because of some young wolves? I believed you were smarter than that, brother."

"Remus. Quiet now. It's done. I'm here and an attack is going to start on the Cities. You know what you have to do," I ordered.

"Come on! You know I just sent out wolves. I need more time to carry out the plan perfectly. You can't give up on it now!" he yelled as he hit the desk hard.

"Look. Complete your end and secure everything before we attack the Council. I have done my part training the rebels as best as I can. You know we couldn't have waited. We were already short on time, Remus."

He remained quiet and still. I glanced at him. He looked tired. The Council had him working hard. He had to do it, of course, if we ever hoped to eliminate the entire Council and expose the corrupted alphas, and gather the support of those who still favored them. Even with the culling of mates, it was hard to overthrow them all. They had power. Even to get this far had taken decades of bloody effort. I saw Remus's angular face cast in firelight, his brown hair fading to grey. His face reflected a mirror image of mine. After all, he was my twin.

The Low Cities had been in our family since whatever some-such treaty had established it, and whenever twins were born within the family tree, the pair ruled over the Cities. Remus and I had ruled the Cities since we were of age. Until I left to join the rebels and Remus planned to infiltrate the Council ranks to change the fate of Vascya, that is.

I sighed. "Look. The Cities will go down. You should leave now, so that you can remain in the shadows. The Council won't have any reason to question your loyalty. The last stage will start soon, and we will finally get rid of Idaos for good. For now, you should leave."

He thought for a moment then slowly nodded in agreement. He got up to leave the chambers. But before he left the room, he turned to look at me. "It was good to see you, Romulus. Take care," he breathed.

My lips turned to give him half a smile. "I remember how we used to play in this room; father's study. Good ol' days, Remus. Without war, without needless death."

"We'll avenge our father. I promise," Remus said.

"I know," I replied. Remus turned and left me alone in the chamber. The old scent of musk and leather brought memories of a happy past.

My eyes snapped open when I heard the first scream. It was from a distant place, but the shrieking was almost too painful to bare. At last, it had finally begun.

The Low Cities will fall, tonight.

JAILHOUSE

Marcus

I followed Eliana with Luthor behind me. The hallways of the castle were dimly lit. They were wide and spoke to the magnitude of the castle. The stony walls covered with lavish tapestries. It was beautiful. If only carnage wouldn't ruin it all tonight.

As we ran, our footsteps echoed in the corridors, and my heart raced with an adrenaline induced rush at the thought of being caught. That wasn't an option. Turning right at the end of the corridor, we quickly found an entry to a staircase. Stopping for a moment, we stood still and scanned for any movement around us. It was dead silent. We were alone. Luthor was ahead now, looking back at us as he took to the steps. Following him, we descended into the bowels of the castle.

While we descended deeper underground, I couldn't believe the sheer number of steps. I don't know how many hundreds of steps we had covered before we came upon a hallway with several guards and a thick steel door.

"You there! Identify yourself right away!" yelled one of the guards. He wore the typical uniform of a Council guard with an emblem of Vascya etched on the breast.

"Where are the damned prisoners!" Luthor roared. He changed into his wolf. He was big. Well over ten feet tall as a wolf. He growled and ran toward the guards. His size and speed were incredible, which matched his appetite for a fight.

The guards moved out of Luthor's way, dodging his attack. They shifted one by one and out of all six guards, not one could match Luthor's size. Eliana stood beside me, ready to launch an attack. "They aren't attacking us. Look," she said.

I looked closer at the guards. They were hesitant. Luthor's size alone intimidated them. Luthor worshiped strength. He wanted to match Belaize, everyone knew... he had heard of Belaize's tales of gore and glory.

But no matter what Luthor did, he would fall short of Belaize's terror. He lacked the one thing Belaize had, the blessing of Liunella. As Luthor launched his next attack, Eliana followed suit, changing into her wolf as well. Immediately, she ran to attack the guard on the far left.

I watched her leap off of the wall, landing on the shoulders of a guard and taking him to the floor. She bit down on his throat, killing him instantly. By this time, Luthor had already killed three others. He was pinned by the last two. One of them had bitten his arm, holding him down, the other had their claws dug into his chest. I ran forward, pushing my weight into the wolf biting Luthor. He squealed and let go, falling to the side. Luthor used his free hand to break the other wolf's arm.

Eliana watched as I stood above the whimpering wolf.

"Where are your prisoners?" I questioned him. He looked at me, his eyes full of fear. "Where!?" I yelled louder.

"In-inside!" he spat out. Luthor viciously stomped on the poor wolf's chest, caving his ribs. The wolf coughed blood but didn't die, and just curled up on the floor in pain.

"Suffer," Luthor said and walked onward.

I stared at him, watching him writhing in pain. "P... p... plea... please," he begged. I watched him bleed out on the floor. For a moment, I wanted to help him.

"Marcus!" Eliana yelled, pushing me forward and pulling me out of the trance. She pushed her claws into his chest and ended his misery. She shot me a dirty look that would have stopped a bear in its tracks. Eliana would kill me if I wasn't in my best form. She turned and ran up ahead of me. I followed her through the door.

We entered a cavernous expanse lit sparsely by torches. However, no guards were in sight. Maybe they thought no one could infiltrate this deep into the Cities. The area was littered with thousands upon thousands of cells. I couldn't believe my eyes. The rows of cells looked infinite. The screaming and howls of wolves were deafening. The smell of feces made me gag. It was so awful that my eyes were watering.

I glanced at Eliana, and she was shaken up as well, nearly keeled over. After a few moments, I noticed each cell had a lever controlling the door. "Luthor. Start pulling these." I motioned and pulled the first one with both hands. Within seconds, he was several cells ahead, flipping every lever he could.

"Follow his lead!" I told Eliana and started unlocking from the other side.

It had been well over an hour, and we had opened hundreds of cells. The people were hesitant to leave the cells, initially. Many cowered inside and refused to come out. Those who did were hesitant to leave the long alley of cells. Others had attempted to run away, but were stopped by the more sensible wolves. "Listen, if we run, we will get caught. These people that freed us got in without raising the alarm. We should follow their instructions," one of them shouted.

Eliana stopped and turned to me. "I'll get these people out. Go ahead and look for Adrian, Marcus. Bring him back," she said fiercely and started giving out instructions to the prisoners. She exuded strength and dominance, and quickly the crowd calmed. She looked like a prophet of Liunella, caught by firelight, and standing above the writhing mass of emaciated, maimed wolves.

I kept pulling the levers and opening the cells, ushering men, women and children toward freedom. My arms ached, my back was knotted with strain. It seemed to take ages, and I was certain that, at any moment, the alarm bells would sound and we would be caught. That kind of tension changes you. It makes you alert, desperate, and deeply focused. *This,* I realized, *this is why we fought.*

Luthor was nowhere in sight. I was getting frantic. I couldn't stop worrying about Adrian.

I heard a commotion behind me where I had left Eliana. *Time was up.* But I kept moving ahead and suddenly crashed into Luthor at an intersection between the cells. We both were panting. "That side is done," he muttered. Before I could answer, I heard a loud scream.

"The guards," he said, cursing under his breath. "I'm going to help Eliana, keep opening cages," he said and dashed in the direction we had come.

I did as he instructed; I opened cell after cell. Yet Adrian was nowhere to be seen. Anguished screams and desperate howls filled the corridors behind me, echoing, amplifying. This was a nightmare. I stepped up to a cell and flipped the lever. "Damn it, where the fuck are you, Adrian."

Suddenly, my wolf perked up and stood at attention. This scent! It was him.

"Adrian!" I yelled, running into the cell at the far end of the dungeon. I saw him huddled in the corner. He was covered in feces and blood.

"M... M... Marcus?" His voice faltered. He looked dazed, puzzled. As he slowly lifted his head from the cradle of his hands, I saw a deep gash on the side of his head. His nose was broken, and both eyes were so purple and swollen I wasn't even sure he could open them. He was barely conscious. They had tortured him.

"We came for you!" I said urgently. "We need to leave. Come."

He mumbled something deliriously. "Marcus?" he said again. I leaned down and tried to lift him up, but Adrian started vomiting black bile onto the floor. He was under the heavy influence of wolfsbane. Anger flared inside my heart. I wanted to lose myself in a blind rage. I wanted to tear apart the cowards who had done this to him. My family. But I beat back the urge. I wiped his mouth and eased him to his feet.

"I'm here for you, Adrian. I'll get you out of this hell."

He was delirious and his head lulled to the side. "Come on, we have to leave," I said to him, lifting him on my shoulders.

"L... low...er... lev...el." he muttered.

"What?"

"What is in the lower level?" He wasn't making any sense. Did he mean that there were more wolves inside?

The commotion had grown into an uproar now. I heard the groans and screams of those that were fighting. I left the cell with Adrian on my back. Together we were going to leave these hellish dungeons.

"Marcus!" Eliana shouted as she found me. She was panting and her arm was covered in streaks of blood.

"We need to leave, the guards, they're overwhelming us," she barked. Glancing at Adrian, she cursed, "Oh Liunella."

"I need to check something, take Adrian and run!" I said.

"But Marcus we need to get out,"

"Just trust me. Take him and go! Make sure he reaches the Sanctuary alive, please Eliana. I think more wolves are trapped, I need to go find them. Don't waste time!" Then I pushed Adrian in her arms.

She nodded reluctantly and changed into her wolf to compensate for the added weight. I turned around and ran deeper into the dungeon. We were going to get everyone out of this godforsaken place!

I ran as hard as I could, my legs pumping hard. My wolf was excited. I couldn't tell why. I turned a corner and saw a staircase. That must be the lower level. Without wasting a second, I continued downward for several minutes. I was deep under the city now. The place smelled of dread and death.

My lungs burned and I had to slow down to a cautious walk. I was drenched in sweat, bile rising in my throat. It was darker here. Fewer torches lit the area. There weren't any cells. Just a long, stony hallway. When I reached the end of the hall, I saw two doors distinct from the darkness. Beside one was carved a name.

I walked closer to it. It was a wooden door etched with the intricate design. It was beautiful and ominous at the same time. "Janus Deathbringer." I read.

I opened the door and my wolf immediately tensed. He was nervous, almost cowering. The room was unnaturally lit. There were no torches yet the room was aglow with haunting light.

The room wasn't large, but it was nowhere near small. There were four pillars that surrounded a sarcophagus. "This is a tomb..." I said aloud. The room echoed with my voice, almost as if offering a confirmation.

My wolf was more nervous now than ever. What was this fear I felt? I studied the sarcophagus. It was scrawled with several winged beings. I didn't know what they were. In the center of the stone sarcophagus was a pebble sized stone that glowed brighter than Liunella herself. It surged with magical power. I lifted my hand to touch it, but before I could, a surge of power shocked me. As the shock coursed through me, it registered. What this thing was. A stone from the Astral Realm.

But how?

The stone called to me, but I resisted its urge. I backed away from the tomb. An eerie breeze, like the sighing of a beast, swirled the layers of dust along the floor. I heard it call me. "Bboyy," the voice whispered.

I jumped and growled. I swiveled around as if to catch the maker of that voice. My head jolted to each corner of the room. There was nothing there. Nothing but darkness. Nothing but for the door that I had come in from.

"What is your name, boy?" the voice said again. It chilled me to my bones. "Come here. You can be my puppet." The voice whispered. I bared my teeth in a snarl.

The room grew colder and darker. My wolf whimpered and cowered. I willed myself to run. And somehow, my feet obeyed. I ran for the door as the darkness closed in.

"Don't leaveeeeeeee." The voice whispered as I ran through the door.

My heart pounded loud and fast in my chest. *What was that?* My mind screamed. That's not possible. My mind tried to rationalize what happened. Yet, I could not shake this feeling of dread. The door to the tomb shut hard, splintering the wood and cracking the frame. The floor under me vibrated as I heard a loud crash coming from inside the room.

Before I could so much as blink, I was at the far end of the hallway, crouching in the safety of the stairs. I gathered air into my lungs and leaned my head against the stonework. I closed my eyes. After a few moments, my body felt like mine again. My mind was no longer gripped by icy fear.

But here, alone in the hallway, my wolf stood at attention once more. He was adamant that we were not to leave, that we check the last door. I couldn't so much as move closer to the stairs. The fighting above was a distant memory, now. My world did not extend beyond the shape of that door. So, I went. And I opened it.

There were around fifteen cells surrounding the perimeter of the room. A singular desk sat in the center.

I heard shallow breathing. For a second, I thought that the entity had followed me here. I turned around quickly and saw nothing. The cells were occupied, I realized.

I looked inside the cell closest to me. The small, huddled form inside was not moving. Not at all. This person was dead.

They weren't the only ones, either. I checked more cells, and one by one found the decaying bodies of more wolves.

I had to get anyone who was still alive out of here!

I flipped through the papers on the large mahogany desk. "Project Bloodmoon." I read aloud. I looked through the document. It detailed notes and drawings of the gruesome methods of torture and subjugation used on these wolves. Flogging, whipping, starving, insertion- I slammed the pages back on the table. What the hell is wrong with these people?

With cold fury I realized that *this* was the Council. Sick, twisted beings lusting for power. I could not fathom how this was possible. How could they not see this cruelty and not do everything in their power to destroy it? How could they hurt others so callously? Monsters. Every single one of them.

I looked at the pages again, and I turned to the end. The last few pages were an appendix that alluded to some kind of key... another document. I moved to open the page. It detailed the process on how... Belaize was turned into a killing machine.

I couldn't believe it. A method of creating weapons. No... turning wolves into weapons. No remorse, no fear. Just killing and bloodlust. The Council was conducting experiments on its own people. Belaize was never given the decency of humanity. He was used like a tool.

"You there...," said a feminine voice. "You're no guard." I grabbed the handful of papers and stuffed them inside my jacket. I turned to one of the cells and saw a woman standing there, leaning against the bars. My eyes went wide and my heart beat loud. Her eyes went wide. A bitter expression covered her face.

"A weakling like you?" she said, and my heart sank. "Liunella insults me."

"I'm more powerful than you know," I said instinctively. I couldn't believe that of all places in the world, I'd meet my mate here.

"Hmmph, you're weak, I can see it in your face." My wolf roared to the surface, growling, asserting its dominance.

"I'm shaking," she said sarcastically. "Get me out, now." My wolf roared.

"Release me!" she said. The dominance in her voice was clear and my wolf obliged. The mate bond had formed and I knew I would never deny her, be it a request or an order. My wolf retreated, and I felt humiliated.

"Erylesia?" said a voice from another cell.

"I won't leave you, Beryl. We will have our revenge on the Council," she said with conviction.

"No. I- My end is near. Let me go in peace, Erylesia. You still have strength left. You will survive. The rest of us never had the conviction," Beryl said, his voice weak.

"You," Erylesia said pointing at me, "Help me carry him out, I can't because of the wolfsbane," she said, averting her eyes. Her cheeks flushed at the words. Not with a subtle blush, either. They were the molten color of fury... and humiliation. *At weakness,* my wolf explained.

I immediately went inside the cell beside hers. The old man was barely conscious. He was light, and frail, but quite tall. Without a word, I carried the man in my arms.

"The rest?" I said, glancing at the bodies inside the cells.

"They have passed on," Erylesia said coldly. I nodded but she had already turned away, walking out of the godforsaken place.

I followed Erylesia as she expertly navigated through the corridors. It was a long, terrible, silent walk. I was careful not to shift the man in my arms. My mind drifted to my companions. I had faith in Eliana. I hoped Luthor, too had made it out of the jail.

We followed the narrow passage until it expanded into the cavernous hall filled with cells. The floor was red with blood. Prisoners and guards alike lay dead or dying. The foul stench of urine and shit almost made me vomit. I held my breath as we quickly passed through the alleys. There must've been over five dozen dead and several dozen more dying.

I suddenly felt an astral distortion on a scale I had only ever felt when Belaize shifted. I looked for the source and my gaze settled on Erylesia. *Impossible! Could she?* It was unheard of.

As we made out of the dungeons, light flooded from the staircase. Bodies of several Council guards littered the steps.

"Marcus!" I heard Eliana scream as she burst into view in tow with Adrian on her back. A look of relief passed over her face.

"Hurry, we have to leave! It's chaos outside." She turned and ran. I turned back to Erylesia, whose face was twisted in a silent curse.

She couldn't change, but that astral distortion showed her monstrous strength. That's when I saw it, two white streaks in her dirty black hair. *Impossible!* My mind swam with confusion. There were no female Kaisers, there had never been, but she so clearly exhibited the signs.

Erylesia caught me looking at her. "Let's go!" she said. I followed her. Running up the stairs with the man on my shoulders was hard, even as a wolf. The sheer number of steps was fucking ridiculous. It took us over twenty minutes of constant climbing to reach the top. The screaming was dreadful. Smoke was in the air, and fires dotted the Cities, glowing in the darkness of the night.

We rounded a corner onto a large balcony. The view allowed us a complete picture of the Cities from above. The fires we saw were small, but the surrounding courtyard filled me with horror. Hosts of guards rallied in the courtyard. There must have been three hundred of them, with more spilling out on streets and houses.

"Keep running, don't stop!" Erylesia yelled.

"This... this is hell!" I said as a group of prisoners stumbled into the courtyard and were butchered immediately.

I was a fool to think the seven of us could pull this off.

TRAPPED

Eliana

The loud crash at the corner of a hallway made me jump back. I turned to the side, immediately dodging the Council guard that aimed to pounce on me. My wolf felt the urgency of the situation. Adrenaline pumped through my veins. My leg muscles were shaking as I moved quickly and slammed him hard into the guard. The momentum of me and Adrian together helped me topple the guard over.

He fell hard on the stone floor, whimpering. But he got to his feet within seconds. I had just enough time to put Adrian down, thankful that he was now unconscious, otherwise the pain would've hit him much harder. The guard's gray wolf was bigger than me. He curled his lips, baring his sharp canines, ready to attack me. These Council guards were always a pain.

I lowered my shoulders into a defensive stance. I felt my heartbeat resounding in my ears. I scanned the enemy. He was waiting for me to attack. "Come on, bitch." He growled.

"You'll regret that," I said and ran toward him. I pushed my body forward with force and swiftly slid past his right side. He was expecting a head-on attack and was slow to adjust. I jumped on his back, slamming him down on the floor, pushing my claws into his neck.

Warm blood splattered on the floor as he tried to get away from me. I had severed his windpipe. He wouldn't live long and would die in agony. He choked on his blood, making horrid gurgling sounds as I stood up. The freed wolves were behind me and saw the dead body at my feet.

I moved quickly to Adrian. I had left him at the corner of the hallway, but he now laid sprawled on the ground. "Fuck," I cursed. I waited a moment, taking a deep breath. I opened my eyes, focused. We were now in the last leg of our mission. We needed to get out. Fast.

I lifted his heavy body up again and began running down the corridor. Marcus, Luthor, and I had released countless prisoners from the cells. I had directed most of the women and children in one direction and ordered those who were capable of fighting to protect those who were weak. Those prisoners were a part of the rebellion now, and they were our comrades.

The Council guards were overpowering the Twin Cities. The sheer number at which the Council had bred soldiers to control Vascya was unbelievable. They had no remorse or guilt for killing us.

As I rounded a corner, I saw a group of freed prisoners staggering down the hallway. They were holding each other up, but making slow, desperate progress. Each prisoner was smeared with dirt and grime, their cheeks stained with tears. When I reached them, I said, "It's alright friends. We will make it. Just keep moving. I will cover you." They gave me nothing but gasping sobs in response. I felt each second inch by, their movement was slow, but I would die before I left any one of them.

The courtyard was enormous. The vast expanse was lush green and littered with fountains shaped in the form of wolves. I don't think I had ever stood in a place so... pristine. But that wasn't what surprised me. The Council guards in front of the gates made me shake in fear.

Dozens and dozens of guards were all armed, armored and ready to attack. We must've been outnumbered thirty to one. I saw a wolf giving orders in the center. He was snarling at them, and they rushed to meet his demands, compiling into small clusters of strike teams. They were planning to retake the city and capture us.

That wasn't an option. Our failure. I couldn't afford to be captured in this place.

My mind was racing with all the possibilities to take them down, but it was impossible. I was alone with a wounded Adrian and handful of prisoners who were already exhausted from the torture they had suffered.

We were too few. Even though I had released over a thousand prisoners, they all were scared, weak, and scattered. We didn't have an effective plan. We were just desperate and unorganized. And with so many guards, it would be next to impossible to defeat them. I couldn't hide here and wait for more rebels to show up. That's not an option either.

Time was ticking fast. I glanced at the wolves who were with me. They were panting. They had suffered and after giving them hope of freedom, I couldn't disappoint them. The best course of action would be to leave this courtyard right now. I turned to whisper the message to the rebels, but stopped midway.

The ground under my feet vibrated with great force. I glanced immediately at the guards. *Maybe it was one of their tricks*, I thought. But they were surprised too. They didn't know what was happening either! The guards were shouting at each other, their leader screaming at them to maintain order, to stand their ground, but some were fleeing. Running away in fear. *Cowards.*

I quickly glanced around trying to find the source of the vibration. It was coming from the middle of the courtyard. Something was wrong. I looked more keenly and saw the ground was boiling upward like some bulging mass was pressing up from below. But why?

More than half the guards had run away, and those who remained looked at the shaking center of the courtyard with morbid curiosity. Suddenly a pillar about fifteen feet high erupted from the ground. Great piles of earth and bush spilled outward as if caught in an explosion. Soil fell on us like rain. The freed prisoners cowered and prayed.

I examined the pillar as best as I could in my partially hidden state. I didn't want to attract any attention to our little group. The pillar was made of steel and had several hundred holes embedded on its surface.

Not a moment passed when the pillar began rotating. With a loud thud, an arrow landed right in front of me. I immediately jumped back, shielding the others behind me. What in Liunella's name was happening?

I shifted to the side to get a better look while ushering others to stay behind. I saw the carnage in front of me. The pillar was shooting arrows with such speed that they were piercing the Council wolves straight through.

Their neat ranks had completely dissolved. The guards had quickly turned on each other, pushing and shoving in a mad dash to flee. Arrows rained down and screams filled the night. Blood and bile and worse soaked the earth. They were slipping in it, stumbling, and screaming as they ran.

But how!? What is happening? Then it clicked in my mind. The guards didn't know about this. Or the tunnels. This was another one of Romulus's secrets. I silently prayed to Liunella. Maybe she wanted us to succeed after all. Within another two minutes, the courtyard was piled with just dead bodies. Those who were alive were maimed by the arrows and struggling weakly.

A great stillness overtook the courtyard, and only then did I finally move from my spot. Adrian almost slipped from my grip, but I clutched him tightly. When the pillar stopped rotating, I gestured for the others. Slowly we made our way through, killing the guards who survived the onslaught of arrows. A small mercy. We had to get out of the castle now. May Liunella let them rest in peace.

Romulus had not prepared us to roam the streets openly. This city was a fucking maze. Fires were spreading fast, and people were fleeing with what little they could carry. It was complete chaos everywhere. I let my wolf guide me and soon the outer gate yawned before us, wide open.

"Get out of here. I will stay. Go! go! go!" I yelled and pushed the wolves out.

"Thank you," one of them said and ran away with others, out of my sight, into the burning hell.

I spotted Alver and Armina at the gates. He was directing the prisoners forward, out of the castle. I let out a sigh of relief and then pushed forward. Armina rushed towards me, grabbing Adrian's arm, lifting him up. Alver came forward too and slapped Adrian's face a few times. Adrian's eyes flickered open. "El..." he muttered.

"You are safe," I said. We'd done it. Marcus and I- No, the seven of us had rescued him.

"Armina will take him back to the Sanctuary. He is in a bad shape, Eliana," Alver said.

I nodded. *At least he is alive*, I thought. "I'll make sure everyone has escaped." I ran through a series of alleys, killing six guards in the process. My mind was shut off from any emotion. I killed without a second thought.

I was fighting one of the guards in an alley when someone pushed me. I fell hard to the ground. I forced myself to open my eyes and the only thing I saw was trouble. Nine wolves had surrounded me, and they were growling nastily.

I glanced around and saw that I had ended up in a secluded lane with no rebels in sight. I silently cursed.

One of the nine wolves attacked me first. I was on the floor but I dodged his attack. *I'll have to defeat all of them.* Romulus had trained me to fight for this day. I would not let him down. I am an alpha, and this was my battlefield.

I took a deep breath and analyzed my opponent. I couldn't take them all at once, but I could take them one by one. I formulated a plan in my head.

Only execution was left.

Another wolf came at me. I dodged this one again by sliding to my left and popping up to my feet. As he slid by me, I dug my claws in his throat, and instantly, the wolf fell on the ground whimpering, blood staining.

One down, eight to go. The Council guards were wary of me now. This wasn't going to be an easy fight, and they knew it. It was a mistake to underestimate me. It would cost them their life. They had made a circle around me, entrapping me. *This would not do*, I decided.

The next wolf tried to attack me. I ran toward him with force and speed. My claw ripped his heart out. I shoved his body aside and ran, breaching through the circle. I had to get away.

I ran as fast as I could. I sensed that they were getting close at my heels. I had only bought myself a second at most. Even with my speed, they could keep up. They weren't the Council guards I was used to in the field, these had experience. They were veteran soldiers. They were able to match rebel warriors. The thought filled me with dread.

I pushed my legs harder, running through a maze of hallways. Suddenly a guard took a massive leap forward. He caught my left foot and we tumbled to the ground. Shit! I fell and gasped in pain as white spots flickered across my vision.

My eyes teared up as I tried to stand. I had broken a rib, I could feel it tug sharply at my skin with each breath. Not only that, I felt dizzy. The strength was leaving my body. That only meant one thing, Wolfsbane. By the time I was on my feet, I was circled by even more guards. They were about fifteen in number. They were growling. They wanted blood. My blood.

"I want this whore," growled one of them. He came forward, flanked by four more guards.

"Fight fair bastards. Four guards for one she-wolf? Is this the might of the Low Cities?" I taunted, as I tried to find a way out. But I found none. I had no other choice but to fight.

I'll fight with my dying breath. "Who the fuck cares about 'might'? Right now, I'll break your bones and make you suck my cock. Your pretty little mouth looks empty without one. We don't care for shit about honor. Your mouth won't be used for lovely words, so shut up." He laughed gruffly and came forward step by step.

I was doomed. He lunged his claw at me. The pain was blinding and I couldn't dodge as swiftly as I would have before. His nails grazed my arm. Blood soaked my fur. The other four attacked me simultaneously. Somehow, I managed to get away, but with their onslaught, I was tiring by the minute. I was bleeding. I was covered in bruises and scrapes.

One of the wolves slammed his body over mine and I fell. I couldn't get up. Three wolves held me down.

The wolf from before laughed as I tried to get away from them but to no avail. I could see torture and death in front of me now. *This is what happens when you dare enter the Low Cities*, I thought. *You lose. You die.*

As the wolf wrestled on top of me, his ragged breath nauseated me. My wolf tried to get away but she couldn't. She hated this feeling of being powerless. She wanted to kill each one of these wolves.

My life flashed through my eyes. Maybe this was the end. My father, my brother, Amae, Marcus, Adrian, Romulus, and lastly Belaize. His sleeping form in the Infirmary came into my mind as I squeezed my eyes shut and the wolves held me down.

My wolf howled and screamed with one thought directed towards our mate. *Belaize*! We screamed in agony as the Council guards began their torture.

PROTECT

Belaize

It had been several hours since I had left the Sanctuary. I was out of breath, sweat soaked completely through my clothes. It ran down my face in streams, my hair bunched together.

"Damn this," I cursed. My wolf wouldn't stir. I had tried changing countless times, but my wolf wouldn't turn. It was trapped.

I had to run fast. The Low Cities were about half a day run from Regvyer. From the Sanctuary, the distance just increased. I couldn't help but wonder about Eliana. They were ahead by a few hours; however, they could run at almost five times my speed. They could change, and I couldn't.

The foolish she-wolf had run along with Marcus to the Low Cities to die. *How moronic was she!?*

But how stupid am I? I thought as I avoided tumbling over some shrubbery. I was running after her to what, possibly, might be my death as well. I grunted and kept moving forward. I would have to stop soon. The thought disgusted me as I panted heavily. In this state I was just a scrawny, uncoordinated mess.

I had to stop when a cough bubbled in my throat as I heaved to catch my breath. Spitting on the ground, I held myself up with my hands on my knees. *So fucking weak.*

Water. I needed water. I began following my nose. There wasn't any water nearby, but I did smell fire. Fire and excrement. I sensed a large hunting party close by. I let the scents completely wash over me. No, I decided. It was larger than a hunting party. It took me almost thirty minutes to find the trail of the massive host. There must have been over two thousand people. It was a shipment. Fresh meat for the Council.

I snuck around to the side and merged inconspicuously into the massive camp. Wolves were pacing about setting up tents and stacking firewood. They jested and hollered amongst themselves as I found my way into a supply tent. There were barrels of food. Raw meats, fruits, and vegetables. I dug into the barrels and took large bites of food. I scarfed down my fill, enough for ten, and drank till my belly was full.

Once I had finished eating, I began looking for fresh clothes in a nearby supply tent. It took several minutes of stumbling around before I found it. There were several soldiers inside. I took the risk of being spotted and I walked in. No one paid attention. Why would they? Who would dare to come inside their tents?

I found a chest full of clothes and picked out the largest size they had. I tore the sleeves off and slipped into it. I let my breeches drop to the floor. I put on the longest set of pants too. They were short by a few inches but they would make do. A few weeks ago, my body wouldn't have fit into a simple soldier's uniform, yet they hung loose around my frame. Weak. I had grown weak.

I turned and gestured to one of the recruits. "The armor, where is it?" I asked. He waved his hand carelessly, "The tent with the big Vascyan insignia," he said.

I nodded and left. As I left the tent behind, I smelled something I had not smelled for decades.

Are they here? I followed my nose toward the end of the camp. A pasture was ahead and I couldn't believe my eyes. Horses! A few dozen of them. All geared and tied sporadically to the makeshift fence. They were massive stallions that could only have been bred for war. I had seen a few in the Low Cities when I lived and trained there. The Council was breeding them and they were successful.

Horses had gone extinct ages ago. Never have I encountered one in the wild. I could use them to get to the Low Cities faster. Glancing around, I saw no one was guarding the horses either. The Council guards was overestimating their strength and numbers.

Quickly, I crossed the pasture and leapt over the makeshift fence. I approached a large black stallion, his mane swooping to the side of his graceful neck. He was powerful. His muscled body was proof enough of his strength. And he knew I was powerful too. I approached cautiously. I stepped closer to him and rested a hand on his neck. He used his body to drive me away, creating space between us. His nostrils flared and I could see the steam of his breath.

I smiled widely. He was a proud creature. I stepped closer again, and before he could move away, I grabbed the reins tightly in my hand. The stallion skittered back, but only so far as the rope would allow. I stepped forward, placing a hand on his head, clutching his lead harder. "Calm down." I growled lowly. We looked on one another, then. I met his great, glassy stare and he met mine. Taking my measure. He let me approach. I stroked his head lightly. "You're a powerful one."

"I dub you, Midnight!" I spoke aloud. He neighed in approval. The black horse reached around and touched my hair with his muzzle. I untied his lead and reached up, gripping the saddle. He was big.

I lifted my foot, and stabbed it at the stirrup, missing the first time. The second time I got it right, and laboriously hauled myself up, but the saddle spun around and I fell hard on my backside. *Oh Liunella.*

I stood up again, dusting myself off. I held the saddle in position and found the buckle was loose. I retied the belt around Midnight's abdomen. Holding onto his saddle, I hauled myself up, my foot resting in one stirrup and then the next. Finally, I had mounted the beast.

He was strong! Exceptionally strong if he could carry me. He didn't buckle or falter from the extra weight. For a moment, Midnight didn't move, taking deep breaths and standing tensely. He turned his head and looked questioningly at me. His brown eyes waiting for a command.

"Let's go." I held his reins firmly in my hands. Midnight didn't move. I cautiously kicked the horse's flank with my heels. Startled, the creature took a few quick steps forward, and then relaxed into a steady gait. There was a rocking motion, yet I found it difficult to balance. Midnight's head bobbed in time with his feet. He took a deep breath and let out a loud fluttering noise.

I pulled back on the reins just so, putting pressure on his bit, and Midnight responded by moving faster. Bumpier. I bounced along with him. With each step, I jolted in danger of being thrown off, and Midnight's ears went up. He went faster, and in a fraction of a second the bumping stopped. The motion was smooth, almost weightless. I found myself smiling abruptly.

I snapped the reins hard, and Midnight took off in a strong gallop.

"Hey! You! Where are you going?! Stop!" I heard someone yell from behind me. I didn't bother looking back as his shouts melted in the swift wind. Midnight and I leapt over the fence and disappeared into the forest.

The wind streamed by me, whipping Midnight's long mane back in my face. His head was up, his ears forward. He was gaining speed. Midnight was incredibly fast and powerful for a horse his size. He vaulted over rocks and logs with ease.

Wind tugged at my dirty hair. The ground rushed by me, and the only sound was the pounding of hooves against the forest floor. I kept a strong grip on the reins. I was balanced on something a mere foot wide, hurtling forward faster by the second. The Low Cities were far. Even with Midnight by my side, it would take too long to reach the Cities.

Riding a horse was harder than I thought. The constant motion chafed my inner thighs brutally. I was constantly aware of my position otherwise I would slip sideways, and Midnight had taken pleasure in the moments I was thrown off once or twice, until I got used to it. I squeezed both legs tightly in an effort to stay with the horse. A few hours later, when I was certain I wasn't being followed, I slowed down considerably.

"Easy Midnight." I patted his neck softly. He was an intelligent creature. He knew my commands, and instantaneously he had accepted me as his master. As the thought completed itself, he swung his head back in protest.

"Easy!" I called as he bucked again in defiance. It was as if he could read my mind.

"Fine, I'll consider you my partner," I said stroking his neck. I dismounted him as he came to a stop. My world tilted with vertigo as I stumbled away. Slowly, my vision evened out and I took the opportunity to stretch. My muscles, especially my backside, throbbed with pain. I took a step forward and wobbled and groaned. Fuck, reaching the Low Cities would be painful. But Eliana's face flashed in my mind. I tried changing again, straining against whatever held me, yet nothing happened.

Midnight was glistening with a white sheen of sweat. He was panting hard. I did my best to wipe him down, and then I guided him to the small stream nearby. Before he could drink his fill, I pulled him away. Too much water too quickly would tire him, I knew that much.

A few miles later the stream flowed into a small alcove. It created a small waterfall that fell several feet into a pool of water. The pool of water further drained into a small pond, and the pond into a small lake. It was a beautiful, serene sight. I spotted a few herbs that were used to mask body odors.

I considered tying Midnight off but he had protested before I could make much of the thought. He grazed while I washed my clothes with a small rock, easing the dirt and grime from them. I hung them dry on a low hanging branch close by. I looked at my reflection in the rippled water. I couldn't even recognize myself. I wondered who the last few weeks had made me. I wondered if I was a person at all, if I was anything more than what had been done to me, what had been taken. Who am I? I asked myself.

But the answer never came.

"Death," I mused. But the word felt empty.

I was deep in thought when I felt a shove and I splashed into the water. I got up soaking, water flowing off my body in tiny rivulets. I looked angrily onto the shore and saw Midnight standing where I stood.

"You mangy beast!" I called with a laugh and proceeded to wash myself. He was a loyal creature. My laugh surprised me. I couldn't remember the last time I had laughed with such carelessness. Bloodlust and murder were my life. But... something had changed since the Astral Realm.

I finished washing myself, the first true bath I had had in weeks. I felt refreshed and energized. My thighs were burning still from riding, yet the bath had subdued the pain for the moment. I walked out of the lake and patted Midnight. "Next time, I'll push you into the water," I said.

I checked on my clothes that I had left to dry. They were still damp. I walked off into the woods naked, searching for some scented herbs. It was a few minutes before I found them. I crushed them in my hands and rubbed some on my armpits. I sniffed, satisfied, I decided to head back to the lake.

As I got closer, I heard Midnight neigh in distress and immediately ran toward the sound. He was struggling with something. I burst through the tree line and onto the shore. I spotted two she-wolves fighting to hold onto Midnight's reins. He yanked his head back and they slipped from their hands. He reared onto his hind legs, neighing loudly and ready to hit them.

The two women cowered back in fear. I hadn't sensed them till I was much too close. I had grown weak. So fucking weak that even my senses had dulled. Weeks in a dark prison cell with my wolf refusing to come to the surface. It had taken a toll on my body.

"Midnight," I yelled.

He thundered backward at the sound of my voice. His stance was defensive and uneasy, his nostrils flared, but he stood towering next to me.

"What do you want?" I asked them.

They were intimidated by my size. The woman who I presumed to be the eldest looked me up and down. Her eyes wide with disbelief. It was then I realized that I was naked. As bare as I was the day I came into the world.

I growled and turned for my clothes. I took my breaches and slipped into them. "Tell me, what do you want?" I said impatiently.

"W... what is that?" The elder one hesitated and pointed at Midnight. I looked at the two of them. The younger one was cowering behind the elder. Siblings perhaps.

"That's a horse. Council breeds them. I wouldn't imagine you have seen one," I said gruffly. The women were in awe, no one had seen a horse in the wild for decades. Who knows what else the Council has been up to?

"You have the red-rimmed... You're Belaize? Aren't you?" the elder woman questioned. I was surprised she knew who I was and hadn't run at the sight of me.

"What of it?" I replied.

"The rumors are that you were killed by Faust," she said nervously. "Other rumors say you deserted the Council..." She trailed off.

"I'm not dead, now, am I?" I replied coolly. "Nor did I desert their ranks. I was betrayed by the Council."

Why was I telling this woman anything? Why did it matter? I rolled my eyes. She took a deep breath, as if to gather some confidence.

"Were you in a vicious battle?" she questioned again. The other girl stayed back. She caught me looking at her and hid further behind the woman.

"Is she a half-wit?" I inquired, gesturing towards the younger woman.

"No, she is not," she said sullenly. "She is.... she is a casualty of this war," the elder woman said with frustration and anger clear in her voice.

"What happened to her?"

She hesitated a moment then burst out. "It was someone like you! Some sick monster that defiled her over and over until she stopped being my little sister and is now a scared child," she shrieked at me and hugged her sister tightly. Her words hit me like arrows, piercing through my skin. I was speechless.

"It's people like you that reap the benefits of war, for you want nothing else but slaughter," she finished with a sob. I stood still while the awkward silence grew into an unnerving wait.

"My condolences," I said softly. I gestured for the older woman to come closer. She warily approached me. I pointed to the trees behind me.

"Through those trees, about six miles from here is a rough game trail. Follow that trail until you see three peaks in the distance. When you find the peaks, travel east and you will come upon a Sanctuary. Tell them you seek shelter. You will find friends there," I said and grabbed my shirt off the vine. *Dry enough*, I thought, as I slipped it on.

I put my leg up in the stirrups and sat atop Midnight. "I wish you good luck, travelers." I kicked the stirrups and galloped off.

The Council was wrong. Corrupt. Evil. I was... am, corrupt and evil. And yet Eliana trusted me... Ronak trusted me. Amae had helped me.

Why? I thought through clenched teeth. *Why?* For the first time in weeks, I felt my wolf stir. Like a wave over the coast, the rush of the Astral distortion subsided shortly afterward, giving me hope, only for it to so teasingly slip away.

"Shit!" I cursed as I pushed Midnight to run harder. It was no problem for the massive stallion. I had wasted enough time resting.

Three days had passed since I had left for the Low Cities. The damned thing wasn't anywhere in sight. The sun was breaking over the horizon. I felt the forest beginning to thin, the trees becoming sparser. Through the gaps in the trees, I saw smoke and the flames licking high onto the castle.

Impossible! I thought with wonder and snapped the reins. "Midnight! Run faster!" I yelled. We broke through the tree line, and I smelled putrid smoke and charred wood. The flames lit up the ever-lightening sky with chaos and death. Midnight ran harder sensing the urgency.

I reached the front gates, which were on the opposite end from where I had arrived. I saw streams of wolves running into the woods. The crowd scattered as I swiftly rode by. Through the blur of motion, I even saw a few wolves stop to watch in awe as the madman charged toward the flames. We flew through the streets.

At the castle gates I, surprisingly, saw a familiar figure. Alver was guiding the throngs of freed prisoners out of the castle. Alver noticed me at the same time, and he stared in awe as I approached him.

"You!" he said, "By the goddess! Is that a horse?" he exclaimed.

"Alver, where is Eliana!?" I yelled. He didn't answer. A sense of dread passed through me. *Where is she?*

I jumped off of Midnight. "Alver, guide these people to Ronak!" I gave him the lead.

"Do not lose him! Or I'll kill you," I said and ran into the oncoming mass of people flooding out of the streets. Hundreds, no, thousands of people.

I ran hard and tried to pick up her scent among the thousands assaulting my nose, but I couldn't find it amidst the chaos and the acrid smell of dead and piss in the air. I tried to change again, leaning heavily into my wolf bond. Nothing.

Not even a pulse of my wolf came to surface as I tried to change. I yelled in frustration. I turned into an alleyway; people were moving out of the way to avoid me. I ran as fast as I could, searching the cobbled streets through smoke and raining ash.

My mind flooded with images of Eliana, bloodied and beaten. But I felt her. Praise the Goddess. I shut my eyes and concentrated. Eliana was struggling against a force I could not sense. She needed help. The blood in my veins was pumping hard. Something was desperately wrong.

Where are you? I called to my mate. Nothing. No response. We shared a connection. But our bond was yet to be completed. It was faint but I knew that I had to find her.

An overwhelming urge to protect her encased my entire being. As I went deeper into the Cities, I saw the bodies. First one or two, and then dozens. Laying in heaps. Wolves set aflame, stumbling out of the burning homes, their bodies charred by the fire. Weeping children clutched at their dead guardians.

A scream echoed in my head. *No!* "Eliana!" I yelled. My mind was flooded with images. This time, I saw her in a dingy alley. She was fighting! Eight... no twelve individuals. She was surrounded. I ran harder.

The images were becoming stronger. They were becoming clearer. It was as if I could see through her eyes for just a moment. I kept moving. I didn't know the way. I just prayed to Liunella that I was right. I turned a corner and saw a group of twelve wolves, and Eliana on the floor.

She was being held down by another wolf as he pressed his weight on top of her. Naked. Laughing. Two others were removing her breeches. Anger flooded my mind as my wolf rose to the surface. I felt stronger than I had ever felt before. I grew in height. Ten... Eleven... Twelve feet tall. I towered over the other wolves.

They felt the astral distortion and turned to face me. Their death was at hand. The clothing I wore tore and fell off in scraps.

"Impossible!" said the one who was on top of Eliana, "Faust killed you!"

I didn't say a word. My wolf had finally come to the surface to aid his mate. I glared at them, licking my lips. The familiar bloodlust flushed my senses. My muscles rippled, poised and ready. My breath was ragged with anger. I howled loud and lunged toward the closest of the wolves.

Before he could react, I thrusted both hands into his abdomen, lifting him over me. He struggled, feebly scratching at my arms, as I held him up high. I flexed and tore the wolf in two. His guts spilled over me, staining my fur red. My chest was no longer silver, but red with the blood of my prey. Red with my anger. The wolves around me were shaking. They feared me. As they should.

I took large steps forward. The group was frozen in fear. I swiped my hand as hard as I could, catching a wolf on the cheek. His neck snapped to the side, his bones tore from the skin through a large gash.

The remaining ten jumped at me at once. I took their hits as if they were nothing. I ripped another's head off his body by sheer force alone. Another aimed to bite my neck. I backstepped and hammered my fist into his skull. One of his eyes popped out and his skull shattered from the impact.

I turned in a fury, looking for the one who had tried to defile Eliana. *My mate.* He cowered to the side of her now. As I found his eyes, he let out a terrible screech, and slid backward on the rough stones.

"Please!" he yelled, "I beg you!"

Four wolves grabbed me from behind. I snarled with complete, animal rage. I tore one arm free and grabbed one of the four with my claws. I squeezed his skull until it dripped like pulp from my fingers. He dropped dead. The remaining wolves let go and backed off slowly. Then they ran away, melting into the alleys of the burning cities.

Only the wolf remained still on his knees, profusely crying like a child.

"Please!" he begged. I looked over to Eliana. She had gotten to her feet. Her expression said it all. She was trembling and terrified. She had finally seen me for what I truly was.

"Stand coward!" I said. He flinched when I spoke. He was still naked, his member hanging limp between his legs. I grabbed it and tore it off, throwing it into the burning building beside us. He screamed loud. Blood splattered on the dirty alleyway. He crumbled flat on the ground in pain. I leaned down, grabbing his hair, and pulled his head up. I looked his eyes. I grabbed his arms with my hands.

"She's... MINE." I roared and tore off both his arms. He screamed more, terrifying screams of pain and shock. I kicked his chest and he rolled back. I grabbed one of his legs and tore it off with ease. He screamed more and more, and I relished it.

I thrusted my hand deep into his chest and tore out his heart. He fell back dead. I threw the heart into the fire, and as it burned, I threw his corpse in as well. I rubbed my hands with dirt, but there was no scrubbing away their blood.

I turned to look at Eliana. She was scared. I was covered in the blood of the wolves I had slaughtered. I approached her but she took a step back.

I halted in my steps. She was covered in cuts and bruises and was bleeding. "Are you well?" I asked gently.

"I'll... you... slaughtered them," she said with wonder.

"And I'll slaughter anyone who tries to harm you," I replied. She looked into my eyes. She was afraid. Of me.

My heart sank as a feeling of sadness overwhelmed me. I shut my feelings out. *At least, she isn't harmed*, I thought. The face of the brutalized woman hugging her sister's legs, flashed before my eyes. I silently thanked Liunella that she guided me to save Eliana in time.

"Where are the others?" I inquired. "Marcus? Romulus?"

"I don't know about Romulus, but Marcus and I were split up." She was warily eyeing the scene of the carnage around us.

"I'll find him. Get to Alver, guide the prisoners out. He's at the front gate," I said and turned to leave.

"Belaize..." she said softly. I paused, my back still turned to her.

"Forgive me, Eliana," I said and ran off, my eyes shut tightly.

"Wait..." She called after me but I didn't stop.

It took almost a half hour before I stumbled onto Marcus. He was panting heavily, carrying an injured wolf on his back. He was following a woman. I sniffed and my wolf grew cautious.

"Marcus!" I growled. He turned to see me and nearly dropped the man he was carrying. The she-wolf stepped between them and me.

"Belaize of the blood moon," she said. I changed into my human form. I grunted in reply.

"We had heard murmurings of your death much to my displeasure," She continued, "But the goddess is good! I can kill you myself now."

She was strong. Incredibly powerful. I sniffed the air again, this time noticing the white stripes of hair streaked through her glossy black hair.

"Impossible!" I said.

"I am the Kaiser who will end you. Fortunately for you, I am under wolfsbane, or I would have slain you right now." She smiled.

"Erylesia, he's with us. We have to keep going," Marcus said timidly.

"Marcus," I said, "You've found yourself a woman that's more than you'll ever be." He growled with defiance.

"This isn't the time for your games!" he said. "Let's go."

"Give him to me, you'll pass out soon," I said, pointing to the wolf of Marcus's back.

Erylesia growled. "Alright, keep him," I said with my hands in the air.

"Are there others back there?" I asked.

"I don't know," Marcus replied. "Check once more, and let's get the hell out of this godforsaken place."

Before leaving, he gave me a nod, a gesture that I returned.

I ran into the ashy ruins of the Low Cities trying to see if anyone had survived, and killing more guards on my way. I helped freed wolves find their way. But my mind was still on Eliana.

She's safe. But she fears me. The thought made feel uneasy.

Who am I? I thought to myself. *What have I become?*

"I am death?" I said aloud. Eliana's face came into my mind. Those beautiful green eyes which had made my heart beat for the first time in my life.

No... I am Belaize. Just Belaize.

INTERLOGUE

Maya

I laid in bed without moving a muscle, waiting for the time to tick by. What was I waiting for? Death? My salvation? Freedom? Ha. Freedom. How naïve could I be in this cruel world? My thoughts consistently took me back into the whirlwind of emotion in my head.

All I had for comfort in this bleak cell was a stiff pillow and a thin sheet. A bucket lay on its side in a corner of the small dark cell. It reeked of feces and urine. Countless times I had vomited my guts out in that same bucket.

There was nothing else to do. But wait. Day in and day out for this cursed child placed by the Council to leave my womb. I used to wonder how the elders could be so cruel. Using me, and countless other she-wolves, as breeding tools. But as they ripped away my children from me, my thoughts had left me.

Die. Die. I wanted to die.

I placed my hands on my swollen belly. How I longed for this child to die. I didn't want this child to see this world. A twisted and corrupt world where I would never find my mate, where I was nothing more than an experiment. Just a womb. Seething rage took over as I dug my nails into my belly. The pain washed over my senses. Only when the feeling was unbearable did I retract. Blood oozed out, trickling over the same fading scars. *Why won't you die?*

I had been stripped of my humanity since the moment I was discarded in here. To them, I was nothing more than a *thing*. An object. I struggled to hold onto the parts of myself that still existed. *Maybe I had once loved the color blue,* I thought. I had even lost my name through the years, nothing of my tactile identity remained anymore, save for what little I could remember. The guards called me bitch, slut, whore... they used these words to define me, to reduce me, and in time I suppose it had worked. A tool to feed the machine that was the Council.

But I used to have dreams. Dreams of running with my mate, of bearing his children, of raising them together. In the early days, I would go there, spend the hours drifting within my mind, building a safe place. But the goddess was cruel, and I could hardly recall the rays of the sun. This was my fourth child. I remember looking at the faces of my previous children sucking milk from my breasts, just as the Council guards snatched them from my arms, never to return.

A single tear streaked down my face. "Die," I said silently to the child kicking ever so intently inside of me. She, I had a feeling it would be a girl, was full of life, but did that even matter anymore? Maybe if circumstances were different, I would have raised her myself, but no. I knew better now. I knew not to name her. Not to sing her to sleep. I knew that she would be gone before my tears healed and my milk dried.

"Maya..." I heard a voice say softly, pulling me out of my thoughts. I turned my head and saw exactly who I had expected to see. Merritan. The only guard that had a vested interest in me. The only one that had bothered to learn my name.

"What is it?" I asked him, colder than I had intended.

"Are you feeling better? Does your chamber need cleaning?" he questioned softly.

"Leave me be!" I said and turned to face a windowless, gray, brick wall.

"Call for me, if you need anything," I heard him say, defeated. Soon his echoing footsteps disappeared down the hall.

Here I was again, left alone to my thoughts once more. And again, they dove into the turbulence that was my mind. The cycle continued.

I opened my eyes, realizing slowly that I had fallen asleep. I got up and stretched, holding my belly while I waddled toward the bucket. I straightened the bucket and emptied my bowels into it. I cleaned myself off and waited for Merritan to return.

When he reappeared, he carried two buckets of hot water and a set of clean clothes. He opened my cell, took the dirty bucket and then left. I had done this hundreds of times, yet it was no less embarrassing than the first time. I quickly washed and dried myself in the same urine drenched corner. I changed into fresh clothes. In that time, Merritan returned.

"The guards made venison today. I saved you some." My mouth watered as I heard that. Meat... I'd get real meat for the first time in months. I looked at him, hoping my desperation wouldn't show so clearly.

He smiled and practically ran down the hall. He returned shortly with venison steak, untouched and steaming. I knew he hadn't eaten at all today. He left his meal for me, again. He just smiled. I took the plate and gorged on the food.

"She will come anytime now," he said looking at my swollen belly.

"It'll be better if she dies," I said morosely.

"Don't say that!"

"She will grow up to become a disgusting excuse for a wolf. Obeying the Council's orders, and someday she will commit atrocities far greater than those being done! So, it's better if she dies now!" I sobbed and screamed. Tears filled my eyes. Merritan's face shifted then. His brows furrowed and his mouth went tight. He looked like he might cry.

"Maya..." he mumbled. "I'll get you out of here! I promise." He pulled me into a soft embrace. I struggled, but he held me. I felt my walls breaking and cried in his arms.

We stayed like that for a long time. Despite where I was, Merritan made it bearable. He had for years now. Every time my child was taken away, he would console me. He would sit with me and hold me. He showed me kindness in my dark, dingy cell – something I had forgotten.

When he left to return to his duties my mind returned to its dark home. Hours passed. Or maybe entire days melted by. It made no difference. I drifted, I paced, I slept. I told the time by the functions of my body. And when my hunger was desperate, I would wait for Merritan. But he did not come. Instead, a fat wolf by the name of Bernard appeared before my cell. He was notorious for a short temper. "You there, whore..." he called. I bowed, submitting to him. He hobbled in and sat at the foot of my bed.

"Sit," he said, promptly gesturing toward his lap. I hesitated and saw his brow furrow. "Now bitch!" he yelled, and I sat on his lap. I felt a bulge between his legs. Disgust filled my body. I wanted to vomit. But I had no choice. My body was not mine anymore.

The thin cloth that passed for clothing did little to conceal his bulge. He pulled up my shirt and his hands gripped my swollen belly. A tear streamed down my face. His hands moved higher until he groped my breasts. He pinched and pulled, making me wince.

He smelled of sweat and dirt and ale. He was so large that he couldn't have taken his breeches off even if he tried. Just sat me atop and pushed into me.

He was panting now; this was exciting to him. I felt him tense, and he squeezed my breasts hard, making me scream. And then he was done. He pushed me off of him and stood. His breaches had a stain on them. Foul pig. *But what was I?* He got up and left my cell without a word.

Merritan came to stand at my door with a grim expression on his face. He had a split lip and bruised cheek. The guards had beaten him. They knew he favored me, and this was just a show for him. Tears flowed freely now from my eyes. He knew what they had done to me. They used me to show him what I was. He knelt and reached for me, but I cowered away from him. I was scared. I wanted this to be over. I wanted to die! And today, I would do it. Be over with this humiliating existence.

"Just kill me, please," I whispered, as I fell unconscious.

I opened my eyes again, groggy from sleep. I felt my wolf stir for the first time in the last three years. I was shocked. My wolf... Merritan. He must have found a way to avoid giving me wolfsbane doses. *That's why he was giving me his meals*, I thought. He wanted my strength, my wolf's return. He had waited for the wolfsbane to wear off. A tiny flame of hope bloomed inside of me. I knew I could change soon!

I sat down and waited.

I felt the child inside me kick harder than ever. I felt the blood drain from my face. *No! Not today!* I panicked. I could hear desperate wails coming from my throat. And then Merritan was there, and he was unlocking my cell.

"Let's Go! Quickly!" he said firmly and took my hand and pulled me out.

He led me through the halls. I took great, gasping breaths as waves of contractions threatened to seize my whole body. But we kept moving. When we exited the building, I saw the chaos. Flames, smoke, dead and dying wolves. The Cities were under attack and Merritan was dragging me out. He turned into his wolf. Golden fur, that's what I first noticed. He swept me off of my feet as gently as he could and ran to the side of a building into a narrow alley. He was strong, stronger than I gave him credit for.

We had turned into several smaller alleys when I felt my stomach twist again. A slight groan left my throat. *Shit, not now!* The pain in my belly was increasing by the minute. I held onto Merritan tighter as he led me through the alleys. He turned to a small rusty building and entered quickly inside. He glanced at me with a look of worry on his face.

"Are you alright, Maya?" he questioned as soon as he changed into his human form.

Before I could say a word, I fell to my feet as the pain tore through me. He hurriedly picked me up in his arms. He moved me desperately through the house until he could place me on a bed where I laid down, writhing in pain again.

As the wolfsbane effect was receding, my wolf was coming to the surface getting ready for birth. Another scream broke past my mouth as I twisted on the bed.

"Maya! Tell me. Is the child coming?"

I nodded my head as pain took over my body once more. He shuffled out of my sight immediately. Vaguely, I heard him shuffling through draws, slamming cabinets, gathering supplies. The pain receded again for a few minutes, and I was able to catch my breath. I was drenched in sweat, and I felt its kicks in my womb, eager to get out and be part of this wretched world.

I panted heavily. For a moment, I thought that maybe the pain was false. Maybe it won't come out today. That this was some nightmare. But the Goddess is cruel. I knew it in my bones. She had no luck to spare me.

I felt my underpants soak through. The water was soaking the bed sheets. A tear slipped down my eyes as I realized she was going to come. It was time.

"Merritan. My... my water... it broke. This thing will be here soon," I muttered.

I remembered the first birth alone in the cell. My water had broken, and my screams of pain were echoing all through the dingy cells. My child was born and stolen from me in the same hour. *Die!*

"We have about an hour," I said as the contractions started again. I gasped in agony clutching the sheets tightly with my hands.

With each wave of pain my screams raised in pitch. It was as if they weren't enough. I could never scream long enough, or loud enough to make it stop, to battle away the pain. I was panting and twisting, but this child was taking its sweet time.

Merritan clutched my hand and handed me a piece of cloth. "Maya put this between your lips. We... can't be found. Not now," he breathed.

I took the cloth and bit down hard.

It was hard. Harder than before to push the baby out. I pushed and pushed with all my strength. My legs were spread wide apart, blood was soaking the mattress. My thoughts were a mixture of anxiety and despair. Tears streamed from my eyes. *Damn you! Die. Just die before you ever take a breath.*

Help me! I called out to my wolf. *Lend me your strength!*

I felt her on the surface, and her strength flowed in my veins, and I pushed again. It felt like a weight was pulled from my body as the baby breached. I heard its first cry.

I closed my eyes and panted heavily. It was out. It was finally out. My thoughts were clouded from exhaustion, but Merritan was shaking me.

"Maya! Maya! It's a girl! You were right!" He yelped in surprise and happiness. He cut out the cord and cleaned the baby with the spare cloth he had. The baby was in her wolf form. Just a tiny pup. So tiny. Her fur glistened. Her eyes roamed the room wildly. And as I breathed her in, her little body shifted in my arms into soft pink flesh. She changed her form for the first and the last time till her teens.

I was still in pain. A few minutes later, more contractions pushed my body towards passing the afterbirth. I was drained. My eyes were closed. It felt like all my bones had been broken.

Merritan cleaned her and placed her on the floor over the soft clothes he had laid out. He pushed my legs apart. He had done this before. He had stitched my insides after the birth of my last child. I didn't feel the needle piercing. I just stared at the cracked paint on the ceiling, while all I heard was my child wail on the floor. Merritan was done in a few minutes. He used another spare cloth to clean the blood away.

"Here, Maya. Hold her." Merritan came to me with a bundle in his arms.

"No. I don't want her."

A look of sadness crossed his face. "Maya. Please. She's... innocent. Please, Maya. Don't deny her your love," he whispered as he knelt beside my bed. He held her as she cried loud and hungrily. He looked at me, his eyes pleading. Take her, his eyes seemed to beg. I turned away and pulled the covers up to my chin and huddled away. He stood up, defeated, and attended to the crying child. He disappeared into another room.

He came back with the infant happily suckling on a bottle filled with what I thought was warm milk. My eyes slowly closed, my final thoughts of the infant in his arms.

Loud crying awoke me. The infant was seated alone on a small couch wrapped tightly in white cloth. I rose from the bed. My body was stiff. I stretched lightly. My body was regaining its strength; however, I was weak. I walked to the bundle of cloth and watched it from above. She was a wrinkly mess. Her cheeks were flushed red. My heart throbbed. Longed for me to hold it against my chest.

"Pick her up!" he said, startling me. "Please, Maya!" he begged. He had a bag strapped over his shoulder.

"I will not pick her up!" I said, "It'll be better if she dies. The world will chew her up and spit her out without a second thought," I said and turned away, leaving the room.

"Maya!" He called behind me, frustrated. I left the door open on my way out.

He appeared a few minutes later with the babe suckling on more milk. He wrapped an arm around my collarbone and held me close.

"If you want to die, then die, but I won't let you take out your frustration on this child!" I was astounded at his words. I didn't know what to say.

"Follow me!" he said, turning away with the infant in hand.

I was dumbfounded. I had never seen Merritan angry. I walked behind him, slowly, cautiously. We left the safety of the ransacked house. It had been several hours since I had birthed the baby. The buildings were still burning. I was weak, barely able to walk. My insides were burning with every step, yet I moved ahead with Merritan. We came across the occasional body here and there.

We walked on; he kept a slow pace to allow me to keep up, but even with a large pack and a child, I was still slowing him down. He turned a corner and his form disappeared momentarily as a changing of the wind swirled smoke around us. He disappeared from my vision. I lurched forward desperately. *Please don't leave me.* Suddenly his body was pressed to mine. He was here. But so were others. There forms stood black against the smoke.

"Maya, take the child and run!" he said. He dropped his pack, it landed on the flask of milk and snapped open. The white liquid flowed out onto the ground. I peeked from behind him to see a fat wolf and three others staring us down.

"Oh Merritan, you proud fool." The fat one spoke. It smelled of Bernard. Had the circumstances been different, the vile man would have looked comical, but here, he was deadly.

Merritan turned and thrust the child into my hands. She began crying loudly.

"That belongs to the Council!" Bernard said. His voice sounded as if he was choking.

"The Cities are burning to the ground!" Merritan said, "Just let her go, and you can have me."

Bernard laughed heartily, his cronies laughing with him. "But I can't fuck you! Can I? I like that bitch. I want to put my pup in her next, now that she is ready."

"Run!" Merritan said. He changed into his wolf. Blond and beautiful. "Run!" He screamed and launched at Bernard. The last glimpse I ever had of the beautiful blond Merritan was his jaws wrapped around Bernard's neck. Bernard's face was twisted in agony. His cronies attacked viciously, and I heard Merritan's death throes as his anguished cries filled the sky. Tears streamed down my face, but I turned my back and ran.

Sensing death in the air, the child began wailing. I cursed. "Shut up!" I said as I ran as hard as my frail body would carry me. The wailing never stopped. I turned left, then right, left again. I felt blood trickling down my legs as the stitches Merritan had set ripped apart. I looked ahead of me and I saw one of Bernard's cronies blocking my path. There were two others with him. I stopped in the middle of the alley.

I ran backward and slipped into a larger street. I heard the wolves behind me. I felt a searing pain in my back as one of the wolf's claws dug into my skin. I stumbled but stopped myself from falling atop the infant. She cried louder and louder.

"Shhhhh little one," I cried. "Be my hope!" I said.

The wolves surrounded me. I fell to my knees holding the infant. She had no name. The little one had no name.

"You filthy whore!" one of them yelled and kicked my ribs. I felt them break. The intense pain raked my body. I crawled backward, away from my assailants. I crawled until my back met a stone wall. I would die in this back alley. We would die in this back alley.

The bundle of mess was squirming and wailing in my arms. I focused on her small, wrinkly tear-stained face. *What should I name you? How wrong I was about you. You're my innocent child, why did I want you to die?*

I heard a scream but kept my eyes closed, hugging her close. I felt the pain all over my body; my blood mixing with the ash and dirt. I couldn't breathe. It throbbed to just breathe.

I heard one of the wolves speak. "Impossible!" Another screamed in agony. I opened my eyes, and I saw two of the wolves run away, disappearing into the streets and alleys.

Before my eyes stood an enormous wolf. His size was incomparable. Before my eyes he shifted into a human and knelt beside me. His hair hung loosely around his face, and he was aglow in the light of the flames behind him.

"You won't survive," he said bluntly. I nodded. I knew my death had arrived.

My breathing was growing shallower. My baby cried. Her cries echoing in the morning mists.

"Take her... please..." I begged, holding her up feebly. He slowly took her in his massive hands. She was so tiny, but she was healthy, at least.

My eyes were heavy. The rays of the morning sun did little to warm me. What I felt now was the icy embrace of death. It wouldn't be quick, but instead a slow, bitter death. The large wolf looked at me. Pity reflected in his tender, red-rimmed eyes... no, it was sadness. Long white hair, and a scraggly black beard. He wore only breeches. His body was covered in scars, one especially gruesome across his chest.

An angel.

"I can make it easier."

Peace. At last.

My child's cries pierced me out of my lull, "Oh child, you don't have a name yet?" I whispered. The human morphed into his monstrous wolf again. He pressed his claws between my ribs and slid them into my heart, puncturing it. There was a sharp pain... followed by peace. My eyes grew heavy. "Your name..." I muttered. My voice getting softer.

"Ni... ha... ra..."

HOPE OF LIFE

Eliana

I stood with Alver as the throng of people exiting the Low Cities thinned. Every few minutes a straggling group passed the threshold. Maybe a few dozen, at most.

Luthor had returned several minutes ago. He was missing an ear and was heavily bruised and beaten. His shirt was tied around his waist as a makeshift bandage.

"You should wait for Romulus. I will go ahead and make sure everyone escapes. We cannot handle a surprise attack from the Council," he said and moved ahead. I was stunned, but I stayed. Work needed to be done.

"Father must have sent a few warriors our way. I am sure you will meet them somewhere. Make sure the rebels are rightly dispersed and they take people to different Sanctuaries," I said.

Luthor nodded and limped away.

Eric soon appeared. He was in terrible shape; it was as if dozens of wolves had mauled him. His arm was broken in several places. I told him that Armina had rushed Adrian back to the Sanctuary. He left shortly thereafter. To say he strode from the capital gates would be a bit of an overstatement, but he carried himself with the unmistakable confidence of a job well done. Through the chaos and madness, I couldn't help but smirk.

I stood there, reflecting on our journey. It was folly, for a few days ago simply getting one person out of the Low Cities was an impossible task. Yet, seven wolves had taken down the Low Cities and burned it to the ground. It wouldn't have been possible without Romulus.

I watched a building collapse, sending cinders arching into the morning air. I turned to Alver. Seeing him hold that beast beside him was quite unsettling. It was a horse, I guess. A massive beast. I had recalled a picture of this animal in old, yellowed books I had read as a child. I was astonished to know the Council still breed them. He was dark as a moonless night, and occasionally kicked the ground and flared his nostrils. Behind its armored exterior was a beautiful creature. Alver would occasionally stroke its chin, and it gleefully nudged Alver. It was fond of affection.

I approached it slowly; it looked into my eyes, peering into my core. I gently placed a hand on its snout. It shook my hand off and turned its great swooping head back to Alver.

"Eliana!" I heard and turned to see Marcus running to me, stopping several feet away when he laid eyes on the horse.

"W... what is that doing here?" he asked. He was carrying a wolf. A woman with him laughed merrily and approached the horse. She set her hands on his cheek and patted its muscled chest. It neighed in approval. I was shocked. *Why was it showing affection to her?*

"What a beautiful creature. Whom does it belong to?" she asked commandingly. "What is its name?" she questioned, her gaze directed at Alver.

"I was never told," he replied. The horse nuzzled its head closer to the woman. I felt a tang of jealousy.

"Eliana, is everyone out?" I heard a familiar voice say.

It startled everyone. "Romulus! We have been waiting for you," I replied. He looked as crisp as ever. Not a wrinkle on his clothes or a scratch on him. Not a drop of blood in sight.

"The arrows, was that you?" He gave me a knowing smile.

"Belaize went in there looking for survivors," I said. He scowled in response. I knew everyone was cautious of him, hated him. Yet he had come. Come here. *Belaize had saved me*, I thought, and not for the first time.

"It has been a few decades since I have seen one like you," he said, finally noticing the horse. He smiled and clapped the horses' back. "Magnificent creatures, these are," he said. The creature skittered to the side and shook its head in unmistakable approval.

"Alver, help mount the injured onto the horse, and let's make haste," he said.

"Marcus, put the wolf onto the horse," Romulus instructed. Marcus obliged. The woman that had come with Marcus watched him work with a keen eye.

Belaize, hurry.

I peered inside the blackened gate of the Cities and I saw a shirtless man with a bundle of clothes clutched to his chest appear from behind one of the burning buildings. The heat distorted his image, but I knew it was Belaize. I *felt* it. He held the small bundle delicately in his great hands. As he got nearer, I realized they weren't clothes, but white sheets. It was odd. The bundle of sheets moved. He approached us and walked to the horse.

"Midnight, come!" Belaize said and began walking away. *The nerve of him.*

"Belaize! What are you holding?" I yelled behind him. The woman beside Marcus watched him walk, too intently for my liking, and the horse followed.

"Eliana..." Marcus yelled, I looked back at him, but Romulus interceded holding up a hand to stop Marcus. I turned and ran to Belaize.

"Belaize!" I said, approaching the tall man. "Why are you just walking away?!" He turned to face me, his eyes were red, more than usual, and tear stained. He had been... crying.

"What?" he barked. "What do you want?" His ferocity stung. I couldn't say a word. "I'll drop this one to the Sanctuary, then I'll leave," he said.

I heard a small cry from the bundle of clothes, followed by a full-blown tantrum. He opened the sheets and revealed a naked baby. She was just hours old. My heart throbbed for her.

"She's so beautiful," I mumbled. I looked up at Belaize. For the first time, I felt genuine about my feelings for him. He had rescued a new-born pup.

"Belaize... where is the mother?" I whispered.

"Dead," he replied. My heart sank. I yearned to hold the little one.

"Nihara," he said. "Her name is Nihara." He held her towards me. I took her in my hands gently. A tear dropped from my eye. She cried feebly, clutching at the air. I cooed and put my finger within her reach. As soon as she could, she wrapped her small hands around it and tugged it toward her mouth. She suckled at my finger greedily. She was hungry.

"Belaize, her food?" I questioned him. He shook his head. "We need to find her some milk," I said. I searched frantically through the crowd of people leaving the Cities. Most were smeared with ash or worse, hobbling, with that glassy-eyed look I was all too familiar with in this war, when the loss is too great to comprehend. Most were injured. However, I spotted a she-wolf carrying an infant as well.

I approached her, "Please, would you kindly spare some milk for the little one? She's got no one to feed her. Her mother is dead," I said. The she-wolf nodded. She handed her infant to Belaize, who was standing beside me. Belaize looked bewildered but said nothing. The she-wolf looked around, and she took Nihara in her grasp. She walked towards a tree and sat with her back against it. Lifting her shirt up, she tucked baby

Nihara underneath. She fed greedily, suckling at her. Belaize watched her with an unwavering gaze.

Several moments later the lady handed Nihara back, taking her now sleeping infant back from Belaize. "Thank you so much," I replied, bowing graciously. The lady adjusted her shirt and hurried along with her companions. I held Nihara upright against my shoulder and patted her back softly.

"We should go," Belaize said. He held out his hands. I hesitated, but passed on Nihara to Belaize. He held her upright and patted her back as well, copying me. She playfully cooed and burped loudly seconds later. I couldn't help but laugh at her.

Belaize smiled as well, and for once it wasn't a malicious smile, it was genuine. Baby Nihara rested her head on his shoulder. Soft brown hair crowned her head. Her eyes were a light amber, they were burning with an unearthly fire. Soon, she was asleep.

Belaize covered her with the sheets once more and handed her to me. Nihara, the Low Cities, Belaize, Adrian, all of us making it out alive... these were victories. Nihara gave hope of life.

The others had caught up to us. Marcus was speaking to the woman. The woman must be an alpha. I felt her powerful aura, similar to that of Belaize. It was dangerous. Fierce. Alver was strong too. The horse stayed close to Alver, but eyed Belaize. Then it clicked, the horse. He seemed to respect those he considered equal. I felt that familiar tang of jealousy.

"Erylesia, no!" I heard Marcus say as the woman stepped in front of Belaize. Her silver eyes were glaring at him, her mouth turned in a sneer.

"Why are you here, Harbinger? I should kill you. I will kill you," she threatened.

Belaize's stance changed instantly. He returned her sneer with one of his own.

"No. I don't know who you are. But Belaize has helped us. Helped me. He deserves a chance," I said defiantly.

Erylesia turned and stared at me. Chills shot down my spine. I knew in my gut that she was strong. I stood my ground. The heat between us crackled. Alpha on alpha, the fight for dominance. My wolf was on the surface, ready to put this woman in her place. "How dare you defend a murderer, girl? Who gave you the authority?"

"I am not just a girl. I am the daughter of Ronak," I shot back.

"That self-proclaimed title is unworthy. Do not speak to me. I am a Kaiser." She huffed with pride. She tried to change as well. The astral distortion was vigorous, but it dispersed as soon as it came. She cursed under her breath.

"You are not the only one blessed with the blood of the old," I challenged back. "Regretfully, you were imprisoned in the Low Cities.

You do not know of what has happened in your absence. Do not jump to conclusions." I huffed in anger. Everyone had gone silent and was watching us.

"That does not wash away his sins, girl," Erylesia shot again.

"Think what you must, I don't care," Belaize interrupted before I could speak.

"If I could turn, I'd tear both of you apart," Erylesia said. Belaize's eyes grew dark. A challenge of an alpha is never easy to let go. He clenched his free hand. I saw his teeth elongate.

"Belaize!" I yelled. The noise awoke Nihara, who bawled loudly. Romulus looked up at me. All eyes were on me and the bundle of white sheets in my arms. Belaize recoiled instantly. The challenge, the anger, forgotten. He was looking at Nihara.

"Who is that?" Romulus inquired.

I wrapped the sheets around Nihara and held her to Romulus. Romulus took the infant, holding her in his arms, and inspected her. As he brought the crying infant closer, she reached up grabbing his nose. The entire group laughed; the tension lost. Romulus held her, and she snuggled up to him.

"Eliana!" Marcus said, looking at me, and back at Belaize.

"No, you moron!" I said groaning, my cheeks heating. Prick.

"Belaize found her with her dead mother." I looked at Belaize. He looked tense.

Marcus held Nihara next. He played with her gently. The entire time, Belaize watched him like a hawk. I realized he was watching everyone who held the child. He was her guardian. Her father. He felt parental affection toward Nihara, however would never admit it. Nihara turned her head and reached for Belaize. I saw him moving quickly and taking her from Marcus. He held her in his arms, gently rocking her. Everyone was stunned, looking at Belaize and at each other. He had a fearsome reputation as a savage killer and heartless assassin. Yet, here he was rocking a child back and forth.

My wolf was in the back of my mind. It thrilled her that Belaize, our mate, was showing such a side to us. She always had faith in him. Maybe even I did too, but his reputation was hard to see past. It clouded my mind with doubt.

I wondered if he would accept me. I wondered, not for the first time, if he were beyond redemption. In the cell, during our conversation, he was unwilling to fight for our cause, yet here he was. Belaize was lethal, yet... he looked like a giant, holding the small baby in his hands tenderly. He was now her protector. Could someone change so quickly?

But these were deeper questions of my heart and would have to be set aside till the world was a calmer place. The act of organizing resources was something I was more familiar with. It was a deep comfort to me, offering aid to those who needed it. With the tension retired, at least for now, I was able to direct our little group into teams and clear out the Low Cities. The ancient castles of the city were in ruins, burning apart from the flames.

Shortly thereafter, large scores of troops arrived. They wore the rebel insignia with renewed valor. Father had sent reinforcements after Belaize had left. The warriors helped maintain peace and order. With more competent warriors we made sure that we rescued every single man, woman, and child out of the depths of the prisons and slums.

After the attack, all the wolves just wanted food, and shelter, and a place to be at peace, as quickly as possible. But the journey home was a desperate struggle. Hundreds of wolves were gravely injured or atrophied. We hunted all that we could and paused as often as we dared. But it wasn't enough. Many went hungry. Many died. We had to dispose of the dead and cover our tracks as well. We carried on that way. Each morning we would rise again and bury those who had died in the night. The river was not wide enough, nor fast enough, to give a proper Liunella send off. There were simply too many. And all the while I thought of father. I was eager to get back to him, to thank him.

I wanted to tell him the tale of our victory myself. I imagined his face when I broke the news that we had secured the Low Cities for future operations, though I was sure that rumors swirled already. With the Council's main arsenal destroyed, we could begin to plan another wave of blows. And by the time the Council would have any idea, its strongholds throughout Vascya would be nothing but memories.

Looking back, it seemed like getting to the Low Cities had been one of the hardest things I had ever done. I was grieving the fate of my friend, and trying to maintain focus enough to stay quiet, stay hidden. Stealth was of the utmost importance. But we had done it. We had saved him and countless others.

After a long and gruesome journey, we crested a small hillock, and there, in the distance, I saw three jagged peaks. Home. While we were the last party to arrive, and I was more tired than I could've possibly ever imagined, I felt a blessed wave of relief wash over me. I turned to look at Belaize, who wore a serene smile. Something he reserved for Nihara. *And me,* my wolf amended.

Belaize was walking beside me with Nihara in his arms. He refused to give her to anyone except me. He would delicately extend her into my arms as she slept soundly. His actions were so different. This was a side that had never surfaced before, I could tell that much. They had developed a special bond.

I looked ahead and spotted Marcus as well. He was walking with

Erylesia. She was an alpha. Female alphas were rare, and female Kaisers had never been recorded in the history of Vascya. The Low Cities had many secrets hidden inside.

"Belaize." I said as I pressed closer to him. He slowed to match my pace, shifting the sleeping Nihara in his arms.

"I have a question for you," I said.

"What is it?" he said, his voice ever so gruff.

"What made you go there, to the Low Cities?" I inquired. "I am grateful that you did. You saved me. Thank you. I just... you weren't keen on coming before."

"Are you sure you are Ronak's seed, Eliana?" He looked at me, his eyebrow arched in a question.

"Because you're a fool if you don't already know the answer. I came for you."

"But why?" I asked again.

He let out a deep sigh. Nihara opened her eyes once, but when she saw Belaize, she closed them again. Belaize started rocking her back and forth.

"You should have more faith in the bond that Liunella graced us with. I am who I am. I have killed countless with no hesitation. And I will do so again. The only difference now is that I couldn't let you walk to your death alone. Liunella made sure of that. Right now... my only purpose is to keep her safe." He gestured towards Nihara.

"But... why? Why do you care so much about her?" I wondered.

He remained silent for a few minutes. I didn't know if he would answer me either.

"She... is innocent. She reminds me of myself. He... gave me to the Council as a child. My father tore me from my mother's arms deliberately selling me to the Council. I'm not innocent. I have taken so many lives that my hands will always be stained red with blood. But it is my duty to protect this girl, yet untouched by war. It was her dying mother's wish," he said.

I nodded and remained silent as we walked along the path. We were both lost in thought by the time we finally reached the Sanctuary.

Everyone was waiting for us. The rebels were gathered at the entrance with smiles on their faces. It was victory for us, and the fall of the Council was within our grasp.

Prisoners were welcomed by open arms. Some were carried and others were eased into makeshift Infirmary tents that lined the main thoroughfare. And everywhere, survivors looked eagerly at the incoming wolves, hoping to find a familiar face, a lost loved one. Hope died in the faces of many but rose up in others. It was a heart aching, joyous return. Belaize and I were one of the last ones to enter. I heard the deafening cheers of our people echoing loudly along with wondrous sighs of the wolves who witnessed Midnight for the first time.

"Oh goddess, what a majestic beast is this? Wait, who is that on his back? Is he dead?" I heard a familiar voice. Turning around, I looked for its source. I saw the familiar old woman with her gray hair tied in a bun.

"Amae!" I called out. She was ordering a couple of wolves to carry the wolf on Midnight's back away to the Infirmary.

"Amae!" I called again. She finally noticed and walked toward us, immediately ushering me into a tight hug.

"I was so worried, but then the rebels started piling in. Goddess, how many did you free from that prison? We don't have space or supplies to hold so many. Ronak has been busy all day to provide for everyone. The sick are being treated, and so many pregnant she-wolves are giving my old bones a headache." She smiled, wrinkles deepening on her face.

"Amae. Where is Adrian?" I asked. Luthor had taken him out of the Cities first. He was bruised and beaten, last I had seen him. A sad smile crossed Amae's face.

"Armina. Liunella bless her. She brought Adrian back in time. Honoria has been treating him. He will live. But it will be a long recovery ahead."

My eyes glistened. I silently promised myself to go to the Infirmary after I talked to father.

A moment later, Amae's attention shifted towards Belaize. "What is that?" she inquired. Belaize didn't budge, but Amae's scrutinizing gaze made him lean down, showing her Nihara's face.

"A baby?" she exclaimed. "Where?"

"In the Cities. Her mother is dead," Belaize replied in a monotonous voice.

"Give her to me. I'll take care of her." Amae raised her arms to take Nihara. Belaize immediately took a step away from her.

"No. She stays with me. I'm her guardian," he said stiffly.

"Child. Be quiet and give her to me. I will take her and feed her. You can't enter a room full of milking she-wolves now, can you? Be my guest, if you have the courage to do so," she finished.

I had never seen Belaize look so flustered in my life. A smile tugged my face. Immediately, he handed Nihara to Amae. She cooed at the baby.

"Don't worry. I'll bring her back to you. Meet Ronak in the meantime," she instructed and walked off with Nihara.

I looked at Belaize with a grin. His eyes looked everywhere but me. I pushed aside the toil of the last few days. I shoved my anger and my fear, and even my hope, as far down as I possibly could. It was time to meet my father.

"Let's go," I said and led him to Father's quarters.

On our way to meet father, I saw plenty of new makeshift tents littered along the Sanctuary. The Sanctuary was bustling with activity. So many rebels were in one place now. As we rounded the final corner, I saw a string of wolves going in and out quickly. Father was probably assigning them various tasks at hand.

We both stepped inside his makeshift office, and I felt like a lifetime had passed since I last stood here. I felt aged, somehow, weary and worn. My father was sitting in his chair, plans and papers laid out in front of him as usual. He looked tired. He was instructing a wolf about patrol duties when he saw me.

"Go. Now," he said.

He got up from his seat and came toward me, pulling me into an embrace. I wrapped my arms around him and only after a long moment we separated.

"You did the impossible," he said proudly.

"We have Romulus to thank for that," I said with a smile. "Belaize helped, too," I said with little pride in my voice.

"Associating with the enemy. Eliana, I thought you were smarter than this." I heard a venom filled voice. I looked in the corner and saw Rayne standing there.

We haven't been talking much after I had taken a stand for Belaize. After his failed assassination attempt, Rayne had avoided me like the plague. Clearly, he wasn't over it.

"He isn't the enemy anymore. He has a purpose, and also, a grudge against the Council. That makes him our friend, not our foe," I said.

"He still is the enemy. Just because you don't see it, doesn't mean I am blind as well."

"Rayne. That's enough. I believe Belaize has proved enough that he isn't a threat to us anymore." Ronak said it with a firm voice.

"Just because El smeared honey over it doesn't make it the truth, father. You don't want to see the truth hiding in plain sight, either. The love for your daughter has affected your senses."

"Says the coward," Belaize muttered. He had been silent, just watching Rayne.

Rayne stepped closer towards Belaize. "What the hell did you say?"

"You're just a fucking coward, Rayne. You always will be," Belaize said coolly.

"What do you mean, Belaize?" I questioned. *How did he know Rayne?*

"Don't believe him. He is a fucking liar." Rayne yelled and pushed Belaize backwards. Belaize rocked a little but didn't move a muscle.

"I have a reputation to uphold Rayne. If I become a liar and coward like you, where would that get me? Nowhere. I am anything, but that," Belaize said.

"Rayne, stop it! Belaize, why are you talking in riddles?" I asked.

"On the Council's orders I had attacked one of the Sanctuaries Rayne here handled. I was fighting the rebels when Rayne showed his face. Instead of facing me like a man, he tucked his tail between his legs and ran away, leaving his comrades to die for him, sacrificing their lives for this insignificant cockroach," Belaize said, his expression serious.

"No. Rayne would never do that." I couldn't believe Rayne would ever do something like that. He has pride. Yes, we had a sibling rivalry, but Rayne was better than that. He was an excellent leader. He told us the Council attacked the Sanctuary, and that he barely got out.

Belaize looked at me. I held his gaze. His eyes were cold. There wasn't a shred of dishonesty or hesitation in them. He was telling the truth.

"Rayne... how could you? You let wolves die?" I whispered as the realization hit me.

"Really, El? You are going to believe this murderer over your own brother and blood?!" he yelled at me. "He was the one who killed them all, yet you stand here questioning my allegiance?"

"You left people to die. You sealed their fate with your selfishness. Why, Rayne?"

"For the last time Eliana, are you really fucking going to believe him out of anyone? Why?" Rayne screamed.

I finally lost my temper. "I trust him because he is an asset. He is capable, strong and he is the one who will change the tide of this war. Yes, he did murder and maim innocents. Belaize is riddled with his sins, yet Council hunts him. Belaize has done things. Terrible things! But it's not for you to decide how he answers for them. Because you ran away. Like a fucking coward. My brother who did nothing but help people, who fought in the rebellion, ran away when it mattered the most.

"Whether you like it or not, he has helped us now. He has switched sides to us. And he is more of a man than you'll ever be, Rayne." I finished. I could feel my face flushed with blood and anger. Silence graced us for a moment, but it was short-lived.

The realization stuck Rayne in seconds and he sneered, "That clears up the confusion! I wondered why you were so keen on keeping him alive. Because you had whored yourself out to him. Free pass to those who sleep with my sister, all sins are forgiven. Kill whoever you fucking want, eh?" Rayne said angrily.

"Rayne. That is enough," Father said.

"But fath-" Before Rayne could say anything, my father lifted a hand.

"Leave. I can't believe I couldn't raise a better son," Ronak replied, turning his back on Rayne.

Rayne stayed quiet for few seconds. His mouth was agape in shock. "You believe her, too. I should have known that I have no place here where the Navars decide our fate. You should know, even if I ran for my life, it was the murderer you're siding with that hunted and killed those innocents."

Rayne walked towards us, and as he steps forward a chill settled inside me.

"You'll pay," he whispered, as if death himself was speaking, and he wandered off into the dusk.

ARCHIVES

Idaos

Dusk came sooner than expected, the last of the sun's rays hid behind soft gray clouds. Looking out of my window at the serene sunset, I found a momentary, transitive peace. The birds were chirping and returning to their nests. As the evening grew dark, the stars were like brilliant pearls cushioned upon pure black velvet. The night was a perfect one with a warm gentle breeze.

I sipped warmed wine in the lavish comforts of my estate, nestled behind thick walls, and well stocked with books and scrolls. War is a profitable venture, after all, and I spared no expense. The simple, unavoidable fact of the matter was that the gift of foresight is invaluable when times are perilous. My desk was flooded with letters from worried nobles and nervous merchants. *Idaos, will my harvest turn out this year? Idaos, trade has suffered, and my allegiances are strained, when are you next available for another reading?* Power, I had learned very early, only comes to those with the will to use it.

It was perhaps an old trick passed down through the journals of my ancestors. A long, adaptable bloodline of *Vouyens* that served to guide Vascya by filling their own pockets. I tipped my glass and gave a silent prayer, *Blessed be the goddess, eh?* When I was a much younger man even the first king of Vascya gave call to my chambers.

When I had stood in his presence, I knew that there would be nothing good to come from his ruling. He was much too honest. Much too just. And the longer he stayed in power the less relevant I became. What followed, the downfall of the old Council, and the rise of the new, was unfortunate at best, but better than a boiling mob of peasants at my door. And, to be fair, I did warn the Good King of the doom he bought when he accepted glory. But my words fell on deaf ears.

Even though this new Council was a bastardize form of the old, I still found relevance. Sure, the first Wolf, Fenrir, had given the Four their powers to rule over Vascya, but that was shortsighted – of course the masses would feel under-represented, it was only a matter of time before we would've been forced to expand. Amid the chaos, Elder rites were bestowed on those outside of the original four, the bloodlines of old. So be it. Better that I had a hand in it.

I had always loved the history of Lycans, the knowledge of our elders, bestowed upon by the moon goddess herself. Often, I would visit the underground levels of the city to access the archives and read to my heart's content, lost in the scriptures, the vast knowledge left by our ancestors.

I had been reading through old, yellowed journals when I forged the path that would remake Vascya. A high-ranking alpha named Aserion, another Vouyen, and long since dead, gave me the idea. He was highly respected in my family. Growing up, my mother would tell me his tales each night as sleep overtook. The tales of his greatness, the prophecies he had foretold which came true. How the Council sought his advice and followed his direction.

Aserion ran Vascya during his time. His decisions, his prophecies, helped others achieve greatness and bring peace and prosperity to the land. The small period of peace ended with Aserion's death. He died during another wave of protests against the old Council. And now, nothing remained of him besides moldy leather and fragile paper. *That would not be me,* I vowed.

Still, it had appealed to my senses, and I had opened the journal carefully, flipping open its wrinkled pages. I read the first page with interest under the glow of oil lamps.

My writings on this paper are a testament to my thoughts. Prophecies pass through my mind in a constant whirl. I write them down in hopes to guide the wolves of Vascya on a path of self-salvation. Only then can Vascya prosper in the future.

Liunella has bestowed me with the gift of sight. I have been chosen for a purpose and without fulfilling it, I cannot ascend to afterlife. For years, I have sought death, but it has never shown its face to me. Death plays, it hunts, but his face will always be a mystery, ever-changing. Will it ever?

I have had many visions in my long life which have come true. I have foretold war; I have foretold peace. I have told many about their demise. But something greater is coming. It compels me to hide away as its power is so great. I fear him and the visions I witness him in. I wonder what are we being warned against?

The entry ended with that question. I turned the page to read more, but realized pages were torn from it. More than half of it was missing. I closed the old journal and moved to put it back in its place. As I stood, a loose piece of parchment fell out on the ground. I leaned to pick it up. As soon as my fingers traced the paper, dread and doom filled me. I fell in sudden shock.

Tremors of fear seized through my body. My heart was gripped with great danger. Darkness. All my senses had gone dark. My eyes went blurry and my vision blackened. I fell to the ground, my breathing increasing rapidly. I was panting on the ground like a dog. I tried to open my eyes, and the void engulfed me further, suffocating me. Pain shot through every nerve of my body.

After a few minutes, my breathing calmed. I opened my eyes again and this time was met with the low glow of the oil lamp. Confusion coursed through me. The piece of paper was lying in front of me. I softly gripped it and pulled it closer. Pain shot through me again, but I tried to keep it under control.

My eyes glazed over what was written on it.

When blood turns on blood,
the cull will begin,
Lycans will fall,
dammed be the sin.

I was horrified. No! The great elder Aserion had predicted the doom of our land.

Tears formed in my eyes and slipped down on my cheek. *This means... Everyone is in danger. I am in danger! I'll die?!? No!* I continued to read the prophecy.

There will come those that rise from the depths of destruction,
To restore what once was,
the bearers of the God of Death.
Two there shall be and their guide will be extermination.
Rise will they holding the key to endless death
To low upon this world,
should the two ever mate.
The power and strength will be in their bond,
the lycans will bow.
The stink of death surrounds us all,
to storm and fire Vascya must fall
Prosperity will follow against all odds,

dwelling between the death's claws.

I read through the prophecy. Once. Twice. Hundreds of times. My mind was in an uproar. A feeling of dread had settled in the pit of my stomach. I shifted to the side and vomited my guts onto the floor. I'd never had such a reaction to a prophecy before. This wasn't my own, yet...

I glanced at the paper, reading it again.

I was going to die. I knew it.

A sudden calm came over me. My body went numb. A cruel idea tinkered in the corner of my mind. What if I prevent all the demise that would befall us, that would befall me?

I... will be the light for Vascya. I will take the Lycan race to a new height. But first, the society we have created will be destroyed. Burned. From its ashes will rise the new beginning. I will be the pioneer. The light.

Taking the yellowed paper between my fingers, I folded it into two parts, creasing it, and tore the lower one off.

I read it over. To stop a fire, start one.

I finally stood. My knees were shaking. In the old archives, where the history of Vascya existed, I felt the gaze of my ancestors searing on my back. I moved towards the table, my hand clutching the paper. I took off the hot glass which covered oil lamp, my fingertips burning. I moved a hand and lit the paper aflame as I read the last words again, as it turned to smoke and ash.

Prosperity will follow against all odds,
dwelling between the death's claws.

A loud creak of the door pulled me from my thoughts. I stood at the window ledge. The dark night had fallen, the vast gardens of the castle lay barren and quiet under Liunella's light.

"Forgive me for the intrusion, Alpha. But the elders have summoned you to the Sanctorum." I heard a voice of a Council guard.

"They have called for you right now, alpha," he insisted.

"Okay," I said. I moved and grabbed my crimson robes which lay on my empty bed before walking out of my chamber.

The guard accompanied me on the way of the Sanctorum. *A call of the Council at this hour?*

A few minutes later, the guards outside the Sanctorum pulled open its heavy door, and I entered. I glanced around the massive room; the chalk white walls once again lit through the light rays entering the Oculus. Out of ten chairs of the Council, four were empty. Evette and Illari had refused to come back to Regvyer since the last meeting. They had claimed a neutral position in the war. They denied our armies entry in their states. Even though the sisters were not of a bloodline, they were excellent leaders. It was a shame to lose them.

The guards closed the door behind me. I moved and took my seat in the center along the table.

"Where are Valio and Olegario? Should we wait for them?" I questioned.

"I had sent for them, but the rebels have blocked their path. They will not be joining in the meeting tonight," Canagan said from my right. Each elder had a somber expression. A call to convene at this hour worrisome. The tension was palpable.

"We should proceed regardless of their absence," Eyolf said, scratching his beard. "What has happened?"

Remus cleared his throat, "I have received grave news."

We all waited silently. He took a deep breath and said, "The Low Cities have fallen."

"What?!" Alpha Eyolf gasped in horror. "How!? The Cities?"

It was chaos. Utter chaos.

"Stop! Everyone!" I yelled, banging my fists on the table. *No. No. The prophecy will come true. No!*

"Remus. How? What happened? Please tell us everything," Esteve said after everyone quieted down.

"In all honesty, I don't know. Liunella only knows how they infiltrated the Cities. The females of the breeding program and the prisoners have now joined the rebel ranks. They killed our best trained soldiers," he said with an edge to his voice.

"What about the Cities? What do we have left?" I mumbled. My insides were in turmoil.

A pained look crossed Remus's face. He lowered his head in defeat. "Nothing. We have nothing. They burned cities to the ground."

"The rebels? Any signs? We should be able to track them!? Such a large number!" Amarog wondered.

"They burnt everything, every soldier, every lip that could tell their location. It was a massacre. There is no sign of rebels. The warriors have covered their tracks well. Even with the weak and wounded, they knew how to handle it," Remus said in a monotone.

"I found out too late about the attack. By the time I arrived, all that remained were burning and decaying bodies. They attacked right when we had released a shipment to Regvyer," Remus said.

A pain began behind my eyes, my head was throbbing. "What should we do now? One of the major sections of our power is gone," I said with despair.

"Where were you when the attack happened, Alpha?" Eyolf pointed at Remus, a sneer on his lips.

Massaging my temples with my fingertips, I said, "Now is not the time to blame each other, Eyolf. If we do not trust each other, then who is left? How can we win? How will we prevent destruction and death that is to come? We have to be united!"

"Have you lost your eyesight, Idaos! Look! Look around us! United? Together? That is a wishful dream." Eyolf fumed. I glanced at the empty chairs around the table in the Sanctorum.

"I ask for your forgiveness, Alpha. I was with the said shipment. I had business in the Capital and sent word to Idaos that I would arrive here. When I found out about the attack halfway through my journey, I rushed back, but the rebels had already disappeared. I have failed you. I have failed the Council. Ronak... he has bested us, that Navar." Remus said.

"Not all is lost," Alpha Canagan said. "We can still overwhelm the rebels. Although, our numbers have decreased exponentially. We have to remember; we are the alphas. We will rally every able wolf from our packs to fight against the rebels. So long as we have the strength, we'll fight the rebels. For Vascya."

"I have a suggestion. Let us put our trust in Faust and hand him the reins of the next attack. Janus's blood is in his veins. With all his might, he'll bring us victory," Remus said thoughtfully. There was no objection against Faust. He was the next best thing after Belaize. Belaize...

"What about Belaize?" I questioned.

"It's rumored that he was fighting for the rebels now," Remus replied solemnly. I cursed under my breath.

"What in the world is happening? First the Cities and now Belaize too is in the hands of the rebels? We have to work fast!" I continued, "Alphas. I suggest we task a group of efficient soldiers to eliminate Belaize. It will be hard, but it can be done. We have to kill him otherwise our doom is guaranteed." Everyone was quiet for a while, lost in their own thoughts.

"We could stop the entire war," Amarog said slowly. I looked up to meet his steely gaze.

"It's nonsense to continue with it. We can stop the war. We don't have to kill the rebels or the mates," he finished.

"The prophecy. Don't you remember it well when you read it with your own eyes?" I countered.

"We've been at this war for years. Lycans are suffering. Liunella's heart bleeds because we are killing our kin because of her gift. We have to stop. Let the prophecy take its own course," he said.

I was agitated. I clenched my fist as my head throbbed harder with pain. "You say this now? Where were these protests against our actions when we decided the fate of our race? The prophecy is the prophecy of death. Our actions are to prevent the death across our nation. We-"

"I haven't seen the wolves of the prophecy yet, and the only killing around here is the one we are responsible for. The blood is on our hands, not those wolves." He furrowed his eyebrows, the veins in his forehead throbbing in anger.

"What do you suppose we do then?!" I raised my voice. My temper flaring.

"Alpha, we respect you and your bloodline, but this is certainly becoming foolish day by day. Who are these wolves? We'll never know. The war is pointless."

"I have a hunch at one of the wolves in the prophecy. But, I cannot be certain," I said finally.

"If you know, why this war!? Let's stop the killing and eliminate that one wolf."

"It's not that easy. Because... we let the wolf go." I said.

"Do you mean Belaize?" asked Remus. I nodded slowly. I felt anger pulsing through me. I was losing them. Fifty years of hard work, muddled by those insolent rebel dogs. The silence stretched.

"Why did you hide this from us, Idaos?" questioned Eyolf.

"I had already put an order to kill him. But the mission failed," I responded.

"We need to kill him. We'll pool our resources to target and kill him," said Canagan.

"It's not that simple now, is it? He has sided with the rebels. He has Ronak's protection. We can't kill him so easily now. But maybe... we can make an exchange. One life, in an exchange of thousands," said Remus.

"We need to send a message to Ronak, discreetly. I don't believe he will side with us so quickly."

"He preaches about stopping the war. If he doesn't give up Belaize, we can make sure that he will lose the support of his allies. After all, no one will miss the Blood Moon Harbinger," Canagan said.

"We will need a different plan of action if Ronak disagrees," said Remus.

"The war will continue as long as the said mates are alive. We need to make sure that Belaize is the one, otherwise, Ronak will call our bluff. He can never know that we are basing this on speculation alone. Our army's primary focus should be to eliminate Belaize at all costs. Would you agree to this, Amarog?" I appealed.

There was no opposition this time.

The Council meeting concluded. I exited the Sanctorum and headed back to my chamber.

HOPE

Marcus

She is here! I felt my wolf's happiness. I hadn't noticed the dullness in my senses until she had returned. A shroud of joy covered my mind whenever Erylesia was nearby. Her presence made me better, happier. Yet we had a long road ahead as mates. She hadn't acknowledged our mate bond yet. In my heart, I knew I didn't deserve her. A powerful alpha, she was. And what was I? Weak.

Erylesia had gone with Ronak, traveling to different Sanctuaries in different states. It had been a few weeks since I last saw her. In her absence, I had been responsible for training rebels in the dance of combat. It was important to mold the untrained rebels who we had freed from the Low Cities into warriors for our next battle. We had been lucky to survive. Liunella had blessed our victory that day.

Belaize, too, had been coming to the grounds. Initially, he would use our sparring grounds for his own athletic discipline and then leave, after all, he needed to get his strength back. What was astonishing was that many prisoners he had helped release joined him and sought his advice for close combat against the enemy. Belaize being Belaize took that opportunity to throw wolves around like toys.

There were many rebels who still were against Belaize. His reputation exceeded his reach. They didn't like that the Blood Moon Harbinger was harboring amongst them, roaming and living freely. Some of these rebels had encounters with him through the years, and they never ended well. I knew many had approached Ronak, begging to execute him, yet Ronak was rigid in his decision. Ronak trusted Belaize. I think it was because he trusted Eliana. The change in Belaize was clear to those who knew the truth about Eliana and Belaize, but I knew he would not hesitate to cover his hands in blood.

"Erwin! Come here!" I called the sandy-haired kid toward me. He ran towards me from the opposite corner of the training grounds.

"Yes, Marcus?" I ruffled his hair.

"Did you finish your training for today?" He nodded enthusiastically.

"Yes. I did. I can perform all the exercises you assigned me now, without the use of my arm. I can even do push-ups!" Erwin dropped to the ground, pushing the balls of his feet back and keeping his back straight. He pushed his body up with one arm.

"Good. Starting tomorrow, we'll move on to the next level of your training. It will be hard," I said.

"Marcus, I need to know. Will I be able to fight alongside everyone?" he prodded. I knew this question was coming soon. Erwin had to grow up in the harshness of this war, which doesn't show innocents like him any mercy. The bitter truth would kill him, but a disabled wolf is a burden on the battlefield. I sighed sadly and looked at him.

He was gazing at me intently, hope shining in his eyes. "Erwin. I do not want to give you false hope. I know... you work harder than the rest of them. Yet... I don't think even after your training Ronak will assign you to the front lines," I stated.

He lowered his gaze and looked at the ground. I saw a tear drop onto the dirt. Oh, Liunella.

I leaned down on my knees and raised Erwin's chin up and rubbed his tears away.

"But... I'll keep helping you to become strong. You may not be out there, but the Sanctuary still needs protection. We need our prisoners to be guarded by powerful wolves to protect the innocent living here. That's why you'll have to strive to protect them. Understand?"

He sniffled a little and rubbed his face clean. "I'll try my best!" he said with resolve.

"That's all I need from you, Erwin."

"I didn't tell you this, Marcus, but I turned three days ago. I can finally turn into my wolf!" he said with a grin.

"That is marvelous! Why didn't you tell me sooner?"

"I wanted to change on my own. It was painful but I... want to be strong. Strong enough to challenge the harbinger. But when I turned, I wanted to be alone," Erwin said.

My heart went out to him. So young and experienced so much suffering. I wished... I just wished for things to get better for him from now on. No one can change the past, but we can change ourselves. *She's here*, my wolf whispered in my mind.

"You know what? I'll help you tomorrow after the festival. Meet me here at dawn. Get some rest and finish your chores and enjoy to your fullest tonight at Lunaire. You deserve it. We all do," I said, standing up and dusting myself off.

"Thank you, Marcus! I'll see you, tonight!" Erwin said and ran out of the grounds.

"You are too soft on him." I heard her melodious voice coming from the shadows of trees.

"I'm not. No one wanted to train him, but he was too stubborn to be sent away," I said and turned toward her.

"I knew you came back, Erylesia," I said, a smile tugging on my lips automatically. Walking toward her, I took a deep breath, I smelled her delicious scent. My wolf was howling inside of me in delight, flashing images of my naked mate through my mind, but I cast them aside. I just wanted to be closer to her.

"I returned a few minutes ago with Ronak. We traveled all over Vascya," Erylesia said with a hint of pride in her voice. They had kept her imprisoned for two years in the Low Cities. She relished the freedom. It had breathed new life into her.

"Any interruptions by the Council?" I inquired.

"Twice. Council is laying low after the fiasco with Low Cities. It was a bite to their asses anyway, I don't expect much from them right away. A few alphas on the Council have retracted their support of the Council. Rumor has it the sisters have recalled their packs, sent them back to their states, but the idiots won't help the rebels. Neutral. My ass," she scoffed.

"We still need to be on guard. Can't trust them or the Council. I have been training some wolves. We need to increase our security and patrol," I said.

"Yes, I noticed. What is with that child, anyway?"

"You already saw that he is missing an arm. His mother was killed. He tried protecting her but lost his arm. Ever since he arrived, I've been helping him," I said with a trace of sadness.

"Come on, Marcus. There are many wolves out there who have suffered the same fate. I do not see you showering them with affection. There is more to it," she stated in a demanding tone.

I lowered my eyes. Erylesia was honest. And prideful. I looked at her. Her fierce violet eyes, her proud stature, and brown hair parted in the center with a silver streak running on both sides of her face. Beautiful.

I didn't deserve her. I would never be on her level.

"You're right, Erylesia. I was a spy for the rebels, and I had infiltrated a Council raiding party. I had been sending crucial information to Ronak while I was there, so he could save as many as possible. On the way to attack the next Sanctuary, Belaize-" Erylesia took in a sharp breath, listening intently.

"Uh yeah. I had been stationed right beside Belaize. I was leaking information out right from under his nose. But, on the way to Sanctuary in the north, we encountered Erwin and his mother. Belaize killed her in front of my eyes and I couldn't do anything. I couldn't stop him. So, I feel... No. I am responsible for Erwin's disability. Because I wasn't strong enough. That's why I try to help him as much as possible. Because, right now, that's the only thing I can do to atone for what I've done... or couldn't do at that moment."

"It wasn't your fault," Erylesia said with a sudden softness that caught me off guard. I looked up and caught her gaze. Her violet eyes showed me a glimpse of emotion that I didn't think I would ever see. It disappeared as soon as it came, and she averted her eyes.

"But I'll always bear its burden," I said.

She clapped my back. "Come on, let's go see Ronak. We have a festival to prepare for," she said as she turned away. We walked through the makeshift houses and tents. Several hundred freed rebels had been resettled into other Sanctuaries, but there were still over fifteen hundred wolves here. It was a daunting task. Still, seeing them make a home in the Sanctuary inspired hope.

Wolves were buzzing with excitement. Everywhere I looked, people had soft smiles on their faces. Children were shouting and laughing with each other or sitting around knitting crowns from flowers they had picked this morning for the festival. A few wolves were helping decorate the large courtyard with sweet-scented jasmines. Some were assembling wood in a gigantic pyre for tonight's bonfire. It was different today. People were different today. Care free.

It brought a sense of normality. The fall of the Low Cities was the desperate win we needed. We had many more battles to fight, yet tonight, everyone wanted to celebrate the festival of Eclipse, Lunaire. It was an annual festival in Vascya for centuries, where we waited for the first rays of Liunella to bless us after the dark eclipse. Thinking back, it had been two decades since Eliana, Adrian, and I had last celebrated it.

We were almost at Ronak's tent when I found the courage to brush her arm, slowing our pace. "Erylesia," I said. She paused, turning to look at me. "I know you think that I'm weak, but I'll prove myself to you. I don't want the only thing between us to be that the Moon Goddess paired us together." I paused, gathering my thoughts.

"Marcus..."

"No, just please listen," I interrupted her, "I will show you I'm not weak," I said with vindication.

Her face was an expressionless mask. So, I waited.

"I know that the Moon Goddess has paired us, but Marcus, I am never settling down, whether that is with you, or another wolf," she said almost apologetically.

I nodded meekly and began walking again. *We will show our mate that we're worthy of her,* I heard my wolf say. *Someday, perhaps*, I thought.

We walked in silence for a while longer, braiding through the busy wolves, when we saw Belaize laid out under the shade of a large oak in a secluded area. Nihara rested on his belly. The two of them were sound asleep. I couldn't help but smile, Belaize, of all people.

"That coward. Pretending to care about an orphan. How can one stoop so low?" Erylesia spoke between gritted teeth.

"I don't believe that's an act. He is changing, perhaps," I mused.

"Murderers don't change, Marcus. I should know. The bloodthirst consumes us. Eventually, he will revert to his old ways," Erylesia huffed.

"You are an excellent fighter. Your blood sings in battle, just like his. Yet, you foolishly choose to ignore the change he is going through. I know he is the harbinger, yet... when I see that innocent soul in his arms, I see what he is now. What he was—"

"What was he, Marcus?"

"Lost," I said and turned away. I nodded at the wolves stationed outside and entered Ronak's tent without a second glance.

"I was expecting you here sooner!" Eliana said. I grinned at her. She was almost back to her old self. The same cheerful girl I remembered. She was sitting next to Ronak. Piles of papers, maps, and books sprawled in front of them.

"I was talking to Erwin. Everyone's excited for tonight," I said.

"Come sit." Ronak signaled to the empty seat opposite him.

Erylesia finally entered the tent, and with no hesitation, went straight for the seat Ronak had offered to me. I felt my ears redden but sat beside Erylesia silently instead. I caught Eliana's eye, observing us curiously. I just shook my head and relaxed in the chair.

"You made it back for the Lunaire, I am glad, Ronak," I said.

"I wasn't planning on it, but with Erylesia's help and confidence, it was much easier than anticipated. We had trouble with chieftains of other Sanctuaries, of course, but we actually created three more. I will have to transfer some people to other places," Ronak said.

"I have compiled a list and schedule for those selected who can travel with warriors. They can start moving out in teams in five days. Moreover, the lack of resources to care for the pregnant she-wolves. Over three hundred, and almost ninety are ready to give birth in the next two weeks. The healers are overworked, and our medicine stores have nearly run out," Eliana informed us.

"I will get more supplies tomorrow. I'll take Adrian as well. He's been whining like a pup to go out of the Sanctuary." I chuckled.

"How is Adrian now?" Ronak questioned, a hint of a smile on his face.

"He has almost healed. He's a bit slow to the draw, but I think getting up and movin' about will be the best medicine for him. The Council guards were cruel to him. Which reminds me, we should thank Armina, El."

"We will do it tonight." Eliana winked at me.

I heard a deep rumble from Erylesia, which she disguised as a cough. My mate was jealous. I willed myself not to laugh. Knowing Erylesia, this will be a disaster.

"Ahem- Why the sudden Lunaire, Ronak? It's pointless unless we have won the war," Erylesia said stiffly.

"No, Erylesia. It is not only for morale, but for hope. It gives us hope to look forward to a happy future. So many rebels have spent their lives running. Lunaire is not just to celebrate and wish for the Goddess's blessing. It is a ray of light for so many. I couldn't deny them that. Not this year. So, I have made preparations. Security will remain tight, and knowing those old bastards, the Council won't act for another few weeks. Too busy licking their wounds clean," Ronak said.

"So, tonight, we get to live carelessly. Adrian will sing," I said.

Eliana groaned in her seat. "Don't remind me. And we can't stop him this time either."

"You both are fond of him," Erylesia said slowly.

Both Eliana and I looked at Erylesia. She was... curious. "Yes. We have grown up together. The four of us. Rayne, Eliana, Adrian, and I," I said.

A pained look crossed both Ronak and Eliana's faces. I bit my tongue. I shouldn't have said that.

"Ronak, are you still on about your child?" Erylesia asked matter-of-factly.

"Aye. Perhaps I was too hard on him." Ronak's voice was sullen.

"Listen, pops, have the coward imprisoned. He betrayed you and your entire cause when he fled. And to make matters worse, he did not even deny a single thing Belaize said."

"Erylesia! Coward, maybe yes. But, Rayne doesn't have an evil heart. He has always proved his worth. Ronak made him the Chieftain of the Sanctuary in Walka. It was unfortunate, but really, do we all not run away from the fight sometimes? He should have a chance at redemption, too," I defended.

"It is only cowards who run, Marcus. Just them. A soldier faces the enemy regardless of the consequence," she said proudly, but her words pierced my heart.

A coward. "I should be imprisoned as well. I ran. I ran away to save my life. I was knocking at death's door and so I ran, Erylesia." I stood up, and twice in a day, I left Erylesia speechless as I walked out of the tent.

A coward. I'm just a coward, and I'll always remain one. The words rang loudly in my mind as I kept walking. My legs were moving on their own, and before I realized where I was, I had already climbed the stone steps of the iron-gated Infirmary on the other side of the Sanctuary.

I went down the stairs. Moving through the well-lit hallway, I finally entered Adrian's room. "The prince returns!" Adrian announced, his arms raised above his head in mockery.

"Oh, be quiet, you bastard," I said dryly.

"I have Amae's gift now, and I can see in your mind. I see... a lover's spat."

I remained silent and sat beside his bed. His injuries had healed except for two or three yellowed bruises. He was back to his cheerful self. I had hated seeing him injured. It reminded me of my helplessness back when he rescued me.

Still, if we hadn't gone for Adrian, we wouldn't have taken the Low Cities. And we'd be damned if he ever let us forget it. He held bed-locked parades dedicated to his own importance. And I suppose we humored him, for now anyway.

"What? Don't tell me I am right. Erylesia hasn't been back five minutes and you're already fighting?"

"I don't want to talk about it," I drawled.

"You are mates, Marcus. For what it's worth, Liunella has put the two of you together," Adrian said.

"I know that. Yet, I will never be right for her."

Adrian smacked my head with his bandaged hand. "Have some trust in Liunella. You both found each other in that hell, if that is not a sign, then Marcus, I should blind you with a stick."

Rubbing my head, I scowled. "Stop taking advantage of your injury, rascal."

He burst out laughing. I couldn't help but laugh with him. Ronak was right. We needed a night to be carefree. To cherish our loved ones.

Getting up, I said. "Well, it is your last day here. I'll tell Honoria to let you out by evening. Which song will you sing tonight?"

Adrian feigned shock, "All of the old ones which we used to sing, of course!"

I groaned. I shook my head and smiled.

"Lookin' forward to it," I said, before leaving the room.

LUNAIRE

Eliana

The Sanctuary was buzzing with palpable excitement. The children, she-wolves, even the warriors, all dressed in their best clothes for the Lunaire. The Sanctuary was beautifully decorated, laden with flowers and lined with torches. In the night, once again, the goddess has come to the sky as a mother comes to sing a soft lullaby, to ease her children into the star-filled dark.

Lunaire was an age-old tradition. The lycans celebrated the festival of eclipse since Liunella had created us. Many celebrated with their packs, some even used to travel to the temple of the Sundara and worship Liunella. Beauty, grace, hope, and life. That is what the eclipse meant. The light that shone brightly after dark.

There was still some time left before everyone was to gather beside the pyre in the courtyard. Cooks had tirelessly prepared for a feast. I knew it would cost our food stores, but for tonight, that was okay.

I stood waiting for Adrian at my usual spot near the Infirmary. The tree was an old comfort. Marcus had gone inside to fetch him and I had insisted to go as well, but he had ignored me. So, I was waiting. The minutes ticked by. My thoughts drifted to Belaize, how I wished he would join us, but his curt refusal was answer enough.

"I do not frolic, Eliana," Belaize had said and taken Nihara with him to Liunella knows where. I had decided I would enjoy it nonetheless.

My wolf had insisted that I ask Belaize again, urge him on, yet I had left him to his peace.

I heard faint footsteps and looked up at the steps of the Infirmary. There stood Adrian, dressed in a white, loose shirt and tight pants. Donning a long jacket with gold embroidery, he looked well. He had finally healed. "Belaize will kill every wolf tonight who so much as stares at you a moment too long." Adrian whistled, looking at me. I had missed his voice. I had missed my friend.

I was wearing a floor-length gown. It was a soft blue, verging on turquoise, cinched at my waist with a silvery, floral pattern, and flowing outward in soft waves. The off-shoulder cut of the dress showcased the pearls that Amae lent me. I had never worn something so delicate, feminine. Growing up in the middle of a battlefield, I was most comfortable in combat clothes, yet for tonight Amae had insisted that I dress well. My hair was loose and cascading down my back.

I folded my arms in front of me, tapping my foot on the ground, "You are late." I feigned annoyance.

"Blame Marcus! He was whining about Erylesia." Adrian rolled his eyes.

"I did no such thing. He," Marcus smacked Adrian's head, "was busy wooing Honoria, who by the way, has no interest in you, Adrian." Marcus side-stepped in front of Adrian and grinned. He had worn similar clothes to Adrian's, but instead of white, he wore a soft crimson shirt paired with black pants. Adrian and Marcus were similar in height, towering at six feet two, just a few inches taller than me.

"Adrian, did you at least invite Honoria to the Lunaire?" I asked, shaking my head. *Fools.*

"She is assisting in three births tonight," Marcus said. "Liunella bless those pups."

"I want to go already. I have been held prisoner in there. It is my night of freedom!" Adrian half-shouted.

"Let's go. The eclipse is almost upon us." I looked up at the luminous moon, shining bright in the starry sky. Magnificent.

Adrian and Marcus came to either side and held my hand. Just like when we were kids, the three of us moved ahead, giddy with joy. Lunaire reminded me of the innocent times when we were just children, running around with no worry. Yet, so much had changed in the last two decades.

Walking through the Sanctuary, seeing every wolf dressed in fancy attire just like mine, was a rare treat. We gathered in the courtyard. The children who had worked hard decorating for the festival came to us with baskets filled with flower crowns. I smiled at them.

"Here, have a crown!" said a young girl, no older than ten. All three of us kneeled down, and the sweet girl placed a white flower crown on our heads.

"Thank you," Marcus said and kissed the girl's cheek. I swear, I saw her cheeks flushed as she ran to her friends with her basket.

We burst out laughing. Getting to our feet, we made it to the courtyard finally. The wolves had done a magnificent job decorating. Sweet white jasmine garlands hung down from ropes tied throughout the courtyard. Lanterns flickered with the soft glow of small flames. The pyre in the center of the courtyard was yet to be lit. Tables and chairs were placed in the corner near the Kitchens. I eyed the table longingly, but we would have to wait until during the celebration.

People gathered in loose clusters in the courtyard, laughing, talking to each other. We navigated our way through the crowd, finally finding Amae. I stepped ahead, hugging her first, followed by Marcus and Adrian. Amae had her hair up in a braided bun with little white flowers weaved in the braid. She was wearing a matching white gown, which shimmered in the light. She smiled at us. "May Goddess bless you all with the first light," she said.

"And with you," we answered in turn. The words felt timelessly familiar.

"Where is father?" I asked.

"He will come soon, dear. He is busy working with the patrol. Any news about Rayne, child?" Amae questioned.

My shoulders hunched reflexively. "No. He left the Sanctuary. Marcus and I had gone to find him, we scouted for the last two days, but he left without a trace. His friends don't know where he went either," I said. It was too painful to think about it. Rayne... I shut away those thoughts. No. I would only focus on joy, tonight. Adrian gripped my hand in reassurance.

"Where are Belaize and Nihara?" Amae prodded again.

"He is not coming either," I replied.

"It is that beautiful girl's first Lunaire! Wait here." Amae fumed and stormed out of the courtyard. I looked after her in surprise. No one knew what went on in her head. Maybe age was like that. The world was just more prone to bending for you.

"I bet she will drag Belaize by his ear," Adrian said, and I giggled. The image of Amae dragging the enormous Belaize was comedic genius.

As I wiped the tears away from my eyes, I felt Marcus stiffen. Both Adrian and I followed his gaze and saw Erylesia entering the courtyard.

She was wearing a gown as well. It was a caramel-colored gown, hugging her bodice and flowing down in fuller pleats on the length. A broad ribbon wrapped around her waist. Her hair was tied in a bun except for the familiar silver streaks that framed her face. This was the first time I had seen her look so... feminine.

Marcus took a sharp breath but stood his ground. We watched Erylesia take the flower crown from the sweet girl and placed it on her head, herself.

"Stop drooling, Marcus," Adrian mumbled. I shoved my elbow in his ribs.

"Honoria just released me. You want me to back in already?" Adrian laughed.

I glanced at Marcus. He was still staring at Erylesia as if he could look at nothing else. I nudged him. "We should ask her to join us. She looks lost," I said as I watched her silently stand at the edge of the crowd.

Despite Marcus's attempts to stop me, I dragged both the males across the courtyard toward Erylesia. She saw us coming, but her gaze only found Marcus. A sense of loneliness washed over me. I wanted Belaize here too, but he was too stubborn.

"I am happy you came, Erylesia," I said smoothly as we approached her. She looked at me, expressionless.

"Ronak insisted I come," Erylesia grumbled.

"I am Adrian. I don't believe we've met properly." Adrian elegantly lifted his hand and Erylesia ever so graciously shook it.

"I am Erylesia," she replied.

"I know. That one doesn't stop talking about you." Adrian pointed at Marcus.

Marcus cleared his throat. "Uh-you... you look beautiful," he said awkwardly.

Erylesia went rigid. I noticed her flushed cheeks as she turned away, trying to regain her composure. Mates. Definitely mates.

"Thank you," Erylesia said. An awkward silence settled between us.

"Erylesia, please join us for Lunaire. It will start soon; my father is coming as well," I said.

"Okay."

Together, the four of us walked back to the pyre. Adrian was telling me about the nonsense that Honoria put him through, when someone in the crowd shouted with excitement. "It's starting! The eclipse is starting!"

All of us looked at the night sky. It was darker than before. A shadow was slowly stretching across the surface of the moon. The moonlight was dimming, and the moon was tinged with red.

When the moon's brightness had almost vanished, my father appeared with Romulus. I hugged both of them dearly. My father was dressed in an emerald jacket with black pants. Chains were loosely drawn across his lapels in a style that was bit old, but fashionable. Romulus was dressed well as ever, nearly identical to my father's attire.

"Where is Amae?" Father asked.

"She will be along in a minute," I replied.

"We should start the ceremony. Everyone is restless," Romulus said. My father nodded.

My father went ahead to the center of the crowd. When people saw him, they quieted down. We formed a circle around the pyre.

"I could've never imagined that we would celebrate tonight, not until we had won." My father's voice echoed in the silent courtyard. "We haven't won, but with Liunella's blessing, we will! So tonight, everyone celebrate. Be free. Cherish each other and live." His voice boomed.

We looked up at the moon. The shadow completely covered it now. Only a faint outline of the ringed moon remained among the starlit sky. *Any minute now!*

That's when Amae rushed beside us with the bundle of joy. Nihara was giggling in her arms, suckling at her thumb. In the time Amae was away, she had dressed Nihara as well in a blue frock and a big flower crown on her head. As soon as she reached us, I smelled Belaize behind her. He had come. Amae had made him come. He hadn't changed out of his usual breeches, towering over us all, yet I smiled at him. He was clearly distressed.

"What did you do, Amae?" I asked her pointedly. I took Nihara from her arms and she snuggled right into my chest. I kissed the top of her head.

"I snatched Nihara away, obviously. Belaize was with Midnight outside the Sanctuary. The stubborn fool wasn't listening. I took her, anyway." She laughed as Belaize stood silently behind us. Before I could greet Belaize, I heard my father's voice again.

"Everyone! Let Liunella's light bless us all into a better future."

Together, we knelt on the ground. It was quiet. I bowed my head, looking into Nihara's wondrous eyes. *Bless us, Liunella. Bless my family*, I prayed.

Then the chanting began,

"Bless us, Liunella.
Enlighten our path to future.
Pardon our sins,
Accept us with open arms.
Liunella, we praise you, honor you
Oh, gracious goddess.
Mother, comfort us.
Give us strength.
For even in darkness,
we seek thy light."

The first ray of light hit us all, bowing in Liunella's grace, blessed by her light. And finally, the drums started. The torches lit brightly all around the courtyard and the bonfire in the middle was lit at last.

We rose from our knees, Amae assisted by Belaize, and circled around the fire to the sound of drums and music. Everyone cheered as wolves began dancing to the beat.

Somewhere in the cheers, I heard my father's voice again, "Eat and dance the night away! It's the Lunaire!"

Our little group broke off as well. Adrian jumped in the center of the crowd, swaying to the drumbeats. I smiled. Erylesia went toward what I suspected was the Kitchens, followed by Marcus. Amae and Romulus had melted away in the crowd, leaving Belaize and me alone with Nihara.

Nihara crawled up in my arms, putting her hands on my shoulders curiously, looking at the flickering light of the burning fire. Belaize was looking at me. At Nihara.

"You should have changed, Belaize," I said, smiling.

"It is Amae's fault. She took..." He waved his hand at Nihara, who was now jumping in my arms, excited by the drums.

I started swaying slowly, dancing with Nihara, as Belaize stood there.

I didn't ask him to dance. Silence hung between us as Nihara and I moved. Words weren't needed. I had already seen what I wanted to see.

I had seen his red-rimmed eyes beaming at us. Beaming with hope.

May Liunella protect that hope, I prayed, dancing through the night.

THE FIRST KING

Ronak

The Lunaire was in full swing. The music, the dance, the heavenly food, it was amazing how the wolves of the Sanctuary pulled together to celebrate the festival of the eclipse. The wolves danced in the flickering light of the pyre. I was strumming my feet on the ground to the beat of the drums, sitting on one of the many chairs that lined the courtyard.

The contagious smiles of the children running and singing the old songs made me smile. *Adya would have danced alongside everyone*, I thought as the loss of my mate washed over me. Sometimes the hollowness swallowed my heart.

I was sitting alone when Amae came to join me with Nihara squirming in her arms.

"Nihara," I called softly. The baby cooed and gurgled happily. I fixed the tilted flower crown on her head. She looked at me and jumped into my arms. Amae laughed as I held her.

"Belaize, let you take her out of his sight?" I questioned, raising an eyebrow and smiling at Nihara. She was a beautiful baby girl. Her soft, unruly auburn hair had grown a little since I had last seen her. She held onto my finger tightly. "A firm grip for such a little creature," I said as some of the tension eased from my mind.

"Yes. I snatched her and told Belaize to change, otherwise I would not return Nihara to him. So, Eliana is going to lend him some clothes. My word, skipping on festivities and making the poor child miss the fun."

I looked at Nihara, who had now removed her flower crown again, tearing it apart piece by piece instead. I plucked a leaf out of her mouth and shook her playfully, making the baby giggle.

"Such innocence. I wonder why Belaize protects her."

"Eliana said he plucked her out the arms of her dead mother. You have seen the number of pregnant she-wolves the Council bred. No wonder the poor child had no one." Amae frowned.

I stood up from my seat and walked with Amae. "Where is Romulus? I saw him with you earlier."

"Luthor dragged him to a drinking game. Kaiser or not, Romulus can't deny his star pupil." Amae grinned. I wiped the drool away from Nihara's lips. The celebrations had been raging for hours, and the pyre was all but burned. The chill of the night had settled in, and many wolves had retired to their tents, tired after the celebration.

A few dozen were left in the courtyard. I spotted Adrian singing in an awful voice, "Standing tall, I am the one, you bow beforeeee..." grooving and singing in a drunken state. I chuckled.

"He never changes," I said.

Amae agreed. "I told him to stop, but he yelled louder than before so I left him alone."

We roamed the courtyard, talking and greeting, blessing each other with a better future. It had been ages since we celebrated anything. I was happy with my decision. I wouldn't be a leader if I dared not listen to the recommendations of my own wise woman. She hobbled along beside me, spritely as ever

"If only Rayne was here," I mumbled after we sat down on the benches near the fire, heating in its warmth.

"You mustn't blame yourself, Ronak. He made his choices, and in our world, those choices are of life and death. No one could have imagined or predicted this."

"He is my son!" I said with conviction. "I should have seen it coming." I shook my head with remorse. Nihara sensed my unease and cried. I rocked her back and forth to quiet her down, but she wouldn't stop.

Unexpectedly, Belaize appeared near the entrance, a look of anger plastered on his face. His body had regained some of its old strength. He had finally changed out of his filthy breeches. He was clean shaven, dressed in a white shirt that barely fit him, paired with a set of black pants, and he stormed toward us. Eliana wasn't far behind, almost sprinting behind him. "Belaize!"

Some wolves paused, eyeing Belaize warily. He took Nihara from me and sat on the wooden bench across from us. Nihara immediately ceased her crying. I had to admit, this was a side of Belaize I had never thought

I would see.

Amae said with a laugh, "He loves that child more than anything."

I nodded in agreement. "Perhaps that child saved us from the Low Cities and maybe even this war. With Belaize having something to protect, he may fight with us," I said, more to her than anyone else.

Eliana sat beside Belaize, and Nihara crawled back and forth between the two. Mates. Who would have thought Liunella paired those two? But the war was cruel, and peace was a stolen moment of reality.

I missed Adya too much, tonight. Eliana and Rayne. Even after decades of war, I had failed them. I knotted my fingers together, trying to shove aside my bitter thoughts.

Soon, a drunk Adrian joined us as well. He was about to sit next to Eliana when Belaize glared at him. Adrian shot backward and hiccupped merrily.

"I know, I know," Adrian said and moved to sit beside Amae, he nearly tumbled to the ground and rested instead against her legs.

"Amae, tell us the stories of the old wolves!" Adrian slurred.

"Young man, this is not the time!" Amae hit his head. Adrian shot his hand up and held it dearly.

"Please! Pleaseeee! I want to hear some."

"Why not, Amae? It will be like the old times." Eliana smirked.

"You are not children!"

"We are! And Nihara wants to hear one." Eliana cooed at the little baby in her arms.

"Alright! Alright!" Amae shook her head. Adrian cheered at her feet. I glanced at Belaize, who was staring at Adrian.

"How about the story of the first wolf?" I suggested.

Amae shot me a glare and cleared her throat. "Once upon a time, our gracious Liunella decided to bless the barren land of Vascya. Vascya was nothing an expanse of endless forest. Liunella chose a place that was later known as the Altar of Liunella. There she created the first wolf, Fenrir, the magnus. She created the first generation of a thousand wolves. Fenrir was the leader of those wolves. When he thought the wolves could reign on their own, he chose four among them of note. Do you know which ones?"

More people had gathered around us and sat on benches. They had taken an interest in the folktale. The children were sitting on the ground in front of Adrian. One of them chimed, "I know. I know. The four winds. Mugiri, Draxus, Çatall and Beleotell!" the boy said proudly.

"Correct! Fenrir chose the first four winds. He tore his own power apart, and with Liunella by his side, gave Muigiri the gift of strength, Draxus the gift of intellect, Çatall the gift of future sight and lastly Beleotell the gift of ghost. Together they formed the four winds of Vascya."

"My father said that the four winds were the greatest!" another girl chimed. The group felt surprisingly intimate. From the corner of my eye, I saw Marcus and Erylesia join as well.

"They were, child. They formed all of lycan civilization, the Vascya we know. The alpha bloodlines that still exist today are their descendants," Amae said.

"What happened to Fenrir?" A small girl wondered aloud.

"They say he died, but I believe he is lost in time, existing somewhere away from us," Amae said.

"But the wolves only live for two hundred years! My father told me." The previous boy frowned.

"Yes," I said, "But… but Fenrir, who knows. He is a myth to us, a story passed through the generations. Amae said that to sound mysterious." I smiled.

"Another one, Amae, please!" The children, along with Adrian, begged her.

"Silence," Amae said loudly. For a tiny woman, she had quite a voice. The buzz of the crowd subsided. The fire flickered around us; wood crackled.

"The year was 1680, I think. The Council was lost, not strong enough to keep the general populous in check. Riots and looting were ripe throughout Vascya. The countryside was plagued with hunters that drove bovines to extinction. Even now, the wilds have yet to fully recover. Without a proper governing body, Vascya was doomed. It was a time darker than even now. They saw not even the moon graced us."

A chill had settled around us as we listened. I knew it well, because all of us had suffered from the aftereffects of that time.

"In that time of chaos, appeared Alistair. An alpha, the likes of which had never been seen before. He was said to be as white as the mountainous snow with eyes like red roses. Gallant and beautiful beyond comprehension. He took charge of the broken Council and guided Vascya to prosperity.

"In a few short years he set the entire country straight. Many challenged Alistair throughout the years, and each time he emerged victorious. He never killed his challengers but instead befriended them. And in return for their life, his challengers served him gratefully. Happy to keep their heads on their shoulders, they dutifully obeyed the great Alistair. When Alistair had repaired the state, he resigned, hoping that his efforts were enough, but again the Council was lost without him. So, they granted Alistair the title of First King."

"As king, Alistair spent his days serving the country; with the Council and his followers by his side, he thrust Vascya into a new age. Crafts and artisans were in high demand. Vascya flourished under his rule. He ordered wolves to expand into the frigid north, the tropical south, the western desert. Soon he was bonded and wed to a beautiful wolf by the name of Arialla. Almost a year later, their child was born. Jonan. A young white wolf, like his father, but with his mother's blue eyes. After a reign of a century and a half, demise befell the great king."

"It was around this time that Idaos joined his ranks. Idaos was young with a fire in him to excel. His lust for power was clear. With him joined his ever-eager follower, Eyolf."

"Idaos solidified his hold on the Council that reigned below the king, gaining the support of alphas from the previous reign. When Alistair was touring the countryside, Idaos launched a campaign to smear the name of the Good King. Alistair was gone for twelve weeks, and in that time, Idaos had convinced the population of Alistair's underhanded behavior. All of it was lies. He presented false proof, testimonies from the alphas that joined him.

"It is said that Idaos threatened death on the other alphas and their families. Idaos blackmailed, backstabbed, and strong-armed his way to power. He bought debts and traded secrets. Eyolf and Idaos made a dangerous duo. They strategically conquered the Council, and when they had used their puppets, they disposed of them. When Alistair returned, his ferocity knew no bounds. Alistair, a normally well-thought and articulate individual, was distressed by Idaos' cold cruelty."

"If he was a bad person, why does he sit on the Council?" asked the small girl, teary-eyed.

"Because dear, he cannot be taken or removed so easily. Many have tried," I mumbled. It was a cruel reality, as long as some wolves supported him, Idaos would always have the power he craves.

Amae cleared her throat and continued, "By the time that Alistair arrived, the entire Capital had gathered for what was set to be a public spectacle. The execution of Queen Arialla and Prince Jonan. Alistair surrendered and begged for their lives. He promised retribution, revenge, money, power, he even offered exile. But, Idaos was smart. He knew that as long as Alistair lived, he would be a threat. They pierced the Queen and Prince through the heart with a spear. Alistair's cries were inconsolable. He ran red with fury, but his fury died instantaneously when he realized that the public was cheering for the execution. The same people he had devoted his life to. He cursed Vascya and turned his back on the Capital and all of Lycan-kind."

"Idaos sent his hunters, among them was Darren. A hunter with a vicious reputation. Only Darren returned from the several dozen sent to pursue Alistair. Alistair was never seen again. Rumors spread that they had killed him. But no one knew with certainty where he had gone. With him left Vascya's hope for a better tomorrow. The last chapter of the life of the great White King was closed."

Amae finished her retelling. "Of course, I left out some details," she said with a smile.

"The dawn is almost upon us, everyone. It is time to hit the hay," I said, clapping my hands. A collective groan rose from the children and adults. No one wanted the festivities to end, but sluggishly, the courtyard emptied. In the deepest part of the night, as I walked Amae to her tent, she turned to me.

"He is alive, Ronak. The White King is alive," Amae said slowly.

"How? He is certainly dead, Amae."

"I have no proof except that I witnessed him. In Belaize's memory. I saw flashes of white light. I am sure that was Alistair," she said with conviction.

"Why did you not tell me before, Amae?"

"Because, it would have been pointless. There is only one person capable to stand tall with our king, and that is Belaize. Yet, when he was captured, he was lost. Now that he has found his light, a will to live in this war, he will help us," she said.

I looked into her aged face. She looked older than she was. I knew this was because of her gift. It sapped her life slowly. All the time she had spent in the Astral Realm had added up. She had mentioned once that spending a day in the Astral Realm could take months off of a wolf's life. It was different for all who visited, but those with the blood of the ghost were stricken with the worst of it.

"You think Alistair will come back to us?" I wondered. Amae pondered for a bit. She twirled her fingers in her hair absently. Her habit left me smiling a bit. She was wise and aged, and yet had the habits of a young woman.

"He must. It's been more than a century. If Belaize is the only one to have encountered him in recent times, then it has to be him. We could send Eliana with him," Amae said.

"It's too dangerous for both of them to make the journey. Eliana is needed here to prepare for our next move. But maybe if we can convince Belaize..." I trailed off. I allowed Belaize to live in the Sanctuary, yet his mind was fickle. The only reassurance that he would hurt no one was Eliana.

"It's worth the risk. We need Alistair," Amae said more drastically as we arrived at her tent.

Through the long hours of the night, I sat alone, thinking of my options. Alistair could be a powerful player in this game of war. Idaos had yet to retaliate for the sacking of the Low Cities. We must move carefully. Any minor oversight could destroy our resistance. Suddenly, the entrance to my tent raised. My head snapped up.

"You!?" I questioned the hooded figure standing in shadow.

"Idaos sends his thanks," the figure stated, removing his hood and stepping inside.

CONTACT

Belaize

It was early morning. The usual buzz of people walking, training, and working was absent today. It was deserted. Many people had celebrated late in the night and for today, everyone was resting inside the tents they called home.

I had changed my clothes as soon as I had left the Lunaire with Nihara. She had fallen asleep in Eliana's arms after playing and listening to Amae's tales. I had grown up listening to some of them too, but I had paid little attention, because training with Janus had been taxing enough to not bother with folklore. All I had known at that age was fighting and killing. I was the Council-bred assassin.

Walking toward Ronak's tent, I wondered why I had been summoned so early. My gut told me it was no good. I had dropped Nihara at the Infirmary to be fed by her usual wet nurse, when a wolf told me Ronak had called for me. I didn't like to be called at all; I had killed people for less, yet I went anyway.

Making my way through the courtyard, I saw the pile of ash of the pyre. The flowers that bloomed beautifully last night were now shriveled and dried. It looked an odd mix of training ground and afterparty.

I reached the tent that served as Ronak's office and entered inside. I saw Ronak wasn't alone. Eliana, Marcus, Adrian, Erylesia, Amae, and Romulus were present as well. Ronak looked up at me, nodding.

Erylesia's nostrils flared as she huffed at my arrival. "He is here. I do not understand why we had to wait for him."

"It is imperative. His presence was requested," Ronak said, running his hand through his hair. He was agitated.

"Bring him," Ronak instructed Romulus, who got up from his seat and went outside.

"Why the secrecy?" Eliana prodded. Ronak stayed silent instead.

Within a minute, Romulus was back with... *what?*

"Remus," I said coolly. "The Council is making a move," I concluded.

Eliana looked back and forth between the two. She didn't know.

"Your twin. Romulus, that's your twin!" The others were stupefied as well. Besides Amae, and Ronak, no one knew anything, I realized.

"You didn't know that Remus was his twin?" I asked Eliana. She shook her in denial.

"He never told me. But why didn't YOU say anything?"

"I deduced they were working together. I didn't want to expose their relationship. Why did you think the Low Cities fell? It is the Twin's heritage," I remarked.

"Why did you hide this from us, Ronak? We could have overthrown the Cities much earlier. Why were we made to fight and lose every time?" Marcus clenched his fists. He was fuming.

"Because you didn't. With every attack, I released information, hiding it from the Council. I will not claim that not a single life has been taken in this ruse, but it has saved thousands. Only a select few know about the relationship between the Cities and the rebels. We couldn't risk it."

"But we could have used the power, the army, if it was always under our control," Marcus said.

"The Council is more than an enemy we fight against. It has more sway than you realize. This is not war. It is deep-rooted politics. The ruling alphas sit on their silver gilded chairs and, with a flick of their wrist, change the course of the country," Eliana said.

"Take a seat, everyone." Ronak sighed.

Everyone settled down again. I pulled a chair over and sat as well. The tension was palpable.

"Why now?" Adrian wondered. "Why did you come here now?"

"Council wants to meet Ronak," Remus replied. "They want to stop the war."

"Nonsense," Amae mumbled. "You have strolled in here with a white flag in hand, is that it? The Elders will never lose. They paint illusions for the masses. What is the real reason?"

Remus sighed in defeat. He was pale compared to Romulus, but they had the same face, same body.

"They want to negotiate with you, Ronak. In exchange for stopping the war, ceasing the culling and raiding of mates, they want you to hand them Belaize," Remus said.

Blood drained from Eliana's face. She clenched her fists and shifted in her seat. Her eyes darted toward me.

"Why? Why would the Council go to such lengths?" I said. They had wanted to kill me, sending Faust and his squadron, but this? I didn't expect this. I thought they wanted to eliminate me because I had defied their instructions time and again. But this?

"Because... Idaos has concluded that you are one of the mates mentioned in the prophecy, Belaize. The reason for this culling. He says his gift does not lie," Remus said.

My wolf, my instincts, were overwhelmed with the need to protect Eliana. *We are the prophesized mates? How? The Council doesn't know about Eliana. She will be safe.* I glanced at everyone. The horror of the situation had left everyone speechless. We were the answer, the key, to end this war. To stop the fighting. And to stop the destruction.

"No," Eliana said. "No. No!"

She shot up from her seat. Agitated. She started pacing back and forth in the tent. "No. The Council. They will never stop. Never. They will hunt each rebel to the ends of Vascya, even if they have Belaize in their clutches. We cannot have this exchange. The price is too high."

"High? The Council wants you to surrender the Blood Moon Harbinger. Use your wits, girl, one life against countless others," Remus said.

Eliana almost growled at Remus. "Remus..." Romulus mumbled beside his brother.

Remus looked at Eliana again. The realization hit him as he glanced back and forth between us. "Oh, Liunella."

"Liunella is cruel. To lose both children to fate, Ronak. I pity you," Erylesia commented.

"Do not add fuel to the fire, child. Ronak is at the end of his line. Do not push him," Amae warned. I had never heard the small woman use that voice. She was angry at Erylesia, rightfully so, yet that was the blatant truth.

"The Council is prepared to publicly demean Ronak and his leadership. They know that Belaize harbors here. They will use every dirty trick to their advantage Ronak," Remus said.

"Eliana is right. The Council will harrow us till every rebel is on their knees. Although you are right, handing over Belaize might reduce the number of casualties, but how can they be sure it's Belaize? The Council has never made an assumption before. Idaos has been known to manipulate the Council," Ronak said.

"Yes. Truthfully, I also bear the news that half of the elders have sided with rebels now. Illari and Evette are neutral, but that gives the rebels advantage. Valio, Olegario and Amarog will be on our side. They haven't outright declared their allegiance, though. But when the last battle is on the horizon, their support will turn the tides in our favor," Remus said.

"Ronak. It is time." Amae placed a hand on Ronak's shoulder. She looked at me, her gaze pierced my soul. I averted my eyes.

"To end this war, we need to eradicate the Council completely. We will not bow, Remus. We have yet to find our secret weapon," Ronak said, "The news that Belaize and Eliana might be the mates of the prophecy changes nothing. The Council has and always will see us as an enemy. You might be the mates that they hint at, but we can't be sure. We don't have the time to squabble over this, either. When that wretched prophecy comes true, we will know, till then, this war is the one we fight."

"Belaize." Ronak called my name. "It is time you prove your allegiance to us. Yes, you are Eliana's mate, and you have been invaluable in the Low Cities. I have witnessed the change in you, but I am to give one task that you must fulfill. Both of you and Eliana, in fact," Ronak said.

Eliana stopped her pacing and stared at Ronak. A feeling of dread settled in the pit of my stomach.

"Your greatest weakness, Belaize. You will have to face it again," Ronak said.

"No." I said sharply. The only fight I had ever lost. I looked at Marcus, who sat in his chair, stunned at the revelation. *He did an excellent job as a spy. So we have come full circle, back to this,* I thought.

"What are you talking about?" Eliana asked.

"Belaize, Eliana. We need you to go into the forest of Sundara, again," Amae said.

"No," I repeated. "That is no place for her." My heartbeat rose as the dread intensified. Flashes of the white stormed through my mind.

Amae placed a hand on my shoulder. "We wouldn't send you there if we could help it, child."

"You don't have such luxury to refuse," Ronak said matter-of-factly.

"What's in there?" I asked Ronak. "What almost killed me?" I felt my blood rushing through my body as flashes of that day entered my mind again. I shook myself out of those thoughts and steadied my breathing. Thinking of Nihara helped calm me.

"Alistair," Amae said and paused. The air grew still.

"What the hell, Amae! You are joking, right?" Adrian exclaimed. I glanced at everyone again. All seven of us, besides Amae and Ronak were shocked. Secrets were spilling out, each revelation shocking me to my core.

"Impossible," I said, astounded. "He died ages ago."

"I have seen him in your memories, child. He lives," Amae assured us.

Everything made sense then. I finally understood why I feared that place. Why I was so hilariously outmatched against that white flash. The old King Alistair.

"We will go," Eliana said finally. "We will search for Alistair."

"No," I said again.

Eliana glared at me. I wanted to look away, but I held her fury-laden gaze. "You do not decide for yourself, Belaize. I understand our bond. But look ahead. Open your eyes and look into a future. A future without war, where peace exists," she said.

I was about to refuse again, when she held her hand up, stopping me. "For Nihara," she finished.

The word stuck in my throat. She was right. I was her guardian. Nihara's protector. For her, for them, I would face my fear, and enter that wretched forest again. Eliana knew that well.

I stiffly nodded in agreement. Everyone was watching us. "Someone will have to take care of Midnight," I said.

"We will find him, father. Then, we will stop this war, on our terms. We have lost too much to play into the Council's hands." Eliana folded her arms in front of her chest.

"Now, Remus. I understand the Council wants us. But that is not a reason enough for you to enter our Sanctuary to meet with my father. What is going on that has shocked you enough to run here?" Eliana said, straight to the point. She was in no mood to riddle away.

Remus swore but regained his composure. Eliana's question had struck hard.

"Navars. The same as always. Ronak asked me the same question when I arrived." He smiled, but the smile didn't reach his eyes.

"I came because..." Remus took a deep breath, "Because Janus is alive."

Amae grew pale, and I imagined I mirrored her reaction. Another storm brewed in my mind. My past was standing in front of me again, yet I was helpless. Janus. Janus was alive.

TO FIND THE KING

Belaize

The city of Rylsk was bustling, which was refreshing as we had spent three weeks traveling, finally to arrive here. I looked around, trying to spot any Council guard that might be patrolling. I craned my neck to see Eliana who was looking through the crowd with suspicion as well. On our way here we had encountered a few Council guards. We had changed our path quite often, throwing anyone who was following us off our trail.

"Don't worry. We'll be safe here. We just have to lie low," I said, bending down to speak softly into her ear.

"How long do you think we will have to stay?" Eliana mumbled over the shouts of a vendor selling fruit on the street corner. She tugged at her dark gray cloak that matched my own.

"A day at most. Then we enter the forest."

If it were in my hands, I would have headed straight to Rylsk, but I was on Ronak's mission. He insisted that I follow his instructions perfectly. Following Council rulership had its perks; I'd to admit. I could have wandered to any city or village in Vascya and the guards would fall at my feet to serve me.

I took Eliana through a series of alleys until we ended up in an old rusty bar. The door creaked as I pushed it open. I headed straight for an empty seat in the back corner. I heard the clank of the glasses as the bartender poured liquor in them. A moment later, Eliana joined me.

A server girl came up to our table and said, "Welcome to Malcolm's. What would you like?" She was a mousy girl dressed in rags. I didn't expect much from this dump.

"Do you have Moonwine?" I said. She just nodded.

"I'll have one glass," I said, dismissing her.

She turned to Eliana. "And for you, miss?"

"A plate of roasted pork and some lager would be great," Eliana said.

The girl left us alone. I looked around the place. It was nearly empty, except five wolves scattered talking among themselves. The bar was a small and shady one.

I glanced at Eliana. She had her hands in knots and was staring at them intensely.

"Relax a little," I muttered.

She shot a glare at me but took a deep breath. "So... what now?"

"Now, I'll have a drink."

"You know what I mean," she said while narrowing her eyes.

"We find a place. Tomorrow we'll be on our way," I said.

The server returned with our drinks and set them down on the table. I immediately sipped the wine. The burn in my throat always felt good. Eliana silently ate her food and sipped at her lager. Things felt a little stiff between us despite the hours journeying together. I wanted her near, but at the same time, I didn't quite know what to say. I was used to soldiers for company.

I supposed that other types of people would make idle chat. Entertain her with tales of friends, old memories, or blushing stories. Liunella, she deserved a night of, oh, I don't know, dinner and a play. But I had none of that to give her. It made me want to fidget in my fuckin' chair. My wolf paced restlessly in my mind.

We were soon finished. I paid for the drinks and stood up. Just as we were about to leave a wolf stood up and made his way to us. I stiffened and raised a hand to Eliana as he approached.

The wolf waved to us and said, "I couldn't help but overhear, do the two of you need a place to stay?"

"We weren't talking to you," Eliana said.

"Yes. But you still need a place to stay," he said with a laugh. The motion did odd things to his full mustache and jowls. Even his round belly shook merrily.

"My friend owns an inn down by the alley. I'm actually just heading down there. Would you like to join me? I can get you a great price. Just thirteen dira!" he said with another pompous laugh.

"No," I said and exited the bar. Eliana followed suit. We had only taken a few steps into the street when the wolf approached again.

"Come on! The night has fallen. Where will you find a place at this hour? Come. I'll lead the way. Only twelve dira!" he said again in his chirpy voice.

"I do not repeat myself. I have already said no," I said. My senses were on high alert. I took a breath. Six wolves lurked nearby.

"But please! The young lady needs to rest at least! What if something untoward were to happen? These are troubled times, and this city after dark is not a place, you'd want to find yourselves in!"

"Are you threatening me?" Eliana remarked. I looked at her. She clenched her fists, glaring at the wolf. This might just get interesting.

"No, no! Sweet lady! I am not. I'm just offering you a place to stay with your man," he said.

"No. You ARE threatening me." She huffed angrily. Stepping closer to the wolf, she fumed. It was almost comical as she was a head taller than him.

"Well... I am not. But if you don't want the Council guards sniffing around, we at the inn can help you!"

"Aren't you a persistent little dog?" I said mocking him.

Eliana grabbed his arm and twisted it around his back. She pushed him to the ground. He tried to get up but couldn't. Eliana put her hand in the pocket of her cloak and pulled out a few diras. She tossed them to the ground at his feet.

"Here. Get out of my sight. And take your lackeys with you. If I sense one, I will snap all of your necks. Understand?"

He nodded through a groan of pain. She quickly jolted up, pushing him to the ground. Her steps were purposeful as she led us away.

"I don't want to hear a word about it," she muttered.

"I didn't say anything," I said with a smirk. My wolf inside me was proud of her. I repressed the feelings, and we walked along the lonely streets of Rylsk.

Toward the outskirts of the city, we finally got a place to stay for the night. Eliana was friendly with the innkeeper, and as far as I understood, Marvel was a rebel ally. He provided aid to those sympathetic to the cause. He didn't ask questions and gave us a damn good rate, too.

Our room had a double bed with two side tables. On one side of the room a table and chair were placed by the window. I sat in the chair and looked outside into the night. Here, the streets were dim and empty, though reflective light from the heart of the city blocked the stars from my view. My head ached with tension. I knew that if our mate bond was discovered we would be handed in for gold, but worse yet was the forest. I couldn't shake the oppressive dread.

Eliana took a seat on the bed, resting against the headboard. She had removed her cloak and placed it on the rack behind the door. I could reach out and touch her if I dared. But I couldn't. I... wasn't sure why.

"What do you think about the prophecy?" Eliana drawled.

Her hair fell down her back in waves with a few locks framing her face. But her striking emerald eyes were trained on me, waiting for my answer. I didn't reply for a few minutes. The silence lingered between us as we sat there in the small room.

Finally, I stood up and removed my cloak as well. I proceeded to hang it on the hook beside Eliana's. I unbuttoned my shirt and removed it. I had regained most of my muscle by now. I felt fuller, restored.

I turned and took one step closer to her.

"I don't care about it." I traced the deep scar on my chest with my fingers. It still reminded me of that searing pain I felt that day.

"I am here because Ronak chose me. Because of this."

"I never asked, but how did you get it?" Eliana said. She had an incredulous look on her face.

I laid down on the bed, near her feet, staring at the ceiling. I folded my arms above my head. "The forest we are going to enter is that of Sundara. It's not far from here. About three hours run, south of Rylsk. I have been there before. The ruins of moon goddess's altar rests at the heart of it. I know that centuries ago it used to be a place of pilgrimage. Thousands went there and worshipped Liunella. But now that place is barren. A monster lives there."

"Or that's what I thought. The Council had sent me there to eliminate that monster but I ended up with a scar. To this day, I am... afraid, I think. I am afraid to go in there." My voice was lower than a whisper, yet it echoed around the room.

"Father shouldn't have asked you to do this, Belaize. I am sorry," Eliana said softly.

I closed my eyes and just took a deep breath. Eliana's scent calmed me. I don't even know why I was saying any of this, but it felt... liberating.

"Amae. She has the blood of the ghost. She... entered my mind and saw the monster. I don't remember much, if I'm honest. But I saw a white flash with red eyes hungry for blood. That's all. And then I was knocked unconscious. I know that Amae thinks its Alistair, but I'm not so sure. I... don't know what to think," I said.

"Do you think we can win this war?" Eliana shifted towards me.

"When Ronak asked me to choose the rebels, to bring Alistair back— if he exists at all— in exchange for my life, I thought maybe we could win. I don't know. Does Alistair even exist? We are grasping at threads. I just... Nihara. She has given me some meaning to live for. When I plucked her out of her dying mother's arms, I vowed to protect her. If ending this war somehow keeps her out of harm's way, then I'll do it," I said. My eyes were still closed.

"What was it like? The Council?" She asked.

A question that I had been dreading for the past few weeks. I knew she would ask me someday, but no amount of time could have prepared me for it.

"I don't know where to start," I mumbled. I sighed. A rush of memories came into my mind, drowning me in the past.

"I don't remember much. Amae... she helped me remember some things. I didn't have a memory of how I became Council's assassin before. I just remembered that the Master of Arms, Janus, had trained me. It was like a switch that had been flipped in my head, and all these memories of my childhood became clear. My father sold me to the Council. I don't think he knew I was a Kaiser. My mother never knew that I was sold. He lied to her. I don't understand why... but that's my first memory."

"I'm sorry, Belaize." Eliana took my hand and squeezed. I felt tension leaving my body in euphoric waves at her brief touch. I cleared my throat.

"Yeah. Well, after that Janus took me in. I had a roof over my head for the first time, but I had to pay the worst price. Janus starved me for days. I think I went two months without food. He would hit me. With chains and whips, whatever he felt was necessary for my training. He would make me run for days without a break until I lost consciousness. I was weak. He said he would make me the incarnation of death, and for that to happen I had to go through pain so I would know what it felt like when the soul leaves the earthly vessel and departs into the heavens. Day after day he would torture me. I remember... I used to cry. But... I stopped. Because no one heard my wails." I felt another squeeze of my hand and this time I gripped her hand hard.

"A couple years later, his torture methods weren't effective anymore. I didn't feel the pain as I used to. He changed tactics. He introduced his son, Faust, to me. Faust hated me from the beginning. Janus tortured him just as he had me.

"But something was different. His only goal was to make his father proud, and Janus only wanted one thing in life: to create death. When he was solely focused on me, he ignored Faust. So Faust assumed I was the reason Janus didn't favor his own son. Who was I to convince him that his own father was a monster?

"Janus made both of us compete. We would fight till we were both bloody. We would fight through concussions, broken bones, it didn't matter. I hospitalized him multiple times. In the end, I always won. I always had the upper hand; I was better than Faust because of my bloodline.

"Janus had the perfect candidate to complete his project. But... only one flaw remained. I lacked that killer instinct. I didn't want to kill. No matter how much he starved me, hit me, dragged me around the forest, or left me tied upside down from a tree for weeks, it never happened. I couldn't kill Faust." I released a breath that I didn't know I was holding.

"What happened afterward, Belaize?" Eliana questioned after a couple minutes of silence.

"I'm not so... sure. I remember... a dungeon of sorts. He had me tied up, and touched a glowing stone on my head. I think that's when the switch, it shifted something in me. I don't remember much afterward. But he commanded me to kill a Council guard and without hesitation, I did. I didn't feel guilt anymore. No, it was like I couldn't feel guilt anymore, or anything, really. It was so much easier. I was invincible.

"To test my limits Janus demanded the one thing I was afraid of doing. He told me to attack him, but I hesitated. So he kept provoking me until my world was red. I was driven mad by bloodlust. I attacked Janus, who I had grown to fear. I attacked him and I killed him. The fucker died laughing. I remember his vile laughter. He had finally done it. He had created the Blood Moon Harbinger."

"After his death, or so we thought, the Council began using me. I carried out their missions and had enjoyed killing. I was undefeated. Wolves across Vascya feared me. I was death. Until the Council tried to kill me. I was too strong to be in their control and now, with this prophecy... Eliana, my past is filled with horrors. I know I can't be forgiven for my crimes. But, when I see Nihara, she reminds me of that young wolf who was torn from his mother's hands. I just... can't bear that thought." I stopped speaking. I couldn't go on.

"I didn't... know. Belaize, I am... sorry. I wish you didn't go through all that pain," Eliana said with sympathy clear in her voice. Her hand was still in mine. It felt nice, her calming aura. She genuinely wanted to... protect me?

"We're mates, Belaize," Eliana whispered as if answering my unsaid question. She shuffled her body and laid down too. The space between us now was so small. My wolf wanted to get closer to her, but I refrained. I laid completely still.

"Yes," I said.

"I will always protect you," she said.

"I don't need that."

"I'm your mate. I will die to protect you. Liunella has given us a gift. Maybe, you don't need it, Belaize, but I'll do whatever in my power to protect you and Nihara. Because she means something to you, to me. I understand you don't trust easily. I know you don't have a plan for the future except providing for Nihara. But you need to see that... I am here for you. I will be... no matter what. I have tried everything in my power to show you that I have accepted you as my mate, whether you see it or not. The question remains... do you accept me too?" Her voice was soft but trembled, full of insecurity and sincerity. Afraid to hear my answer.

In the silence, my throat felt dry. Somehow, I made my lips move.

"I... already have," I said in a hoarse whisper.

"I saw you... in my mind. You were crying and sitting beside me in the Infirmary as I laid helplessly in bed. In that moment, I knew I could never part from you. No matter what, I told myself. No matter how much I restrain myself, even now, my wolf just wants you. It will as long as it lives.

"I just don't want to hurt you, Eliana. Being with me means being surrounded by death constantly. I have the ability to kill anyone at any time. But you, you are good. You're not a murderer, and I don't belong beside you," I said with remorse.

"I am an alpha, Belaize. Blood of the old runs in my veins. I have struggled with war. I have seen people die. I lost my mother to the war. I was raised to be a warrior. I have killed people. I am my father's right hand, and yet, you think I am innocent?" Eliana chuckled. "I am stronger than you think Belaize. I have seen and felt pain as well. Set aside your simple notion of goodness, the world is more complex than that."

I moved to my side. My body was close to her, nearly touching. I felt her breath hitch as I came closer. I slowly opened my eyes and was met with her gorgeous emerald depths. I lifted my hand and traced her cheek with my finger as it turned to a rosy pink.

My heart, it twisted with sadness. Eliana had seen the horrors of the war and yet...

"Your eyes, they are pure. You're mature. But, your heart, it's innocent. I don't want to take it away. I pray to Liunella, you don't have to witness what I have."

"What do you mean-n?" She stuttered.

I closed my eyes and let my wolf take over. I knew my eyes had turned. I felt my bones snapping as my face elongated. My fangs grew out of my mouth. Fur started covering my face. I felt Eliana shiver beside me in shock at my distortion.

"Look at me," I said, my voice hoarse.

I opened my eyes. Eliana gasped a little as she saw them. She gazed at me for what seemed like eternity. She leaned her hand against my face, touching my fur softly. Her small slender fingers felt good, leaving me wanting more of her touch.

"If you don't understand now... you will someday. But I hope that day never comes," I said, taking back control. My bones snapped again and my fangs retracted. My fur was gone, leaving just bare skin beneath her fingers.

"Rest now. We won't have a chance later," I said as I shifted a little away from her. A sigh of relief escaped her mouth.

"You confuse me, Belaize," she said.

"How?" I wondered.

"You're not what a mate is like."

"I'm what you get Eliana, in this life, and maybe many more to come," I said.

"I know. I think... I like it. Do you think we really have a future?" She asked again.

"I do," I said with sudden determination.

I felt a sudden shift in my mind. Something had changed. I cleared my mind and slowly reached for it. It was like a connection. I felt Eliana's presence in my mind, warm and gentle. I felt her thoughts. It was like a fog had been lifted between us. I felt her sympathy for me. Her genuine unwavering will to protect me. I felt her... love for me.

I didn't deserve that, yet she had those feelings for me. I felt at war with myself, the view I had of the man who could kill without even a wince, and the man who was worthy of her light. Somehow, it felt right. She felt right. And I would sort out the rest.

You can feel it too, right? I asked her through the connection.

Yes. I do. I heard her sweet voice echo in my head.

I looked at her with confusion. "What does this mean?"

"I... I think... we have bonded." She whispered in amazement.

Belaize, take all the time you need. I'll be waiting for you. I heard her voice echo again.

We had a connection. We have bonded. I have... a mate.

The realization left me in shock. Sleep took over us soon enough as I was lost in a world of dreams with Eliana as my purpose in life. My mate.

I woke up early the next morning. Eliana had begun to stir as well. A comfortable silence had settled between us.

"We should leave soon," I said as I stretched and got out of the bed. I grabbed my cloak and stepped out of the tiny room. A part of me was free now that I trusted someone. Living with no one at my back, though it had been beneficial at the time, had left me crippled socially. Wolves were never created to be alone. I wondered what this would mean for our life together.

Eliana was still not out of our room yet, but I felt an odd presence, something at the back of my mind. I tried to ignore it, but it was persistent.

Suddenly, my thoughts went blank and my vision brightened. It was like the white-hot glow of the sun had blinded me. I growled cautiously. Something was wrong. My wolf tore to the forefront of my mind and I shifted.

"Belaize..." I heard an angelic voice whisper. The voice was coming from inside my head and from all around at the same time. It was smooth and pleasant to my ears. Worse yet, it was completely unbothered. Panic rose in me now. *What the fuck was happening?*

"Who are you?" I growled and spun around. The brightness faded slowly. I blinked my eyes furiously until I could make out bare shapes. I realized that I was outside the inn. However, everything stood still. No one was moving. Everything was frozen in time. I could make out an open door with someone's foot out and the other in, frozen in place. I looked up and saw birds hanging in the air, frozen mid-flight.

"What is this power?" I asked, growing more anxious.

That was when I saw her. She was tall for a woman. She had platinum hair that fell below her waist, pale skin, and her eyes that glowed the color of the lapis stones. Flowing silk robes glided inches above the ground, and six wings arched around her form. I felt a natural subjugation to her.

"Who are you?" I questioned. I fell to its knees and bowed, as if pressed down by a supernatural force. I pressed against it with all my will, but it was like trying to hold up the sky, useless.

"Do not fear me child," she spoke harmoniously. Her mouth did not move when she spoke. Her radiance was warm and inviting. "My child, you were astray, but you have come back. You must protect her." She spoke.

"Protect who?" I wondered.

She gestured towards the inn behind me, the door was open, and Eliana was stepping through. Like everything else, she was also frozen.

The realization dawned on me.

"Goddess!" I said. "Forgive me." I bowed further, my head almost touching the ground.

She smiled and nodded. "You will find the one you search for, but you will also find death. Death follows on sure feet, wherever you go. Protect her, child." A moment later, everything returned to normal. The sounds of the city returned to my ears as everything unfroze.

I looked around frantically as the world simply resumed, as if nothing had happened. The goddess. My mind was a whir. She's real, she exists. *Death follows on sure feet,* she had said.

The words tasted almost bitter in my mouth. "Belaize, is something wrong?" I heard Eliana call.

I debated about telling her but for some reason decided against it. My wolf howled in protest. He didn't want to hide anything from our mate. Yet, I still didn't think it was the right time to tell her.

"Nothing, just wondering where Alistair might be, if that thing even is Alistair."

She put a gentle hand on my shoulder, "All will work out, the Goddess watches over us," she said.

She does watch indeed, I thought and silently prayed.

After leaving the inn we traveled for a few hours. Progress was slower in this form, but we were less recognizable. Gradually, the streets became trails, and then even less than that. We only changed into our wolves once we reached the trail that led to the heart of the forest of Sundara. Damn near impossible to find as it was overgrown. People don't go into that evil forest anymore, yet fragments of paths still existed. That sense of dread I had felt all those years ago returned. A pit had formed in my stomach.

"I... I'm afraid," I stuttered as we stood close to the slight clearing of brush that marked the trailhead. Eliana looked at me compassionately. I felt her trying to calm me down through our bond.

"You could always wait here." She chuckled. I saw a devilish look on her face and knew she was challenging me.

"Eliana, if that thing shows up and attacks, run," I said with all seriousness. She sobered up quickly, and we finally stepped into the eternal darkness that was the ancient forest of Sundara.

Almost immediately most of the light was blocked by the thick conifers and deciduous trees that surrounded us. So little light reached us that it was practically insignificant. We ran through the forest for a few minutes when I sensed someone nearby.

Be on your guard, I said to Eliana through our bond as we ran.

I sensed the creatures of the forest roaming without fear in the woods. It was their home. I was hungry and wanted to kill but otherwise I didn't pay that much attention. My hunger could wait. I used what little memory I had of the place, coupled with my awareness, to navigate the forest, and the hours melted away. The moon rose, and with it, the feeling of Luinella's presence around me.

I came to an abrupt stop. My paws dug into the wet ground in an effort to stop my momentum. The altar of the moon goddess lay in front of us. It looked almost entirely unchanged. The same white stone, the same crumbling gate. The woods cleared and I saw the magnificent structure in front of me. Even in the soft glow of the moonlight, the ruins looked breathtaking.

We're here, I said through our bond. I was ready. I scanned my surroundings for any intruder. Nothing. I stepped forward, climbing the steep steps at the entrance. Eliana followed, looking vigilant and calm as ever.

The old hallways were illuminated by the low light of the moon. Walking through them filled me with certain peace that I didn't know existed. I had to wonder if I felt the space differently, given our mate bond. *Maybe that's why people worshiped in this place*, I thought.

Still, I was afraid, ready for that monster to attack. But I looked at Eliana. She took my hand and gave me a reassuring squeeze.

"We should go and look for him," she said and tugged at my hand.

"This... was a wrong decision. I believe we should leave Eliana. This isn't safe for you," I said with an edge in my voice. My stomach was a bottomless pit. We... we needed to leave.

"No. I'm not backing down," she said with confidence. "We have to do this for the sake of Vascya."

"You should have listened to your mate," boomed a voice. It echoed through the hall, shifting and reverberating. The sound was larger than life.

The hair on my body stood at attention. Fear kicked in, and it took everything in my power not to run in that moment. I felt the astral distortion from the voice in the shadows and saw the familiar red eyes that haunted my dreams.

No doubt was left in my mind. We had found our king.

REBORN

Idaos

"You never cease to amaze me, Idaos," said the cloaked man in a gruff voice. "Time and time again, I am the one cleaning up your messes."

Anger flared inside me, my hands trembled which I hid inside my old robes, "Don't you dare!" I said, raising my voice.

"You should never have come out so early. Your actions destroyed our entire schedule. You have put the entire plan in jeopardy."

Our plan was foolproof, yet the rebels had surprised us at every turn. The Low Cities had fallen at the hands of few wolves. A substantial portion of the army had taken a hit to the morale. Rumors spread like wildfire that Belaize's ghost fights for the rebels. Untouchable and undead.

"You must rea—" the cloaked man was interrupted by the knock on the door. He instantly melted into the shadows of the room, disappearing. I didn't know how, but he disappeared entirely. Even his presence, that feeling of oppressive dread, was gone.

"Enter," I called out loudly. The wooden doors swung open and revealed a guard accompanied by Faust.

"Alpha." Faust lowered his head.

"What is it, Faust?" I asked calmly.

"I-" Faust paused and sniffed the air. An odd look crossed over his face. "That scent?" he asked curiously.

"Don't worry about that, tell me, what do you want," I said.

He frowned and sniffed again. "I apologize, my lord. We have something," he stated. "We have finally found the location of the rebel camp where Ronak operates from."

Good! This was exactly the news that I needed. After everything had gone wrong, this was it. Finally, the rebels would be in our grasp, along with Belaize. *I won't let you be my doom. I will be the light of Vascya. I will outshine my ancestors.*

"Excellent! Take two thousand soldiers with you and finish them! Immediately. We must control Ronak. Even if Remus finds him and convinces him to give up Belaize, we cannot stop our attacks. I don't care about the prisoners. No survivors should remain. Be it the she-wolves or their pups. Kill them all. Especially Belaize, he must not survive," I said. I would not let Belaize be my end. No. Never.

"How did you find them?" I asked.

"That's the thing, we didn't. They found us." Faust had a wretched smile on his face.

"What do you mean?" I asked.

"I found myself a rebel that is more valuable than any weapon could ever be. More valuable than that pathetic pet of yours." he spat.

"Out with it! Today is not a day that I wish to have my patience tested, Faust," I retorted.

"Ronak's son! Rayne. I found him. He has left his doomed father's side for a place on the Council. A lost little pup just looking for validation." He laughed maniacally.

"The son of Ronak the Wise..." said the cloaked man emerging from the shadows.

"Oh goddess! What in the world are you doing?" I yelled at the man. It was as if my position of control and the authority was slipping out of my hands. Such insolence!

Faust stood at attention; his teeth bared at the threat that he didn't notice before. Sniffing the air again, he cautiously stepped to my side.

"Who are you?" he yelled, lunging at the man. "Why do you smell like him?" His voice trembled as he spoke. He was afraid, no, terrified. After all, the ghost of his past was alive and walking in before his eyes. It was pitiful.

"I smell like him, because I am he." The cloaked man stepped into the light of the torch and removed the hood from over his face. His features were illuminated by the light of the torches in the chambers.

"F... fa... father?" Faust was panting and shaking now.

"What sorcery is this?" he questioned. "You are dead!"

Janus laughed out loud. "Silly child, God's soldiers don't die!" Janus touched his child's cheek. Stroking his chin.

"How!?" he asked, "How are you alive?" Faust was in a frenzy. I could smell the fear in the air, which was making my wolf agitated.

"Fret not the details my son, now go on, fetch Ronak's child for me. Won't you, Faust?" Janus said with a sadistic smile.

"I... Yes, father," he said, bowing his head as he left.

"Was it wise to reveal yourself, yet?" I inquired.

"This war is in its final phase, it will be over soon, and when it ends, I will assume control of this land." He smiled, a terrifying smile that left chills shooting up my spine.

"You will not control Vascya. That was not the deal that we struck, Janus. You can't rule Vascya. Only the Council can," I said. He couldn't be serious.

"Oh, you old fool, the Council is done for. And it already rules on my command. Can't you see?" He laughed maniacally. It echoed through the dimly lit space. The shadows flickered around us.

"And you believe the citizens won't revolt again, against your rule? Someone who isn't of the bloodline, working from the shadows, and who is supposed to be dead? Vascya will have none of that unnatural magic that brought you back to life after what Belaize did to you. That was not the deal," I said. Janus had lost his mind.

Suddenly, air had been cut off from my lungs, and I was suffocating. I felt his long fingers wrapped tightly around my throat. I tried to use my strength to loosen Janus's grip, but to no avail. I didn't have a young man's strength, let alone the will to best this *thing*. He was going to kill me; I realized. I felt my vision darkening when a breath of fresh air again filled me.

"I'll answer your question when your soul departs this world, Idaos. And I have known you long enough to know how you love to cling to your wretched life. Although, know that when he comes, it won't matter who revolts. This world and its kingdoms are doomed. If anything remains, it will be in his dominion," Janus's voice rose to a shaking, fever-pitch. He was psychotic.

I took a sharp breath and fell into the chair beside me. Janus... he... I couldn't wrap my mind around the fact that he had almost killed me, and with all my strength I couldn't stop him one bit.

"Who is he?" I croaked.

Janus smiled. "He is a—", again Janus was interrupted. He growled and turned his head toward the door.

"Fath... Lord Janus, Rayne is here," Faust stated, gesturing toward the wolf behind him. A tall wolf walked in. He had dark brown eyes and a mop of blond hair. He had the hint of a beard, and his face was dirty and disheveled. "Come with me son of Ronak," said Janus. He walked out with Rayne.

A moment of silence fell as the rhythmic tap, tap, tap of his steps grew ever fainter until it disappeared.

"Why didn't you tell me he was alive?" Faust roared suddenly. He turned into his wolf, growling madly. Saliva dripped from his mouth like a rabid dog.

"That is a mistake that will cost you your life if you don't back down right now," I said in a low voice. He roared louder, but took a few steps backward. "I didn't tell you because even I did not know until recently."

"But how can that be?" He thundered.

"Janus was in hiding and came to me only a couple of months ago. He claims he was hiding in the Low Cities," I told Faust.

Faust visibly calmed. "After all these years, he lives!"

"Yes, that is him, but there is an unfamiliar stench to him, which he masks with an overbearing aroma of some foreign herb." Faust frowned. We sat in silence for several moments before Rayne and Janus returned.

"In return for a seat on the Council, Rayne will provide us the location and weaknesses of all the Rebel bases he knows of. Well, I'm sure you can 'clear' a spot for our brave friend here," Janus said and scuffed Rayne's hair.

Rayne recoiled from his touch and grabbed Janus's hand. "Do not mistake me for a child now. Or you will regret it." Rayne growled. He let go of Janus's hand and left the room.

Janus laughed wickedly, his voice echoing through the halls. Janus turned to me. "From now on, I will take command of the Council. You've been a good pawn, Idaos."

"What?" I said incredulously. *Did he mean to kill me? It can't be that something has shifted my future.*

"What do you mean pawn?" I questioned, pointing at him.

"Did you really think you have devised every plan for Vascya alone?" he said viciously, smiling.

"Alistair, Belaize, the Low Cities. My massive tomb in the bowels of the Low Cities castles. I've been planning this for more than a hundred years, and you were the perfect pawn to use," he said.

"A hundred years? What are you talking about Janus? My bloodline is that of the Sight. It has been in my family for generations!" I bellowed.

My entire life was put into question. What was happening?

"Oh, silly Idaos. You have always been the pawn in this plan. Haven't you ever wondered why you burned the last part of the prophecy?" Janus asked.

"Wait... how... no. I never... I never burned anything. What are you talking about?" I was in shock. *How did Janus know? I am sure I was alone that night. How?* Questions invaded my mind.

"Don't feign ignorance, Idaos. If it gives you any reassurance, you have always been my favorite pawn. One single thought turned you into a vile man filled with greed, that's quite telling. Representative of the whole lot of you, wouldn't you say?"

"No..." I whispered in horror. How?

"Don't get me wrong, you are a direct descendant of one of the four winds, but your Sight, was a simple illusion. An illusion created by me."

Impossible! I remembered the strange blackness that had taken my vision that night. That had never happened before. I was such a fool! My breathing was labored. That prophecy was not mine!?

Anger flared in me, and my wolf came to the surface. My claws sharpened to a fine point and I threw myself over Janus. *I'll kill him. I'll kill Janus. No one can take my Sight. It's the goddess' gift to me. I can't be wrong in my visions.*

I aimed for his neck, but before I reached him, he flicked his wrist and the next moment, I was laying on the ground, pain shooting up my back. I rolled over, disoriented.

"Now don't get any ideas silly Idaos, you've yet to complete your role." Janus rested a hand on my shoulder. He squeezed at the base of my neck, cutting off the air again. I lowered my head in defeat.

"I am God's will, and you will heed me," he said coldly. My wolf retreated inward.

"Announce my return," Janus spoke out loud, addressing me and Faust. "Call the alphas, and tell them," He paused, letting his words sink in. The walls themselves absorbed his words.

"Tell them… I am reborn," his laughter was terrifying. A sense of dread filled my body as Janus whistled himself to the dusty throne room that had been left unused since Alistair had been overthrown.

IRONHEART

Marcus

The morning was crisp and beautiful. My muscles twitched as I ran. It had been almost a month since Belaize and Eliana left to find Alistair and Remus had returned to the Council to convey Ronak's last message regarding the exchange for Belaize.

Ever since, both Erylesia and I had traveled with Ronak from one Sanctuary to another, helping them set up, and preparing for the fight that was to come. I'd seen the toll sacrificing his daughter to the whims of fate had taken on him. It was a hard decision. He looked haggard and worn.

This morning, too, we were running toward one of the South-eastern Sanctuaries. The forest was thick as we ran ahead, diving deeper into nature. We had been traveling for the last three days. Ronak had commanded Erylesia, myself, and Luthor to accompany him at the meeting with a few other chieftains.

We weren't far from that Sanctuary now. Another twenty minutes and we would reach our destination. Erylesia was leading us, while both Luthor and I surrounded Ronak. He was our leader; we couldn't be too careful. Soon enough, we came across the first patrol. There were three wolves together on the guard, just like in our Sanctuary. Ronak had set up each Sanctuary with similar and efficient securities.

"Welcome." The three wolves bowed their heads in respect. Ronak nodded in acknowledgment.

"Jennifer awaits your arrival," one of them said.

"We won't make her wait much longer," Ronak said, and without another word, the four of us went deeper into the woods toward their Sanctuary.

All of us changed into our human forms. Once dressed, we crossed the gates of the Sanctuary.

This one wasn't as large as ours. The area was enough to comfortably settle about five hundred people, yet in the main Sanctuary, over fifteen hundred thrived. Our numbers had increased after the fall of the Low Cities, but slowly, almost all rebels had been settled in various Sanctuaries across Vascya. Ronak had worked tirelessly to make sure that not even one life was lost in vain. There was no one in this realm I held in higher regard.

"Welcome, Ronak. Glad to see all of you arrive safely," said a short stocky man. He greeted us at the gates of the sanctuary. I could see how well designed the sanctuary was. Easy to navigate and it seemed like our sanctuary, Jennifer too had her tent towards the center easily accessible to all.

"Xyabolt," Erylesia said and sending her hand forward, greeting the man. He shook it, a clear respect for my mate.

"Erylesia, I knew you would come with Ronak," Xyabolt said with a straight smile.

"I'd never miss a chance to scout another Sanctuary, you know that," Erylesia said.

Xyabolt moved, waving his hand, inviting us in. "Come, Jennifer has been waiting. The other chieftains arrived last night. I am sure you are famished, but lunch will be served after the meeting."

We walked with Xyabolt. Ronak said under his breath, "I know better than to keep the Ironheart waiting." Xyabolt gave a knowing laugh.

Both Luthor and I were new to this Sanctuary. It had been set up in place of the one lost in Walka. I had spied for Ronak for over a year and half my skill was that of perfect infiltration, unlike Luthor, who had been mostly trained by Romulus in the front line of the battle. I glanced at Luthor, who had been quiet on the journey. He was missing an ear. The spoils of the fight of the Low Cities.

"What?" Luthor sneered when he noticed my gaze.

I half coughed and said, "Nothing. Just looking around." I waved my hand in the general direction.

Luthor had never respected me. I knew that much. Even when I wanted to single-handedly walk to the Low Cities because of Adrian, he stated I was weak. A nobody. Yet, we had survived, all of us had. But now we faced the next obstacle.

We walked into a large tent. It was humid, and it took a moment for my eyes to adjust to the dim light. Four people sat around a wooden table. Five chairs were empty for us, as well. Three burly men, and one short woman, looked restless. As we walked in, one of the men stood up. He was also dark-skinned, but not as much as Xyabolt. Thick, black curls framed his face.

"Come in. Come in. I can't wait for this to be over. Jennifer is starving us." He winked at the petite blond woman. The other two men groaned in response.

"Sora. Stop," the one sitting on Jennifer's left said.

"I didn't say anything." Sora just flashed a smile. "And who might you be?" Sora directed his gaze at Erylesia.

"Not interested. Can we start?" Erylesia said, folding her arms in front of her, looking bored.

"A feisty beauty," Sora said again.

A wave of jealousy washed over me as I suppressed the urge to hit the man. I clenched my fists, my nails digging into my skin.

"She is out of your league, Sora. Leave her be," Xyabolt said, taking his seat.

"A woman of her charms? Never?" Sora said again.

"Fool." I saw Jennifer roll her eyes, just as Erylesia grabbed Sora by his neck. She pushed him to the ground and snarled at him. I felt her familiar astral distortion. Just like Belaize's. Her fangs grew as she pulled back her lips, revealing her canines. The loose silver streak fell across her half-transformed face.

"I told you," Xyabolt muttered from his seat.

"A Kaiser? Fuck. I am sorry," Sora immediately sputtered out.

Erylesia pulled back, her fangs gone. She moved and took her seat as well. Sora laid on the ground for another few seconds and then stood up, rubbing his neck.

"Settle down, now," Ronak's voice boomed. I sat on Erylesia's right while Ronak was on her left. Luthor took his place beside me.

"What is the news at your end, Theo," Ronak inquired of the man sitting beside Jennifer.

Theo read aloud from a neat stack of papers before him. "The three hundred rebels you sent have been settled in my Sanctuary. We were scouted by a few Council guards twice, but we were able to eliminate the threat. The meat stores are suffering. With so many people, we need more supplies," he finished.

"What about you, Reyes? How many attacks?" Ronak said.

"Three. The Council is restless. We will send more supplies to Theo. Illari and Evette have granted us safe passage, as you said they would in your last letter," Reyes said.

"Ronak." Jennifer's crisp voice cut through the room. I felt a shiver down my spine. She... was composed, yet her black eyes reflected fury.

"Yes?"

"Let us all stop wasting our time and get to the main agenda. Why do you think I summoned all of you here?"

"Not to discuss strategy?" Sora asked quizzically.

Jennifer ignored Sora, and instead stared at Ronak. "My birds in the Capitol chirped that we have what the Council wants. They want it enough to stop the war, yet I have seen no signs of our rebellion ceasing in the past month, Ronak. Care to explain?" Her voice was dripping with venom.

"Do not speak to Ronak in that manner, girl. He is our leader," Luthor said. Luthor's allegiance surprised me. I thought he only cared about Romulus.

"Do you not know what is happening in the Capital?" She glared at Luthor. "Rebels are worried. They are worried that Ronak will lead them to oblivion. Which is why I want Ronak to convince me and every Chieftain that we are not idiotic to follow his word blindly!" Jennifer said as she sat back in her chair, waiting for an explanation.

"Is this true?" Reyes exclaimed, astonished at the declaration.

"He has his reasons," Erylesia mumbled.

"That doesn't matter. Why are we not making efforts to stop the war?" Jennifer continued to grill Ronak.

"You do not know the complete story of what has happened or the gravity of the situation, Jennifer," I said, frustrated with the tight-lipped woman.

"What does Council want?" Theo questioned me, leaning forward in his chair.

"Belaize. They want Belaize," I said. The memory of the day Eliana had Belaize left to find Alistair flickered in my mind. I had made Eliana promise to come back alive from Sundara.

Ronak ran his fingers through his hair. "I wish it were that simple. There are things I chose not to reveal to you and the other chieftains. Belaize has sided with rebels now."

All five of them almost broke out in protest, but Ronak held his hand up to stop them. "Yes. I know he has committed many crimes. His hands are stained with the blood of our comrades. Yet, I have seen him change. I will not barter away a life. Giving Belaize to them will never be enough for the Council. Their promises are empty," Ronak said.

"But if submitting Belaize to the Council lessens the suffering of thousands of people, I want you to do that, Ronak. Don't protect him... unless... you have a plan," Jennifer said.

Ronak nodded in agreement, "I do. But I will not reveal it. It is our hope against the Council, and Belaize is the key. I beg for your forgiveness, Jennifer, but I ask you to trust me. I will lead us to a Vascya without a war."

The chieftains shifted in their seats. Each wore a tumultuous mixture of confusion and apprehension on their faces. The silence dragged on. One heartbeat, then another. The room felt frigid as deep winter.

Impulsively, I stood up. "Ronak can't tell you. But please believe me, Ronak has always fought for us. He raised me as part of his own family. I am grateful to him; I trust him with my life. He is Navar. He has the capability to guide us through this. The Low Cities have fallen, our chance will arrive soon. We have to be ready. We have to be united. Put your faith in Ronak. The time to doubt him has long since passed. He is my alpha. He is my leader," I said. My heartbeat throbbed in my ears, but I couldn't sit passively while the rebellion fell apart.

The five chieftains looked at me, analyzing me. Then they nodded.

Jennifer pulled out a silver thread from around her neck. It was attached to a blue stone in the center. "It is the mark of the Chieftain, Ronak. You entrusted us all with the responsibility to protect the wolves under our care. You trusted us, so I will too, this time. You have our support, Ronak. Lead us to victory," Jennifer said.

I sat down. Erylesia was watching me silently. I caught her gaze, but she averted her eyes. After another hour of talking about the settlements, security, and strategy, we were finally free.

Sora was the first one to leave. "I am starving," he half screamed and ran out. I shook my head, laughter bubbling in my throat. He was one of a kind. He reminded me of Adrian. The others left the tent as well, headed to the Kitchens for the promised meal.

I was the last to leave but found Erylesia waiting for me outside the tent. She silently fell into step beside me. From the corner of my eye, I felt her glancing at me, mustering up the courage to say something.

I waited patiently. I knew not to push her. She was... strong-willed, but awkward with me.

"That was nice."

"What was?" I prodded, masking my smile.

"You. Standing up for Ronak in there," Erylesia said.

"It was the truth. They are the only family I have since my parents died in this war. I will do anything for them. It is hard for Ronak, too. After what happened with Rayne..." I shuddered at the thought, "I am worried about Eliana. Not so much about Belaize, yet I can't help feel sympathy for him."

"Sympathy?" Erylesia wondered.

"Yes. He was a monster. But after everything, I... know he changed. It is in his eyes. They once held fury. They had rage and a hunger to kill. Now? It is just... guilt. I pity him. I shouldn't. I am weak in comparison. I lost to him, yet I can't explain it," I said as I looked at the ground.

"I understand. The notorious Harbinger, he is not what I expected when you freed me, Marcus. You sympathize because you have a heart of gold. You are the good in this world," she said, but her words felt as if they were coming from far away.

"I know you don't desire our bond, Erylesia, yet I want to be strong so that I can walk beside you in this war. I do not want to be a burden.

I want you to be proud," I said nervously.

"I AM proud of you, Marcus," Erylesia said.

I looked at her. She was staring back, her violet eyes striking me down, yet I didn't see the hate and disappointment I once saw. Only acceptance.

I reached my hand toward her gently. This is it. Either she will accept me for who I am, or she will not. I looked at her, waiting.

She glanced at my open palm, then back at me. Another moment passed, and finally she closed her eyes, grasping my hand. I laced my fingers together with hers tightly, sparks shooting down my body. She took the first step.

My mate had accepted me.

ALISTAIR

Eliana

"You never should've come back here." I heard the deep rumble. I couldn't move. I couldn't breathe. Every fiber of my body wanted to bow down at his feet. He is real. Alistair, The King of Vascya.

The sheer power of the astral distortion from his shift was overwhelming. As he stepped into the soft light of the radiant moon, the shadows melted away from his white fur. His every step made me want to cower and run.

Belaize had changed too, but he was shaking. For as long as stories have swirled around him, I have heard that the wolves of Vascya considered Belaize to be humongous. But his size paled compared to Alistair. Belaize was nearly a foot shorter in his wolf form.

"Run!" Belaize said and stepped in front of me. He was afraid that Alistair would attack us. Even so, his stance was protective, urgent. I sensed his desperation.

Go! I heard his thoughts through our connection but stood rooted to the spot.

No! Not when we have come this far.

"Listen, old man, I don't want to fight," Belaize gruffed and lowered his head in submission to the Alpha. My mind was in utter shock, even Belaize was submitting.

No! You have to be strong! I yelled. But he remained still.

Eliana! Go. I'll stop him. Please, his thoughts echoed in my mind again.

I changed into my wolf. In an instant, my bones reshaped, my senses heightened as I grew taller. I still felt small standing in the presence of two of the strongest wolves in Vascya, but I kept my head held high. I wouldn't back down either. I am a Navar. This mission would not fail in vain. Father entrusted us with this task and I would not let him down.

I nudged Belaize's back with my hand, supporting him. "He will not listen until we force him to, Belaize. We have to make him listen, even if it kills us in the end, for the sake of the Lycan race," I said.

I stepped up beside my mate and faced the massive wolf. I readied myself for the inevitable fight. My eyes flickered from left to right, taking in my surroundings quickly. I calculated our exits. Then I shifted my focus to rocks, fallen pillars, tiled walls. If we could use the environment to our advantage, we could wear him down considerably. With my speed and Belaize's strength we might make it out alive. But I had to attempt one last option.

"We need your help!" I said, "The Council must be stopped."

"How can you expect help when you prepare yourself to strike me?" Alistair thundered. His growl echoed in the broken archway of the Liunella's temple.

"We either live today, or we die. But we will not return without you by our side. No matter the cost," I said. My legs were trembling, but somehow, I found the courage to face Alistair. *Or maybe it was foolishness*, I wondered. I shoved the negative thoughts out of my mind.

"We need your help. The Council has doomed us all to our deaths," I said.

"I don't care about the damned Council," said Alistair, baring his teeth in rage. "Leave. And never return."

I studied Alistair. He was not standing too far away. Why hasn't he killed us already? From the fearsome stories I heard, we should have been long dead.

Maybe... I thought, and changed into my human form. My heart was pounding in my chest, but I stared at Alistair. His red eyes bore deep into me, as if he were reading my soul. Alistair cocked his head in interest.

"You're playing a dangerous game, girl," he roared.

Eliana, what the hell are you doing? I heard Belaize's frantic thoughts pooling inside my head.

Trust me.

"Please..." I walked toward him slowly. "We wouldn't have invaded your haven unless it was important."

"Idaos and his Council are killing the citizens callously and need to be stopped."

"Idaos..." Alistair said, tasting the word on his tongue.

"That coward still clings to his life." He huffed. "I do not care about wolves or the Council. I used to, once, but times have changed. You have shown courage, girl. But leave, never come back here. I won't repeat myself again," he said and turned his back to us, shifting into a human. He was tall, almost the same as Belaize, but the years had worn him down. His hair was grey and unkept.

"Old man, we didn't come here to leave," Belaize changed as well. He had regained his lost confidence now, and stood beside me, facing Alistair.

Alistair, however, didn't answer. He turned and started walking out of the empty atrium.

Don't stop me, I told Belaize.

I ran toward Alistair, calling after him. When he was within reach, my hand grazed his thin shoulder. He shuddered and instantly jerked away from me. He spun to face me, his face contorted in anger, "Girl, you've made a second mistake in my presence. Never touch me again," his words were filled with venom. "Just leave."

"Enough of this, you coward! You've been hiding away from this war for far too long. It is time you returned." I raised my finger, anger flowing through me, "Do your duty to this country, you were once its king. And a king never abandons his kingdom."

"Once..." he said, his voice was softer. "But do you know what those in my kingdom did? Disregarded their king who sacrificed his life for them and..." He stopped. His eyes were distant, reliving the worst moments of his life.

"Idaos took everything from me, I would have killed him, but the people turned against me. I do not care if this world dies. I devoted everything to those people, and they turned on me for some spineless liar! How did they repay the Good King? For their crops, their clothes, their order and peace? They shoved a spike through his mate's heart and beat his son to death." His voice was emotionless. He wasn't angry anymore.

He looked like a man who could not swallow another drop of misery. I looked into his eyes; they were tired eyes. He had seen too much cruelty. His pupils were dark red almost like Belaize, but they lacked the black pupil. Just a deep blood red.

"And you never once wanted revenge for the family you lost? They were killed in your place. They deserved better. Just like the rest of the wolves who are suffering at the hands of the Council. They deserve better," I said.

He closed his eyes and said a soft prayer.

"Your words... pierce deep in my heart, girl."

"Come with me and let me tell you the truth of Idaos and his plot." And he walked toward the ruined atrium.

I looked back toward Belaize; he was still apprehensive of Alistair but had eased a little.

I returned to him and touched his shoulder. He met my gaze and nodded.

We live another day, Belaize.

Let's hope so, I heard.

He followed my lead further into the ruins. The ancient murals showed the four winds surrounding an imposing image of Fenrir in the center. I saw Alistair sit on a section of the collapsed roof. He sighed audibly, resting his head on his hands.

Alistair looked older still in the dim light, weary and frail. His shoulders hunched as if he wanted nothing more than to curl around himself. His head hung low. Gone was the imposing wolf from only moments ago. Not even a shadow remained. "I left a long time ago and swore to never go back. I cursed the moon goddess and those that followed her." He spoke without prompting.

"Yet, you live here," Belaize said as he sat down on a broken pillar splayed across the floor.

"Ironic, I know. Yet, this was the only place that remained untouched after the Mugiri's rebellion," Alistair said.

"Yesterday, she appeared to me in a vision. She spoke of you, child," he said, gesturing toward me. "She said that you would be the one to end this timeless conflict. You will be the light of Vascya."

"Who?" I said, intrigued by his statement.

"The Goddess herself."

A shiver ran down my spine. *Liunella? How?*

He continued, "But you do not possess the skill to lead a single person, let alone this country."

He stared at Belaize. "And you are more important than you realize."

I craned my neck sideways to look at Belaize, too. He had a look of astonishment on his face.

Belaize scoffed, "How is it possible that... you and I had a vision of Liunella on the same day?"

"You saw her too?" I said bewildered. That couldn't have been a coincidence.

He nodded slowly. "Right before we left Rylsk. I didn't get a moment to think it over, let alone to tell you. But... how could this be?"

I felt Alistair's scrutinizing gaze on me. My gaze eyes met only blood red.

"In the Goddess' eyes we both are significant pieces in this great game of gods," he said.

Alistair stood and yawned, stretching his arms above his head. "I was going to tell you the story of how Idaos took control of the Council."

Alistair began his retelling. Mostly, what Amae had recited back at Lunaire was accurate. Idaos had used Alistair's absence to turn the people of our nation against him. I couldn't even imagine what it must have been like to lose everything, yet for a moment Rayne's face flashed in my mind.

"The same people that I risked my life for took everything from me. I begged them to just leave my mate and my son. They could take me, kill me, torture me, but they did worse. They left me alive. Imagine the king of the great nation of Vascya humiliated and degraded on his knees." I heard the crack in his voice.

He inhaled sharply, "My pleas of mercy made no difference. They wanted blood, and Idaos made sure that it was my blood they got. I felt her die. I breathed my last breath just as she did hers. After that, I left, vowing never to return."

Idaos... his name rang in my head like a bell. He... was the one responsible for the slaughtering of innocents. And ages ago he was the one responsible for this Civil War. *He will pay for his crimes*, I vowed silently.

"Idaos is a puppet!" Belaize said suddenly, "The real mastermind is Janus."

"Who is this Janus that you speak of?" Alistair inquired.

Belaize explained Janus was the Master of Arms, and through use of his vile methods, the Council ousted the rebelling wolves. "But what I don't understand is how Janus is alive. I know... I killed him with my bare hands. But Remus confirmed he was alive."

"Both are responsible for merciless deaths. No explanation comes to my mind as to why and how Janus is alive. But I know that we need you, your highness, to lead us back into a time of peace. Will you help us? Will you come back to lead the rebels to victory once again?" I pleaded.

Alistair just let out a short laugh. "Highness? No, child. I am not the king anymore. Wolves have shamed my name. I am nothing more than a memory now. Nor will I accept that status back. My time has gone, along with the duty to the throne."

"You need to become a leader, child. It is time for the next generation of Vascyans to inherit their destiny. Tell me, do you have the courage to accept?"

Me? Could I do it? Be the leader? Doubt flooded into my mind. Belaize's voice overpowered the storm of thoughts in my head.

I support you, Eliana.

I glanced at Belaize and saw determination in his eyes.

I finally turned to face Alistair. He was studying me, waiting for me to cower away.

My answer echoed in the ruins of the temple.

THE CITY OF SOLORO

Marcus

It had been several months since Eliana and Belaize had set out to find Alistair. I couldn't help but think this entire mission would be fruitless. I was worried about Eliana. Alistair would have to be well over two hundred years old, hardly reliable for war. Perhaps he had more to offer, maybe he was an expert tactician. Maybe he knew secrets we could exploit. I didn't know what role he would play in the upcoming battle.

I rose from the patch of Acana that I had planted in the small garden behind the Infirmary. Ronak was making this a permanent base. Houses were being reconstructed and stabilized. Part of this meant ensuring we had an ample supply of Acana for medicinal needs. I gave the little garden a quick look, making sure I had watered it enough, and headed back for the Infirmary to drop off the leaves I had harvested.

I was helping Honoria taking care of the patients in the Infirmary. We had always struggled with healers, and at the moment Amae had taken responsibility of Nihara's care. She had insisted, otherwise Belaize wouldn't have left.

Nihara was growing so fast and needed so much attention at such a young age. Her once wrinkled and small face had blossomed into red, rosy cheeks and a blubbering grin. She was hope, all the young pups were. Taking care of Nihara, however, left most of Amae's work to be tended by people who didn't know their own head from their tails.

I reached the familiar brick building and entered inside through the iron gates. I sensed Amae in the building. It was rare that she left her tent these days because of Nihara. But when I had my wolf follow her scent and peeked inside the healer's quarters, Amae was talking to a young, flustered man. She was pacing around the room restlessly.

"Amae, what is the matter?" I asked, announcing my presence.

She looked at me and waved her hand, inviting me inside. "One of the she-wolves is about to give birth, but we have run out of medicine to induce her labor. She is in a delicate situation. If it isn't administered as soon as possible, both the mother and the unborn child may die."

"What medicine is it?" I insisted.

"The Council banned it from public consumption some time ago. They used it in the breeding program. But I have a source in Soloro. I usually get it myself, but I couldn't find the time this month." Her voice was filled with regret.

"I have nothing assigned to me, so I can get the medicine. What is it called?"

"That'd be wonderful! Yes, that would work just fine. Okay, you'll need to go to Soloro. You will be there in two hours..." she muttered. Her hand made scrawling gestures in the air as if scribbling on paper. "Yes, you can be back by nightfall. That works. The medicine is an herb called Dagmiyo. Its essence is extracted and concentrated. It is known as Dagmiyo Milk. You'll have to find the seller first. There's a pub near the outskirts of the town. The owner will have it. He knows me, so he'll give the medicine to you." Amae said everything in one breath.

"Slow down! I'll go right now. Take this." I handed the young man the bag of Acana. He fumbled with it clumsily, and muttered, "Wait, here." He handed me a couple of diras. "Bring as much as you can with this amount, please," and then he practically fled from the room as if he could go another lifetime without ever witnessing Amae's fury. I didn't have time to even pass the coins back, so I set them easily on the small bedside table.

"I'll be back by nightfall. Just take care of that she-wolf," I called as I jogged out of the Infirmary.

First, I went to my tent. It was small and gray like the rest of them. I shuffled my pillow around until I felt the pouch inside. The weight of it wasn't reassuring, but it would be enough. Money was hard to come by, especially in war. We were lucky to even get a hot meal twice a day.

I left my small tent, hurrying through the gates of the Sanctuary, when I sensed Erylesia coming toward me. I turned and saw her walking in from the outer woods. She was glistening with sweat.

"Going somewhere?" Her voice was soft beside me.

"Yes. Soloro. Amae needs me to get her some supplies. Want to come?" I bit my tongue just as the stupid question left my mouth. *Idiot.*

"Sure. It has been a while since I've roamed a city," Erylesia said, and my wolf paced with excitement.

We changed into our wolves. I felt my fur sprout over my skin, my teeth elongating. Erylesia's muscled wolf was nearly as tall as me. Striking silver fur covered her chest.

We cut through the woods at a blinding pace, reveling in the chance to move and stretch freely. I had trained hard these past few months, and I was faster and stronger than before, but Erylesia was always a step ahead. I didn't mind. Chasing her through the woods was exhilarating.

Time went by and the dusk was settling in as we reached the edge of Soloro. We had ran at our top speed and we both were drenched in sweat and panting heavily.

We stopped just outside the city before changing again. As we entered I noticed that, contrary to its size, it was quite busy. Even as evening approached the streets were bustling with people. I smelled the fresh scents of food, spices, and exotic perfumes. Many businesses were open and thriving, which truly was a rare sight these days. We trudged through the streets, trying not to draw attention. Finally, we arrived at a shanty pub run by a short bartender.

"I need some Dagmiyo milk," I said in a low tone, but was met with a sharp glare. The bartender held a finger to his mouth and signaled for us to follow. He took us down a flight of steps and through a dark hall. The hallway opened into a room with several shelves.

"Shamus." The small wolf called. "Do we have any Dagmiyo?"

Shamus? Huh. What an old name, I thought. "Just a moment."

A young woman with spectacles adorning her face appeared from behind a shelf. She was an attractive young wolf, brown-haired, angular chin.

"Dagmiyo... hmmm... I think we have a few dozen vials."

"I'll take all of them," I said, reaching into my small pouch of dira. The woman laughed. Her laugh made her glasses slip from the bridge of her nose and fall to the wooden floor.

"Oh!" I reached down to pick them up for her, and instead butted my head against hers.

"Hey!" She screamed, holding her head.

"Forgive me," I said, rubbing my aching head as well.

I glanced at Erylesia, who was leaning against the door behind me. She was grinning at the spectacle. I awkwardly laughed, running my fingers through my hair.

"You can't have all of them!" she said with a glare.

"They're for someone else." I frowned. "Uh- Amae said she knows you," I said, scratching my head.

Recognition reflected in her eyes. "Oh! Amae sent you? Fine, yes, you can have them!" she said disappearing behind another shelf.

Such an odd woman. She appeared again, carrying a large box in her tiny hands.

"It'll be two hundred diras for the box."

My eyes widened, "No way!" I said shocked, "That's quite a price."

I emptied my pouch into my hand and counted the coins. I only had about three hundred dira in total. But I had wanted to get a few more things as well.

"Yes, two hundred! Two-zero-zero. It doesn't look like much, but keeping this shop running means I need to fill the right pockets. The guards take half of everything I make," she said.

I reluctantly handed her the diras.

"I'll return for the box in a few. There is something I must do first."

We briskly left the small pub. Erylesia was quiet. I navigated our way through the city, going into a stationery shop for parchment and quills. When I exited the shop, I found Erylesia eyeing something in a shop across the street. I walked to her, bags in my arms. "Something you like?"

Erylesia jumped back a step, startled. I looked up; there was a gorgeous velvet box with many stones inside it on display.

"Nothing." Erylesia's cheeks were flushed red. I just smiled. Quite a woman, she was.

"Let's go." Erylesia marched ahead. I shook my head, laughter bubbling in my throat. I followed her as a cloaked man stumbled outside the antique shop.

"Stop him!" an old man shrieked.

I dropped my bags and ran after the thief. He had almost melted in the crowd, turning away into dark alleys when I tackled him down. We crashed to the cobblestones, and he lithely escaped my grip. He skittered to the side and jumped to his feet.

The hooded figure swung a knife at me. I barely had time to react, to move out of the way. I lunged after him and grabbed him by the shoulder and used his momentum to take him to the floor. "You fucking coward!" I said and yanked the cloak away. A disheveled beggar's face came into view. He reeked as if he hadn't taken a shower in weeks. I scrunched my nose and pushed him down. He was frail, with an odd stench, a Jackal, I concluded.

"Please!" the skinny boy yelled.

"Please let me go! The guards, they'll kill me for stealing. Please! I have to feed my sister!" he begged. I realized he was no older than a mere sixteen. My heart gripped with sadness as I opened my hand. *Even they had it rough.* "I will give you money, but hand me that box," I said.

The thief looked at me, panting. He relaxed under my grip and handed me the box. I finally let him loose. I emptied the pouch, now seventy diras lighter, into his hand.

"Find honest work. This will feed you for the next week. If you need help, contact the rebels. They might guide you too," I said. He looked at me and back at the coins. He nodded.

"Thank you. I will not forget your kindness," the jackal said and ran ahead. I watched him disappear into the busy streets.

"That was a lot of money, Marcus. You should have slit that abomination's throat. Even the Goddess curses him and his kind," I heard Erylesia say.

"I know. But, he needed it more than we do," I replied.

I closed the velvet box and headed back to the shop while Erylesia grabbed the bags that I had dropped outside.

I put the box in the old man's palm. "Take care of your things."

"Thank you, my boy. Thank you. Folks been sayin' that lads around here been stealing for weeks. But you saved my treasures. Please take something." The old man said.

"Oh no, I can't," I said sheepishly.

"Please, I insist. Anything in my small shop."

I looked outside, where Erylesia was waiting.

"On second thought..."

Night had fallen when we made our way back to the Sanctuary. It was a longer run, the box and other supplies had weighed us down considerably. We arrived around midnight. Both Erylesia and I were panting when we arrived at the Infirmary.

"Amae," I called.

"Marcus!" Amae came shuffling out a delivery room and took the box of vials from me. "You both went?" She winked.

We nodded. "Outstanding work. You saved a she-wolf with this medicine. Thank you." Amae smiled.

"Go eat now. We will take care of everything here. She is just going into labor," Amae said.

"Is the she-wolf okay?"

"She will be now. Thank you!" She disappeared inside.

"Let's keep these things," I told Erylesia. She nodded and followed me to my tent. She dumped the trinkets on my tiny bed.

"Why are you like this, Marcus?" Erylesia asked out of the blue.

I removed my jacket, which was drenched, and threw it in the corner. It needed to be washed. Removing my shirt, I changed into fresh set of clothes. I glanced at Erylesia. She was eyeing me. I smiled and sat on the floor.

"Because I am. I enjoy helping others," I finally answered her.

"May I ask you a question?" I laced my fingers in my lap and stared at the ground.

"Yes," Erylesia responded.

"How were you captured and imprisoned in the Low Cities? I have always wondered. You are… you. Strong. Yet, they held you captive," I asked. We had a good day. Back in Soloro it was easy to pretend like we were two different people in a different world. I had even made her laugh, and while this was painful, I felt close to her. Closer than I ever had, and tonight curiosity got the best of me.

"I grew up in the eastern city of Gornikulu. When I was young, I lived on the streets after my parents died. I lived and survived with other orphans like me, escaping the Council guards at every turn. After we were proven capable in a fight, some orphans joined the rebels. I didn't want to. I always knew I was Kaiser. I knew my value and how people would fight over me, try to use me. So I hid. And I continued to live that way. Training myself, getting stronger, living in caves in the forests. That's when a tracker squad found me.

"They didn't capture me, I killed everyone, except one wolf. A runner. A coward. It was a big mistake. A few weeks later, a larger host came. I fought hard, but I was one wolf and they were two hundred. Eventually, using wolfsbane, they subdued me. I was taken to the Low Cities. I spent three years in that cell, Marcus. That man, Janus, wanted to create more like Belaize. More killing machines. But their methods always failed with the rest of us. When the Low Cities fell, you came to free us," Erylesia said.

"I am sorry, Erylesia. You have gone through your own share of hardships." I put a hand on her knee, giving it a reassuring squeeze.

"Yes. I never wanted a mate, Marcus," Erylesia said softly.

Her words pierced my heart, yet when I looked at her, in her violet eyes, they were happy.

"Why?" I croaked.

She sucked in a deep breath. She closed her eyes. "My… father was a Kaiser as well. It is rare. We had hidden away from everyone. My parents and me. He told me that our blood, it made us a target in the war. But the Council guards tracked us. My father… fought to protect my mother and me. But he lost his life. There was so much blood…

"Only my mother and I survived. But losing my father was too much for her fragile heart. She locked me away in a dresser, my mother, and she killed herself in grief. My mother lost the will to live and ripped her throat apart with her own claws." Erylesia went silent. A tear trickled down her cheek. I knew she had never told that to a soul. I felt the weight of those words. I grabbed her hand, squeezing it.

"That is when I vowed never to accept a man. Never. Yet, here we are. Liunella has blessed us with a bond that is… beautiful. And I can't help but cherish it," she whispered her voice heavy with emotion.

I stood up and rubbed away her tears. "I promise not to leave you, Erylesia. I will be by your side till my last breath."

I pulled her to me, holding her close. She almost pushed me away, but I held her tight. She had been alone for so long. But not anymore. After a while, I pulled away, kneeling beside her again. I was ready to finally ask her again.

I pulled out a small rufous-colored box from my pocket. I pulled the lid open and watched Erylesia's violet eyes widen with surprise.

"You didn't!" she exclaimed, "You don't have the money!"

"I didn't. But the shopkeeper was generous, so I brought this for you," I smiled. Her cheeks flushed again. I decided I liked the color. Beautiful.

I gazed down at the amethyst ring that sat in the velvet box. Intricately designed with swirls of silver around the stone. Perfect.

"Will you finally accept me as a mate, Erylesia?" I asked. There it was again, the insecurity in her eyes, and the hope that overpowered her.

"Yes," she said.

I slid the ring on her slender finger, placing a kiss on the top of her hand. Mine.

She was mine.

THE ASTRAL REALM

Eliana

Ninety-three. It had been ninety-three days since we first met Alistair but our mission was far from complete. We had one aim, and that was to bring Alistair back. I thought we would die, but never in a million years did I think Alistair would mentor us to become stronger, especially me. Belaize and I had spent weeks honing our abilities.

In the time that we had been under his wing, Alistair had begun teaching me how to access the Astral Realm at will. Day after day, he drilled me with the process. Fighting till I couldn't move a muscle, training, sparring, and pushing me to unlock my mind.

The first time I had seen the transition into the Astral Realm was when Amae guided Marcus with just the touch of her hand. And now Alistair was teaching me to access it as well.

Where are you? I heard Belaize's voice echoing in my mind.

Beside the pond, I replied.

I liked how Belaize talked to me through our connection. The more we talked through it the closer I felt to Belaize. Liunella gifted us with this bond, and finally, we were accepting our destiny.

I sensed Belaize approaching. I looked back and saw him emerge from the thicket.

"Hi," I said, and patted my hand on the ground beside me.

He settled down as well. His scent washed over me, and I felt my wolf's joy. Our mate was with us. After so much we had gone through, we could be with each other this way. Our bond wasn't complete yet, but I knew someday it would be. Maybe when the war was over, and we could roam peacefully in Vascya again.

What are you thinking about? His voice echoed in my mind.

It was typical that he wouldn't speak to me, but his thoughts would always reach me. It was as if he was... afraid to talk out loud. I knew Belaize needed time, and I was prepared to give him that. *The mighty Belaize is woman shy,* I thought. I made sure to keep that one to myself.

"Enjoying a moment of this peace. We have been raised in this war. Don't tell me you don't feel the soothing waves of this place," I said with a smile.

The small pond was beautiful, surrounded by lush forests. The tropical wind created ripples in the pond which touched my toes, washing away stress as the water receded.

"Yes. It is peaceful," Belaize admitted.

We sat in silence for a while. I nearly didn't realize it, but I was holding Belaize's hand. I squeezed it softly. Reaching for him was a gesture I did without thinking.

"How... did you go to the Astral Realm the first time?" I questioned, breaking the silence.

Alistair called it the art of gods. It was one of the hardest things I had ever encountered. It seemed with each passing day my concentration deepened, widened, until my mind was a vast and elastic expanse that I could drown in. Still, my capabilities were novice by comparison. I had learned to transcend into a reality that wasn't ours, yet I was always pushed back, never fully transitioned like Alistair wanted me to be.

"The first time was an accident. I'm not sure how to explain it," Belaize said.

"What happened?"

Belaize fell silent. I felt his muscles tense as he sat up straighter. I squeezed his hand again, staying silent.

"I... went on my first rampage," Belaize said, speaking slowly.

"I remember very little. Janus had done something to me... it was as if... the control I had over myself, my emotions, was shut off. Janus had made me angry. He had degraded my existence, insulted me, and tortured me. But, that day, something had changed inside me, in my heart." He pointed to his chest.

"The anger had overwhelmed me, and I started killing and injuring the wolves that were nearby. A killing spree. Which ended after I pulled Janus's head from his body. After that, I lost consciousness and somehow entered the Astral Realm."

"I'm sorry for what happened to you, Belaize," I said.

"You don't understand, Eliana. Ronak... kept you untouched from the horrors of this war," Belaize said.

"You've told me this before."

"Yes. What... I went through and what I did after that. All the murders and working for the Council. Yes, you have seen some grotesque aspects of it, yet somehow, your heart is untouched. The crimes I committed made me who I am today. Every sin is everlasting." He sucked in a deep breath.

"Alistair teaches you how to transcend into this other realm, yet the way I learned was the hardest one of all."

"I wish you hadn't suffered through that, Belaize," I said. My heart broke for him the closer he allowed me to be. So much misshapen potential. I worried if his spirit would ever fully heal.

"I don't deserve you, Eliana. You are purity that rarely exists in this world. I..." Belaize trailed off.

"I am not Belaize. I have led countless battles and missions. I know death like the back of my hand. I have lost my mother, and my brother to the war. But I choose to look forward to a future with peace. I know... I was wary when we first met, Belaize. You were terrifying. The Blood Moon Harbinger, the greatest assassin of them all. But when I saw you... I didn't care. I was glad that my search was over. I may have not accepted you with open arms but... I fought for you in my own way. I tried... I really did," I said, my voice was wavering.

"I don't deserve the effort, Eliana," Belaize said, sadly.

You do, Belaize. Because no matter what, you are my mate and I choose you above all. Our connection is proof of that. It is proof that I accept you with all your flaws, all your shortcomings. The man you were is behind us now. You are not a perfect mate. Neither am I. But we are enough for each other, Liunella, made sure of that.

The next instant, Belaize pulled me close and his lips found mine. My eyes were closed as I felt him kissing me with a softness I never knew existed. I threw my arms around his neck and kissed him back.

We parted after a few minutes and sat in silence. After a few hours, we went back to the ruins. It was time to train again. Today, we were going to attempt to reach the realm. It would take several hours, according to Alistair.

Alistair had warned me about the risks of the realm. One mistake could leave you stranded and your soul may be lost forever while your body turned to stone. The risks were perilous, but I had Alistair to guide me. The old man had grown on me. He was our king once, and I could see that he deserved the title. He was patient and honest, and, blow for blow, rivaled only the mythical Fenrir in ability.

A part of me was nervous. We had been pushing my soul to the Astral Realm, but what if I transcend and couldn't find my way back? I was yet to even see the realm. Once I caught a glimpse, but my concentration had quickly broken and thrown me back into Tierra.

You will be okay, Eliana. I heard Belaize reassure me.

"The Astral Realm, in its truest essence, is an area where our realm, The Tierran Realm, overlaps over to the Sacred Realm. The realm of the gods. In theory, if you were to train your mind enough, you could visit the Astral Realm; however, it is impossible without divine powers to cross the void from the Astral Realm into the Sacred Realm." Alistair sat in front of me, his deep red eyes looking into mine as he drilled his theory into me yet again. Belaize sat at a distance, watching as Alistair directed me.

It surprised me when Alistair had taken a keen interest in developing my strengths. He was adamant to have me lead but insisted I was not ready yet. I hoped I would be soon. With each passing the day, the Council recovered its forces.

I glanced at Belaize; he was listening intently. He had a cruel force, the boundless fury of a much younger man, throw him into the realm. I had nothing except the will to cross.

"Focus," Alistair said.

He tapped my head. "Your heart is your portal to the Astral Realm. Your mind is holding you back. Your lack of discipline prevents you from achieving your potential."

I focused my attention on myself. My feelings, my dreams. Belaize. I let go of control and felt my soul leaving my body slowly, as I had done these past few weeks. I felt the air, the heat, and the sound of nature. Everything. I kept floating up and felt the white glow surround me. Almost there.

I felt the prickling on my skin, the vibration, the light. I was there. *Almost there.*

The next instant, I was thrown back into Tierra once again. I was panting, my heartbeat racing fast. I slowly opened my eyes but saw only pitch black. Instantly, everything came crashing back down. My soul rushed back into my body.

I opened my eyes and saw Alistair and Belaize sitting in front of me.

"We should have been past this stage, Eliana. You stupid girl, look at Belaize, he has mastered this with his tumultuous heart, and you... you hold him back. Physically, emotionally, mentally. You are a roadblock," Alistair thundered.

Why was Alistair doing this? My heart was beating fast and irregularly. I was trying. Hard.

"I'm sorry. I'll do it this time," I said and closed my eyes again.

"You must harness the power of the realm to stay in it, which you've yet to achieve. Only the strong-willed can roam freely in the Astral Realm. I know, it is hard for you, child. You are not a ghost, nor do you have the strength for it. But I know you will do it. Your mind is too crowded. Empty it. Your thoughts, let them flow out of your mind. Show us you, too, are strong."

I felt a soft caress through our bond. Belaize, he was reaching out to me. My mind calmed. *Alistair is trying to break the mental barriers you've constructed in order for you to see the realm clearly. You won't succeed until you let go. Completely.*

I took a deep breath. I felt my heartbeat slow. It dropped to a singular beat every minute. My legs went numb. The feeling continued. I felt my soul tearing away.

Belaize's voice was gone now. My entire body went numb, and my breathing all but stopped. I felt an odd chill, but it wasn't a physical chill, it was deeper. Something primal.

The wind stopped; the chatter of the small animals ceased. The silence was unnerving. I felt the soft heat surround me once again. I emptied my mind. I felt nothing and everything. My senses dulled as my soul transcended again, toward the Astral Realm. I was almost there. The aura of the realm enveloped me, graceful as ever, like a film encasing me. Peaceful. Like a calm sea.

Then, like an eggshell, I felt my concentration breaking. I felt the realm slipping away, but I held on. I held on to the invisible rope that tethered me to that place, as waves of force crashed against my soul, forcing me back. Almost.

You can do it, I heard Belaize's distant thought.

I was hanging on with all my strength, willing the realm to accept, to welcome me. I will do it, I screamed in my mind and a moment later, it was calm.

It was peaceful. It was majestic. I was there. I was in the Astral Realm. I opened my eyes slowly and stared in wonder at the glorious sight ahead of me. A world shrouded in ever-lasting sheen of white. As if the northern snows had frozen time itself.

"You did it!" I spun around and saw Alistair and Belaize standing behind me.

"This is it?" I asked.

"Yes, this is the Astral Realm," he answered.

"It is beautiful." I saw now why Belaize didn't want to leave. It was peaceful, serene, and there were no feelings here. I was in awe of such magnificence.

"Yes, but it is deadly as well. Those who lost touch with reality wander mindlessly in hopes to return home," Alistair said.

"There's a tree here," Belaize said with a smile.

"A tree?" I asked incredulously. I looked around us, we weren't surrounded by trees.

"Let's go, but be wary of shades," Alistair said.

Belaize led us forward. After walking for what seemed like hours, we came across a monstrous tree that rose into the sky higher than any mountain. A tree so high you could never reach it's top.

The tree had six major branches. One branch was dead, devoid of life.

One that was dying. A rain of leaves falling from yet another branch. But the other three branches were stagnant. Unchanging

"The Ygdrasil, the World Tree. I see you have been here before, Belaize," Alistair said.

Belaize nodded. "Indeed. Several times. Every time, I entered the Astral Realm, I somehow stumbled upon this tree."

"The tree is dying," Belaize added.

"The world tree doesn't die; it changes to represent the state of the world. When this world dies, the tree will rot. But it does not die. The tree will always exist. At least that is what our history tells us. It is said that beyond the tree, across the water of truth, is the Sacred Realm where the gods dwell."

"You aren't wrong," said the melodious voice of a woman. The three of us spun in unison to face a beautiful young woman. She was short and slender with tanned skin. Black hair fell loosely behind her.

"You?" Belaize tensed behind me. Alistair noticed this, and stood in front of us, wary of the enemy.

"Oh! Do you recognize this woman? I thought you wouldn't. I thought you must have forgotten, Belaize," the woman said with a cheerful laugh. She ran her fingers along her body as if her skin were a gown she was smoothing out.

This made no sense. Why was she speaking so strangely?

"Belaize, who is this?" I questioned. I was ready for a fight. But my gut told me she wouldn't harm us.

Alistair stood silent, thinking, calculating.

"This... was Nihara's mother. But I... killed her. I had ended her misery. Who are you?"

The woman smiled, "So you know her! I handpicked her especially for you, Belaize," she said matter-of-factly. "We are friends after all, aren't we?"

"I do not know what you are," Belaize said coldly.

"I am what you claimed to be, of course. Death," she said with a smile, but it didn't reach her eyes.

Menacing. Cold. Something otherworldly existed here.

"I hope the child is faring well?" she asked.

Was this a dream? Was the Astral Realm playing tricks on my mind? But both Belaize and Alistair could see her. This was not a coincidence. I realized; Marcus once told me he had seen someone in the Astral Realm after they had been murdered.

"Who are you?" Belaize questioned.

"I am the end," she said nonchalantly. "The end of every story."

She disappeared. "I am also an ally," the voice appeared from behind us.

We turned to face her again. Her smile didn't waver at all, in fact, it grew. She was having fun.

"Good job, Alistair. I was waiting for the three of you to meet me here."

"You knew we would come?" Alistair asked calmly.

"Yes. I did. I know so much. You could say I have endless knowledge, but I'll only tell you what you need to know. Nothing more, nothing less. The fates let me play, but I am bound by their leash," she said sullenly.

"What is happening with the world tree?" I asked.

"The world is changing, for better or for worse, it's impossible to tell. But I would favor it to change for the better." The woman sat down and leaned back slowly, her feet stretched out in front of us, as if basking in the sun.

"This does not bode well. What needs to be done?" he asked the woman. In response, she yawned.

"A war." she replied, smiling. "This war will decide the fate of your precious country. But it is the first of many."

Belaize was silent, but I felt the tornado of his thoughts.

The women looked at Belaize and I and said, "You are the guides of Vascya who hold the key."

"So, Idaos is right. It is not mere speculation," I said.

"That fool is a mere pawn in the game of gods, child. The game began centuries ago, but the last race comes forth. All of you are soldiers to the new world that will emerge," the woman said.

"In time, everything shall be revealed. Let's see if you can save a doomed reality."

And with that the woman vanished, leaving a chill in the air.

Alistair was silent and unmoving.

That was unsettling.

Before we could even resume our conversation, or make sense of what had occurred, the air shimmered around us. It was almost as if the air was twisting into strings, coalescing together. From the ever-circling air appeared a familiar old woman.

"Amae?" I asked. What was happening today! My mind was jumbled with so much strangeness.

Amae's face lit up as she pulled me into a hug.

"Ahh, I found you. It used to be a lot easier," she said, rubbing her temple.

"Belaize, Eliana, begin making your way back to the Sanctuary. Much has to be done."

"How did you know we would come to the Astral Realm?" I questioned her.

"I felt a distortion in the realm and made my way here. I know you and Belaize, and I can feel whenever you enter this realm. How the realm works, I will never know. Yet, I am glad to see that you both are well," she said.

After a few moments, she noticed the old man with us. "You must be

Alistair." He nodded.

"Pleased to meet you, my lady," he replied, he folded his hands behind his back and bowed.

Amae's cheeks grew rosy but she nodded at him and spoke again. "Join these two and come to us, Vascya needs you now."

Her words made Alistair smile, "Forgive me my lady, but I've left society for a reason. I..." Amae interrupted him promptly.

"Get your head out of your ass, swallow your pride, and do your duty. You and I are too old for such formalities. Time is of the essence here and we require your presence back at the Sanctuary." I had never seen Amae speak so sternly to anyone other than Belaize. It was almost comical.

Alistair looked shocked. Scratching his head, he nodded his head in agreement. "It will take a few weeks. They aren't ready yet."

Amae smiled, "I must go now. Finding someone in the Astral Realm is taxing, especially since I have not done it in ages. Hurry back now."

"How is Nihara?" Belaize asked quietly.

Amae smiled at Belaize. "She misses her father," she said.

"I'm not her father," Belaize stated. He sounded almost sad at the statement.

"Foolish child, you are her father. In fact, both of you are her parents," Amae said, tapping him on his head.

She disappeared from our sight, going back into our own reality.

The Astral Realm, such a place could only be described as surreal.

"We should go," Alistair said.

"There seems to be a lot of upheaval in the world." I nodded.

Belaize was the first to vanish out of sight.

"It's like waking up. Open your eyes," Alistair said, and he vanished too. I closed my eyes and focused.

"You're going to die! Every single one of you... Hahahahahaha!" My eyes shot open as the haunting laughter followed me out of the Astral Realm.

"No!" My scream caught in my throat as I found myself back in my world. Belaize and Alistair saw the look on my face.

"What happened?" Belaize asked, concerned.

I saw something... But what was it? My mind was twisting in on itself. It was a wolf... but it had grotesque, twisted black wings. But it wasn't there before. Did I hallucinate?

"There was a voice..." I said. "I don't know what to make of it."

"A voice?" Alistair questioned, puzzled.

"Yes, it was a deep ominous voice. It said everyone was doomed." Alistair's brow furrowed.

"Are you sure? The Astral Realm is notorious for making people see and hear things that don't exist. Maybe, you heard something because it was your first time in there," he said.

I nodded, but something in my gut told me that whatever this was, it was real, and it was coming for us.

A New Life

Marcus

Erylesia was out again doing reconnaissance for Ronak. She had travelled to some nearby Sanctuaries on Ronak's order. I had gone on a supply run and returned yesterday. I was eager to see her.

Everyone was busy with something or the other. It was odd that the Council hadn't made a move. All of Ronak's other spies had gone quiet. No new information came.

"Marcus!" Erwin called. He was drenched in sweat from head to toe. Over the last few weeks, after he had shifted, Erwin had grown a few inches. He worked hard. He was determined to get strong. His muscles had hardened, growing thicker and stronger by the day. His face showed only the vestiges of the child he once was.

"I am finished for today. I will go for a run after lunch," he said.

"I will join you again. I want to see if you can run faster than last week." I smiled. But Erwin shook his head in denial.

"No. I want to go alone. I want to scout the area around the Sanctuary on my own." Erwin stood tall; his decision unwavering.

"It is not safe," I tried to argue.

"It never will be, but I know the patrollers and I won't go far. This isn't the first time I have gone alone. I'll be okay," Erwin insisted.

I sighed. It was true. He had been running and getting used to his wolf. I ruffled his hair. He was still shorter than me.

"Okay. Don't tread off too far, Erwin," I said.

"Marcus, can I ask you a question?" Erwin was looking at the ground nervously, one hand clenched beside him.

"Yes?" I waited.

"The... Harbinger." Erwin spit out the word, "Will he return?"

My heart clenched. My gaze shot to his stump. I took a deep breath and calmed myself.

"He will, I'm afraid," I said and watched Erwin suck in a sharp breath.

He had suffered at Belaize's hand. I didn't blame him for resenting him, but Belaize was a changed man. But did that fact rid him of his sins?

"But I do not think he will return for another few weeks," I offered.

I put a hand on Erwin's shoulder, he flinched, yet didn't step away. He could've sat in torment for the rest of his life, grieving over what was over and done with, but he wouldn't, I knew. He was made of stronger will than that.

"I am sorry, Erwin. Hang in there. We have to use every ally in the war, and that is the only reason Belaize now works with us. You don't have to like it. But it will not change the fact we will need Belaize to fight with us."

"I know," Erwin said in a monotone. "I will go on my run now." Turning away, he marched out of the courtyard.

"What was that all about?" Adrian came from the Kitchens nearby, munching on an apple.

"Erwin suffers. His state is the constant reminder of what he lost," I said sullenly.

"Belaize did that, didn't he?" Adrian asked mid-bite.

I nodded. "It was unfortunate."

"He will live. I hope he gets better and moves on," Adrian said through another bite.

"You are a pig," I said.

"What? I am hungry." He swallowed his bite and smiled.

"So, when is Erylesia coming back?" Adrian asked with a knowing smile.

My ears turned red, and I averted his gaze. "Soon. She is on her way back."

Adrian wiggled his eyebrows. "You can't wait for her to get back."

"Shut up, bastard," I mumbled. Adrian loved to tease me ever since Erylesia and I had officially mated. We had a small ceremony a few weeks ago near the river. Erylesia had looked beautiful that night. Ethereal. Amae dressed her in a lilac gown, pearls adorned on her neck. Her hair loosely braided into a bun, lined with a string of flowers.

Only a few people witnessed our union in Liunella's light. Ronak, Amae, and Adrian were present. I had wished that Eliana was there to support us as well. We had exchanged our vows. To be with each other till our last breath.

That night Amae had welcomed Erylesia to be part of our little family. Ronak had given us a private tent in the living area for mates. They provided the illusion of privacy. Although no one bothered anyone here, we could sense each other's presence. We were a pack. It was a comfort. It was enough.

An invisible tension left my body as I sensed Erylesia enter the Sanctuary.

Erylesia, I said through our bond.

Without a second's delay, I heard her voice echo in my mind. *I am here.*

I am eager to see you.

I have to report to Ronak. He is working me to the bone. I will be free in an hour.

I'll wait for you, I replied.

"She is here, eh?" Adrian inquired.

"Yes. Wait, how?"

"You had a look come over you. Erylesia is that great?" Adrian smiled.

"It is all Liunella's doing. I am glad I found her." I smiled again.

We started walking toward the Infirmary. Amae had called us to help a few wolves settle into their tents. Finally, many were healed and most of the she-wolves had given birth. The healers had worked hard, and the wolves in the Sanctuary had come together to help whenever needed.

"I didn't have much trouble on yesterday's run. The Council guards aren't interfering either. It's good that the Council has split," Adrian said.

"Yes. Soon the Chieftains will prepare the rebels to march. We are waiting for Eliana's return. I hope everything is okay," I said. Thinking back, I was shocked when Remus said that they might be the target of this war. The sweet girl who we grew up with... I couldn't help but wonder what the future held.

Amae was waiting at the Infirmary gates with ten wolves. Four she-wolves carried their pups in their arms. The wolves looked exhausted and weak. Without a word, both Adrian and I got to work, leading them away toward their new tents.

Finally, after a few hours, I returned to the Infirmary. Adrian had already gone to eat in the Kitchens. He was always starving.

"Ba-buh." I heard the sound and looked around. Erylesia, and she was holding the beautiful Nihara.

"Nihara!" I called as I approached her.

"You are Ba-buh now," Erylesia said laughing. It had been six days since I last saw her. As I approached the two ladies, Nihara reached for me with her tiny hands. I took her in my arms and she snuggled up to my neck. It made me jealous of Belaize whenever I would see him holding Nihara. No other feeling was better than holding a new life.

"What are you doing here?" I asked Erylesia as I gave my finger to Nihara, who started sucking happily.

"Oh, nothing." Erylesia smiled. Her cheeks were rosy. Goddess, she was beautiful. "I came to see a healer."

My eyes went wide. "Why? Are you okay? Are you hurt?" I asked. Before Erylesia could answer, Nihara bit hard on my finger. "Ouch!" I pulled the finger away.

"She will start teething soon." Amae came from the gates.

Amae took Nihara from my arms and coddled her. "Go eat supper. I will give Nihara to a wet nurse." She ushered us out of the Infirmary.

So, we left, and I grabbed her hand, lacing my fingers with hers. "Are you okay?"

"Come with me," Erylesia said, and lead me toward our tent. I stayed quiet. I waved goodnight to a few patrol wolves here and there as we made our way to the living area. The field was littered with small tents.

I tried to imagine the days when all the wolves lived in different packs, under the guidance of the Council. It used to be a family, where everyone thrived together. The Council helped people divide their territories and guarded not only those areas but the borders of Vascya as well.

I believed this is what a pack should look like. I smiled at the thought. We made our way to our little tent; it was small yet spacious. Enough for both of us. I shut the opening as apprehension welled up in my stomach. I finally turned toward her. My mate.

"Erylesia," I mumbled.

She made her way to the soft straw bed and sat down, sighing. I sat beside her and felt her lean on my shoulder.

"It feels like I haven't seen you in weeks," she said. I felt her hands running through my hair.

"It's Ronak. I should tell him not to make my mate work so much," I said.

"If only you could. The new settlement in the northwest is taking its toll on both of us. But it's okay. I like to help Ronak. He is an outstanding leader."

"Yes, that he is. They don't call him the Wise, just for laughs."

"Come here," I said and pulled Erylesia in my arms. My wolf was happy and content. I felt her love through our bond.

I closed my eyes. This is one of the moments that I had longed for all my life. And after a lot of struggle, she was finally with me.

It had taken a lot of persuasion and patience, but Erylesia had accepted Liunella's gift. Erylesia, a powerful warrior and a Kaiser, had love in her heart.

Now, will you tell me? I tugged at our bond. I felt her relax in my arms.

"Marcus."

"Yes?"

"I have something for you," she said.

"There is no need, Erylesia. But please, what is wrong?" I pulled away and looked into her violet eyes. I put my hand on her forehead, checking for fever. I glanced at her arms and legs for cuts and bruises.

Erylesia grabbed my hands and put them in her lap. "I am okay. You are not listening to me."

She laced her fingers through my hand. I saw the glint of sapphire. Mine.

She moved my hand and placed it on her belly.

That's when it struck me. I focused on my senses and closed my eyes. How I had not felt it earlier shocked me. There were three of us.

You're going to be a father, her words echoed in my mind.

I pulled Erylesia close and kissed her.

"You'll have to keep away from Ronak, now. He can rely on someone else."

I love you, Marcus, I heard her say, her soft voice ringing in my mind as I drifted in thoughts of our small family.

THE ROAD HOME

Belaize

Four weeks. It has been four weeks of Alistair teaching Eliana to go to the Astral Realm. He takes her there every day.

She was picking it up quickly, no doubt. It used to be just the wolves of ghost lineage who could transcend into the Astral Realm with that ease. But I believe the stronger you are, the easier it is.

We hadn't encountered Amae or Nihara's mother again, nor did Eliana hear that voice. It confused me at first. But the fact remained that it could not be overlooked. What could it be? All these years, whenever I entered the realm was when I lost control. But in the last couple of months, everything had changed, along with my hold on the realm. Especially, my memories.

I watched as Alistair and Eliana sat cross-legged facing each other. Their eyes were aglow with an unnatural silver hue. Today they had been gone for several hours.

I crossed my legs and closed my eyes. I took a deep breath, and I felt my legs go numb, then my belly, followed by my entire body. I opened my eyes, and I found myself in the Astral Realm. I tried to recreate the hallway I had once visited in my mind with Amae's help; however, it wouldn't materialize. I focused on Eliana, Amae, Nihara, something that might take me back into my memories. I saw the realm begin to shimmer, and then the hallway appeared around me. The familiar doors and crumbling stone were a welcome sight.

I had told Eliana about the hallway, yet she never encountered it. This was a place all my own. I lost myself exploring my memories. Reliving the fight of the Low Cities. Finding Eliana, fighting Faust. The months that I spent rehabilitating from the fight. The deeper I went, the more the memories darkened. Along with the memories, emotions that I had repressed all those years ago came back to haunt me. The encounter with the she-wolf I had beheaded. I remembered seeing her pup in the Sanctuary. The armless boy. *Should I apologize? No, he didn't need a reminder of his shortcomings, but didn't he deserve one*? I wondered.

It wasn't long before I ended up back at the shattered door. But the door was not as crumbled as it had once been. A memory that was no longer lost. I relived the fear my parents felt. I relived the horror of being sold to Janus for a fistful of coins and the false promise of safety. More than anything, though, I tried to find memories with my mother.

I searched for some time, eventually reaching the golden door. It refused to budge. I was curious what was behind this golden door. I tested the door nearest to it. It opened to a small meadow. The woman was there. She held a wailing child. The child had bright red eyes and a head of messy blond hair, almost white. I was once that happy child with bright eyes.

My mother held me, and she sang softly. She had a beautiful voice. It was soft and warm and familiar. That memory wasn't altogether special, but it was something I had never known that I had in me. Fresh memories would spring up every day that I visited. But this memory of my mother in the fields singing to me was as far back as I could access.

I opened my eyes in the actual world. Alistair was still in the Astral Realm with Eliana. I walked around the ruined temple. It still boasted a history that had not been witnessed in decades and I found myself entranced by the scrawled tales. The goddesses, the winds and Fenrir. These murals could not explain the disappearance of Fenrir. He was present in every image then, at some point, he was not. There were several great "searches." Attempts to find Fenrir. A myth. A story concocted by parents to entertain their children.

I walked out of the temple and deeper into the forest. Deeper than Alistair had ever taken us. It grew louder. Animal sounds filled my ears. It was calming. Soothing. I sat beside the pond, resting at the base of a tree when I smelled Alistair.

"She's still in the temple," Alistair spoke.

"Let's return then," I said. I stood up, dusting myself off, and walked toward him. But he raised his hand to stop me.

"Fight me," Alistair said.

"What?" I asked confused, "I can't fight you, you're far stronger than me." He chuckled lightly.

"And if you come across another that is more powerful than you?

Would you say the same? Come on, Belaize of the Blood Moon," he taunted. I didn't move.

"I will kill you and Eliana. I will hunt down everything you've touched and burn it to the ground," He had a maniacal look to him. Something had finally snapped in the old recluse. I turned into my wolf, my bones snapping, my senses sharper than ever. I saw him turn as well. If he wanted a fight, he would get one.

Alistair was massive, a foot taller than me. He was a brilliant sheen of white. My scar throbbed and burned. "I see you carry the mark I gave you all those years ago."

I growled loudly. "Have you become unhinged, old man?" He laughed out loud, an insane laugh. "I am better than I've ever been. Now, come at me!"

Alistair lunged at me with powerful strides. I jumped back, avoiding his reach.

"Fight me," Alistair yelled.

I ran forward and swiped at his chest; he caught my hand in his monstrous claw. He balled his other hand into a fist and punched me square in the gut. The wind rushed out of my lungs and I dropped to my knees. He was too strong.

"You weakling, you had a taste of strength and you thought you could fight the world. I will show you true strength." Anger boiled inside me. I rose to full height and dug my feet into the ground and pushed. Alistair didn't budge. I growled, straining under the immense pressure and felt as Alistair was lifted into the air. He was surprised. I threw him as hard as I could and he landed several feet back. He rolled onto his feet and laughed.

"That's more like it, show me your raw strength. Lose yourself to your anger and I will pick you apart." That's when I realized what this was. He was trying to train me.

"You crafty bastard," I roared and lunged at him, but he evaded my arm and punched me again in my chest. As I reeled he hit me hard in the jaw. The force of his blows nearly made me black out. I stood upright, trying to keep my eyes open and focused. My vision steadied, and I ran to him, I lifted my right leg and feigned, shifting my weight to a left hook instead. Alistair read the movement and redirected the blow at the last second. My fist grazed his cheek and drew blood. He punched the back of my neck and my vision turned black.

My eyes felt heavy. I tried to open them, but the effort was blindingly painful. A few painful moments later I managed to steady my vision. A whirl of color solidified around me.

"You're up," Alistair said as he appeared by my bedside. I saw Eliana resting above me, her hand to my cheek.

"Alistair told me what happened," she said, and shot a stare that could have stopped a moose in full charge.

"It's fine," I said. "The old fool pointed out my weakness." Alistair smiled brightly.

"Ah so you realized what I was doing. Impressive," he said. He had a look of pride on his face. "Tell me, what is your weakness?"

"Marcus was the first to guess it. But you knew it from your experience as a warrior," I said "It's my ego."

Alistair's smile widened. "I am so sure of my victory that my guard drops when I swing." I gestured with my head to Alistair. "That is also your weakness, old man." He rubbed his cheek. It was bruised, scabbed over.

"You are quite the fighter Belaize, if you had an ounce of fear when you fought, you could defeat me."

"What do you mean an ounce of fear?" I asked him, confused.

"Your fear is part of you, but you do not feel it because of your ego. You believe nothing can harm you. Thus, you fear nothing. But if you incorporate fear, your senses are heightened, and you can evade attacks that are too fast. Your instincts are your most vital tools in a fight." He put a hand on my shoulder.

"Your fearlessness removes your instincts. But there is more to fighting than technicalities. When you conquer this weakness, you will be a warrior unlike any in the history of Vascya."

Two days after when we set out on the long road home we came upon a crossroads town. One road led to the Capital and the other to our camp. The town was ransacked. The market was destroyed, the once busy streets were empty, save for a few desperate looters. Both Eliana and I looked at each other. Something was wrong.

"What happened here?" Eliana questioned a woman who tended to her child near the end of the street. The woman looked at us suspiciously and held her child closer.

"The Vascyan army came this way," the woman said.

"The army?" Eliana tensed.

"Aye, I reckon bout two- no three hundred of 'em came through a few days back."

"Which way did they go?" I asked her.

"They headed them ways," she said, pointing to the direction that would lead to the Sanctuary. I felt Eliana's thoughts whirling.

"Relax, we can't afford to panic now, let's get going," I said to her.

She looked at me, terrified to her core. This was an extermination squad, and there wasn't a speck of doubt in my mind where they were going.

"Alistair, we are running the rest of the way." Alistair nodded, and we all simultaneously turned. The woman's eyes widened in shock at the sight of Alistair. The white wolf. His size and chest of silver were striking. We took off in a dead sprint toward the Sanctuary. Eliana's mind was lost in distress.

We will get there soon, I told her through our connection.

Let's hope so.

We kept on like that, running through the night and much of the next day. Our training, both physical and mental, had allowed us to push beyond fatigue. Still, when we stopped to rest, Eliana would do nothing but pace. Alistair was silent as ever, but his face said enough.

We finally approached the Sanctuary in the early hours of the following morning. Dawn had graced us with little light. We had encountered nothing that had suggested an army had come through. No tracks or forgotten campfires. But as we crested the last hill the horizon was aglow in a faint, red light.

"The Sanctuary!" Eliana called.

"Liunella help us," Alistair said as the smoke in the air spoke of what we all feared.

The Sanctuary was burning, and with it all of our friends.

RETROGRESSION

Ronak

I awoke with a start. Sweat was covering my body. I felt a cool breeze that left me shivering in my bed. A heavy feeling settled in my chest. It wasn't a new feeling. It had been growing for a while and made its nest right in my heart, the feeling of hollowness.

I closed my eyes and my thoughts immediately went to Adya. She was my life, and yet here I was, left in this wreck of a world without her.

Flashes of Rayne came next. My boy... how could he have gone so astray? It seemed only yesterday that Rayne and Eliana played right outside my tent. Their giggles and laughter would echo around the first small Sanctuary I had established. Everyone would smile when they saw my two children enjoying a little bit of their childhood. But now... everything was a mess. Eliana was out somewhere with Belaize, and Rayne... Rayne was gone. I trusted my own blood and paid for it dearly.

In front of the others, the survivors, I couldn't grieve, but here, alone, I knew that his departure from the Sanctuary had left a hole in my heart.

Perhaps I was too hard on him; perhaps I should have paid more attention to him. For that was all that he wanted. I felt disgusted by my bloodline. This... bloodline was the cause. If only it had skipped Eliana, then maybe I would still have my family by my side.

I got up and slipped into some clothes. I made sure my collar was smoothed and my shirt wrinkle free. I washed my face in a basin of cool water and only then was I ready to face my people. Walking out of my tent, I felt the cold air biting my skin. Goosebumps decorated my bare arms. It was a calm morning. The sun began to peek over the horizon. The first rays of the infant morning caressed the trees, creating streaks of warm light through the leaves and branches.

"Sir, you're up early today?" I heard a voice call from behind me.

"Ah, Adrian, come join me," He was dressed in combat attire and drenched in sweat. He walked over to me and stood silently watching the sun rise.

"It's truly magnificent. It makes me feel small," Adrian said.

"It's because we are small, son," I looked at him, he had healed well over the past few months, but I knew he masked his pain in front of others. The Low Cities had been traumatic for everyone.

"This land was never meant to soak in the blood of our conflict, and yet that is all that we have fed it for the past century," I said.

"The war will end soon, right sir?" It was a mix of a statement and a question. I did not have an answer. We began walking together toward the edge of the Sanctuary, near the river.

"We may win, but the cost will be great," I said and turned my back on the ever-brightening land, the water reflecting the soft glow of the sun. "Whatever cost though, we must win, we have no other choice."

Adrian nodded in agreement. "I want to see Vascya without war."

I patted his back. "And you will see it, Adrian. The time is near."

I left Adrian back at the river as I walked alongside it. Inspecting the new enclosures, we had to see if we had caught some fish. I had installed them when the migration had started. They would serve as good food for our soldiers. The result was fruitful. Piles of fish lay trapped in the barrier. I called a few wolves and instructed how to harvest for today's lunch.

Next, I saw to the patrols. The security was airtight. Many wolves lived inside the Sanctuary who didn't have the ability to protect themselves. The old and the young. It was my duty to ensure their safety. On my way, I saw Luthor appear with his guard near the north entrance.

"Ronak, enjoying the nice morning, eh?" I nodded in response.

"It's a beautiful day, after all."

After my daily rounds, I found myself walking toward the camps. Several enclosures had been converted into permanent homes, while others were still tents. Work had slowed since I had split tasks. I had sent several of the masons to other villages to renovate their camps as well.

Our victories over the Council had resulted in a boost of morale amongst the rebels and the wolves were happy. They wanted to build their homes again which were torn down by the Council.

A sudden burst of wind blew, biting at my skin again, and I felt my wolf stirring. It'd been too long since I last let him roam. *Let's go for a run! It's time to relax.*

The sun was setting into the sky by the time I returned. A few people

awaited at the gate to report their findings. I admit that their greetings and chatter fell on deaf ears. All I could focus on was the refreshing run I had. Dipping into the cool river after working up a hot sweat. The thrill of feeling the air whip through my fur. It was exhilarating. I couldn't help but smile. I had spent a whole day on that run and it was worth it.

"Ronak, the harvest is ready, the corn crop is bountiful." The farmer was proud of his work as he rightfully should be.

"Well done, be sure to set a few carts aside to barter with the other Sanctuaries," I said. He nodded and hobbled off. I stepped into my office and sat down.

A few more wolves came and went, finishing the debriefing for the day. But when I was alone in my tent again a chill ran up my spine and a feeling of dread took over.

"Ronak the ever busy..." A familiar voice spoke in a hushed whisper.

"Rayne!" I exclaimed.

"Son!" I stood up looking toward the source of the sound. Something was wrong. My gut told me something terrible was going to happen.

"Son..." I repeated when he stepped into the light from the shadows. "Son... I—"

"You don't deserve to call me that anymore," Rayne's voice cracked.

He walked up to me and stood face to face. He was weak, frail. His face was hollow and the spark of life in his eyes was long lost. I didn't care that he was a traitor or a coward, he was still my son.

"Where have you been? It is okay, you're home now. Come let me get you some food, please." I said gently. I lifted my hand up to put on his shoulder but he smacked it away and took a step back.

"I don't want your fucking food! Don't you get it, I'm not here to make peace... oh no. Your dream of peace, I will not let it happen. You think I can't do anything. It was Eliana who you relied on. Watch as I destroy everything you have worked for. Then you'll be proud of me, father. Proud that you raised a son who is your sorrow." He stopped abruptly. He... was deranged.

Then it dawned on me, the meaning behind his words. "You brought them here."

A sinister smile graced his face.

"It didn't take you long to figure it out. Guess you earned your title of the Wise, father. Watch me and be proud, just like you are proud of Eliana."

He bolted out of the room and out into the world. I dashed after him.

I burst out of the tent, frantically ran looking for Rayne. Trying to find him in the shadows.

"Rayne!" I called out. A wretched scream escaping my mouth. I couldn't believe what was happening. That's when I heard the deafening howl echo across the Sanctuary. Fear gripped my heart. We were under attack.

I looked around for Rayne but he was nowhere to be found. He had disappeared again. I followed the sound of the howl as fast as I could. I saw my people fleeing their homes at the sound of the army's call.

"Ronak, what is happening?" The question consumed me, louder than even the thudding pulse in my ears.

"Run, evacuate to the Western Sanctuary. Leave everything and go, tell whoever you can!" I said with a sense of urgency that bordered on sheer panic.

I ran as hard as I could to the edge of the Sanctuary. Nothing... There was nothing there. No trace of Rayne either. I raced around the perimeter before I smelled blood. I slowed down and I saw piled bodies of two guards sitting in the dirt with their throats cut.

"Liunella help us," I said. I morphed into my wolf and howled desperately. The signal of an assault on the Sanctuary. Danger. This was it, we had prepared for an assault, but not like this. Not with Rayne on their side.

"What have you done Rayne!"

Several of the other guards converged around me. Adrian and Luthor among them.

"The Sanctuary has been infiltrated. We have to get everyone out safely. Two of you, get the children, women, and elderly to safety. Tell whoever you see that they must either fight alongside us or help others get out," I ordered. Two wolves broke away and ran inside the Sanctuary without another glance. They had their mission. They would die completing it.

"Adrian, go with Marcus and lead the others West. Luthor, this is where we make our stand. We have to let the others get away. Buy them enough time." he nodded and turned into his wolf.

"Let's get these fuckers," Luthor snarled.

We split up to spread the alarm faster. In a few minutes we had gathered in the center of town and the evacuations had begun. That's when the wind shifted and with it came the scent of hundreds of wolves. They were rushing toward the Sanctuary and would be upon it any second now.

"Warriors of Vascya, I will not lie to you," I stared into the small sea of faces that looked at me for direction, "We will not live to see tomorrow. But we can ensure that our loved ones will! We will fight till the blood sows the seeds of the future." A collective murmur went through the crowd.

"By the Goddess, Idaos will shake in his castle walls when he hears the cries of our deaths," The few dozen wolves with me nodded and cheered. Others joined our ranks as I spoke. Our numbers neared a hundred.

"Till death!" I said.

"Till death," they repeated.

"For a free Vascya!" I said.

"For a free Vascya!" They echoed.

I heard howls from inside the Sanctuary followed by echoing howls from outside. I laughed.

"Let us make them hear the conviction in our voices and show them the might of the Vascyan spirit that dwells in us," I howled loud, long, and proud; I was joined by the wolves around me. This was it! We march now to our deaths. *May the Goddess bless us.*

The tension welled up in the crowd. Brave wolves poised and ready to give it their all. One minute ticked by. Then another. Soon, the wake of the advancing army became visible on the hilltop. A great cloud of dust rose around them. Everyone was holding their breath. I sensed the army approaching us, their synchronized steps thundered through the air.

"Form up!" I heard Luthor yell. Some of the wolves had managed to get into the armor that we scavenged from the Low Cities. It was finally put to good use. One of the wolves had handed me a dented breastplate as well. I didn't know how much it would protect us, but my only hope was to buy a few precious minutes for the Sanctuary to be evacuated.

"Man, I'd give anything to see my son one last time," one wolf said.

"Mother... father..." another began.

"Alyssa, my love..." spoke another.

"Save your prayers warriors, Liunella will have no room for them when she hears the cries of our enemies." An awkward laugh travelled through our ranks.

It wasn't just men in our ranks, brave women of Vascya, Armina and several others who would give their lives for us, for the rebellion, were among us. I knew their strength and their capabilities, they were the some of the fiercest wolves I had ever seen. There was no way of telling how outnumbered we were until the dust settled, but we would damn well slaughter as many as we could.

A few scattered rows of warriors made up the front lines, and the rest were with me, scattered in small clusters behind tents, buildings, and supply crates. I had set up our camps in such a way that we knew all the hiding spots which we could use for our advantage. Some were assigned to attack from the shadows. The stealth of those wolves would be the deciding factor in tonight's fight.

"Here they come!" I howled as we ran full force into the battle.

The advance was brutal as the army fell upon the Sanctuary. They tore through the worn wooden defensive walls almost instantly. Splintered shards assaulted the front lines, but they managed to hold the army for a few moments.

The scent of spilled blood filled my nose and my wolf grew ravenous. It wanted blood and it would go for the kill. Time slowed, and in the heartbeat pause that the front lines held back the army of wolves, we finally charged the enemy.

I leapt over a wolf and kicked my feet into the back of his skull. I was quickly surrounded by several others. I knew I was the target. They wanted to capture me or kill me, but I wouldn't let that happen.

"We got him! Ronak the Wise!" The man spat. I smiled delightfully. *What a fool.*

I lunged at his neck and crushed his throat. Two wolves swung at me at once. I leapt over them and clawed at one's head, leaving deep gouges in his helmet. He fell to the ground as blood pooled around him. The other managed to land a punch at my gut. It winded me but most of the attack was deflected by the armor.

The two remaining wolves hesitated. They knew that I wasn't to be taken lightly. These two were a lot stronger. They separated and flanked my sides. It would be a challenge. I cycled my gaze from one to the other. They staggered their attacks.

I blocked one but before I deflected him, the second wolf pried at my armor. The central abdominal piece flew off. I kicked at the wolf and hit him square in the jaw, making him howl in pain. The other bit down on my exposed neck. I felt pain shooting through me.

"Arrrghhh!" I yelled and reached behind me to pry his jaw open. My fingers ached as he bit down harder. I lifted him into the air and felt his jaw loosen. I thrust my arms forward, launching the wolf backward. He landed on his feet, but I didn't give him a second to regain his bearings. My hand ripped through his armor and out the back of his spine. He fell limp and I tore my arm out. It was covered in his blood.

"Shit!" I gripped my torn neck.

I took a few steps and my legs wavered beneath me.

"Damn!" I took the armor off and tore my undershirt. I tied it around the wound as best I could to stop the bleeding. The rag was immediately soaked through with my blood. A coughing fit racked my body. Blood spattered the dirt as it spilled from my mouth.

The wind blew and with it came a scent. I swung to the side just in time to avoid blows from a large wolf. He was massive. Must've been ten feet tall, and so near to Belaize in height that I couldn't help but stagger back. A cunning move, too, using currents to mask his scent. If the wind didn't change when it did, I would have been decapitated. "Your senses are sharp," the wolf said.

"They don't call me an Alpha for nothing." I felt blood trickling down my side. I was losing it too fast. I felt lightheaded. My wolf snarled. I faced him and readied myself.

"I thought I would use this to defeat Belaize one day, but I guess you'll have to do. After all, I don't do this often." I focused my strength inward and let my instincts take control. My body rippled. I let the true strength of an Alpha course through me. There were few legends of this strength, and only ever manifesting within the four winds' bloodlines.

The wolf was surprised at my sudden change. I saw the hesitation in his eyes. After all, it was a natural instinct to surrender to their alpha. Despite that, he managed to throw a powerful punch. I ducked at the last second and threw an uppercut, breaking the wolf's jaw.

The bottom of his jaw dislodged completely. The wolf howled in pain, his tongue hanging down against his neck. I threw another punch and his neck snapped. He fell limp onto the ground.

My body shrunk back to my smaller form again. I was breathing heavy. The cloth around my neck had torn off. I felt at peace as a soft breeze washed over my body, cooling the sweat that coated it.

A familiar face appeared in front of my eyes. "Son... Rayne," I felt an intense pain as my own blood ran through me.

He pushed me hard and I fell several feet away. Dead bodies littered the ground and I found myself spitting blood amidst this pile of death. A fit of coughing wracked my body, blood splattering the ground. Droplets of blood glittered in the sunlight.

"Die you damned old fool!" I heard him yell hysterically as he kicked my chest, breaking my ribs. I laid under his feet, undone. Was this my fate?

"For-give me, Rayne... for all the wrong I did... to you..." I said between my deep, labored breaths. My vision thinned and tears escaped my eyes. Tears of regret. Through the last light of my eyes and the last vestiges of strength in my body, I turned to face my child. His rusty blond hair flowed in the breeze. His brown eyes reflected my own. It was as if time had frozen. A look of shock overcame his tear-stained face.

"It is too late father. Too late," Rayne cried, kicking me harder. Blood flowed from my mouth.

"I... was always... proud of you... son," I said with the last of my strength.

"Rayne! You fucking coward!" I heard a vicious cry. I wondered who that was. The pain was vicious, throbbing. The rush of the blood in my veins was aching and I wanted to scream in agony, but I didn't have the strength.

I failed her. I failed Adya.

INTERLOGUE

Marcus

The first howl shook me. It was powerful and desperate and it signified only one thing: we were under attack. I was on patrol tonight when I heard it all the way from the east exit of the Sanctuary. I immediately ran toward the camps. I had to get Erylesia away.

The second howl ripped through the sky. “Damn it!” I looked around. The sun was beginning to set. *Erylesia!* I yelled urgently through our connection.

Where are you?

I reached our tent and found it empty.

“Goddess!” I shot out frantically. I caught her scent and immediately followed her trail. When I finally saw her I took a breath of relief. She was ushering a few children toward the exit.

“Erylesia!” I called.

“Marcus,” she said as she pushed some children ahead.

“Run! Run with the older wolves.” I heard her say.

As I reached her, I grabbed her hand. “Come. You have to leave.”

“Marcus, the Sanctuary. We have to help Ronak.” Erylesia was out of breath. She must have run as soon as she heard the howl to help others.

“No, you must evacuate, you can’t do anything to help in your state. I’ll find Ronak!”

Erylesia began to protest. "Marcus, no—"

I held up a hand to stop her. "Shut up and go, take others with you, they need you to guide them. We don't have much time. You know the way to other Sanctuaries. You can lead them out of here. I will make sure others get out." She paused and looked at me. She knew I was right, no way I would let her into the thick of whatever was going to happen, not like this, even if she was a damn Kaiser.

"Go, I'll follow shortly. I promise, once I know that Ronak and the others are safe."

She wouldn't budge and stood there stoically. So, I did all that I could, given the situation. I took her by the arm and ushered her toward the nearest of the exit

"Go now! Erylesia, please. If not for me, for our child," I said. My heart broke as I forced her out, following the throngs of people exiting in a flurry who, once again, were abandoning their homes and livelihoods.

Erylesia stopped and stared at me. "Come with me!" she begged, "Please, Marcus, you cannot leave me." A part of me wanted to run, to take her and raise our child away from this madness. Go to lands untouched by the Council, away from their influence. But another part of me, a larger part, needed to stand and fight. Fight with my alpha, fight for hope, a better future. To get revenge, to make the Council pay for their transgressions. To stop this bloodshed.

I pulled her close kissed her for a long time. I couldn't get enough. My mate, my life. She was with me right now, and for a second the sounds of life dimmed until only the two of us remained. Our lips parted and I rested my head against hers.

"I can't, my duty is here, yours is to protect our future," I said. I ran my hands over her belly, trying to feel the life inside her.

"I love you," I whispered. Three simple words. The weight those three words held was different today. They hung in my heart, and they stuck in the air.

I placed a soft kiss on her forehead. "Go," I urged. She took a long look at me and finally nodded. She turned her back and joined the fleeing Vascyans.

I watched her leave as another howl broke the twilight sky. It was followed by several weaker howls. An army! *Fuck.* I thought for a moment. I needed to help turn the tide of this battle. Before I go join it, I had to rally everyone I could.

I went from door to door, calling out to anyone that might still be here.

Almost everyone had left. Another deeper and longer howl shook the sky. Ronak! I knew it was him. He was our alpha; my wolf immediately broke to the surface and answered his call.

"I'm coming!" I declared and ran to the next home. I opened the door abruptly. I found an aged couple sitting silently, holding themselves in the far corner. "Davon, Ylma... come, we must evacuate you two." I urged them to get up.

"Marcus..." Ylma spoke sadly.

"We aren't going to evacuate," Davon finished.

"No, don't be crazy, hurry up, let's go." I did my best not to let the urgency of my words strain my speech.

"No Marcus, no more running. We've been running too long. No more," Davon said firmly.

"Son, you must understand that we have run from our home many times before. Each time it gets harder to build a new one. The strength has left us to run. Not anymore. We will face our fate head on, be it life or death," Ylma said.

"This is our home, and we will protect it!" Davon said, resolute in his choice.

"But..." He held up a hand, silencing me. I hung my head and walked out.

Damn this, I thought. I left their home, and I realized that the fighting had started. Agonized screams began to fill the sky. The enemy had breached our front lines. It was time that I joined them.

I ran toward the screams. The scent of blood hot in my nostrils. My focus was solely on making it in time. In time for what, I did not know.

I turned a corner and ran headlong into Erwin cornered by two guards. He was shaking in fear. I rushed toward him and put myself between the attacking guards and the boy.

"Erwin, run, find Erylesia, she will guide you out," I barked. He didn't move. Damn! Why was everyone adamant on doing the opposite of what I say?

The two guards didn't waste any time and attacked. They were fast, but their armor made them clunky. I tore off the helm of one wolf and slashed at his neck. The other tried to jump me from behind, but I dove out of the way and killed him by thrusting my hand through his neck.

I turned to Erwin. I put my hands on his shoulder and shook him out of his trance. "Erwin, you can't falter now, come on get a hold of yourself. We have come too far for you to go into shock now and give up," I said to him. He looked at me with fear evident in his eyes. But after a few moments he calmed down and stopped shaking.

"You wanted to help, so go to the Infirmary to make sure its empty, take as much of the medicine you can and follow the people exiting the Sanctuary." I nudged him toward the right direction. He was still afraid but he had a look of determination on his face. He nodded and immediately ran toward the Infirmary.

I hurried along to the center of the fighting. Sounds of struggle were everywhere, and beyond the tang of blood I smelled fire too.

I ran faster, rounding corners and skirting tents, and saw that Luthor was fighting three wolves just outside the main courtyard. As strong as

Luthor was he was being pushed to his limits. He was surrounded, his stamina waning. I cursed under my breath and joined him.

"Marcus, took you long enough. You were right about these cowards, but they're a lot stronger than I thought," he said. I watched the three of them carefully, they were out of breath too. Two were gravely injured. One of them had a broken arm. Luthor had done a great deal of damage.

"Luthor, I don't know you to be modest. Clearly you have these three on the ropes," I said, mocking the three of them. They snarled at me in reply.

"Watch out for that blond one, he's sporting those wolfsbane gauntlets," Luthor indicated toward the Council guard. I looked at his clenched fists and saw a smaller, sleeker design of the bloodbane gauntlets.

"You need wolfsbane to take your opponent down. Pretty pathetic," I said.

As soon as I finished, the three of them lunged. Two went for Luthor. One of the guards attacked me. He swung with both of his fists, trying to take me out of the fight quickly. I scratched and clawed at him. I tore at his flesh. Sprays of red flew into the air. Eventually he collapsed, dying, as blood spilled from his neck in spurts. I turned to Luthor and found him sitting against a tree in his human form. The other two lay dead at his feet.

"Go on," Luthor said.

"I can't fight anymore, the wolfsbane has done its work. If you hadn't shown up when you did, I would have died." He was wheezing but he would be fine, I knew he had survived worse than this.

I gave Luthor a nod of respect and turned to leave. The sounds of battle were frightening. More prevalent were the screams of the dying and injured. Grotesque piles of poor wolves had been left to rot and die. The smoke hung thick in the air. I ran past Midnight's pasture. The horse was in a frenzy. *I'll come back for you*, I thought and continued forward.

A familiar scent hung in the air, Ronak's. He should be around here somewhere. I sprinted harder past the stone buildings to find Ronak standing afar, blood splattering from his mouth. Someone was standing next to him, their hand inside Ronak. The wolf pulled his hand out with Ronak's guts clutched in his grip. His hair the same sandy shade as Ronak's. I sprinted forward as the horror struck me.

"Rayne! You fucking coward!" I screamed. Ronak's body fell. *No! No! This can't be. Not like this.*

"Get up, you don't deserve to go like this," I called frantically. Adrian came crashing from behind burning tents. He looked back and forth between Ronak and Rayne. "What the fuck! Ronak!" he yelled and ran, punching Rayne in the gut. He staggered backward.

"Rayne, you fucking scum!" I lunged at him as well with venom in my words and my eyes seeing red, but he managed to turn sideways. Adrian and I stood side by side, ready to grab him.

I saw Rayne's face, there were tears in his eyes. "No, you do not get to cry for him you fucking bastard! No, you lost that right when you killed him. When you... you killed your own father." I lunged at him again and he dodged, sending his claws outward to, pierce Adrian's stomach. He fell to his knees.

"No, come back here, face me you fucker!" I yelled after him as he fled.

"Do-n't worry abou-t me. Catch that- bastard!" Adrian yelled. I nodded and left both Ronak and Adrian. I ran after Rayne, but his scent had disappeared, blending with the burning Sanctuary. The smoke assaulted my nose and I coughed. I was running toward the exit when suddenly a rebel wolf's head rolled in front of me. An expression of pain covered her face in the last moments of her death. Stunned, I turned to see a tall wolf headed in my direction. He solidified from the smoke like some phantom nightmare.

"Hmmm, she was weak, I didn't even put my full strength into that attack," the wolf said, his voice was deep and full of malice.

"You seem like you know something, tell me, where is that craven Belaize?" I looked from him to the head lying at his feet. He kicked the dead woman's head again, rolling it aside.

Intense rage and fury filled my veins and my wolf grew. I lost my mind in a whirlwind of malice. The man took a step back.

"You are Marcus, aren't you?"

"I am," I replied with no emotion. The anger seething within me did not find its way into my words.

"Faust," I said, though I had not met him, I knew it was him. Leader of Mortis, the notorious kill squad.

"My reputation precedes me," Faust said, smiling evilly.

"You're nothing but a maggot at my feet." I punched him in the gut. He recovered almost instantly and punched my chest. He followed with another punch to my face. I felt shooting pain, but the anger and adrenaline kept me standing. I ducked low and drove my head into his chin. I grit my teeth and fought through the pain. I felt myself being drained. The world gave a sudden, hazy lurch.

Fuck, not now. I must have gotten scratched during my fight with the guards. My movements were noticeably more sluggish now. But I was still in well enough shape to fight Faust. He would not get away with this.

I punched him in the face, one of his teeth went flying in an arc before landing in the dirt. Faust turned and ran.

No, not you too, I thought and gave chase. Every second drained my power further. I had to catch him quickly.

I darted toward him in a great leap. I caught him from behind. We rolled in the dirt and I ended up on top of him. I roared in his face and began punching him. Left, right, left, right. I kept going, his face was an unrecognizable smear of blood and bone. But he realized that my punches were weakening.

He blocked a punch aimed for his jugular and clamped his bruised mouth onto my hand. I screamed in agony as he bit away a chuck. Instinctively I jerked my hand back. A few fingers made sickening pops.

"Fuck!" I screamed and he got up and began clawing and gnashing his teeth. Picking apart my skin as the wolfsbane took my will to fight.

"No!" I screamed in agony.

"I will kill you," I screamed and rammed my head into his snout, blood began spilling from a fresh gash on my forehead. Faust caught my hand and yanked me forward. The sudden shift in my weight left me off balance and he quickly drove up with this his hips and rolled out from under me. As my world swirled wildly, I saw a dark shape in the distance.

"You fucking bastard, I'm going to slaughter you!" Faust said and thrust his arm forward. He impaled me and I coughed blood.

The shape was growing larger. He pulled his arm out from me and thrust it again, impaling me once more.

"No…" a fit of coughing wracked my body. My vision blurred, the shadow larger now. "I... won... won't die here." I said.

I heard a voice beckoning to me. I felt another fist pierce through me, crushing my stomach.

"Marcus!" The voice screamed in my head.

"You can't die, no! NO!" The voice jolted my vision. The shape that was approaching was now clear.

"Midnight..." I said.

"What?" Faust raised his fist again going for my neck. "You're pathetic," he said and Midnight reared his front legs and smashed them into his head. Faust collapsed. He fell on his side, his legs kicking wildly. Then he was still.

I heaved myself up. Midnight stood with me nudging his head into my shoulder. I walked to Faust's body, stumbling. I grabbed his head and yanked, twisting and wrenching until I uprooted his neck. I tossed his head to the side.

I stumbled again and fell on the ground. I coughed, blood splattering on the ground. My wolf retreated inside me. My body was battered and broken, three holes spilling blood onto the ground. I dragged myself so that I could sit up against a tree.

My eyes shut and the sounds of the world faded.

"Marcus!" The voice was beautiful.

"Marcus, open your eyes please," the voice begged, straining. I urged myself to open my eyes. I was greeted with Erylesia, her tear-stained face. Crying, begging me. I tried to speak but was caught with a fit of coughing, blood splattered onto my chest. A few droplets landed on her silken skin. *So lovely,* I thought.

"I... I... S... s-sorry." The word broke in my mouth, coming out in staggered gasps. My breathing was shallow and short.

"Marcus please, I can't lose you, no! I won't. We... need you." She was hysterical.

There was no pain anymore, her presence, seeing her, had brought me peace. I felt her hand on my cheek. It felt warm and nice.

"Her... n... ame i...s... Co... ra!" I mustered as I felt the last embers of my life leave me. I closed my eyes, the call of closing them so much stronger than my will to keep them open.

Cora, a beautiful name, don't you think my love? I said to Erylesia through our connection.

Please come back, was the only reply before the eternal darkness greeted me.

FAREWELL

Belaize

The thick smoke rose up in the air as fierce fires lit up the dark sky. Alistair sprinted ahead, his white fur flashing in and out of my vision. Eliana was close behind him. I increased my speed as we ran toward the burning hell ahead of us.

"Eliana," I called behind her. "Be careful," I said, almost on the border of Sanctuary now. She showed no sign of changing her course.

Eliana was running wild without being on guard. I felt her anguish through our bond. She was terrified for her father and her friends. I nearly closed the gap between us just before our group was swarmed by Council guards. They leapt at us, attacking without mercy. However, Alistair was ferocious. A demon from hell. His swipes broke bones and tore through flesh with ease. Soon, there were only two of them left.

"Take them old man, I have to stay with Eliana," I said. Alistair responded with a grunt and jumped on the two guards who were taken aback at his size. The fools were too lost in their bloodlust to have noticed earlier. Alistair was as large as, if not larger, than two men stacked.

I left Alistair behind and ran into the thicket of smoke and burning embers. There were sounds of screams coming from all around. The dying and injured.

The smell of blood was so thick in the air that it clotted my nose.

I practically tasted it on the tip of my tongue. This wasn't a fight. It was a massacre. Eliana's scent was all but lost. I had to find her. I ran headfirst toward the carnage. A few fear-stricken wolves barreled past me as they scrambled for the woods. But not everyone had gotten out in time. There weren't that many Council guards either. Ronak put up a good fight.

I turned toward the eastern end of the Sanctuary. The smoke was the thickest there, the tents had caught fire. It was where they had attacked first, I reasoned. I came upon Luthor who leaned against a tree. Bloody and bruised, but alive.

I saw him open an eye. "You bastard, you're too late, the Sanctuary has fallen," said the injured wolf in a weak voice.

"Luthor, where is Ronak, Amae!?" My mind drifted to Nihara. My sweet child.

"Tell me now!" I said. Suddenly, I could understand the frenzy that Eliana had been in.

"Amae hasn't returned to the Sanctuary, thank Liunella. Your pup evacuated with that healer, the stumpy one. Ronak is fighting near the eastern gate. Go help him, this revolution is doomed without him." Luthor spoke bluntly but his words were cold and true. I nodded and ran toward the east, my heart a little at ease, Nihara was safe, at least.

As I rounded the final few stone buildings, I came across Council guards gathered around.

"I think I smell a traitor," I said. The three dozen wolves turned instantaneously toward me. The moment their eyes fell on me, recognition dawned as clear as day. I felt Alistair's presence behind me. The sudden shift of their gazes from me to the much larger and intimidating Alistair could have had a physical impact.

Alistair stepped forward and growled. The weaker willed soldiers turned tail and ran. That's when Rayne stepped from the center of the group.

"I knew I smelled a rat," I spat.

"He smells like her," Alistair said lowly.

"He's her brother," I replied nonchalantly.

More attackers ran, leaving a mere eleven wolves to face us.

"You betrayed your own blood? Unforgivable," Alistair said, deducing the situation. Alistair took a step forward, and half of the wolves standing in front of us stepped back in fear. Perhaps some of them recognized the old wolf from legends, but it wouldn't have mattered anyway. When an alpha demands a challenge, there is little to be done for it. You obey or you die. Rayne stood awestruck; his mouth sealed shut. He couldn't comprehend how someone more powerful than me had showed up.

"Pray to Liunella, pray so that she may forgive you. You will find no mercy here," Alistair roared and the remaining wolves scattered,

Rayne among them. Alistair gave chase, catching up to the slowest wolf instantly and ripping him in two.

"B... Bel... aize..." A weak voice called me.

I looked around to see the source of it. I followed the sound to a dying wolf. He was bloody and laying on the ground covered in dust with an equally bloody Adrian kneeling beside him, pressing his hands to the wound. "Honoria will be here any minute, Ronak. Stay with us," he said.

"Ronak," I said as I got on my knees and assessed his wounds. Blood seeped into the ground slowly, taking Ronak's soul along with it. I glanced at Adrian, he was staring at Ronak, pressing as tightly as he could, but the blood wouldn't stop flowing. Ronak wouldn't recover from these injuries.

"S...some father I... was," he said weakly, his voice a hoarse whisper. He coughed up blood. His eyes closed in pain.

"Just..." Adrian said, his voice already hoarse. Ronak was dying.

"No, Rayne was a terrible son," I said. I tore some of my shirt. Adrian quickly made a bandage out of it, trying to stop the bleeding. But our hands were simply covered in his blood.

"I found Alistair," I said quietly.

"Good... follow Marcus, keep the..." He went silent, I thought that perhaps he had passed on, but another fit of coughing brought him back.

"My daugh... ter. Eliana, she will need you, take care of her. I trust... you." I nodded, he clutched my hand. His grip was weak.

A few of the surviving soldiers had gathered around now. I looked around and saw Alver, battered and bloodied, Armina was missing an eye. There weren't many rebels left. Alistair appeared again too. He smelled of blood.

The wolves separated, clearing a path for him. An overwhelming urge to bow to him took over me as well. His wolf demanded obedience. He took a look at me, and I shook my head. Alistair knelt beside Ronak too. The three of us huddled together as everyone watched.

"Rest well," Alistair said, bowing his head in respect.

"I... stop this war..." Ronak said and closed his eyes. This time I knew there was no coming back. Death had claimed him.

I glanced around. Adrian was still next to me. Bloody and battered. His gaze was fixed on Ronak, whose eyes had lost the light of the living. He lifted his fingers, rubbing them clean of the blood and then slowly closed Ronak's eyes.

"We will stop this war, or die trying Ronak," Adrian whispered quietly, more to himself.

I looked at the tear-stained faces of the onlookers. They were utterly devastated. The last hope to overthrow the Council, to stop the war, to peace, had diminished in front of their eyes.

The crowd began to part as I saw Eliana walk toward us. She was carrying someone. Erylesia was following Eliana, her eyes tear stained. I was a little surprised to see her swollen belly, and her eyes were red and swollen, no less.

"Marcus," I concluded. Eliana had streaks of tears staining her cheeks. Her gaze drifted to her dead father.

A dead silence fell upon the survivors. Adrian stood up slowly and took Marcus's body from Eliana, placing it beside Ronak. Countless brave warriors had died today. Erylesia, sank beside Marcus's now cold body, one hand clutching her belly, the other his cold hand. She was in shock. She straightened his arms beside his body. He had a smile on his face.

Eliana knelt beside me and stroked her father's sandy hair silently. I felt her grief in my mind... no... my heart. I wanted to reach out to her, comfort her, but I knew comfort wasn't what she needed, at the moment. There was no more distress in her mind. It was just a dull and all-encompassing silence.

The silence lasted for what felt like hours, then Eliana spoke.

"The fires need to be put out." She didn't face the onlookers.

"Put the fires out and let's prepare to send off the departed."

A few wolves nodded and began to spread out to complete the tasks. Erylesia started to get up and join the other wolves but Eliana grabbed her hand. "Not you."

"I…we… need to… give him a proper farewell," she muttered.

"No. You will do no such thing, Erylesia. You will stay with Marcus," Eliana said.

"He is fucking dead! I don't want to stay here," Erylesia shouted.

"Adrian," I said. He was standing quietly near us but stepped up. He had a busted lip and a black eye. His wounds had stopped bleeding, though. He was alive but I knew he would rather be dead in Marcus's place. *Family*. The word echoed in my mind. They were a family.

"Yes?" he finally said.

"Will you assist Erylesia to the Infirmary? Get some help with your injuries as well."

Adrian nodded stiffly.

"You can't do this, you damn bastard. You weren't even here during the attack. Neither of you. You cannot tell me what to do!" Erylesia was borderline hysterical.

"Erylesia... not for us. But for your child." Eliana spoke softly. She was looking at her father when she said it.

Erylesia cried in defeat. She bent and kissed Marcus's cheek, wiped her tears away. Standing up, Adrian clutched her arm and they both went away.

"They're all dead, Ronak, Marcus... all of them!" I heard a terrible scream in the distance.

I saw Eliana freeze, "They are," she said quietly. "And it falls to us, the living, to see to it that they are laid to rest," she said. She finally rubbed her face and stood up. She turned around and faced everyone.

"What do you mean? It's all over. We aren't safe anymore; The Council will hunt us all down."

"We won't give them a chance," Eliana said fiercely.

"Let us give them peace. For those that deserve it most are those killed in war," the one who had spoken out stepped back down.

"Alistair, assemble the scattered rebels, and make sure the army doesn't return. Focus around the Sanctuary," Eliana spoke like Ronak. A true leader. Alistair nodded.

"Belaize," I looked at her curiously. My pride was flaring, Eliana was finally becoming a leader.

"Help treat the wounded, you've the most experience in regards to battle wounds." I was surprised at her task. *Me a healer?* It was almost poetic.

"Belaize, make sure they don't suffer anymore," Eliana said somberly. That's when I understood why she set this task on me. I nodded grimly. Those that were too far gone would be put down. I wasn't well liked anyway, and this task wouldn't win me friends either, but I didn't care, she knew that. I held no attachment to these people and that made me the right person to help the helpless.

"What? You can't have... this... this monster kills more!" said an outraged wolf who had heard Eliana's order. He was joined by several others.

Alistair understood the situation perfectly. He let out a soothing grumble. It cut through the din of voices.

"Would you have them suffer more?" he questioned accusingly.

"Those that cannot be saved must not be made to suffer." Eliana spoke clearly and commanded respect.

I saw Alistair look upon Eliana with admiration.

"I need a few people to help me make the pyres."

As the first few hours passed the whole Sanctuary was caught in a choking silence. I had barely seen Eliana in that time, so I did my best to ease her job. Of all the wolves who guarded the Sanctuary during the attack, merely seven survived. Over four hundred were dead. And most of the Council guards. I had to put down over a dozen wolves. I checked the camps too and found a wolf had hung herself after learning of her mate's death. His body rested just below her dangling feet.

Slowly, surviving wolves began to trickle back into the Sanctuary. Many started repairing homes and carrying bodies to the river's edge. After everyone had been accounted for, Eliana led the wolves to the river.

There were almost two hundred rafts and pyres tied to the river's edge, most of them barely afloat because of the heavyweight.

"Let's finish paying our tributes," she called. The bodies had begun to decompose and an unruly scent assaulted my nostrils. Something that had never bothered me before. She walked to a pyre. I saw Ronak's face peeking out beneath a mound of corpses. His eyes were closed and finally at peace.

"We send off our loved ones with the blessings of Liunella. May all of you join her in paradise, beyond the water of truth."

Eliana kneeled beside her father and kissed his cheek. She then took a knee beside Marcus. She removed something from her soiled robes. A smooth, blue stone necklace, "This is yours old friend, rest now. Rest well," she almost choked on her words.

Eliana stood up and stared out into the river.

"Our lives are like the falling leaves. Soon to be carried away by the current that is the flow of time. Rest well those who are departed for your job is done."

She snapped the rope holding the raft. Next to follow her was Erylesia. She had a grim look on her face, yet I admired her courage to stand in front of us. She was letting Marcus go... letting her mate go. I couldn't imagine the guilt and grief she carried in her heart. I knew, though... that she was breathing heavy because of her child that was growing in her womb. And I thought of what Nihara had given me. Adrian walked from the crowd and stood beside Erylesia. No words were spoken but I knew. He was that unborn child's guardian.

Within seconds all the ropes were cut and the rafts started slowly moving along with the flow of water.

Torches were lit and thrown onto the rafts that quickly set ablaze. The stars, the full moon, all paled in comparison to the firelight glow of the funeral. A spectacular sight to behold.

Eliana stood beside me and reached for my hand. My instinct was to pull back from her, but I held her hand.

"It's far too beautiful a night for this. Father... Marcus... forgive me," Eliana said and a single tear fell from her left eye. I squeezed her hand gently. I didn't know what to say, but I felt that she only needed my company right now.

"It is your fault that he is dead." I heard someone say. I turned around and saw the maimed boy. He had grown taller and stronger in the last few weeks.

"If you didn't exist none of this would have happened. We wouldn't be betrayed and Marcus would still be alive." He was staring right at me.

I stared at him silently. Eliana too looked at him, her grip tightened on my hand.

"Marcus said you were on our side, but I don't believe him. Now that this Sanctuary is burned, I will never trust you. I may not be old like you, but I know who my enemy is. It will always be you," The boy spat on the ground, "Harbinger."

"I am leaving the Sanctuary."

"Erwin, please no, you don't know—" but Erwin turned and left, marching out into the wilderness. All around us wolves murmured amongst themselves, but slowly the crowd dispersed. I stayed silent. I didn't know what to say. The fires had since drifted from sight and I felt out of place.

"We should return." Her voice sounded... cold. Eliana finally turned her back on the river and began her walk back to the Sanctuary. She moved with a different confidence now. A leader, the Navar. But it had come at a heavy cost to her heart. She disappeared into Ronak's office. I stopped short. I didn't know if I should follow her.

Come in, Eliana said through our connection.

And so I did, it still smelled of him. But he wasn't in his chair, instead Eliana was seated in his place.

"We have all suffered a loss. But I am sorry about Erwin," she said with a hint of sympathy. "We need to look ahead, move forward. Father left us something," she said, a soft smile on her face. One full of gratitude and conviction.

"What is it?" I inquired. She gestured to his desk where several maps, diagrams, and plans rested. A quick glance through them told me everything I needed to know. The plan included diagrams of the Great Castle, home of the Council. There were details of every nook, hidden passage, and chamber throughout the entire castle. For the Sanctuary, it was hope.

"It's his legacy," Eliana said.

"His final plan to achieve peace. He organized an assault on Regvyer and the reinforcements will be here in a few days, the first of which should be arriving soon. He... never counted on us to bring Alistair back. He still planned this attack. It was his last hope to overthrow the Council. With or without us. Our chances are better now though, with you and Alistair on our side."

"Me?" I asked in confusion.

She nodded, her arms rested on the desk as she read yellowed papers.

"Yes. I know... you don't want anything to do with this war. Neither do I. Not after... losing my family. But... I will have to. We will. You don't want Nihara to grow up in the same way that we did. So, I know you will do everything in your power to stop the Council once and for all."

I stood awestruck. Almost as she said the words, I realized she was absolutely right. I had changed.

"Yes. I'm with you, Eliana. I believe we can win. But... what happens next? After the war."

She stilled for a moment and took a sharp breath in. She caught my gaze.

"We... will go somewhere and raise Nihara as our own."

Eliana stood up wrapped her slender arms around my waist and held me. I hugged her and felt the tension in her body. She laid her head against my chest. I felt tears wetting my shirt and I stroked her hair softly as I held her close. It took several minutes before I realized that she had passed out right in my arms, leaning against me with all her weight. I lifted her easily and took her to Ronak's bed. I laid her down and covered her with a white sheet. She was beautiful. I sat across the room against the wall, watching her sleep.

Ronak you clever dog, even in death you have won us this war. Janus, Idaos, whoever is responsible, I'll make sure you're dead for sure this time, no matter what.

In a few minutes, my vision darkened and a dreamless sleep took over me. All I remembered was Eliana's soft breathing.

COALESCENCE

Eliana

My eyes slowly flickered open. I stretched on the small bed that I was laying in. A moment of peace filled my mind until the waves of memories hit me from the previous day. My heart... it felt heavy.

Father, Marcus... I didn't have time to mourn them right now. I had to avenge them. Somehow. Rayne... Idaos... I'd take everything from them.

I sat up in bed and found Belaize asleep sitting upright against the desk. His long white hair fell over his shoulders. It was longer than before. His beard was thicker too. For as long as the two of us had been together, he had never rested completely. He always slept lightly. A twig snap or a rustle of leaves would wake him.

"You're up," Belaize said. It saddened me a little to know he never slept well.

"Mmhmm," I said and got up, rubbing my face with my hands, wiping the residual sleep away. We left the tent together in complete silence. I did my best to shield him from my hollow heart, but it left our bond feeling stiff and uncoordinated, tense.

"The first of the reinforcements will be arriving soon," I said. Belaize grunted in reply. He scratched at his beard. "I'll catch up with you," he said and melted into the bustle of the busy Sanctuary. Had he not done that often, it would have been unnerving. One might have even mistaken it for disinterest. But I knew that wasn't the case. He wasn't used to this new role. His was not a life of comfort. We were adjusting.

It was late into the morning. People were out repairing the damage done to the Sanctuary. I cursed myself for not rising earlier, not directing them. Liunella, I hadn't even looked in a mirror. For a moment, I saw my father's crisp jacket, his freshly laundered shirt, no matter the time, no matter the day. "A leader must look the part," he would tell me. My vision blurred and I shoved the memory away.

"Catalogue the food we have left and ration it. Make sure the available wolves report to me. We need to send a scouting party for provisions. Berries are in season. Make use of that—" I was almost finished when a rebel came running to me.

"The warriors are here."

I nodded and walked to the entrance of the Sanctuary, or what was left of it. The trees were uprooted, the ashes and the debris of the community that once prevailed, were all that remained. I met with the chieftains of the Sanctuaries that arrived, notably Jennifer. She was a stone-faced wolf, notorious for her ruthlessness.

"I travel all this way and Ronak doesn't greet me himself," Jennifer huffed. The immediate silence around us was uncanny. *That fuck—*, my wolf snarled before I pushed her away.

"Ronak is... he has passed on," I said sternly. I knew I was glaring at her, and it felt good. Immediately Jennifer dropped her hostile attitude.

"Forgive me," she said and bowed her head. She took a look around and saw the state of the Sanctuary. Her eyes took in the destruction the Council guards had left in their wake.

"It happened yesterday," I filled her in.

"We've let the deceased pass on to the next world with their respect and dignity, this is all that is left of the Southern Sanctuary," I finished.

"And who is Ronak's successor?" she questioned.

"I assume you mean to ask who holds his amulet," I said. A wave of sadness threatened to spill forward inside me but I stood rigid. Jennifer nodded.

"He too has passed in yesterday's battle. The amulet was sent with him to the next world. He was worthy of its possession. Come, we can continue this chat indoors, forgive us, our food stores are depleted, most have been burned to the ground. With the fields salted, they are unable to bear any crops for future generations. The Council was thorough in their ambush. They came to kill and destroy. They did not imprison anyone," I said.

Again, she nodded; she had not come here expecting the leader of the rebellion dead. This was the greatest setback of our time. Since the beginning Father had led our rebellion. I caught her looking around the Sanctuary, she wasn't only taking in her surroundings, but she was also looking for something... someone.

"Where is the Blood Moon Harbinger?" Her question was one that I had expected.

"He is here; you will see him soon," I said.

"Ronak spoke of a secret weapon, I assume it's someone other than him." She was rather blunt, but I could tell she was a good Chieftain. Leadership required detachment, stoicism. I knew that now. Knew it deeper than I ever thought knowledge could go. It sat with me, and turned my heart to stone.

"The old King of the Vascyan Nation, Alistair," I said as matter-of-fact.

Her jaw practically hit the floor.

"That is not possible," she said.

"It is, he was alive and lived as a recluse for more than a century." Jennifer was still in disbelief. I took note of her circle of trusted; they were worn and weathered soldiers. I recognized another Chieftain as Xyabolt. He was an even more experienced wolf than my father. He had opted to lead a Sanctuary in the north, last I recalled.

I saw Alistair and Belaize approach from behind the group. Alistair was shorter than Belaize in his human form, but he commanded more respect from the wolves. A legend in the flesh.

It took a second to realize that Belaize had rid himself of his beard and cut his hair short. His face was near stunning. Normally, it was covered in a beard, but without it masking his face, he was practically another person.

Jennifer and Xyabolt turned in unison, wary of them both. I knew they were in an internal struggle because their wolf wanted to submit to their alpha, Alistair. I saw the recognition flash on Belaize's face as he saw Xyabolt following us.

"So, you survived, you old dog," Belaize said.

"Belaize of the Blood Moon," he said, "I heard to the dismay of my foes that you had joined Ronak."

He held out his hand and Belaize and Xyabolt clasped hands in a warrior's salute. They had met on the battlefield before but there was no bad blood between them. Xyabolt understood he had been outmatched, and yet now he was willing to put aside any personal enmity to face the bigger problem.

I led the group to father's war room. There, neatly laid out, was a map of Regvyer. Wooden wolf heads were adorned in a semi-circle around the Capital signifying the combined rebel forces. Our entire strength represented by merely seven pieces, compared to the thirty of the Council. More than eighteen thousand soldiers remained in allegiance to the Council. It was a frightening thought. Or at least it would have been. But Remus commanded a faction of the Council that would attack from behind. But even then, it wouldn't be enough.

"In two weeks, there will be a full moon. Our strength will be enhanced, as will the Council's. We can use this time to regroup and fortify our defenses and prepare for the siege of the Capital," I said, all attention was focused on me.

I looked around, there were still several commanders that were not in the room. They would be joining us soon. Romulus was bringing Sora, the Chieftain of the Western Sanctuary. Joraiel, of the South-west. Velamier from the East.

"Let us adjourn till the other Chieftains arrive," I said. The others nodded, and slowly cleared the room. *Father would've noticed that. He would've waited*, I thought. Belaize remained with me.

"Even with the leaders all assembled here, it'll be near impossible to face those odds," he said. I couldn't help but smile.

"My father had an ace up his sleeve," I said, "There are several among the ranks of the Council that fear Idaos and have been working with an elder to help us. When the time is right, they will attack from behind." Belaize nodded.

He was tense, jaw clenched, staring at me, observing my every move. "What is it?" I prodded him, looking up at him for an answer. Whenever I was alone with him, I was struck by how tall he was.

"Your brother, can you do what needs to be done?" he stated bluntly. I thought for a second, anger flared within me, but I kept it at bay. I nodded.

"If... I fail, make sure you complete the job." Belaize nodded in reply. *Could I though? Would I be able to put him down? It doesn't matter, Rayne is surviving on borrowed time.*

I engrossed myself in one report and then the next, and before I even knew it, the hours flowed by like the river tide. I was pulled from my work when another commotion started near the eastern entrance. Sounds of greeting and shuffling steps. More rebels from the other Sanctuaries had arrived.

Thank you, father, I said silently as I approached the travel weary wolves.

"Welcome," I said and greeted the six wolves who led the vanguard. Our numbers neared seven thousand now. The camp had grown nearly ten times its original size. I felt as though I stood in my father's shadow, in the ashes of the home he built, as we prepared to fight the Council.

"Eliana, it's good to see you child," said a jolly fat man by the name of Zeltram. He was one of the funniest people I have known. He captured me in a massive bear hug and I felt my ribs creaking.

"Here are the soldiers your father requested as I promised," he said, his bearded face flushed. He let me go and I sucked in a deep breath.

"I've heard some dire news on the road little one, tell me it's not true," he said. I shook my head.

"Ronak is martyred," I said, my heart heavy. His face, with its deep smile lines and mischievous eyes, grew somber.

"My condolences," he said, resting a heavy hand on my shoulder.

The others with him each expressed their condolences as well. Noland and Greta, Zeltram's children, each in turn bowed their heads.

Nearly a half hour later, father's quarters were bustling with activity. Every leader from every standing Sanctuary sat around his large table. They had washed from their travels and appeared rested enough. I knew that I couldn't put this off any longer, and slowly rose from my place at the crown of his table.

"The next few weeks will be some of the toughest we will have ever faced. The threat is far greater than just Idaos," I said, everyone had fallen silent. "Our final count of our strength leaves us at a disadvantage to that of the Capital. Regvyer, even in our most conservative estimates, numbers near thrice our size." A quiet murmur travelled through the room.

"We are outnumbered," I continued. A nervous energy emanated from the group. "This could be the end," I said. "But... we owe it to our future," I said "We owe it to the countless widowed, suffering, and dead, to put everything on the line."

Jennifer cleared her throat, drawing attention to herself.

"I agree. But I have one concern, which I believe other Chieftains also share," Jennifer continued, "Ronak has passed on. All of us grieve for him, for he was the one destined to take us to victory. But now, that is not the case. He passed his amulet, his leadership, to someone else, and not you Eliana. Sadly, he is dead as well. What does this indicate other than the fact that Ronak believed that you aren't ready to lead, that you are incapable? I do not think you should lead us, or this Sanctuary."

"I am not here to satisfy your concerns. They are dead, yes. Marcus was supposed to be our leader, but he is gone too. The fall of this Sanctuary was complete chaos. There was no stopping the onslaught! Who did you expect to take the lead? There is hardly anyone left."

"Where is Amae? She is the senior adviser. Or Romulus? I believe we would be more comfortable discussing our attack plan with them rather than you," Jennifer countered.

"Not only that, but it is clear you are mated to the Harbinger. He was the Council's right hand in the slaughter of our people. Now, suddenly he is on Ronak's side. I don't believe it, not for a second. What guarantee do we have that you are not driving us all into a trap? Especially now that Rayne has turned against the rebels and his own father's cause! How can we ever trust another one of Ronak's seed?"

Her words felt like knives to my heart. Yet, I stood there, taking each blow. She was right, wasn't she? It was clear why she doubted me and my integrity.

"I cannot say or give you the proof that you require. Everything you say is true. But do not forget that the Council didn't only kill your leader, they killed my father. I am going to lead to the best of my ability. I possess my father's blood. I am a Navar. I will not stop until all who are responsible are screaming for mercy. I understand your doubts. But the most I will ever do is acknowledge them. That's all. I will lead the attack on the full moon, with or without your support."

A chill settled in my father's chambers. They were all silent. Alistair watched me from the corner. Thankfully, I didn't get any opposition after that. Their acceptance was hesitant at best, but there was nothing to be done for it. An hour later, everyone left the room, except Belaize and Alistair.

"You did alright, Eliana," Alistair said and left the room. Finally, with Belaize alone, I let out a breath.

You were born to rule, Eliana, he said through our connection.

"Where is Nihara?" I asked. I missed her soft smile. "Oh, and Midnight?"

"Back at Infirmary with Amae. And after the attack Midnight ran into the wilderness in frenzy, but as things settled down, he came back on his own. Adrian volunteered to tend to him, make sure he is not wounded," Belaize said.

"He is grieving in his own way," I said, the void in my heart grew, yet I knew… now was not the time to grieve them. We would have that time. Now, we needed retribution for our broken family. I nodded and stood up. It was time to see Nihara. We moved out and headed toward the Infirmary.

Surprisingly, the old brick building didn't suffer any damage. Wolves were there helping the injured ones, buzzing around carrying supplies, muffling cries, and wrapping wounds. We moved inside and saw Amae and Honoria tending to a woman. We waited anxiously. The room was far from tranquil, far from a place of healing. It smelled of blood, and sweat, and worse.

After she was done, cleaning her hands on her clothes, she came to me and hugged me hard. "You poor child."

I wrapped my arms around her. A soft sob came from my mouth as I rubbed my tears away. I had to be strong.

"When did you both return?" I asked them.

"An hour ago, Eliana," Honoria said, stitching a cut above the woman's eyebrow.

As soon as she put the last stitch in, she washed her hands in the water bowl beside her and came to embrace me as well. "Thank you. For keeping Nihara safe."

"She was with a wet nurse when the attack happened. It was the least I could do. I wouldn't have left a child behind," Honoria said softly.

"Where is Nihara?" Belaize asked stiffly, trying to hide his urgency to see her.

Amae chuckled. "Rest up," she said to the injured woman. "I'll be right back." Amae told Honoria and strode outside the room.

"Come with me," Amae called.

I thanked Honoria again, and Belaize and I followed Amae. She took us through a series of corridors and then paused outside a room. She put a finger on her lips, signaling us to remain quiet. Through the glass window, I saw Erylesia, sitting in a chair with Nihara resting in her arms comfortably, resting on her swollen belly. They had fallen asleep.

Belaize stood rooted in place, watching them both. I grabbed his hand and pulled him away softly.

"Let them be together for a bit. Erylesia needs Nihara more," I said.

Amae smiled weakly at us and we left them in peace.

"I saw Erylesia in her state and told her to keep an eye on Nihara. I could tell... that she had lost Marcus. It's always such a dangerous time after the loss of a mate. I've seen so many follow, over the years. Even after Adya... I have seen so much death, child. You'll bring back the peace of this land, won't you?" Amae sighed sadly.

"We will." Belaize and I replied in unison.

I looked at him, a determination was in his eyes. A need to protect Nihara. They were all I had now. Amae split from us and we headed out of the Infirmary. I looked up at the sky. Stars were twinkling brightly and a thin crescent moon was in the sky.

"Not much time is left. Less than two weeks and all of this ends."

"We will win, Eliana," Belaize said.

"You're right. We will win, because I will do anything to protect my family, and that's a promise," I said with the fiery determination that sparked within my heart. *I will make you proud, father.*

THE SETTING SUN

Romulus

It had been nearly six days since everyone had arrived at the ruins of Ronak's Sanctuary, and four since we began the march on the Capital. In that time, the plan had been drilled into each of us, soldiers and Chieftains alike. This was it. All of it: decades of mass murder and extermination, the fight for Vascya, had at last reached the final stages. If we win the night, we could usher in a new era of peace under Alistair.

Time was not an ally in this fight. There was still some hesitation among the chieftains, especially without Ronak's assurance and strength, but our window of opportunity was short and all our doubts had to be put aside. Our only focus was freedom. That's all we could afford.

I sprinted ahead of the vanguard. I led a charge of two dozen wolves to comb our path from the village to village, spreading the word. We had hundreds of wolves join us as we marched to Regvyer. Farmers, smiths, retired soldiers, young and old, men, women. There was no discrimination. The four days of marching had been in near silence. For a host this size, it was practically a whisper.

The elders knew we marched to them, however. No force this size could go unnoticed by the guards. We ascended a hill and I stood watch over the rolling fields. They stretched far and wide and beyond them, lay the Capital.

"Romulus, we are getting close," said Eliana. Sure as night follows day, Belaize was always near her. I took a long look at the man, his long white hair was now trim, his beard gone. He was a man reborn. One with a bloody past that no amount of change could hide or wash away.

"Yes," I said. I looked back at the bottom of the gentle slope. Ranks upon ranks of soldiers emerged from the trees. They all took formation at the bottom of the hill, ready for our command. Eliana stood with me at the peak of the hill with Alistair, Belaize and Adrian, and the other commanders. Amae and Erylesia had stayed behind with the others who couldn't fight.

We approached the massive outskirts of the castle town. In front of us, spread far and wide was the Vascyan royal army welcoming us at their gates. A massive host of wolves stood on guard and ready, staring at the approaching mass that was the entirety of the rebel force. All was quiet. This was it.

The castle spires tore through the sky like sharp teeth against the soft cloud cover of the fading day. As we came to a halt my men began to lay down their packs and make space for a temporary rest. The Council loomed in the distance, separated only by thousands upon thousands of guards.

Without ever turning my back on the great force, I made my way to the other Chieftains, motioning Eliana, Belaize, Adrian, and a few others to follow. The walk was like a dream. I knew that it was real, my heart was thundering in my chest, but even so, the world passed in a blur.

We occupied a small, makeshift tent on the eastern edge of our forces, close enough to the gate to answer the call to arms. Candles were lit to stave away the fading light. Each of us were dirt-smeared and sweaty; there was a restless tension to the room.

"This is it, Romulus, see if you can go around the army and infiltrate inside. Make sure Remus knows when to attack," Eliana said. I nodded.

"I will not sully this day with goodbyes," I began, "Many of us will not see tomorrow. We cannot give the slightest ground. Momentum should not swing in favor of the Council."

My words were held in the air. That nervous, bubbling tension shifted to me now. I caught the command of the room. "We do not have the resources to support a long war. The truth is that this campaign will be over in less than a day. You know that as well as I do.

"One Day!" I said aloud. "If we cannot win the battle in a single day, it will all end, and Vascya will never see light again." I saw the resolve of my comrades. Behind the resolve, however, was fear. We could not fail. Not with the entire country counting on us.

I took another long look at the generals. I could only imagine something similar was occurring across the battlefield in the camps of the Council.

"To victory..." I said and turned my back on them.

I spent the next few hours meditating. I sat in an open area as the tents were put up, several fires were set, and small portions of food were cooked and distributed between the ranks. I smelled fire-smoke and sweat.

I didn't know what to focus on when meditating, as whenever I had before, I had focused on myself and developing my awareness. But today was different. I felt the odd need to pray.

Liunella, The Moon Goddess, The Queen of The Tides... guide us from this torrent of darkness into the dawn.

I finished my prayer and couldn't help but feel a little childish. I had not offered a prayer since I had first left the Twin Cities. But if she was watching from the land beyond the tides, then perhaps she would hear me. Perhaps she would lift her hand in our favor but I heard nothing in return.

I stood and stretched a little, running my hand over my hairless head. I slipped away from the camp and headed toward the rear of the Capital. It would be less heavily guarded, and a lot easier to slip past the guards.

Before I knew it, I found myself walking through the streets. They were deathly silent. Shops and homes had been boarded up. The occasional guard would walk through on patrol, simple enough to avoid, especially since they didn't bother to conceal their steps. As I made my way toward the Capital I glanced at the sun. It was dipping ever lower; I could not see it but for its faint glow beyond the screen of buildings.

"It will begin soon," I said to myself.

I turned a corner and saw a child no older than seven standing by a door. A look of sheer determination plastered his face.

"You there," I said. "Go inside." I spoke harshly but did not conceal anything from him.

The boy growled at me and stood fast before the door. I walked up to him and looked down toward him. He looked up, not dropping the determined look.

"You're protecting your home, eh kid?" I asked. He nodded in response. Suddenly, he was pulled back and a she-wolf put herself between me and the child, pushing him inside.

"It is getting darker by the minute. Close the door and guard it from the inside," I warned and backed away from them. I understood her hostility. It was in the damn air, and I knew the citizens couldn't trust the Council guards completely, either. They lived in Regvyer because the Council provided a roof on their head.

I slipped back into the shadows and made sure I wasn't being followed. Sometime later, I passed the famous fountain of the four winds in the heart of Regvyer. I stayed hidden in the shadows and waited.

The sun had set and the sky was a blood red. It was foreshadowing the night on which history will be made. The place was quiet. Not a soul in sight. That's when I felt him near me. I looked down the alley to my right.

"Remus."

"Come," I heard his whispered echo.

I gave the mesmerizing fountain a last glance and followed Remus. After a series of twists and turns we paused in a dark corner. My senses were heightened tonight. I couldn't feel anyone around me.

Remus was wearing a thick hooded cloak. He pulled his hood down and faced me. He looked tired and older since the last time I saw him. In contrast to me, he had a thick head of hair, and a scar on his neck.

"Is everything ready?" I inquired.

"Yes. The Alphas will be monitoring the fight from the Sanctorum. Illari, Evette and Esteve had deserted the Council. The remaining alphas are here tonight. Some will fight us and some will fight for us. They have taken every precaution to avoid the rebels. Romulus, Idaos, and Janus know that the rebels don't have the resources for a prolonged campaign. They plan to hide in the castle till rebels can fight no more."

"You know what needs to be done," a grim tone clear in my voice.

A sudden chill set along my spine. I felt the collective howl of the rebels resonating in my ears. Their voices rose to a frightening pitch, for Vascya. For a moment I was deafened by it, my heart slowed, and my blood sung in response. My wolf was desperate to answer.

The battle has finally begun.

Remus looked at me and nodded in understanding. It's now or never. Remus walked to the end of the alley and pushed a pile of refuse aside.

"I carved this way into the castle. Not an easy task I have to say. The alphas are wary of me because I commanded the Low Cities, but they weren't overly suspicious. I knew this would come in handy one of these days."

I grunted in response. We ruled over the Low Cities but ever since the Council began its extermination campaign, we split up to infiltrate the Council. The alphas would pay; the way to crack an impenetrable egg was from the inside, after all. The Council have been allowed to continue this for far too long. This ends tonight.

Our steps echoed in the empty cave. It was dark and smelled putrid. Remus had made this way out of sewers. Finally, we reached the end and climbed out of the tunnel and heaved a breath of fresh air.

Remus closed the pit in the floor with a heavy stone plate covered by a soft, thick-weaved rug. We were in an old storage closet of some kind, by the smell of it. In the dim light I saw old furniture covered in white sheets. Dust. Cobwebs. The place wreaked of unuse.

He proceeded to open the door, that's when the hair on the back of my neck stood up. We weren't alone anymore. I closed my eyes and I sensed... five... six... no, eight wolves. Right outside the door. I put a hand on Remus's shoulder and held him right there. He had sensed them too.

"There is no need to waste time now, Remus. We have surrounded you. Moreover, the other end of that passage is sealed. There isn't a way for you to go," a voice called from the other side.

Remus cursed under his breath. A moment passed. I heard the approach of muffled footsteps and went forward and pulled the door open. The number of wolves had increased from eight to fifteen.

"Remus," an old gray-haired wolf looked at me confused. The old wolf eagerly peered inside the room. He wore a smug look.

That's when Remus stepped from behind me. The wolves took a step back.

"Eyolf, you remember him, don't you?" Remus said.

"So, the rumors are true. You never had the spine to kill him, then. You always were a coward Remus. Pretending to win the great duel of the twin Kaisers. I am disappointed. I knew you were feeding rebels information, but this? Disgusting."

"I did what I had to. You've desecrated the Goddess and Vascya for too long now," Remus said with conviction.

"What about you, Remus? You handed us the damn soldiers, didn't you? The blood is on your hands as much as on mine. Do not pretend to be a messiah or savior when you did nothing but whatever we asked of you. You have always been a coward, working and plotting from the shadows. At least I am true to a side, but you are the one who stabs your own in the heart."

"The Goddess will never forgive the atrocities that I have committed to ensure this day arrives. You on the other hand," he said, "You will find no solace in this world or the next."

"It doesn't matter. We have you in our custody and by the morning every rebel will be dead." Eyolf laughed.

"We will not go down that easy," I said and changed into my wolf. Waves of power emitted from my body as fur covered my back, chest, and arms. Remus, too, changed simultaneously.

I lunged for the throat of the Council guard to my right. I crushed his throat and thrusted my fist under his arm and into his chest where the armor didn't cover. A moment later he was dead on the floor. Remus was wrestling with three wolves to my left. One of the wolves slumped over and was dead before he hit the ground.

Other guards lunged at us. It was a fight unlike any I'd ever been in. We were larger than most of the wolves; however, they were many in number. I lunged and attacked, wolves fell, but more took their place. Even with my strength and skill their number was overwhelming.

A wolf bit my shoulder, making me groan and grunt in pain. I tore my arm loose and snapped his neck. My arm was out of commission, bleeding profusely, but I kept fighting.

Eyolf was old but he had the strength of an alpha in his veins. He changed and aimed his gaze at the struggling Remus. He ran toward him. I pulled away from the wolves around me, trying to shove Eyolf out of the way, when – with sudden speed and grace – another wolf slammed Eyolf into the far wall.

I analyzed my surroundings, and the guards now littered the floor in bloody heaps. Our backup had arrived just in time. A set of twenty to thirty wolves scattered around us taking care of the mess. Remus had a few cuts and bruises but he was alright.

I went to Eyolf. His breathing was labored. He probably broke a rib or two. The wolf stepped beside me and changed his form.

"What do you want to do about him?"

I squeezed my hand around his throat. "This is what you get for dismissing the right from the wrong, Eyolf." I crushed his throat and watched the life drain from his eyes.

I looked back at the wolf. "I didn't think you would join us, Amarog," I said and looked at him warily.

"Idaos's rule has gone on long enough. Now, with Janus in the picture, it was about time I picked my fight. Remus merely gave me the opportunity to act." I shook his hand firmly.

I called everyone around us. "It's time, we take back our country and our right to live as we please. You know what you have to do. Attack the city's defenses from the inside and open the gates to the castle. The alphas cannot hide anymore. May Liunella bless us all."

I held my injured arm and shoved my shoulder back into place. This was no time to be injured. I tore my sleeve and tied it around my wound quickly. Outside I could hear the battle raging. Screaming and howling. The clanging of iron on iron.

"Remus, the time to join the battle has arrived."

Somewhere in the cavernous halls of the castle the sound of manic laughter filled the silent void. An unnerving and sadistic laugh.

Janus... you're next! I thought to myself and ran in step with Remus and Amarog.

DARKNESS DESCENDS

Idaos

The scent of war surrounded my castle. Sitting in the dimly lit Sanctorum, I was alone, waiting for others to join. Right outside the castle's doors was the rebel army. Ready to attack us. Ready to obliterate the Council once and for all.

Rebels were getting restless. I heard the soft hum of the army outside, suiting up for the biggest fight of their lives. Our army was three times bigger than theirs. I knew we would win. Their attempt to attack us was futile, yet the tight feeling in my throat only grew stronger.

Canagan and Esteve walked in and immediately head for the wine. I nodded in acknowledgment but no one uttered a word. The rest of the seats were empty. I knew everyone's stand now. I was alone fighting this battle. The tension in the room was growing. This was my Capital and my men were strong defenders. We would stand. We would hold. I would not die.

The door of the Sanctorum opened with a loud bang and Janus walked in. He had a stench of decay around him. The others recoiled in fear from the man who stood before us. Their reactions were not much better than the first time they'd seen the *thing*. But Janus had quickly silenced them, by magical, or by other means.

After that, there was no protest among the Council members.

I had sworn that our dealings were finished after our last meeting.

The man was unnatural. He was more creature than man, even. His aura worked some enfeeblement on me, I was sure. In his presence I felt weak. But this would be last of it. I was Çatall's chosen! I was born for rule. He would not unmake me! I drained my goblet of wine. The world was closing in on me as the minutes ticked by.

He clicked his fingers and the Council guard posted outside guarding the Sanctorum rushed in to pull his chair out for him. He sat down on it with grace. We were filth at his feet.

Damn him, everything was falling apart. Decades of work and planning only to have him appear and usurp all that I have done. I was seething with anger, but I was helpless. In front of Janus, I was nothing. The stench around him, and his incredible aura that surrounded him, exuded death.

"What are you so lost in thought about Idaos?" he said with a malicious grin.

I was going to bellow that this was *my* city. This was my plan and my vision. I was the light of Vascya. I was the maker of the new world. But before I could, my throat constricted. I gasped weakly for air.

He easily dismissed the other alphas and they rose to leave. As the door shut behind them, he stood from his chair. The shift in movement exposed a small medallion. My fingers went numb.

My eyes caught the metal and widened. His face twisted in a smirk and suddenly I could breathe once more. I took great mouthfuls of air.

"What is that?" I found myself saying. He looked at me again and smiled a nasty, evil grin.

"So, you've seen it," he said. He slowly let his robe fall to the floor.

"You... yo... how are you alive right now?" I said as I stared dumbly at what was once Janus. His naked chest was covered with deep wounds, which were bleeding. His neck was slashed.

"You can't be Janus," I stuttered out. The pendant caught the light. That's when I realized what it was, what he had done.

"That's the moon stone!" I exclaimed.

That smile didn't leave Janus's face. "So, you know of it," he stated. I nodded. "It's... a myth but... how do you possess it? And how can you even wear it? Its power is like no other! Janus..." Fear had struck my heart.

A loud crash echoed into the Sanctorum. A wolf stumbled in. He was injured.

"They're here," the wolf said and fell on the floor, smashing the table beside the door.

I turned to Janus but he had vanished.

"No! This can't be!" I yelled at the empty space. Just as I finished my sentence, my vision shattered, and my soul was launched into a vision. I had never experienced such a powerful reaction. *Could this be his work too?*

Then I saw it, it was a monstrous wolf, the size of which I had never seen. A familiar scar adorned his chest.

"Bel... aize." I cried with pain.

Belaize snarled, my vision was beginning to falter. I was being dragged back into the present.

"Stop it, Janus!" I screamed but no words came out of my mouth.

"Let me show what Death really looks like!" Janus said as his body twisted and snapped. He changed into a disgusting creature.

My vision cleared, and I was on my hands and knees panting. Immediately, my stomach emptied itself on the floor before me. The stench was atrocious. The taste of bile stung my throat. I heaved more and more until nothing remained. I dry heaved until my body ached.

I stood up, wiping my mouth, and looked around the room, no one was here anymore, save for the wolf that had stumbled in. He was lying unconscious on the floor, blood pouring from a wound. His eyes were wide open, an expression of fear etched on his face as he took his dying breath.

"This is what you have reaped," a voice said.

"Who's there!" I yelled. Tears filled my eyes as nothing made sense anymore. I looked around feverishly. No one was in the room.

"You have brought forth the end, not of Vascya, but of your own."

"Who are you!?" I yelled.

Before me, a beautiful figure materialized. Deep, starry blue eyes speckled with white. They mirrored the sky. Her pupils were like the moon. Before her power, I fell to my knees.

"Goddess!" I screeched.

"Forgive me!" I yelled hysterically.

"You, child, are a pawn in the large game of fate. Forgiveness, is not mine to give, but it belongs to Vascya, and Vascya approaches."

"No! No!" I yelled.

"Save me... from that creature!" I begged.

"The time for repentance has passed. The end approaches."

The apparition vanished as soon as it had appeared.

"Please..." my voice weakened and despair surrounded me. "Ha..."

"I said help me!" I commanded with last of my strength. "Ha ha ha ha!" I couldn't stop laughing. "I'm going to die!" I said out loud. My laughter bubbled in the halls of the castle as night fell over the raging battlefield.

In the descending darkness, rose the moon. Blood red. A bleeding moon meant only one thing. "Death walks among us," I screamed while madness encircled me.

RETRIBUTION

Belaize

The first howls echoed through the empty expanse of the battlefield which lay before our troops. The silence that had gripped the land slowly released its hold as battle cries and howls filled the black void. The ground began to thunder and shake beneath the paws of the rushing soldiers who made their way into the last battle of their lives.

The faded pink moon climbed ever higher into the sky, as if the goddess was looking down at her children. The moonlit battlefield was the river of sadness flowed amidst us. The screams and grunts of wolves fighting each other resonated deeply within me. It was a sound I knew better than anything. It was pure chaos. All this blood, this death, only to achieve one single goal. Victory over Vascya.

The front lines of both the armies clashed heavily now, and it was almost time for us to join the fight. From our high vantage point, I saw the space between the armies grow ever smaller. Only shrinking pockets remained. The red armor of the Council guards glinted in the moonlight. *The color of blood. Fitting,* I thought.

A few guards almost penetrated our defense and were running along the outside edge of our camp, fighting and killing their way forward. But, before I could lift a finger, I sensed Luthor in his wolf form leaping forward and jumping right in middle of the group. He slaughtered them in under a minute. A few swift, well aimed swipes at their necks and it was done.

Blood covered his paws. He shook his body and laughed with triumph. "It won't be that easy to win against us!" he said.

The soldiers manning our defense cheered him on. The morale was high. *But at what cost*, I wondered.

"It's time," Luthor barked. I turned to face the group that had now assembled near him. Eliana, Alistair, Luthor, Adrian and sixteen other wolves that would be the crux of this attack. I took a long look at the battlefield. I was filled with a strange sensation. Something that brought back feelings of the Astral Realm. Eliana saw me and approached.

"Belaize?" she questioned seeing the look on my face.

"What is it?" she asked, placing a hand on my shoulder.

"This feeling..." I said. "I can't put it into words."

"I feel it too," she replied softly interlinking her fingers with my own.

"Our bond is strong," she said as she looked into my eyes.

This feeling is hope. Her voice echoed in my mind through our connection. Then gently released my hand and turned toward our team. Her face went hard.

"We know our mission, we do not have the luxury to fail! May Liunella give you the strength to change Vascya forever!" she commanded. The group nodded.

"We will win this war. For Ronak. For Marcus." Adrian said with conviction.

"Scatter and win the day, for our future!" Eliana said and the group parted to complete their tasks.

There are three entrances that needed to be breached. Eliana, Adrian, Luthor and I were to attack the western wall and find our way to the Sanctorum with very little bloodshed.

Scenes of battle were visible in the corner of my eye as I soar passed the soldiers. The stone and dirt beneath my feet rose up in clouds and shards as I bolted past. My fur whipped in the wind, the glowing silver on my chest gleamed in the pink moonlight. *Tonight, I am the incarnation of the blood moon.*

Eliana was ahead of me. I felt her strength and determination.

We descended the final hill before the great walls of the Capitol. There were ranks of soldiers running amok, some carrying wounded soldiers beyond the walls.

I looked to my side and saw Luthor diving headlong into the battle. I couldn't help but smile. He loved to win, no matter what. Adrian, with surprisingly equal vigor leapt, into the battle. I had sensed a change in him. Marcus's and Ronak's death had brought a change in them all.

As we approached the wall, one of the soldiers practically screeched in alarm. A few of the wolves that were still able defend against us but were driven back by our rapid onslaught. Like Ronak had originally planned, we would not attack the fleeing or injured. This wasn't a war won by the number of casualties. This would be won with Idaos's head on a spike.

I thrusted my arm toward a guard, shattering his shields and armor, piercing his skin. I felt the wet, sticky touch of blood as it matted my fur. Soon anguished screams had filled the western entrance and wolves ran for their lives, fleeing the Blood Moon Harbinger.

A few courageous wolves surrounded me, though. But the burning desire to kill didn't fill me anymore. These were just people. They didn't know anything else, how could they?

"Surrender and you won't be harmed!" I roared.

"Fuck you, Belaize of the Blood Moon," one of them said.

"You've a keen eye, soldier. You're lucky tonight. I only want Idaos. Run away with your life," I countered.

"For Vascya!" one of the wolves said and ran toward me. I sidestepped, letting his claws meet empty air. I punched him hard between the helmet and chest plate. His legs faltered and he dropped, his armor clanging against the ground.

Seeing him fall, the other wolves resigned to their fate. They weren't a match for my strength. "He isn't dead, take him to our tents and surrender," I said. They rushed to pick up their companion. None of them met my gaze.

I saw Eliana fighting her own battle. She was surrounded by five guards. I saw her kick one of them down and rip his heart out. The other's attacking hesitated as they saw the guard writhing in pain as he breathed his last. They looked at each other and threw down their weapons.

"Surrender yourself and you will be granted mercy." The few who remained fought valiantly and gave their life to their cause. There was nothing to be done for it. We moved passed the unattended gates. When everyone was out of harm's way Eliana looked at me.

Let's go. I conveyed through our connection.

Just beyond the main gate there was a wide stone alley sprawling in two directions. I tried the nearest door, but it wouldn't budge. With all my strength, I ripped open the wooden door that manned the castle. And my hand to Liunella this is true: the guards had piled layers and layers of stone against the fucking door.

"Let's attack together," I said.

Both of us backed away a few steps and with great momentum kicked the rocks blocking our way away. There was a glee to it. Something about it felt profoundly silly, like a child playing with blocks. We struck again and again, until, finally, we entered the Capitol.

It wasn't long before the sounds of battle were drowned out by the thick stone walls that surrounded the Capitol. We had entered the western side and were running through the streets fast. The alleys were empty. As we moved closer to the castle, the scent of blood thickened.

We finally entered the castle through a small door. It had been left open. Eliana and I ushered in and witnessed the dead guards inside.

"Romulus has been successful. It won't take long now," I muttered.

Romulus cleared out the castle well enough. The few guards we did meet were keen to keep their lives and scattered away. We bounded up flights of stairs and down echoing hallways. I sensed Romulus and Amarog nearby. Changing course, we found them shortly. "Glad to have you on our side, alpha," Eliana said to Amarog and shook his hand.

"Save your pleasantries for after our victory. We have to hurry, Janus has been forewarned." Romulus turned and headed deeper into the castle with urgency in his steps.

We turned a corridor and ran into some guards. They were big, stronger than most. As the bloodbath began, screams filled the halls. No use in convincing these righteous fools to surrender. Everyone had scattered down different corridors, fighting their own opponent. As we moved forward, my senses perked up with familiarity.

"Elianaaaaaaaa..." An estranged voice called slithering through the halls.

"Is that you, dear sister?" The voice was taunting and urging her forward. I felt the sudden shift inside Eliana. She stiffened beside me. Her determination faltered, overpowered by rage. Revenge. Her soul sought revenge for the father she had lost.

I saw the look of intense anger in her emerald eyes. The fire she felt, I felt it too, burning me. My wolf wanted control and to rip his throat apart for our mate, yet I knew this was a battle she had to fight on her own.

"Eliana, focus!" I said, jolting her from her trance. She met my eyes and nodded. I followed her through the halls as she followed the goading voice that was calling her.

"Is father with you?" Rayne asked. His laughter was an echoing cackle. The sound of a madman.

"Can you tell him, I loved him, Eliana? Can you?"

We came upon an empty room and Rayne sat hunched in a dark corner. His eyes glinting with something otherworldly.

"Sister. It's really you!" He was filthy, covered in red rags. His once sandy hair was now shaved. His face covered in deep purple bruises.

"You know, I wanted to kill you! But I killed..." He caught my eye, "No! It was him!" he yelled pointing a crooked finger at me. "He is the one who killed father," he screeched.

"Him! Look at him!" he said as spit dripped from his lips.

Eliana tensed again. I stepped forward.

"You've brought this on yourself," I said. And I looked toward Eliana. Her eyes had tears in them but they refused to spill.

"Retribution is yours," I said. I backed out of the room though it nearly killed me to do so. I knew that she could do it, I knew that she would. Moments later, I felt a stabbing pain in my belly and knew that Eliana had been hurt. I fought through it.

I have faith in you. You're the one that will change this nation's fate for the better, Eliana.

I turned another corridor and saw the main stairwell. I ascended as fast as I could. I heard the howls as I smashed down the door of the Sanctorum. Gone was the round table of the Council. Instead, what remained in the holy chamber was a single throne made of gold. Janus lounged lazily, and my wolf raged that this was our fight, now. Idaos stood in dirty robes beside the throne.

"My disciple!" Janus said gleefully. I froze. My body tensed, and his words made my bones creak. I smelled death in his scent. A putrid, reeking scent.

"So, you survived did you," I said.

"Janus! He will kill me!" yelped Idaos as he registered my presence. "With our army we were supposed to win but he is still here!" he yelled.

"I created him, Idaos. He cannot be stopped by a mere army. I have been waiting for you here, Belaize," Janus said with a menacing smile.

"Save me, oh lord!" he pleaded, falling to his knees before Janus. I sensed someone approaching from behind me.

"Alistair," I said.

Janus's eyes went wide with surprise. "King Alistair!"

"No no no no no! Janus! I killed his family, I did, I did, I promise! Save me from him please! These ghosts, they won't stop haunting me!" Idaos groveled now. Janus kicked Idaos like a dog and strode toward me, his robe flowing behind him. A crown rested on his head. He had made himself king.

"You never should have returned here. You are a relic of the past. You have no place in the future." Janus said, pointing a finger at Alistair.

Idaos regained his footing. "Idaos, deal with Belaize, end him! And I will deal with the Forgotten King!" Janus yelled.

In a flurry, Idaos changed into his wolf and ran toward me. Alistair had already grasped Janus and the two were locked in a death match. Alistair had the clear advantage.

Idaos began his onslaught howling and drooling madly.

"I will end you!" His voice echoing with madness as the final battle of the era began in the holy Sanctorum.

THE DARKEST HOUR

Eliana

I was seething with rage. I wanted to rip Rayne's throat out this instant. When did my older brother turn into this vile thing? As children he had protected me from everything. He came running when I would scratch my knee. I knew he had loved me. But this... jealousy made him cruel.

"You know he did it right? You believe me, don't you sister? Belaize killed father," he said like he was lost in his madness.

"You have lost the right to call him father, Rayne. You lost it as he took his dying breath. Belaize was with me when you were killing my father."

"But don't you get it, El. I only wanted to kill you!" he said with some remorse.

"You should have challenged me, Rayne. Attacking the Sanctuary was not the way."

"No. But, I'm an alpha! Don't you see? I'm an alpha on the Council. Look at me! I'm finally an alpha!" He circled in his spot showing his torn red robes. "I don't need the blood of Draxus like you or father. Don't you see my power? Haha!" And he broke out into a fit of laughter. He giggled like a child. He rocked onto the balls of his feet.

"Janus made me an alpha! I've always wanted to be one. Do you sense my power, sister?" He turned into his wolf and swung at me. I faced him head on, not faltering for a single second. He lunged at me and hit me in the stomach, drawing blood. A simple, light scratch that wouldn't even scar.

"Rayne, you are pathetic. You let your jealousy make a fool out of you. Janus turned you into a beggar."

His expression changed in an instant. He growled, lunging at me again. I grabbed his shoulders and smashed him to the ground. He was lost in madness. Killing him would bring no retribution.

"You're not worth killing," I spat and turned my back on him.

He got up and howled as he again tried to rip my head off. I leaned down just as his claws came into view from the corner of my eye. I grabbed his hand and launched him over my back into a wall. I heard the crack of his bones as he crashed against it and fell to the floor.

"Eliana! What do you want..." A coughing fit racked his body. He spit viscous red blood onto the floor.

"You want me to admit it!" he said. He staggered to his feet.

"I killed him!" he screamed. "He begged for his life after he took everything from me. He wanted to embrace me, Eliana. He had forgiven me." He took a step toward me but then groaned in pain.

"Ronak the Wise! I don't need his forgiveness. All I needed was the same acknowledgment he gave you, the blood of Alpha." He spat on the floor. His teeth were smeared red. It dribbled from his mouth in great rivulets. My anger grew to new heights. But it wasn't a hot, bubbling rage. No. It was stone cold fury.

"Silence!"

"Ronak the Wise, not even wise enough to know never to let his guard down. He got what he deserved. Impaled through the heart! I'm glad I brought his death. Pretending to be the great wolf, yet he died a simple death!" he yelled.

I ran toward Rayne and slashed his chest. Blood sprayed my face as he screeched and reeled back.

"I'll kill you, you traitorous bitch!" Rayne jumped forward growling. I ducked under him and punched his throat. My fingers wrapped smoothly around it. He held his throat and gagged and coughed.

"Fucking stop!" I said. Tears welled in my eyes and fell without my willing them. I twisted his neck and heard a sickening crack. Rayne fell limp in my arms.

"I'm sorry... I couldn't be more like father," he whispered as the embers of life drained from his eyes. I cried. I didn't stop. I wailed louder than I ever did as a child. I was left alone in this world. My family was... gone. When the tears finally stopped, I let out the most triumphant howl I could muster as I cradled my dead brother in my hands. Hands that were covered with his blood. The coldness in my heart diminished. All that remained was a deep, hollow sadness.

I stood up. The war isn't over yet. I closed Rayne's eyes.

"I hope you find peace in the afterlife, Rayne. You... had a good soul once. I hope you find the light once again." I pushed his soft sandy hair away from his forehead, kissing it gently. He reminded me of our father.

With one last glance on him, I sped down the corridor that Belaize disappeared in and followed his scent. I felt that Belaize was engaged in a fight. I turned down one corridor and saw dozens of wolves dead and dying. Sitting against a wall was Luthor. His body was covered in bleeding wounds.

"Luth..." I called. I ran toward him and realized. "Luthor!" I yelled at the golden wolf. But he did not stir. I stood up, shocked and numb.

"Eliana," Romulus called from behind me.

"He's gone," he said. Romulus's eyes were red. He had been crying too. Luthor was a son to him. I nodded, pushing my feelings aside.

"We have to keep going!" he said. "Jennifer should be breaking through the southern wall at the armory. We have to get to her!" he yelled and ran. I followed him after taking a last look at the wolf that had nearly rivaled Belaize in strength.

"Rest in Peace, friend," I said and focused my attention ahead. I looked outside and could see some of the fighting had poured into the streets. The citizens were fleeing. I realized in horror that they had no one to guide them. Our forces were funneled into one mission.

Damn it, we can't help them until this is over.

When we arrived at the armory a fierce battle was ongoing. Jennifer was missing an arm and a gaping hole in her chest stared back at us. Still, she fought ferociously. But she was overwhelmed.

"Jennifer!" I yelled as I tried to push through the wolves separating us. I attacked ferociously. Slashing, clawing, biting, and kicking.

Romulus had reunited with his brother Remus. "Remus. You can feel it!" he said to him. Remus nodded grimly. A fierce battle was taking place in the Sanctorum. The astral distortion made me nauseous. The world swum wildly for a moment.

"He will need help," Romulus said and Remus nodded, breaking away from the battle. Romulus took his spot. The tide of this battle was turning. Soon, the enemy wolves had retreated. The hall was littered with bits of broken armor and weapons.

"Jennifer!" I yelled and looked around for her.

I found her buried under a few wolves. Even in her last moments she had killed half a dozen other wolves.

"Romulus, there is nothing we can do for her now! We have to help Belaize! I've never felt distortions this intense," I said. He nodded and we left the proud she-wolf amidst the dead bodies. We passed the room where Rayne's body lay. I didn't stop. A few moments later we were in the holy Sanctorum. Belaize was fighting Idaos, he was injured and bleeding profusely from his stomach.

"Belaize!" I yelled and nearly ran for him before Romulus pulled me back.

"Over there!" He pointed. I looked and saw a shattered and broken wolf fighting Alistair and Remus. The two weren't able to hold him off. Leathery whips of darkness leapt from his body and tore at them. They were in bad shape. I couldn't believe my eyes, that frail wolf was overpowering Alistair!?

I saw Romulus jump to help them. He ducked and dodged those tentacles spiraling from the wolf's chest.

Help them! Belaize said through our connection while still engaged in a battle with Idaos. His voice tore through my mind like a blast of energy. It shook me from my frozen state. He snarled at Idaos and punched him in the chest. He was gaining the upper hand. The man looked ragged and half conscious.

I nodded, leaping into battle with the three other wolves. I slashed his tentacles away and swiftly aimed for his throat, but they were too strong. They curled around my waist and threw me down. The four of us had cornered him, yet he managed to fend off our attacks.

The wolf's robes had torn and what I witnessed was grotesque. A frail wolf, merely skin and bones. The cord like tentacles were coming out of his chest as if they were an extension of his ribcage. Blood oozed and dripped on the floor. What was most astonishing was the fact that his throat was already ripped apart. *How was he alive? What in the world is this creature!?*

"Is it too late to ask for forgiveness?" The broken wolf grinned as those tentacles lashed around Remus's throat. I tore through the leathery tentacles quickly. And all the while the creature laughed as it regenerated.

"You deserve nothing but eternal death, Janus!" Remus snarled.

"Then you can be there to greet me!"

Remus rushed forward again, attacking Janus head on. He wanted to make it quick. The war ends with their life.

Janus snapped swiftly and all of the tentacles shot toward Remus at once. Before anyone could even move, with lightning-fast speed, Romulus dashed forward and tackled his brother out of the way. The outgrowths of Janus's body tore through his body, lifting him into the air.

"You'll die!" Romulus said as his body was suspended in the air. Blood gushed from his wounds.

"You are the one taking your last breath, Remus. Or Romulus? I can't differentiate between you two twins, really. Never mind, only one of you left anyway!" he said gleefully.

"Romulus!" I yelled.

He turned his head to me. "You will make your father proud little one," he said as the snake like tentacles tore him in two. Janus threw pieces of Romulus's body against the wall like trash.

The man that had been my guardian and friend and family... he was gone... *I'm all alone*, I thought as my mind went blank.

THE BATTLE OF THE BLOODMOON

Belaize

Idaos lashed at me wildly. He was flailing his paws randomly. I dodged most of his attacks but some made contact and the blood oozed out of my wounds. My fur was doused in blood, some of which was mine. I had hit Idaos too, yet he got up like a madman and kept hitting me.

He was an old wolf but I'd admit he wasn't an alpha for nothing. He leapt off the floor snarling and baring his teeth like he was ready to tear at my flesh. I grabbed him, wrapping my arms around him, lifting him off the floor, and then slammed his body down on the stony floor of the Sanctorum. I heard a few cracks.

I glanced at Alistair from the corner of my eye. He was struggling against Janus.

Janus was frail and broken but he was holding his own against Alistair. He was fighting using odd reddish black whips, which emerged out of his chest, and reminded me of blood. They lashed out hard, tearing away all that they touched. Alistair was covered in wounds from the tentacles Janus used, yet he kept on going, tearing at them one by one.

"Urrfggghhh" I grunted as Idaos plunged his hand into the left side of my abdomen. He twisted his hand once before I tore myself away, leaving a deep bloody gash in my stomach.

"Bastard!" I growled in fury. Idaos merely grinned with his tongue hanging out of his snout and drooling on the floor like a rabid dog.

"You have always been a puppet. First mine, and now Ronak's!" he said. He swung his left arm at me in an arcing swoop. Before he could land a blow, I kicked him hard in the chest. He absorbed the hit and only staggered back a few feet. That kick could have killed a bear but he just took another lunge at me.

I heard some commotion and sensed Remus. He had joined the fight against Janus. The three of them were fighting hard. The number of tentacles doubled from two to four.

I focused on Idaos again. He was screaming and running at me. I punched him in the jaw, sending some of his teeth clattering on the floor. Blood sprayed out on my hand. I felt a sharp pain in my abdomen as he clawed inside my wound.

"Fucker." I clenched my teeth and took another vicious kick to the leg.

"Belaize!" I heard Eliana's voice. I dared a glance at her; she was scraped up but relatively uninjured. She tried to come toward me but was stopped by Romulus. Janus was the bigger enemy, after all.

I silently thanked the bastard. "Over there," Romulus said and the two joined the havoc.

"You have some strength behind you. For an old fool I never would take you for such a fighter," I said as I circled Idaos. It was time to end this fight. No more Idaos, no more killing.

He took another swing at me. We clashed again. My hands grabbing his, locked in a tense battle of strength. I took a deep breath and let my wolf take over my senses. The strength of my ancestors, the Mugiri, came flowing through my veins.

I stood taller than Idaos, and used all of my power to dominate him. Idaos bent to one knee, then both. I snapped my arms down, releasing my hands and kicked Idaos in the head, sending him sprawling to the other end of the Sanctorum.

He was out cold. I spit out the blood in my mouth and turned my attention to Janus and the four fighting him. I saw Romulus suspended in the air, six of the tentacles had pierced him. Janus barked an order and tore the proud wolf limb from limb.

For a moment everyone stilled in the chaos that followed. I felt Eliana's fury as she dashed for Janus. She dodged his tentacles with newfound speed. One of the tentacles tried to catch her and throw her away, but she slipped away at the last moment. Another one of his tentacles attacked her and she chewed it off. She was going in for the kill.

She jumped high and with all her strength went for Janus's throat. She bit down hard tearing a chunk away. I thought it was all over in that moment, but that slippery bastard used his tentacles and threw her against the wall.

Blood dripped from his neck where Eliana bit, yet Janus was standing tall. He laughed maniacally.

"What the hell are you?" I heard Remus's stunned voice.

Janus was a living dead body. He was in pieces, yet he had the power and strength to fight against us. I ran toward them, but I couldn't stop Alistair from being hurled through the air, too. "You bastard!" I yelled.

Eliana, Remus, and I faced Janus as he laughed and taunted us. "I am your reckoning!" he said.

The three of us attacked together, and for the first time I felt those tentacles clutch at my throat and I knew why they were a match for three of the best fighters in all of Vascya. When it wrapped around my flesh, I felt like it was taking something from me, pulling me away, pulling me down into the black. I snapped the tentacle and made my way toward their core, Janus, who wouldn't stop laughing. He was toying with us.

As the sickening things swirled in the air above me, I grabbed all four with both of my hands in an iron-clad grip. It was like holding snakes in my hands, and I fought to keep them from slipping out of my grip. I used my upper-body strength and pulled Janus closer. He tried to move away but he was no match. I wrapped them around my fist and with his own tentacles, whirled Janus off the floor and into the ground.

His tentacles retreated for a moment. He stood up with staggering feet. That blow hurt him, I could tell.

After that he went into a tantrum. The tentacles shot everywhere. They were damned hard to fight. Alistair had risen to his feet, but he was struggling. Eliana kept fighting, trying to get closer to Janus again.

Alistair huffed as Janus threw him beside me. I tore his tentacles again, keeping them away from Alistair. They kept regrowing. No end to them.

"Belaize! Are you aware of the alpha force?" he inquired lowly, panting for air.

"No," I replied. Alistair smirked and got to his feet.

"I'll end this." he said, stepping up to our foe. He grew ever larger and his fur extended. He stood near fifteen feet tall. His muscles bulged and his eyes were red with a large pupil at the center. It looked like the moon. I wanted to surrender to his astral distortion. Me! The Blood Moon Harbinger wanted to bow to it. The raw strength and the power of an alpha, of a Kaiser, was in front of me. He was once a king, and now I knew why.

He bared his teeth and growled. He sped toward the center of Sanctorum where Janus stood and attacked. Janus's tentacles hit Alistair to no effect. Alistair powered through, cutting them off before they regenerated and grabbing them by the roots in Janus's chest. He tore out great chucks of rotten flesh. He pulled Janus's arms, tearing them off. His head was last as Alistair – with his mighty strength – separated it from Janus's body.

Janus, who had given us so much trouble, was gone. He laid on the ground, his eyes wide. Blood did not pool as I was used to. In fact, it didn't pour from the wounds at all.

Despite his body lying limp, he laughed. "Oh you, poor poor fools," he said. His limbs zipped across the floor and reattached to his body. He grew in size. His robe tore away, and I saw just how truly shattered he was. Gashes and wounds, bite marks and stripped flesh, littered his body, leaving it a graveyard of scars and injuries. Bones were visible where the gashes were deep enough.

As he was stitched together by some terrible force, he slowly rose to his feet. And then his form rippled. From one blink to the next, his broken, mangled body was no more. Left in its place was the body he had in his youth. The gashes were gone. Only smooth skin remained. And out of his back sprouted brilliant, giant black wings.

"Impossible!" Alistair said in clear despair.

"What the hell is he?" My voice quavered.

Remus growled, Eliana stood beside me completely stunned at the creature in front of us.

"Don't you get it?" Janus said. "I am your death!" He flew toward us. Even with Alistair's alpha force, we were unable to hold a candle to him. He decimated us.

He took hold of Remus and launched him against the wall. He was rendered unconscious on impact. Alistair was taken into his arms and he flew up, holding the large wolf as if he were a straw doll. He crashed through the roof, bathing the Sanctorum in the moon's light. At the peak of his flight, Janus changed direction and plunged to the castle with Alistair headfirst. He crashed into the floor with an incredible power that vibrated the floor beneath our feet.

The dust slowly settled. A slow, echoing clap filled the chamber.

"Belaize, you are my perfect experiment. I shaped you to become my perfect puppet," he said. His form was lost in the great cloud of debris in the air.

"Show yourself, whoever the fucking hell you are!" I yelled and growled. I was at attention and my senses were overwhelmed with the creature's presence.

I heard the clapping intensify and the dust parted to show Janus elegantly standing within a pocketed crater on the floor. His magnificent wings folded against his back. His foot resting atop of Alistair's head. Alistair was conscious. He survived a meteoric fall. He was incredibly strong, but even his alpha force wasn't enough to defeat him.

"First, it started with your coward father," Janus said. "Well, he wasn't really your father, the impotent pig. He was eager to seek the symbol of his mates' promiscuity for a quick profit," he said, grinning savagely.

"And when your father was dead, I turned my attention to your *whore* of a mother." I roared at him to stop. I lunged at him, but every time I did he flew out of reach, mocking me.

"I loved every bit of her sweet body. Oh, how she moaned my name!" he taunted. "And then I left her to die," he said.

"And you were the fool who followed my orders. Every instruction I gave. I have total control over you, Belaize. You weren't birthed into this world, no. I created you with my own hands with this stone," he said, gripping at a purple stone hanging around his neck.

"I told you to kill and you obliterated villages. Admit it, Belaize, you loved having the power that I gave you. Power and strength made citizens of Vascya fear you. You were my most promising experiment. I loved playing with you. Until that bitch came. She... oh, she changed you."

He flew toward Eliana, clasping his hands around her throat. She kicked him repeatedly in the chest but he didn't feel a single kick. He flew out of my reach.

"This she-wolf. It was her who ruined you, Belaize. Tell me, was her cunt that sweet?" Janus taunted.

I roared louder than ever. Anger gripped my heart as I saw my mate in Janus's grip. I could feel her suffocating. I heard my heart beating faster as the blood pumped in my veins. The adrenaline made my body shake.

Then, it stopped.

My vision widened. I felt myself growing larger. Larger. I was massive. My wolf had grown and a new strength enriched my body. My injuries healed in an instant. My fur was aglow in a silver light. I saw Janus's eyes go white with fear.

I was aware of my surroundings like I had never been before. I heard the war cries of thousands of wolves outside the city as they fought for their life. I heard Eliana's soft heartbeat growing ever so slower. Remus's shallow breathing. I felt Idaos rise and stare at me in fear and awe.

"What are you!?" he yelled.

"I am Belaize of the Blood Moon!" I yelled and lunged. My legs sprung into action. I felt so light, I could nearly leap over the castle. Before Janus could react, I had his head in my paws. My fingers wrapped around his neck. He released Eliana from his clutches as he struggled against me.

I threw him as hard as I could before I landed. He smashed into the ground, collapsing the sanctorum floor, plunging into the depths below. The sound of the crash echoed in the vast expanse. I ran for the cavity and found Janus soaring out. I jumped against a wall on my left and vaulted into the air.

I landed on his back and bit down onto his shoulder. He screeched in pain and terror as we plummeted to the ground.

"Fahther give me strength!" Janus yelled.

I gripped his massive wings in my hands and tore them from his back. His arms were severed as well, the sound was like tearing paper to me. I lifted him up and held him by the throat. He was terrified.

"Let me go! I can't go back!" he said.

"Belaize! I helped you get strong! Please you can repay me by letting me live! I can't go back!" He pleaded and begged for me to release him.

I didn't. I wrapped my jaws around his neck and bit down, severing his spine and tearing him loose. I tore every bone apart and threw them out of reach. He wouldn't get those parts back. He wouldn't regenerate this time.

A great snarl exploded from my chest, but the song changed. It rose in pitch and lifted my head along with it. The sound greeted the moonlight in the holy chamber. Alistair stood up, wide eyed. Eliana and Remus too were staring at me. I felt their gazes like a touch brushing against my skin. Dimly, I was aware of the battle noises dying away. It was like the world had paused completely to take a breath. They felt my power and every single wolf in the Capital was bowing for me.

When my lungs burned, I inhaled sharply. My vision waivered and I felt lightheaded. But slowly the world was solid once more. I felt nothing but overwhelming euphoria. My mind drifted to Eliana.

The three of them fell to their knees, even Eliana, bowing their heads. I turned my attention to Idaos. He was kneeling too.

"Belaize, you are the one who will destroy Vascya. I have seen it. You are the wolf in the prophecy," he said as he tried to scramble away from me in fear.

"You... you will destroy Vascya! I did all this to kill you and yet here you are! The end of Vascya is here! The battle of the gods will commence and it's because of you! I have seen it! I have seen it! I have seen it! You will end the wolves! Haha!"

Just as I was about to kill Idaos, Janus's broken body lurched. From the core of Janus's being sprang a creature so frail it might have been a child. Malformed and ugly, it crawled to all fours and stood. Scrawny and weak. It looked at me with intense hatred.

"When Fahther comes you will pay with your lives," it spat. It spread its wings, the same that Janus had, yet smaller in size. A peculiar third eye present on his forehead.

"So, you are a parasite," I said with disgust.

"I am Spyros! One of Faerie Kings Generals. You have been warned! Fahther will come for you! And with him your death!" it said and took flight. But I was faster, and I was stronger, and I pulled it from the sky. The frail thing writhed in my hands.

"I am warning you, Fahther will destroy your beloved country, destroy Vascya. Let me —" I didn't wait for it to finish talking. I crushed its head in my hand. A green liquid oozed from my hands onto floor. That fucking thing was dying for the last damned time tonight.

"Fahther!" Idaos said. "Fahther is the end of everything! You will destroy Vascya! Prepare Vascya, seek the other tribes. For it may be too late to recover. Fahther will be angry!" Idaos said shakily.

I felt my body begin to shrink. Soon, I was a man again. Exhausted and broken. Eliana was at my side.

"You did it!" She kissed me. I felt her warmth and gratitude through her lips.

Idaos was still blubbering about tribes of men. Alistair picked an old Vascyan banner and tore it into a makeshift restraint. He tied up Idaos and dragged him out.

"Where are you taking him!?" Eliana asked.

"To show Vascya that this war is finally over!"

Eliana grabbed my hand, interlinking our fingers together and for the first time, I didn't feel that being mates was a death sentence anymore. It was Liunella's gift.

I PROMISE

Eliana

The streets of Regvyer were full of cheering citizens and rebels alike. The civil war in the country came to an end the night Idaos was captured.

Wolves all over the city had surrendered under Belaize's massive alpha force. Each wolf present had accepted Belaize as their alpha. The battle had ceased. We had dragged Idaos through the streets and outside of the city walls. As Idaos was paraded through the battlefield, the Royal Army dropped their arms and surrendered.

In the aftermath I made the accommodations to heal the wounded, no matter their alliance. The corrupt Council alphas were taken prisoner, awaiting their fates in the same cold, dark prison cells that they had kept countless others. And with that, Vascya entered a new era.

Two weeks later, the news of the end of rebellion had reached all corners of Vascya. Wolves who had left their home returned to pick up the pieces. Mates rejoiced, bravely expressing their love for one another without fear. Pups were safe once again.

The population of Vascya had declined, but in a few years it wouldn't be a concern. A sense of hope and happiness flowed through the citizens. It was a childhood dream come true.

But it had come with a heavy price. Many died in the great war: over half of the rebels and the Council guards alike. A massive funeral was arranged to honor those who lost their life outside the Capital. The bodies were burned together and the ashes spread in the holy sea.

But everyone was waiting for today. I was wearing a long, beautiful silver colored robe, made with the finest materials, the likes of which I have never felt. Draped on my shoulder was the cape with the insignia of Vascya, a wolf intertwining with the moon. I was feeling nervous. I felt Belaize's hand over mine as he softly squeezed it in reassurance.

"I wish my father would have seen this day," I said.

In front of me thousands of wolves were gathered in front of the castle at the center of the Regvyer. The gates of the castle were decorated with beautiful flowers.

"He did everything so that you could see this day, Eliana."

"Belaize, what was it like?" I questioned him as we stood upon the dais in the center.

"I don't remember," he replied.

"You made even Alistair bow before you," I said. He simply shrugged and nudged me forward.

I took a few steps and mentally prepared myself. Anxiety bubbled in my chest, but I took a deep breath and stood straight, facing the massive crowd.

"I am Eliana, Daughter of Ronak the Wise. He was once one of the leaders of Vascya!" I began.

Thinking of my father nearly brought tears to my eyes. "He died believing that one day Vascya would be free. Free from the tyranny of Idaos and his Council. And today with all of your effort, we have done it." I said and gestured to the executioner's platform beside me.

Three alphas had survived the War of the Blood Moon. Canagan, Esteve and Idaos. The rest had turned against the Council when we had rallied so they were pardoned but their titles were stripped away. They were lined up with their heads in guillotines.

"What they have done cannot be forgiven. Nor can it be forgotten. With the death of the leaders of old who led us astray, we usher in a new age. An age where we will not forget the ones we are leaving behind." I looked over the crowd.

"We will love one another, cherish one another. We will help one another. But, most importantly, we will live," I said. A roar of approval went through the crowd.

"Our past is what defines our future and our future will be one that is bright!" I yelled over the crowd. "This is inevitable, as they are the ones who brought darkness to our land. With their blood we wash our land clean!"

"Executioners!" I yelled. They nodded in waiting.

"Idaos!" I called out. "You are charged with treason, murder, conspiracy to usurp, conspiracy against the crown, abuse of power, and seventy-nine other charges. You will receive no remorse, you will receive no quarter, for your death is our leap into a brighter tomorrow."

Idaos was one of the few that kept his dignity in the hour of his death. "I said this before, I don't deserve life; however, that does not change what comes from beyond the horizon. Find the other tribes. For that is our only hope. You will be the key to the destruction of this bright future of yours." He said and hung his head down, resigning to his fate.

I nodded at the executioner. A deafening roar erupted from the crowd as thirteen heads dropped simultaneously. Alistair stepped forward a few moments later. He held up his hand and let the crowd silence.

"I was king once. And like Eliana said, the old must pass, for Vascya belongs to the next generation."

"I Alistair, former King of Vascya, with the power vested in my title and hopes of Vascya, do appoint Eliana, Daughter of Ronak, Leader of the Rebellion of Generations, as Queen of Vascya!" Silence settled in the crowd.

"The Council is no more. Will you Eliana, the beloved daughter of Ronak, take the title of Queen?" Alistair said.

"I do," I said confidently. I stood in front of Alistair facing him, watching him intently.

"Do you promise to put Vascya first, before your needs, to guide and serve as protector of our nation?" He stated, looking into my eyes.

"I promise!"

He picked up the beautiful crown with an intricate pattern of phases of the moon in its center. He placed it softly upon my head and backed away, bowing respectfully before me. Banners waived and trumpets played. The crowd hollered and cheered. They rejoiced and they sang.

"Father! Mother! Thank you for everything. Marcus, Romulus, Luthor, Jennifer. I promise! We will never forget you. And you the countless, nameless martyrs. You will never be forgotten. That is my promise."

A few days had passed. The citizens were living happily and with peace. Businesses were flourishing once again. Titles and rewards had been granted to those who had been an accessory to the castle siege.

A new government of was formed with Amae, Alistair and Erylesia as its guides. More warriors were given new titles, Adrian, Master of Coin; I made him promise not to decimate the economy of this country with his drinking. He was back to his old self again. Remus became the Master of Statecraft, and Sora, Master of Arms. I had contemplated reinstating the old tradition of the Fenrir's winds, but part of my promise was to do away with a damned Council, after all.

We had suffered from the war. But, the prophecy loomed a dark shadow over our future. Belaize and I were the key. Hence, we decided that we will prepare. Prepare for the tragedy that will arrive at our doorstep someday.

It was a beautiful evening. The sun was setting spreading its rays across the pink sky. We were in a beautiful garden within one of the castle's courtyards. The scents of spring flowers filled my senses as everyone I knew and cherish were gathered here.

I was wearing a simple emerald gown with workings of gold glowing down to my feet. Belaize, too, was standing in front of me, his eyes only finding mine in this crowd.

Alistair, Remus, Alver, Xyabolt, Erylesia, Adrian and Amae had come today. It was a dream. From a heartless murderer to the savior of Vascya, Belaize truly had a good soul. He was the silent Savior. One who would take no credit. One who would carry hate on his shoulders for the rest of his life. But, we would weather it together, because he was mine.

Amae was talking to others. She held Nihara in her arms. She had grown over the past few weeks and her personality had blossomed. She had a head of black hair and beautiful hazel eyes. She was clinging to Amae's shoulder and babbling in gibberish. She gurgled and cooed, suckling on her little fingers.

Erylesia held little Cora, Marcus's daughter. A beautiful girl with the same head of silky hair as him. With Erylesia's eyes. She was Erylesia's hope. She was born after the war ended. All of us mourned Marcus's loss, but Erylesia was strong for her new-born daughter who needed her most. Adrian was trying to convince Erylesia to let him hold Cora, but she turned a blind eye to the poor man.

Amae broke away from her conversation and handed Nihara to Alistair. He held her awkwardly in his burly hands until she snuggled against his chest. I saw a tear fall from his eyes. He hugged her as if she were his lost child. I couldn't help but smile. Nihara had been the change we all needed.

Amae stepped in front of us. Everyone quieted down. She looked at Belaize with love.

"You've come so far, my son."

"Amae, must you do this here," he said shyly.

"Oh, you fool!" she laughed as she adjusted his garb.

She ushered me forward and join our hands.

"In the Eyes of Liunella, be bound, be loyal and love one another. Cherish one another, protect each other, for this is Liunella's gift to you," she said the words and the vows.

"I promise!" We said together in one voice. Amae tied a delicate silk string over our wrists and then around our hands.

Belaize leaned down, kissing me. His soft, warm lips against mine felt like the first time. It was the start of our new lives. When we parted, barely audible above the murmurs of congratulations of the onlookers, I heard him say it.

"I love you," Belaize whispered softly in my ear.

The celebrations were hearty and lasted well into the late evening, with Adrian singing his famous songs in his worst possible voice. Though Belaize's marriage to me made him King, he did not want the throne, he simply wished to support me on it. He even refused to have another throne added beside the one that existed.

"Subjects must stand before the Queen, and your husband will stand beside you, as you rule," he had said ever so stoically.

Later in the evening, I sat atop our bed as Belaize walked into our room. My mind was moving a mile a minute. I felt his love and dedication for me through our bond.

I stood up, meeting him in his arms, which instantly wrapped around me. Our lips meeting in a warm kiss. His strong hands encircled me and lifted me off the floor with ease, carrying me back into the bed. He laid me down, gently undressing me, sliding my robe from my shoulders and letting it slide from my body. I had never given much thought to my body, but a few of the maids had cleaned me thoroughly. I felt truly beautiful. I had the luxury of feeling beautiful now.

Belaize lifted away from me, my body yearned to feel him. He undressed himself and finally for the first time, skin met skin. I felt electrified. My skin sensitive to his touch. It made me tremble having him so intimately close to me. I felt his hands caress my body. Tracing my skin, caressing every curve. I couldn't keep away from him. My body demanded him.

He kissed me lovingly while our bodies moved. I felt him press against me, making me moan with excitement. I felt the electricity. My senses opening up to him as we finally completed our bond, promising me the eternity of our life.

"Be..laize," I said as ecstasy blinded my every sense.

EPILOGUE

A Scrawny Man

I walked into the run-down tavern. It was filled with other drinkers. My red elemental stone bounced against my chest. The fire within it burning hot, flickering like true flame. After years of searching, I had finally found it.

The shapeshifters of legends. Monstrous beings of terrible and frightening power.

“Drinks for my friends and the friendly folk of the tavern!” I said loudly while slapping the table. “No one will go home sober tonight!” I exclaimed. Cheers of joy went around the tavern.

“What’s the occasion, stranger?” a man said.

“The occasion...” I smiled at the man. “The occasion is that I’ve found what I have been searching for all of this time,” I replied.

“Oh, and what’s that?” he inquired.

“I’ve been searching for werewolves!” I said. The man raised his glass. “To the fuckin’ werewolves!” he said and the entire tavern echoed.

“Here, here!” They said, and soon the songs started.

“Don’t go o’er the mountains for that’s where the wolves hunt.”

The song continued and soon the entire tavern was abuzz, singing and dancing to the old folklore.

I sat back and leaned against the counter. “Bartender! Will five gold coins cover the cost of the tab for a week?” I asked.

The bartender practically beamed. "It will cover the tab for two weeks!" he said and held out his hands. I dropped the coins in his hand and he quickly disappeared behind the door to lock away his haul.

I turned to my subordinates, who were present with me. "Let's go," I ordered.

They followed me out of the bar and once out, I turned to face the tavern again. I held my hands outward and a flame appeared between them.

Dancing between my hands.

"Ignite!" I said and a pillar of flame shot towards the tavern. In mere seconds, the jovial tavern was a blazing inferno. "Ha ha ha ha!" I laughed as I heard the screams inside, vanishing one by one.

Soon not a single voice was heard.

"There's no more music, so no reason to stay here," I said and mounted my horse. My subordinates each mounted their own and we took off towards the greatest kingdom of Man. Escalia!

THE CHRONICLES OF ZASTRERIA

Lycus: The Prophecy of Annihilation
Humik: The Age of Inferno
Upir: The Legacy of Darkness
Siren: The Melody of the Vanished
Basilisk: The Tremors of Hellfire
Faery: The Wrath of the Dark King
Zastreria: The Tale of Gods and Monsters

AUTHOR'S NOTE

Hello everyone, Its I.S. Knight here. You have either just finished reading *Lycus: The Prophecy of Annihilation*, or you've skipped through the pages and come to the end to the Authors Note. If you are the latter, then go back and finish reading this note will still be here. Thank you for purchasing our novel. This novel was the culmination of 3 years and involved the tireless work of several individuals. As Authors, we cannot thank you enough for giving us a chance. Being Self Published means that we do not have the seal of approval that comes with traditional publishing. Does that make self-published authors any less valid? No. It does however make it harder for Self-Published authors to get to the mainstream.

So yes, thank you again. We hope you loved reading the novel and fell for the characters like we did while creating them. Stay tuned for our new works and please leave a review on Amazon, Goodreads, Barnes & Noble, Book depository and more. Wherever you can! so that others can too find the novel and enjoy it as you have. Thank you again, and may Liunella rain upon you her blessings.

Visit *www.isknight.com* and subscribe to our newsletter for updates about our next books.

Drop us an email at: authorisknight@gmail.com

Follow us at @i.s.knight on Instagram.

ABOUT THE AUTHORS

SAUMYA SINGH
has devoured books since she learned to read. Raised in a world of fantasy, she found her calling as a zoologist and her love of science and animals translates beautifully to her writing. In her down time, she can be found reading, bird watching, and traveling. She hopes to connect with readers and inspire the same love of reading she herself discovered as a child.

IPEN SINGH
used to sit as a wide-eyed child taking in every fantastic story his grandmother told. Her stories inspired his imagination and instilled a love of storytelling in him from a very young age. When he's not writing, Ipen enjoys reading, playing soccer, volleyball, and watching movies and anime. He hopes to share a love of stories that allows others feel that same sense of wonder he did as a child listening to his grandmother.

Together, they are
I.S. KNIGHT

CPSIA information can be obtained
at www.ICGtesting.com
Printed in the USA
LVHW081938041121
702453LV00013B/673/J

9 781777 595913